DETONATION

A
Brick Morgan
NOVEL

BURR B. ANDERSON

outskirts
press

This is a work of fiction. The events and characters described herein are imaginary and are not intended to refer to specific places or living persons. The opinions expressed in this manuscript are solely the opinions of the author and do not represent the opinions or thoughts of the publisher. The author has represented and warranted full ownership and/or legal right to publish all the materials in this book.

DETONATION
A Brick Morgan Novel
All Rights Reserved.
Copyright © 2018 Burr B. Anderson
v2.0

Cover Photo © 2018 Burr B. Anderson. All rights reserved - used with permission.

This book may not be reproduced, transmitted, or stored in whole or in part by any means, including graphic, electronic, or mechanical without the express written consent of the publisher except in the case of brief quotations embodied in critical articles and reviews.

Outskirts Press, Inc.
http://www.outskirtspress.com

Paperback ISBN: 978-1-4787-4976-9
Hardback ISBN: 978-1-4787-5170-0

Outskirts Press and the "OP" logo are trademarks belonging to Outskirts Press, Inc.

PRINTED IN THE UNITED STATES OF AMERICA

To

Kenneth L. White
Remarkable husband, father, and friend,
Whose short time on Earth
Made a lasting difference to so many
And from whom came the concept of this novel

Chapter One

The bow of the massive cruise ship sliced easily through the blue-green Caribbean waters, creating a rainbow of phosphorescent colors for its appreciative passengers lining the ship's railings and upper decks.

As the propellers of the great vessel churned the tranquil waters, millions of microscopic sea creatures known as *Pyrodinium bahamense* reacted to the intrusion by emitting flashes of red and bluish light against the eighty-one-degree seas. The *Bernini Under the Stars* was five hours out of St. Thomas in early evening and steering course two-seven-zero toward her next port of call, San Juan, Puerto Rico. Many of its 2,650 passengers with cameras were capturing the beauty of the shimmering light show, while others merely sipped their cocktails and smiled their appreciation.

Assistant Purser Melanie Harris had just completed a reconciliation of the food and beverage receipts for the *Bernini*'s second day of its seven-day eastern Caribbean cruise. Harris was pleased with her career so far aboard the 115,000-ton liner. The cheerful twenty-eight-year-old, blue-eyed blonde had recently signed her fourth ten-month contract with Nobility Cruise Line with the stipulation she could continue in the *Bernini*'s purser department. In her future, she hoped, would be a full purser's job aboard one of the line's 135,000-ton *Renoir*-class superliners. But she worked hard and smart and believed that promotion would come in time.

Melanie decided to reward herself for completing her task by walking down to deck five for a cup of "real" coffee. A lounge on the deck was home to a kiosk that sold real brewed coffee instead of the vile liquid made from concentrate that was served in the dining rooms and food court. That brew often led to critical reviews from passengers that resulted in cranky emails to Nobility's Operations Department in Fort Lauderdale. The cruise line "officially" was working on the problem.

Walking out of her office and passing by the service counter, Harris noticed an incoming call from a passenger's cabin.

"Purser's office, Melanie speaking. May I help you?"

"Help! My wife is acting crazy! Send help! Send security to help me! I don't know what to do! Please hurry!"

Harris instantly felt the panic in the caller's voice. After hearing the first few words, she jammed a finger against a blue button on the side of the phone console, activating the digital recording software that was part of the office phone system. Her heart was racing as she tried to compose herself before replying.

"Sir, I show that you are in room Aquarius seven-oh-nine, is that correct?" Melanie could hear a woman's voice in the background as the caller repeated his urgent call for help.

"Yes. A-seven-oh-nine. Hurry! She's just run onto the balcony—oh no!"

"Sis, put that book down and get out here! The waves are absolutely glowing," pleaded Theresa Fey from the balcony of cabin B-707. Earlier in the evening, she had purchased a bottle of Luisa Ribolla Gialla at Noble Wines aboard ship, and now seemed like a good time to open it. This week marked a year since the death of her sister Marcia's husband, and it hadn't taken much arm twisting to convince Marcia to join her on the cruise.

Marcia had remained by the side of her husband, Allen, for eight months as he fought a courageous but losing battle against pancreatic cancer. Theresa felt fortunate that her home was barely thirty minutes from her sister's and that she was able to provide her with needed emotional support during Allen's illness. The sisters had spent every

Tuesday together after his death as Marcia adjusted to the life of a fifty-five-year-old widow.

Marcia wiped her eyes, retrieved the wine and two chilled glasses from the room's refrigerator, and stepped onto the balcony. The soothing evening breeze seemed to cheer her as she handed Theresa the glasses and took a seat at the little balcony table.

"One day at a time, honey," said Theresa, noticing her sister's red eyes.

"What would I do without you?"

"Can I help?"

"I'll be fine. I'm getting better, but certain things trigger flashbacks to the good times with Allen. They probably always will."

"I'm so sorry, honey."

Marcia sipped her wine and then reached across and squeezed her sister's hand. "I was reading the ship's event schedule and saw that an Eagles cover band is performing in the Luminosity Bar on deck six. Allen loved the Eagles. We attended a concert on our third date."

"Shall we go?" responded Theresa, startled.

"I don't know; this cruise has been wonderful therapy so far. Thanks for giving me a little push to come along."

For the next few minutes, the sisters sat quietly on their balcony as the *Bernini* slid through the Caribbean, her lights ablaze against the darkening sky.

Nobility named each of its ten ships after European artists and then added "Under the Stars" to each name. Every deck on the ship was named for a celestial constellation, and most of the bars and lounges had galactic and astrological identities as well. The Bootes deck provided Theresa and Marcia with a standard cabin, but a balcony that was much larger than the balconies on the Aquarius or Cassiopeia decks.

The women alternated between sipping their Italian varietal and absorbing the angelic heavens and phosphorescent sea. "You know, Allen and I had often talked of taking a Caribbean cruise but never did. I still regret it. I know I need to get over the guilt and move on with my life."

"Maybe we should have a drink in the Luminosity and—" Theresa was suddenly distracted by what appeared to be a person falling from above. Her reasoning went into overload as her brain tried to process what she just saw. She was certain a woman had dropped from the decks above and passed just in front of their balcony toward the sea. She jumped up and looked over the balcony rail as the body splashed into the rushing waters that she and Marcia had been appreciating moments before.

Chapter Two

"This one redefines the word beautiful; it's absolutely gorgeous," the older man declared, gesturing toward a stunning red Chrysler 300G on display at America's Car Museum in Tacoma, Washington. "You just can't find a car like this anymore, and that's a hell of a shame."

Adjacent to the city's massive Tacoma Dome sports and recreation complex, the museum holds the collection of the late Tacoma businessman Harold LeMay, who had developed it after World War II. The ornate structure opened in 2012 and showcases 2,400 antique autos on a revolving schedule that changes the display each month. The second man opened his mouth to speak, but the first was on a roll.

"It's a sixty-one—the first year that the quad headlights were positioned at an angle and the last year of the exaggerated rear fins," the man continued. "Chrysler made less than thirteen hundred of these two-door coupes. We could have bought one in the sixties for under six thousand bucks."

"Easier for you than me," Brick Morgan responded dryly. "I was born in seventy-six." The car was beautiful all right, but Morgan had more on his mind than the Chrysler. Why did the president of the Tacoma Port Commission want to meet him here?

Morgan, owner of Morgan Maritime Investigations, had returned a week earlier from Cabo San Lucas, where he was instrumental in breaking up a scheme to smuggle cocaine into the United States aboard the Diamond Cruise Lines ship *Crimson Diamond*. The vessel had become a major player in a drug ring using ship's crewmen to traffic cocaine on the US West Coast.

Four crew members had used hollowed-out watermelons to smuggle Baggies of pure cocaine into the ports of Los Angeles / Long

Beach, California, and Portland, Oregon, assisted by two key dockworkers in each location. All were captured by Port Authority police in each location and faced federal drug-smuggling charges and sentences exceeding thirty years.

When Brick returned to his Tacoma home from Cabo, he had a message from Barry Mott awaiting him. The men had met at a few civic functions, and Brick knew Mott had retired from commercial real estate and had successfully run for the Tacoma Port Commission, of which he now was president.

At the moment, however, Mott was explaining the finer points of the '61 300G.

The gray-haired executive, natty in a single-button Brioni sharkskin, directed his Allen Edmonds oxfords to the front of the Chrysler and pointed to the grill. "In sixty-one, they changed the grill design and made the top larger than the bottom—terrific idea. And that engine was a work of engineering mastery—three seventy-five horsepower and ran like a Swiss watch. Today this baby would fetch seventy thousand bucks, and a convertible would bring in a hundred and thirty, easy."

"Oh well," Mott said with a shrug. "That's too much for me to spend on a hobby these days, Brick. Besides, it's better that a car like this is in here so everyone can enjoy it. C'mon, let's get some coffee, and I'll explain why I wanted to meet with you."

Morgan accompanied the seventy-year-old commissioner to the mezzanine level of the car museum, where they located a table and chairs in the cafe.

"How familiar are you with the Port of Tacoma?" Mott asked after the men sat down with their coffees.

Morgan had done investigative work for a few of the shipping lines that called on the port, but he decided to keep that information to himself until he knew the direction of the meeting. "Mr. Mott, my knowledge of the port is limited to what I read in the paper and some trips down Port of Tacoma Road to visit a few cargo ships."

"Okay, here's the deal," Mott began, slowly clasping his hands on the tabletop. "While I was growing up here during the sixties, the big act in town besides Weyerhaeuser Timber was the American Smelting and Refining Company—ASARCO for short. For almost a hundred years, smoke from that damned copper refinery contaminated a thousand square miles of the Puget Sound area—and everyone in it—with lead and arsenic poison that poured out of its smokestack in the north end.

"That sulfur-tasting garbage made people sick every day, and who knows how many died from it over the years? Hell, even lawns and plants died. Oh, the company would send out a couple suits now and then to pay off complainers who yelled loud enough, but that was it. Government didn't interfere because the place produced jobs.

"While you were growing up, Brick, we had ASARCO, the St. Regis Paper Mill, and Hooker Chemical all at the same time. They stunk up the environment so badly that newspapers around the country referred to the stench as the Aroma of Tacoma. City officials pretended they didn't notice. It took changes in state environmental regulations to finally get rid of those companies in the seventies and eighties.

"Renovation of downtown Tacoma began in earnest in 1980 when construction of the Tacoma Dome began near Interstate 5. It proceeded with projects by Weyerhaeuser, Russell Investments, the University of Washington, new hotels, banks, and other businesses, and millions of dollars in federally funded renovation of numerous office buildings, theaters, and bridges. New freeways around the city began in the late eighties and continued. The city's face and its attitude started changing with them.

"Look where we are today," Mott went on. "The Port of Tacoma is the second-largest container-shipping center on the West Coast, behind only LA / Long Beach. The health-care industry is booming here, and the UW campus is changing the whole character of the city. The Dome attracts the biggest acts in show business.

"Tacoma is turning around, Brick. No city should be defined in the present by events in its past. It should be defined by the future vision of today's civic leadership. Having said that, I'd like you to become part of that future vision."

Morgan's mouth fell open. "Mr. Mott, I'm—"

"Please call me Barry."

Collecting his thoughts, Morgan gazed out the mezzanine windows toward Thea Foss Waterway, observing a passing seagull dropping a load of whitewash as it flew by. He wondered fleetingly whether the airborne dung had splattered his pristine BMW parked near the building.

"Okay, Barry, you're president of the port commission. I'm a self-employed maritime investigator. How do I fit into your vision of civic leadership?"

"Damn it, Brick. That sixty-one Chrysler I showed you was cutting edge—push-button transmission, power steering and brakes, and swivel bucket seats. Shit—a great car from a great company. In the sixties, Chrysler was on top of its game. Ten years later, they were on the verge of bankruptcy because they couldn't recover from the oil crisis of seventy-three. A few years of ups and downs, and they merged with Daimler-Benz.

"Today, Fiat owns the company. Can you believe that? Fiat. How could they possibly build the Chrysler 300G, and then lose the company to the Italians? I'll tell you how, Morgan; they didn't have a plan B." Mott paused and gestured with his right hand toward the huge landmass north of Thea Foss Waterway, ships now anchored where roads once existed over tidal fill.

"You're looking at a massive economic generator for this region and for the country, Brick. Secretariat was just another horse until the right trainers came along, and then he won the Triple Crown. I view the port in the same way."

Morgan was intrigued with the Tacoma history lesson and Mott's version of the demise of Chrysler's American ownership. The man was razor sharp and clearly in his element at the port. Fine so far, but where was this going? Brick's stomach was starting to growl.

"The port's a jewel, Barry, and I appreciate the work that you're putting into it, but let's stop dancing. Why did you want to meet with me today, and why here?"

"You're being a little modest, Mr. Morgan. I've been aware of your work for some time through contacts here and elsewhere in the maritime industry. You're good at your profession—quite good— and I need that kind of talent."

Morgan concluded that a point was en route. *And it's still daylight*, he thought to himself.

"Let me be direct, Brick. I'd like you to work with the Port of Tacoma to reevaluate our security system and do two things: first, develop a plan to fill every hole you find, and second, determine what new wrinkle may *still* be out there that we haven't even considered. We need the best port security in the world. I've seen some of the systems elsewhere, and they're damn good. So is ours, but it needs to be better.

"Look, poor security planning has hurt this country over and over again from the Revolution to Pearl Harbor, and from Nine Eleven to the Boston Marathon. That's got to end and fast. The growth we've encouraged and enjoy today has made the port a target."

Brick excused himself and walked to a nearby restroom. His fourth cup of coffee of the morning had given the visit singular importance. Taking a moment to wash his hands and straighten his tie, he contemplated the skeleton of Mott's plan and how he might approach it. Morgan knew one thing for certain: he would direct such an operation or refuse to consider it. The other thing was simple: How would he feel if he turned down the proposal and the port was severely hit and people were killed?

The "ayes" had it. Morgan left the restroom and returned to the table. Mott picked up in stride.

"I've given this a lot of thought," Mott said. "If terrorists wanted to put US ports out of commission, I think they would arrive by ship not by land, and they might just strike nationwide on the same day, fouling the shipment of goods across the country for months, perhaps years, and creating havoc like we've never seen before. The Port of Tacoma needs the best security net available to keep us in business and our people out of harm's way."

"From what I've seen, Barry, your visible security presence appears decent. What else do you have besides requiring credentials from every employee on shift?"

"We use the three-tier Maritime Security Levels, or MARSEC system, and also coordinate with the Homeland Security Advisory System. But that's not enough—not anymore. We need our own plan B. Having only enough security to meet minimum federal requirements is an invitation to disaster. Do you know what a TEU is?" Mott asked, switching topics in the same breath.

Morgan gave Barry a little smile as he nodded. "Of course. It's one of those metal cargo boxes that are lifted on and off big container ships." Morgan knew that when shipment of containers from international ports began in earnest during the seventies, the cargo boxes were twenty feet long to fit on truck trailers built to handle that size. Numbers of containers moving through US ports at the time were measured by what were called twenty-foot equivalent units, or TEUs. That measurement method continues despite most containers now being forty feet long. These now are counted as two TEUs.

Mott explained that the Port of Tacoma off-loads nearly two million TEUs annually for shipment primarily in the Pacific Northwest, with about 30 percent bound for the Midwest. Together, he said, the ports of Tacoma and Seattle off-load about 3.5 million containers annually, third largest in the US, behind only New York / New Jersey and Los Angeles / Long Beach.

"Let's just say minimum isn't as up to speed as I want it to be," Mott added. "We've got work to do, which is what I've been driving at today. I expect the commission will authorize a request for proposals soon for a company to do a thorough threat assessment of the Port of Tacoma, Brick. I would hope your firm would bid on the project."

"I would be very interested in your RFP, Barry," said Brick, already quietly concerned that a legal issue could preclude him from responding.

Whether being told about a future RFP by a port official might be unethical for himself and Mott would have to be determined first by reading the Tacoma city charter's competitive-bidding regulations. Morgan liked what he saw in Mott—bright, on his game, passionate—and he knew Morgan Maritime Investigations could handle the job. The fact that the project was in his hometown would be icing on the cake. But first things first.

Mott said a timetable for issuing the RFP would be on the commission's agenda later in the week, and that if it was approved, Morgan could expect to receive a copy by late the following week. Brick believed the timing should give him plenty of time to research any legalities. He had studied the process of municipal procurement and unfair practices while in Stanford Law School, and what he recalled for sure was that if he was given an advantage, he could be found guilty of an impropriety for unfair dealing in the award of a contract.

Morgan carefully steered the conversation away from Port of Tacoma business and to Mott's prior life in commercial real estate. Ten minutes of that was about all he could stand, and he opted to wrap up their meeting.

"You win the lottery tonight, Barry. What car do you want from LeMay's collection?" he asked.

"Easy. The sixty-three Corvette Stingray. The split-window coupe with three hundred horsepower and the three twenty-seven small—"

Morgan answered his phone on the first ring and found a text message waiting from Nobility Cruise Lines. He read it twice.

"Brick. urgent. call me. rob."

Chapter Three

A late-afternoon shower pelted Gaston Rizzo's sedan as he turned north at Sixth Avenue and Pine Street and proceeded down an alley behind the popular Dolphin's Whistle nightclub in Tacoma's north end. He slowed as he passed the gleaming maroon Buick of tavern owner Irv Kelso that was backed into a parking spot near a rear door. The direction in which the car faced signaled Rizzo that a message awaited him.

Satisfied, Rizzo headed through another alley in the next block to avoid suspicion before turning back onto Pine Street and driving quietly away. His unrelated afternoon meeting across town had gone well, and he hoped the message awaiting him would cap off a great day.

Organized crime was as much a part of western Washington's colorful landscape as Mount Rainier and the inland sea that is Puget Sound. Seattle's King County and Tacoma's Pierce County had shared the on-again, off-again focus of the FBI and Justice Department since the 1940s. A new crime wave struck with fatal efficiency beginning in early 1977 as a series of arson fires began destroying nightclubs across Pierce County.

An investigation launched by Sheriff George Janovich went nowhere. The sheriff seemed mystified about the blazes during public meetings and in interviews with the press. The FBI and the Federal Bureau of Alcohol, Tobacco, Firearms and Explosives quietly joined the case, but before their office chairs were warm, the landmark Top of the Ocean restaurant and discotheque in Tacoma was firebombed into history on April 3.

Fear became a common concern of club owners, customers, and investigators alike in the months that followed. After kissing his wife and daughter goodbye on the morning of November fifteenth, state liquor control board investigator Melvin Journey was gunned down in his driveway, shot four times before he could pull his gun.

As the clock ticked into 1978, homes of club owners who were reluctant to sell their nightspots erupted in flames. Authorities acting on a tip found the body of a club bouncer frozen solid in an ice-covered lake in suburban Tacoma with an anchor chain wrapped around his neck. A county fire marshal's son was shot dead and dumped in a field near Mount Rainier, and arsonists tied a screaming night watchman in another club to an inside post before turning that establishment into an inferno.

Federal agents finally zeroed in on Tacoma nightclub owner John Carbone, whose own beachfront residence in nearby Gig Harbor was burned one evening while he was away. Carbone had portrayed himself as a simple businessman seeking to buy out other club owners. His scheme of burning his own home to divert lawmen's attention might have been more convincing if he had not moved a vehicle and numerous family heirlooms from the house before the fire began.

In November 1978, the Feds dropped their net over Carbone and fourteen others, including Sheriff Janovich, who had been bribed to keep the trail cold. All were convicted of federal racketeering charges in 1979. Janovich died a broken man in 1985, and Carbone breathed his last in a mental hospital in 1998.

The FBI turned its attention from Tacoma to Seattle in 1979 when it began a long probe into the Seattle strip-club empire of racketeer Frank Colacurcio Sr., whose legacy would include a 1971 racketeering conviction, 1981 tax-fraud conviction, and a 1991 guilty plea for tax fraud. He also was under another federal racketeering indictment when he died in 2010.

Colacurcio's troubles in 1979 had left a vacuum of criminal leadership in western Washington, and thirty-seven-year-old Gaston (Gas) Rizzo was determined to fill it. For now, he would concentrate on Tacoma, went his theory; Seattle would come in good time. The stocky, six-foot-two, onetime collegiate wrestler was a decorated Vietnam War veteran with expertise in explosives. His war exploits were tempered by two reprimands in-country for slicing off the ears of enemy soldiers with his bayonet, once while the victim was still alive. When his fiancée broke off their engagement during his deployment, he mailed an ear to her home.

The Kansas City native was hospitalized during his last two months of service while undergoing surgery and then therapy for a fractured left kneecap suffered when he tripped and fell on the tarmac while rushing to catch his plane home from Saigon in March 1967.

At just twenty-five and out of the service, Rizzo had a decision to make—return to Kansas or remain in western Washington, where he enjoyed both the climate and what he considered as Tacoma's fertile turf for making money. It was no contest. Rizzo planted his flag in Tacoma and returned to school, using the GI Bill to study electrical engineering at a local community college that offered an extension arrangement with Central Washington University. He supplemented the GI Bill with funds earned as a runner for Colacurcio, resulting from a thousand-to-one parking-lot mishap with an associate of the Seattle crime boss at a restaurant in the Tacoma suburb of Fife.

By 1971, Rizzo had his engineering degree with honors and began looking for opportunities. Small jobs were followed by larger ones, as temporary employers recognized his expertise and paid well for it.

His bank account grew along with his experience and reputation, and by 1975, he had enough for a down payment on three acres of land near the Port of Tacoma, where he opened Mercury Electric Company, a legitimate enterprise that bid on the construction and maintenance of infrastructure needed to transport electricity through high-voltage substations for home, commercial, and industrial usage.

Mercury underbid three favorites within its first year and landed a sweet $4 million contract to develop infrastructure for a gas-fired, combined-cycle power plant in the Port of Tacoma. Both the company and Gas Rizzo were on their way.

Rizzo was an appreciative man. His part-time job with Colacurcio had made the difference in affording his college tuition. In 1978, he repaid the favor without charge by assisting Colacurcio ally John Carbone with a problem he was having with a nightclub operator in Tacoma. Four nights after meeting with Carbone, the posh Hippadrome Lounge burned to the ground on the city's waterfront. Rizzo, the former army explosives expert, was in his office the next morning, quietly reading the newspaper as his employees arrived for work.

Rizzo had struck gold, as he saw it. Over time, he carefully padded each of his winning bids, and Mercury still brought in every project under bid, earning him community acclaim while also fattening his bank account. At age forty-eight in 1990, he took it upon himself to begin forming what he viewed as an investment operation in western Washington. Crime was such a dirty word, he believed, and after all, the investment of time and creative thinking certainly were as important as cash in the business arena.

With Carbone's crew in prison or dead, and Colacurcio embroiled in troubles of his own, Rizzo began building a list of trusted associates who might be persuaded to join him in developing and expanding local business "opportunities." Rizzo saw opportunity nearly everywhere he looked. It merely needed to be managed. If necessary, certain public and private officials could be cajoled into understanding their need for positive responses to carefully worded requests.

Just avoid the spotlight, went Rizzo's creed, and don't get greedy. Over time, the men had contemplated such roguish organizational names as The Ravens, Black Ops, and even The Family as self-descriptors before finally settling on simply The Business since the other three monikers lacked the innocence and finesse if they were ever revealed in courts of law.

DETONATION

But some things can't be helped where money is concerned, and within a year the spoils became worth the risk to Gas Rizzo, who knew that proper planning is always the key to a successful venture; he'd learned that in the jungles of Vietnam. In turn, the key to proper planning would be the planners themselves. And with correct planning, risk to everyone involved could be reduced to virtually zero while serious money was being made and shared indefinitely.

Rizzo had no intention of shouldering any remaining risk alone, of course. The potential partners he began warming to his ideas over time were men he knew well both within and outside the business world—men who understood how to get things done. Running a successful enterprise outside the law required associates with more than $1,000 suits and big balls. It required intellect, education, and finesse. There would be no names, places, dollar amounts, or meeting notes ever recorded regarding group activities.

Remnants of the Carbone and Colacurcio families could be called upon anonymously for certain favors, but none would ever be linked to the leadership. In time, these men would deliver messages to certain business owners and officials, persuading them to participate in upcoming events in exchange for cash and their remaining good health.

Four other men besides Rizzo would form the executive tier of The Business. Former dentist Carlo Conti became Rizzo's first choice in May 1992. He and Conti had met in January 1980 while playing handball at the downtown YMCA and became fast friends. Conti had been a successful oral surgeon and civic activist before a fall while cleaning cedar needles from the gutters of his dream home ended his lucrative dental career. The fall had broken his back, fracturing his C8 vertebra, and Conti never was able to completely cure the numbness in his thumbs.

The fall may have scuttled his primary vocation, but it had done nothing to change Conti's appreciation for the finer things in life, things that Rizzo's proposal could very possibly make happen. Conti was in after one meeting with Rizzo, who believed Conti would be the most intellectual member of the fledgling organization and was beyond compare in his ability to search out internet information.

It had taken Rizzo the rest of the decade to recruit what he considered his dream-team operation that would use brains over brawn—at least most of the time—to extort money from every imaginable source, public and private. Government contracts presented exceptional opportunities, as Rizzo knew from experience, as well as carefully planned political "irregularities." Bribing public officials and wealthy barons of industry was almost laughably easy, particularly when young women and gay men were used in the right ways under the correct circumstances.

Rizzo's military background as an explosives expert had made his destruction of the Hippadrome Lounge a walk in the park. He knew real estate owners could be made to understand how arson of competitors' or of their own properties could become moneymaking propositions or utter disasters. It merely depended on how one looked at it.

A controlled burn was what fire departments called an operation to remove ramshackle buildings or other rubble from a neighborhood. Rizzo chuckled as he turned left from Division Avenue onto a side street. He viewed arson in the very same way.

Minutes later, Rizzo drove up the driveway to his home on Yakima Avenue overlooking Commencement Bay, an area of Tacoma where large old-money homes abounded. His residence, while attractive and well kept, was smaller than the opulent mansions surrounding him. No point in standing out in the crowd, he had reasoned.

Rizzo's six-thousand-square-foot home had been built in 1911 and had been in two generations of the same family for all that time. After Rizzo bought it in 1977, he brought in contractors to restore and add to the lavish wood interior that was created originally from stands of old-growth fir cut outside the city for use in a large school built on the south side in 1883. Rizzo's contractors had reclaimed much of the vintage wood from that school when it was disassembled—not carelessly torn down—in early 1977.

The beams, braces, and flooring, prized for their size, strength, and character, were perfect for Rizzo's applications for an open-beam parlor, a beautiful rustic mantel for the living room, reclaimed mahogany flooring, and a magnificent staircase to the second floor. The completed effect was jaw-dropping.

Rizzo's home also had a maid's quarters. He didn't need a maid, but he had his contractors renovate the area and then carefully conceal its entrance from the kitchen, making it appear to be part of a pantry wall. He would then use the room as a hiding place for the twelve most valuable of his collection of nearly sixty vintage clocks, a hobby he acquired as a boy and reestablished after leaving the military.

He extracted a cold glass from his freezer and liberated three fingers of Black Jack and two ice cubes from his bar to fill it. He nudged his air-conditioning system upward this warm late-summer afternoon, slipped off his shoes, and took a seat in his private screened porch facing the bay just in time to see an immense 140,000-ton Maersk container ship from Copenhagen being maneuvered to its pier by a pair of seemingly angry Foss tugboats. A smile creased his features as he wondered how he might hijack a container now and then. All in good time, he concluded to himself. All in good time.

While reviewing his day, Rizzo made a mental note to have his runner return to Kelso's car later that evening and remove a note that had been placed between pages ninety and ninety-one of a hardcover book and then move the book to the Buick's front seat. The runner had never met Gaston Rizzo or any other members of The Business and never would. Upon receiving a text message, always from a disposable and untraceable burner phone, he would retrieve a note from a designated car backed into a parking spot at the rear of the Dolphin's Whistle. The runner would then send a text message to a phone number on the paper and go home, his work done for the day. Within a few days, an envelope containing $500 in twenty-dollar bills would appear in the runner's vehicle.

The following afternoon, Rizzo was in his office when another burner phone beeped at the receipt of an incoming text message. He wrote down the number, removed another prepaid phone from his desk, slipped on his suit coat, and left Mercury Electric, driving north on Interstate 5 toward Federal Way. Not until he was north of Highway 167 on I-5 did he dial the number. On the third ring, the call was answered by a male voice.

"I understand you need some professional work done," said Rizzo as he continued driving north on I-5.

"Yes, I need to cause major—"

"Not now. Be at the Cloverleaf Tavern at two o'clock tomorrow and look for a ten-year-old green F-100 truck. In the truck bed, near the tailgate, will be a plastic bag containing a prepaid phone. Retrieve the phone, drive to Point Defiance Park, and call me at exactly two thirty at the number taped to the phone. If you call five minutes late, I'll be gone. Are we understood?"

"Yes—"

Before the man could say anything else, Rizzo disconnected and began looking for the next exit to reverse his direction and return to Mercury Electric. He then removed the battery and SIM card from the burner phone.

The following morning, Rizzo arrived at his office shortly before seven and noticed the cars of his shop foreman and equipment manager already parked. He smiled as he surveyed his forty-two white-and-green work trucks bearing the bright-red Mercury center logo parked in the lot. His gaze floated over International Durastar boom trucks, digger derricks with Terex Commander 6000 cranes, a Hogg & Davis cable puller, reel, and pole trailers, and over a dozen pickups and service vans. Average value was nearly $75,000 apiece.

DETONATION

This morning Rizzo had a meeting with his job estimator, big Bo Harrison, to review a bid to upgrade three miles of 230KV overhead transmission lines that bring high voltage from the east side of the Tacoma Narrows Bridge to a local substation in Gig Harbor.

As Harrison outlined his proposal line by line, it became clear very quickly that he had done his homework. The bid was going to be as close to perfect as Mercury could make it. Harrison droned on with a few details, and Rizzo's thoughts began turning to his phone call the previous afternoon. He thought it would be prudent to include another member of his "investment" group in his future contacts with the caller.

Rizzo shook Harrison's hand for an excellent bid before entering his office and dialing the phone number of Carlo Conti.

It was 1:15 p.m. when Rizzo pulled his silver Lincoln Navigator to the curb in front of Conti's Ruston Way condominium. Conti got in, and both men remained silent as they merged with westbound traffic along Ruston Way past more than a mile of trendy waterfront restaurants and nightclubs. Rizzo entered the Black Velvet parking lot five minutes later, turned the Lincoln around, and headed for an exit that would take them south toward the sprawling Tacoma Mall.

"Okay, Gas, what have we got?" Conti finally asked, breaking the ice as they rolled through afternoon freeway traffic and exited to South Thirty-Eighth Street and then to a boulevard skirting the mall.

"Not a repeat customer, CC; a new lead from Irv Kelso. We only spoke briefly yesterday, but the guy was an older male. White, I think, and no accent." Rizzo discovered a crack in a fingernail and absentmindedly bit at it.

"Why not just tell him we start at a hundred K for fixing a parking ticket, and after that he could be looking at real money?"

Rizzo glanced at the digital clock on the Navigator's dash and turned up the radio. "I have the guy calling me at two thirty and thought we could find a quiet spot here in the mall while we listen to his proposal."

"You really shouldn't do that, buddy," said Conti.

"Do what?"

"Chew on your fingernails like that. I've had to operate on a couple people who developed mouth infections from chewing nails that had dirt under them. You could wind up in a hospital if you're not careful."

"And you could wind up in a morgue if you ever lay that bullshit on me again."

"Just sayin' . . ."

At two twenty-five, the men parked in a large lot adjacent to the J. C. Penney and Firestone Tire stores. Both removed the batteries from their cells, and Rizzo turned on the burner phone and placed it on the leather console that separated the Lincoln's large seats. At two twenty-eight, the phone rang.

"Thank you for your promptness. How can I help you?" asked Rizzo, placing the caller on speakerphone.

For the next twenty minutes, he and Conti listened to a proposal so bizarre that at first they believed a friend, or friends, were playing an elaborate joke on them. Rizzo never told the caller that Conti was listening, or that he had moved the car twice during the call to minimize any curiosity. The men gazed openmouthed at each other several times. Rizzo smiled as his colleague put his hand behind his neck and shook his head in disbelief. Finally, Rizzo picked up the phone and glanced at Conti, who shrugged.

"Here's the deal," said Rizzo. "I want ten days to research and evaluate your request. That ten-day evaluation will start after you provide me with a fifty thousand dollar cash down payment. The money will be refunded to you, minus ten thousand, if I turn down your project. If I accept it, I'll present you with the financials. We're talking millions for a project of this magnitude. Are you comfortable with what I'm telling you?"

"Yes, but I need time to arrange the cash."

Rizzo gave a thumbs-up to Conti. "Understood, and please take your time. But let's be clear, my friend: this is serious business, and I'm a very serious man. Don't fuck with me. I accept clean cash only. Your first job is to understand that and avoid the money-laundering regulations that the banks now follow."

For the next few minutes, Rizzo provided instructions for the caller to make the $50,000 drop. He then gave him a new phone number to call and instructed him to destroy his prepaid phone in his backyard barbecue. After Rizzo hung up, he took apart his own burner phone and handed it to Conti, who would make it disappear.

"Tell me straight, CC. Have you ever heard anything so preposterous in your life?"

"Not in this lifetime or the last two either. The bastard is dead serious. He didn't hesitate for a second about this being a million-dollar ticket."

"We're talking about an undertaking that would challenge the CIA or the Pentagon," replied Rizzo, driving out of the lot and heading toward a northbound freeway on-ramp.

"Well, either that or you were just talking with the FBI."

"I don't think so, but give me a few days to check this stuff out and then let's have a full partners' meeting."

Conti nodded and then added, "If the NSA was able to sniff out any part of that conversation, they'd be calling for a meeting of the whole national security team right now."

Rizzo grinned. "I think my life has a new purpose, CC. Do you remember the Spanish treasure ships that were found by explorers off Florida in about thirty feet of water back in the eighties?"

"Yeah. They were carrying millions in gold and silver back to Spanish royalty. Why?"

"Well, I think we just might have stumbled on a king's ransom of our own."

Chapter Four

Anxious to return Rob Spencer's message, Morgan thanked Mott, left the auto museum, and walked to his car. The brief text had startled him, and as he slipped into his dark-green BMW sedan and fired the engine, he hit speed dial for Spencer's phone, only to reach an answering system. Morgan left his name and then turned up the car's air conditioner.

Morgan settled back in his black leather seat and reflected on his conversation with Barry Mott. His four years as an investigator with the Seattle Police Department and three years with the Justice Department often helped him fine-tune what his intuition told him. At the moment, however, it appeared that his intuition had taken the day off.

What was Mott's motivation in giving him a heads-up on the port security proposal? Or was there one? Morgan didn't have either answer, but he did know that the expensively tailored port commissioner had just stiffed him for their four-dollar coffee tab.

Morgan was getting antsy. He hated delays, and twelve minutes had passed since he returned Spencer's text message. Like Morgan, Spencer had a law enforcement pedigree. As a retired major and chief criminal investigator with the Miami Police Department, he was well qualified for his position as director of fleet security for Nobility Cruise Lines. Corporate protocol required that whenever a serious incident or legal issue occurred aboard any of the line's ten ships, that vessel's security officer would contact Morgan first.

Nobility had four options available to its crews when dealing with problems aboard any of its floating resorts. It was a matter of degree. The liner's onboard security office handled minor issues; either Spencer or authorities in the next port of call could be reached by phone or radio for escalating situations, as could the Federal Bureau of Investigation and US Navy and commercial ships in the area. Ship officers also could contact Morgan by satellite phone if other communications channels were blocked, and although that rarely happened, the ability to request or provide crucial information through Morgan was a valuable asset in a world being set afire by terrorists in some quadrants and weak political leadership in others.

Morgan drummed his fingers against the steering wheel. The urgency in Spencer's voice had suggested that Morgan would be on a plane very soon.

As he reached for his phone to redial, it rang with Spencer on the line from Nobility's corporate headquarters in Fort Lauderdale. The pleasantries were short, and Spencer got to the point. "We've got an overboard from the *Bernini*. No luck on the search. She's gone."

"That's Marwah's ship, right?" Raju Marwah had been assistant security chief aboard the *Matisse Under the Stars* three months earlier and had assisted Morgan and the FBI to stop a near-catastrophic terrorist attack onboard using poisoned food at a restaurant buffet table. Marwah had saved the life of the ship's security officer by jumping into the path of a terrorist's gunfire.

"Yep, our favorite Gurkha. His bullet wounds are healed, and we promoted him to chief security officer on the *Bernini*. It's now in port at San Juan, Puerto Rico. The jumper went over last night when the ship was between Grand Turk and San Juan."

"Does it look like suicide?"

"It looks like it, yeah; we have a note. But the cabin steward says she and her husband had been fighting since they first boarded, Brick, and I don't like the sound of that at all. They board the ship, argue nonstop for two days, and she decides to take a swan dive after dark. Now that's convenient, isn't it?"

"Who was the jumper?"

"Wife. Name is Cristiana Bianchi. Husband is Patrizio Bianchi. On the surface, it appears cut and dried, but I'll wager my watch to your Beemer that it isn't."

"Okay, what's below the surface?" It was a question born of Morgan's work with veteran police detectives whose years of investigating crimes often helped them analyze new circumstances and develop perceptions for how those circumstances came about. Different crime categories frequently take similar paths as they develop. Morgan respected Spencer's thirty-plus years with the Miami Police Department and knew there would be a good reason for his suspicions.

"The suicide note was typed. Understand from Raju that the husband called the purser's desk just before she jumped. Raju also says the guy—Patrizio—doesn't appear distraught. He's an attorney from Miami."

"You want me to catch up with the *Bernini*?"

"I've already notified the FBI, but I would be more comfortable if you could make sure that Raju and his people haven't missed anything. The damn media still has the cruise industry on its radar. It's hard to blame the bastards, though. We had that terrorist calamity on the *Matisse* ourselves, and then the *Grand Princess* had two overboards on its Hawaii run last April, and the *Carnival Triumph* still is in the news for losing its rudder off of Cuba and nearly causing an international incident. Now this."

"What's the *Bernini*'s itinerary?"

"Today she's in San Juan. Then she sails to St. Maarten, a day at sea, and on to the Bahamas."

"I have time zones working against me, but I'll grab my go bag and try to meet her in St. Maarten." Before disconnecting, Morgan asked Rob to call in however many old favors it took from his Miami sources to learn what he could about Patrizio Bianchi.

DETONATION

As he made the transition from Schuster Parkway onto Ruston Way, Morgan glanced out the passenger-side window of his BMW and observed three hulking cargo ships anchored in Commencement Bay waiting their turns for a terminal berth. Bumping up against one of them was a small personal fishing boat with the lone man aboard furiously trying to restart the craft's outboard motor after apparently losing power and drifting into the 140,000-ton Maersk *Carolina* anchored barely a hundred yards offshore. Two crewmen aboard an adjacent ship could be seen roaring with laughter as they watched the man looking over his shoulder nervously at two approaching tugboats.

Morgan rolled along, grinning at the spectacle for a moment before his thoughts returned to Barry Mott, TEUs, and security at the Port of Tacoma. "Patience is a virtue, Barry," he said to himself.

Before packing and heading to the airport, Morgan decided to make a quick stop at the Point Ruston Condominiums residence of Rilee, an ingenious computer guru and reclusive friend who Morgan often referred to in jest as his high-priced hacker. Rilee was so skillful at hacking unnoticed into private, corporate, and even some government computer systems that Brick had engaged her to ferret out crucial information for several previous investigations. She had never failed to deliver, and he needed her expertise once more.

It was just after one o'clock as he passed the restaurants of C. I. Shenanigans, The CodFather, and Prawnbroker, whose overwater decks appeared to be doing brisk business with temperatures hovering in the mid-eighties. Morgan turned into the condo complex, checked in with security, and found a parking spot in partial shade near a manicured bed of pink and lavender roses encircling a miniature blue spruce tree. It was his first visit since Rilee had held a small party upon moving in four months ago.

Morgan stepped from his Beemer and glanced toward Rilee's driveway where a cherry-red 2009 Rolls-Royce Phantom convertible graced her parking spot. "Well, at least she's still keeping a low profile," he muttered, heading for the elevator.

The classy, ninety-seven-acre development stretched along a mile of reclaimed and reengineered beachfront once occupied by the gone but unlamented ASARCO smelter that belched its last burst of sulphur gas three decades earlier.

Ignoring an abundance of security cameras, Morgan left the elevator at the penthouse and walked to Rilee's door but found no bell. In its place were two round brass sand dollar replicas that visitors tapped against a brass backing. Brick did so.

Rilee opened her door and stifled a little scream.

"Nice knockers you have there," Morgan said with a grin, as she erupted with laughter.

"So I've been told," she responded, throwing her arms around the big man, who easily lifted her off her feet as he returned the hug. "I installed them myself yesterday."

"You could have fooled me," said Morgan. "I meant the ones on the door."

"So did I," said Rilee, sliding back to her feet and opening the door with a flourish to her new kingdom. She was tall for a woman at five eight, and her 130 pounds were well distributed over her medium frame. Rilee wore a red jumpsuit rolled up slightly at the ankles, displaying short pink athletic socks and low-rise white tennis shoes. Her smile was radiant.

Morgan stepped inside and was unnerved; Rilee had redecorated. Black slate facing now graced the living room wall containing her custom gas fireplace, and a digital faux aquarium adorned an east wall with the rich and bright colors of tropical fish that were not actually there. Two Chesterfield baroque leather love seats enjoyed forward views of freighter and pleasure-boat traffic, a heavy Huard leather ottoman covered with a pair of interior decorating magazines sat in front of one; and knickknacks and family photos rested on a small bookcase near a hallway. Next to the bookcase was a three-foot alabaster statue of fifteenth-century Sultan Mehmet II, founder of what is now Istanbul, Turkey. Rilee's eyes met Brick's, and both gazed back at the statue.

"Well, it was in the catalog, so . . ." she began, her face turning slightly pink before she offered Morgan a lemonade from a crystal decanter atop her custom granite bar. She raised the decanter silently so Brick could see it gleam. "I bought this one at the mall," she declared. He nodded, and she poured.

Rilee was a brilliant and complex woman all rolled into a beautiful, auburn-haired package. During her undergraduate days at MIT a decade ago, she left potential suitors perplexed by noting in the school yearbook that her favorite turn-on was "public-key encryption."

Boeing hired Riley during her junior year to ensure it would have the first and only offer for her when she graduated a year later. The company's investment paid big dividends during her eight years in Seattle working on design-development issues for the company's defense, space, and security divisions' network firewalls.

When Morgan first hired her cybersleuth talents, she was known as Titus—no last name. Her most recent assignment from Morgan involved hacking the computer system of a Middle Eastern terrorist group involved in the *Matisse* attack. A tiny miscalculation, however, and she found herself on FBI radar. A stern warning from the bureau was followed by a $5 million tax-free check and an immediate job offer since her computer skills had been instrumental in eliminating the terrorist network.

Rilee turned down the job on good terms and moved her operation from her suburban home to her new condo. She changed her given name to Rilee—again, no last name—and returned to her private world of secrecy and seclusion. A week after cashing the government check, she was reading ultrasecret, deep-background information involving CIA turning of an FBI mole.

"Were you followed?" Rilee joked as she handed Brick his

lemonade, receiving a wink in reply.

Morgan explained the call from Rob Spencer and his need to fly to the Caribbean this afternoon. He also volunteered details of his coffee meeting with Barry Mott.

"I need two things while I'm gone. See what you can dig up on Miami attorney Patrizio Bianchi and his wife, Cristiana. Then, see if you can find any security-contract proposals at any of the nation's ports. My guess is there are over a hundred; maybe focus on the fifty largest. Concentrate on the RFPs first, and then see if you can find any actual proposals that have become public record."

"Okay if I look under the covers a little?"

"With the shipping port project?"

"No. The Bianchi guy," she answered as she wrote on a pad.

"Go for it," he responded, while pretending to ignore the plunging neckline on her crimson jumpsuit.

"Relax, Brick, you're not wearing one either," Rilee said, eyeing him closely as she took a sip of lemonade.

"Wearing what?" he asked, hoping she wouldn't say . . .

"A bra," she laughed. "You're not wearing a bra either, so relax."

"I am relaxed."

"Not from where I'm standing."

"Uh, well, it's just, uh . . ."

Saying no to temptation had never been one of Morgan's strong suits, but the *Bernini* wouldn't wait if he missed his flight.

Rilee finally saved Morgan from himself. "Before you go, I want to give you a new set of code sheets. The NSA's Bluffdale project is up and running; now nobody has any privacy. By the way, always pull your battery when you're done using your cell."

Brick accepted her five sheets of codes and vowed to be security vigilant. Rilee had always been over the top concerning government intrusion methods, but recent NSA spying disclosures had proven her correct. Her code sheets contained over five hundred verbs and nouns, each assigned a different number. If the code sheets were used only once, the code was unbreakable, even by the CIA or NSA.

"I also created a Faraday cage by moving all my computers into the other bedroom and covering the windows and walls with copper mesh grid."

"You did what? Now you're beginning to worry me. I gotta see this."

Rilee led him to her computer room where he took stock of one wall covered almost entirely with a copper matrix.

"And all this wire will do what?" he asked.

"Have you heard about the Narcissus Project?"

"Enlighten me."

Rilee stood, adjusted the top of her jumpsuit, and proceeded to give Morgan a course in electromagnetic radiation. "When you look at the window on a microwave, you see that it's covered with a fine wire mesh. That's a Faraday cage, and it stops the radiation from escaping through the glass. Then we have the Narcissus venture."

"I'm still listening," he responded, taking a seat in her computer chair.

"Narcissus is the government spying project that followed the Tempest and Black Owl endeavors," she began. "Tempest was a classified study about the susceptibility of some computers to release electromagnetic radiation in a way that could be used to reconstruct understandable data. I know how far-out that sounds, so I'm not even going to discuss Black Owl with you.

"But—stay with me, Brick—Narcissus goes deeper to gather data by using oblivious people to gather leaking emanations from our keyboards, computers, and monitors by attaching RF receivers to commercial delivery trucks that visit homes and offices all over the country. Every time one stops at a house, it's likely that it has inside it a small, built-in parabolic high-gain antenna that is capturing electronic emissions leaking from nearby cables and even LCD monitors to try to understand full conversations. The truck drivers have no idea they are being used by the Feds to gather information."

"You're telling me that when a package is delivered to your condo, Narcissus has equipment inside the truck to intercept info from your computer? Give me a break, Rilee."

"It's no joke," she said. "And it's not just computers, but copy machines and cell phones as well. My work comes very close to crossing the line of cyber legality, and it wouldn't be healthy to have the government monitoring my day-to-day keystrokes. Putting up a Faraday cage prevents any access to my computer system."

"Got it, but who or what specifically is Narcissus?"

"Once the NSA site in Bluffdale, Utah, came online, Congress quietly began the first-ever serious investigation into details of NSA spying since that agency opened. Think about it, Brick. President Truman quietly approved formation of the NSA on November 4, 1952, the same day Eisenhower was first elected president. The country was awash in political news that day and for days afterward. People didn't even notice that they had a new agency for a long time.

"Back then, Americans were patriots, and the idea that a top-secret agency designed to protect the nation might someday be snooping into their private business was far beyond their horizon. Do you realize that the NSA does not have a real budget to show to the public or even to Congress? It's exempt.

"Look, there's no agency or organization in the world more powerful than the NSA, Brick, and what I know about it is like a small grain of sand on my beach outside. But Narcissus itself is a private company that's owned by the US government but hidden a mile deep under a zillion LLCs and overseas trusts. The NSA can tell Congress that they're not spying on citizens, and yet all the spying shenanigans continue, outsourced to Narcissus.

"Even here in Tacoma the police have at least one StingRay device that tricks cell phones into thinking it's a cell tower. If they're looking for a major drug dealer, for example, they can get a warrant that allows them to only hear communications in one specific home or office where that person is believed to be located."

Morgan stood and turned to Rilee. "You know all that, and you're only one grain of sand on the beach."

"Scary, huh?" she responded, arms folded across her chest.

Three hours later, Morgan was waiting for his flight to JFK and then on to St. Maarten. While at the Sea-Tac gate, he received a text from Rob Spencer. Patrizio Bianchi had left the ship in San Juan and was flying home to Miami.

Chapter Five

Morgan finished rereading the email. He counted on Rilee—the hacker for sale—to keep him up to speed, and she had come through again, providing him with his first look inside the lives of Patrizio and Cristiana Bianchi.

Morgan could control many things in his life, but time wasn't one of them. His American Airlines 777 ER still was four hours away from Princess Juliana International Airport on St. Maarten. The first half of the flight from JFK had passed quickly. He had shelled out the seventeen-dollar subscription fee for the airline's international Wi-Fi, and Rilee's uncoded message arrived right on time.

Pat Bianchi was fifty-five and an honors graduate of the Syracuse University College of Law. His father, Victor, was an Annapolis graduate and Marine Corps major, who was killed in action in March 1968 during the Vietnam War. Government financial assistance to the major's family helped pay for Pat's education. He graduated third in his class in 1986 and accepted a job offer in Miami from a law firm that specialized in patents and trademark services. Within five years at age thirty-one, Bianchi had expanded his role into copyright infringement and intellectual property law—a perfect transition at a perfect time for an ambitious man.

Bianchi was a good conversationalist who came across well on the job, at parties, and in meetings attended by senior business-community members who were impressed by his intellect and breadth of knowledge at such a tender age. Rilee's message added that he was outgoing, and as circumstances presented themselves, he schmoozed easily with experts in industries ranging from manufacturing to health care and from natural gas to telecommunications.

Bianchi's investment portfolio contained growing positions in

ExxonMobil, Walmart, and Lockheed Martin. His father had left him $10,000 in savings bonds that Pat sold in 1985 and invested in Microsoft. All in all, Patrizio Bianchi was doing well as he entered the fourth decade of his life.

The near-overnight growth spurt the law firm enjoyed with Bianchi aboard became a gusher by 1991, and Bianchi's income grew with it. He was made a full partner at age forty-one and was elected senior partner a year later when his friend and benefactor, Hal Sutton, was killed in a Lockheed 1011 crash in the Florida Everglades while preparing to land in Miami. Sutton's wife, Deena, also died.

One of Bianchi's associates at the firm was Atlanta native Cheryl Higgins, hired by Sutton away from a Boston firm and assigned to work with Bianchi on intellectual property law, where her star rose quickly and very brightly as well.

Cristiana had met Patrizio at a fraternity party when she was a nursing student at Syracuse, and the two built a relationship that lasted through his final year of law school. With more than two hundred friends and relatives in attendance, they married in front of the university's student union building the day of his graduation and departed for Miami three hours later.

Cristiana completed her master's degree in orthopedic medicine at the University of Miami and joined the school's orthopedics department a year after the couple arrived in the city. Her father, businessman Herbert Bonn, was a widower whose company had pioneered Innovorbonn, a substance similar to Teflon used to produce nonstick cookware and for in-flight experiments by the NASA space program.

Her fourteen years with the university were as fulfilling as they were busy, and in 2001, she accepted a position with the Miami School District as an orthopedic nurse, where her professional skills made her a perfect fit for the district's new sports-injury education and prevention program. Eight years later, she took early retirement at forty-five to devote more time to personal pursuits, one of which was collecting toy dolls dating from the early 1950s, an amusing pastime she learned from her mother.

As was her custom in preparing background files, Rilee had dug deeply into Cristiana's financial records and found a treasure, literally. When Herb Bonn died in 2010 at eighty-four, he left Cristiana a trust fund of $8 million.

"Ladies and gentlemen, as we start our descent into St. Maarten, please make sure your seat backs and tray tables are in their . . ."

Morgan shut down his iPad and closed his eyes as he tried to imagine Cristiana's last few minutes aboard the *Bernini Under the Stars*. It was an exercise in futility; he needed far more information than he had right now.

Twenty-two minutes later, the triple seven's twelve wheels touched and squealed against the St. Maarten's tarmac, and the captain's slow thrust reversal on the plane's two GE 90-115 turbofan engines gently roused Brick from his catnap. The plane taxied to Gate A-2, and as passengers began to disembark, he had a decision to make: walk straight to the terminal's storied coffee bar first or pick up his luggage. The latter won out after he considered where his case might end up in if he left it on the baggage carousel while enjoying a coffee. New Zealand and Paraguay were a couple of destinations that came to mind.

Morgan was still holding his large Panama coffee minutes later while doing his best to flag down a taxi that would take him from the airport to the cruise ship docks near Philipsburg in the Dutch section of the island where he could still use his US dollars if necessary.

St. Maarten is in the northeast Caribbean, roughly a 190 miles east of Puerto Rico, and is divided in ownership between France and the Netherlands. The thirty-three-square-mile vacation paradise is most often visited by well-to-do travelers and celebrities seeking a tranquil and tropical location to unwind.

Many consider it curious that the Dutch and French could coexist on an eight-by-nine-mile island resting in a much larger ocean. Morgan didn't particularly care, but he was grateful that a cab had finally pulled up and stopped at the curb. He plunked his luggage into the trunk and slipped into the back seat, pleased that the vehicle's air conditioner was functioning as they drove off.

"Sir, if yuh want marijuana, yuh better stay on the Dutch side, the French is stricter," suggested the shaggy-haired cabbie, appearing to be a man of experience in that form of relaxation. He was in perhaps his midfifties, short, wore a yellow T-shirt over brown khakis, and held his left hand over his eyes while weaving through light traffic. No sunglasses were in evidence. Or seat belts.

The cabbie changed lanes, eliciting a loud honk from another cabbie trying to pass. The second cab returned to the left lane and passed, and as he did, both drivers yelled at the other and shook their fists. Another ordinary day on the streets of St. Maarten. "He is meh cousin, too fast driver," the cabbie began again. "Now, about da marijuana . . ."

"I gave it up for Lent this year," Morgan responded. "Question: Why are all the casinos on the Dutch side?"

"Dat because the French side is little bit bigger. We get casinos, and they get to talk French and drink wine. Sir, yuh know story of how island was divided?"

Morgan held back a little chuckle. "Go for it, my friend."

"Sir, meh tell yuh the story. It was sixteen forty-eight, before meh was born. They was arguing about where is dat border. So Frenchman and Dutchman have race around island. The Dutchman drank much gin, yuh know, and he keeps falling down. So Frenchman runs dat farther, so they got more land. Dat's okay because we got casino and they have to talk French."

"How many times a day do you tell that story?"

"You the sixth one today."

"I'll remember not to drink too much gin tonight," Morgan replied, paying the driver and tipping him for the story. Brick retrieved his bag and headed toward the *Bernini*, its gleaming white presence looming over the A.C. Wathey Pier, known by locals simply as the Big Pier. The cabbie turned around and drove back the way he had come, perhaps polishing his Frenchman-Dutchman tale for his next passenger.

As Morgan approached the *Bernini* gangway, he recognized the voice of the ship's chief security officer, Raju Marwah.

"Sir Brick, welcome to the *Bernini Under the Stars*—Nobility's grandest."

"Officer Marwah, thanks for the invitation to your new ship." The men shook hands warmly as Morgan arrived on deck.

"I found you a nice mini-suite—A-twelve-oh-four on the Aquarius deck. It's a nice cabin near the bow. Let me know when you want to review our evidence file and crime scene records of the jumper lady."

Morgan was tempted to challenge Raju on his choice of words, but decided to bite his tongue for now. "Give me thirty minutes to freshen up, Raju, and I'll meet you in your office."

"I'm sorry to tell you, Brick, but the husband decided to leave the ship while we were in San Juan. I must be honest, he was a real ass-jerk."

Morgan assumed that Raju was trying to say that Pat Bianchi was an asshole. Having not yet examined a shred of evidence, he pondered why he had already developed the same impression.

Chapter Six

Armed with fresh coffee, Morgan took the stairs from deck five to deck four at the ship's waterline level. The ship would depart St. Maarten in fifty-four minutes. Morgan strode past the infirmary to the door of the ship's security office, tapped twice, and entered Raju Marwah's domain.

"I hope you found your cabin hunky-dory, Mr. Brick."

"Thanks, Raju, and quit calling me mister. It will be fine for what I hope is a short stay." Morgan was a contracted investigator and had been aboard most of Nobility's ships, but only briefly on the *Bernini*. The chief security officer rose from his desk holding a folder and nodded toward a wooden worktable in the center of the room.

"Here's my case file on Cristiana Bianchi. It includes the suicide letter, a statement by Mr. Bianchi, a compact disc copy of his call to the purser's office, and statements from passengers. One of the statements is from Marcia Parker, whose cabin is B-seven-oh-seven on eleven, one floor below the Bianchi suite. She saw the body fall past her while she was sitting on her balcony. Her sister, Teresa Fey, was with her but didn't see it."

Morgan picked up the file and pulled his iPad from his black and well-worn Bally briefcase. "How are the balconies configured on decks eleven, twelve, and below? Are they flush or do any jut out from the ship?"

"You mean project out?"

"Yeah, stick out."

"They're all flush. The Bianchi cabin was a mini-suite with a small balcony. Below on the Boötes deck the cabins are smaller, but the balconies are larger."

"How many starboard cameras picked up the overboard?" While

Marwah retrieved another file, Morgan recalled an operation eighteen months prior when Nobility hired him to assist in upgrading its fleet video-surveillance network. The *Bernini*'s internet protocol (IP) cameras were part of four systems. Its Six Sixty cameras, supported by nearly three hundred wireless access points, maintained general ship surveillance, casino security, back-of-house, and departmental monitoring.

"Of the eight cameras starboard, two picked up her fall," said Marwah. "Most of the general ship cameras feed video data at one frame per second, but the ones monitoring an overboard are set at twelve frames per second."

"Let me take a look," Morgan said, spreading the stills out on the table. He located the time stamp and entered into his iPad, "00132009112015 (CUT)." "From deck twelve to the water is twenty-two meters." He then used a splat calculator on the iPad to enter the meters and sixty-one kilograms for the victim's weight and made the calculation. "It would have taken just over two seconds for her to hit the water." The coarse term "splat" is used by investigators in reference to the sound of a falling body striking a surface.

Morgan glanced at Marwah and was sure he saw the man's face turn red. The security officer appeared confused but made no comment.

The two cameras had captured only a third of the fall and produced just eight frames, none of which showed the start of the descent. Morgan picked up his tape recorder and asked to be shown to the purser's office.

Marwah locked the security office door and led the way to an elevator that quickly ascended to deck five. The men were proceeding in silence down a passageway and had passed a metal stairway connecting decks three, four, and five when Morgan asked what had become of the large Gurkha knife that had saved Raju's life aboard the *Matisse* the previous year.

"It has a big dent in the blade where it stopped the first bullet. The ship's carpenters made me a nice holder to display it, but I need to keep it locked in the department's security cage because it's considered a weapon. Wish I could show it off, but . . ." He shrugged.

Morgan was involved in the shootout with a terrorist aboard the *Matisse* that came within a whisker of taking Marwah's life. The probable fatal slug had struck the knife held in Marwah's belt and ricocheted, missing by less than an inch. Leaping in front of a bullet was either brave or reckless, depending on one's point of view, but after witnessing the incident, Morgan was certain that by doing so, Raju had saved the life of Yvette Fuentes, chief of security of the *Matisse* who had been the terrorist's target.

The men arrived at the office of Assistant Purser Melanie Harris, who was expecting them. Her mouth fell open when she spotted Morgan, who towered over her five-foot-one, 110-pound frame. Marwah introduced them. Melanie stuck out her hand in greeting, which Morgan enveloped with his.

"Mr. Morgan, it's a pleasure. We're glad you're here. This situation has been a ball-ache for us, or as you Yanks call it, a nut-buster." Melanie was British, properly charming and very attractive, but a woman who acted as though that description had never occurred to her. A prize one day for some lucky man.

Introductions complete, Morgan suggested the trio move to the Aurora dining room, where they would have more space to compare case notes.

"No, they're playing bingo in the Aurora. Let's go up to six and use the Nova bar instead," Melanie replied over her shoulder, leading the men past the long service desk toward an elegant spiral staircase that would take them upward one flight. A young couple dressed in shorts and sea-blue Nobility T-shirts passed them, holding hands and laughing, seemingly oblivious to others.

"Honeymooners on a budget," Morgan said to himself.

Once seated in a corner of the bar, Harris opened her laptop and located the digital audio file of Bianchi's urgent call to the purser's office. "Mr. Morgan—"

"Please call me Brick. Mr. Morgan makes me feel old," he replied, glancing at Marwah. He moved closer to Harris for a better view of her file and detected a hint of lilac in her hair.

Harris made a few keystrokes and highlighted the file on her Mac. "All our audio records are saved uncompressed and in a raw audio format. The ship's servers dump to Florida every twenty-four hours. We converted the file so it would be compatible with our department's Macs."

"Let's hear the call," said Brick, leaning forward. They listened to Bianchi's frantic shouting twice before Morgan asked to hear the final ten seconds.

"Sir, I show that you are in room Aquarius seven-oh-nine, is that correct?"

"Yes. A-seven-oh-nine. Hurry! She's just run onto the balcony—oh no!"

Brick made some notes on his iPad and leaned back in his chair. "We'll need to have the file sent to an audio lab, but I'm certain that the background voice—the woman's voice—says, 'You're an asshole! You'll always be an asshole! I'm not taking it anymore!'"

Marwah had listened to the recording several times before Brick arrived onboard. "That's what I thought I heard," he said, nodding. While he spoke, the *Bernini*'s engines rumbled to life as preparations neared completion for her departure from St. Maarten.

"What do you think happened to our victim, Raju?"

"I'm thinking, 'Let eagle shriek from lofty peak; the never-ending watchword of our land. Let summer breeze waft through the trees; the echo of the chorus grand,'" Marwah responded, quoting John Philip Sousa's "Stars and Stripes Forever."

DETONATION

Morgan groaned, having endured the man's off-topic ramblings several times during his investigation aboard the *Matisse*. He set down his notes, folded his hands, and gave Marwah an exasperated stare. "Raju, have you ever fallen overboard from a ship—a *moving* ship, I mean?" he asked calmly. "I enjoy sonnets, too, but not when I'm working, as you well know."

"But they're part of my East Indian heritage," Marwah responded, indignant.

"Well, let me explain part of my American heritage, Raju. That would be the part that doesn't have time for bullshit. So if I hear it one more time during this investigation, I'm going to ask Miss Harris here to help me carry your ass down to the stern and throw you into the ocean. That would give us two overboards in the same week, and I would be investigating both. Are we clear?"

"Okay, okay," Marwah replied, smiling weakly. "I think Mr. Bianchi was a jerk. His wife couldn't take it anymore, so she jumped. It's a suicide, Brick."

"Melanie, look at these two date-time stamps," Morgan said, handing them to her. "What do you see?"

"The stamp for the phone call indicates it was made at zero eight thirteen thirty-eight Zulu on September eleventh, the day after the incident," she replied. Zulu, or Coordinated Universal Time, is the primary standard by which the world regulates clocks and time. The term "Zulu" is used by the military and in commercial navigation.

"Eight thirteen thirty-eight is the next day per Zulu time," Morgan said. "My question is, why do the IP cameras have her going over the side at eight thirteen twenty local time here and our time of the call is eight thirteen thirty-eight?"

"Eighteen seconds after she actually went over," Harris observed, nodding. "We seem to have a tad of a problem."

"*We* don't have a problem, Melanie. But Patrizio Bianchi has a *big* problem."

"You sure know your onions, Brick," she said with a smile as she shut down her Mac.

Harris left the Nova Bar and returned to her office while Brick and Raju took an amidships elevator up to deck twelve. As they walked toward the victim's cabin, Marwah signaled Morgan to stop. "I'm confused. What did you mean that because of the time thing Bianchi is in trouble?"

Brick stopped just short of cabin A-709 and looked Marwah in the eye, concerned at how little the ship's security officer seemed to understand about routine investigational procedures. "Raju, how could the ship's starboard cameras clearly show Cristiana going over the side eighteen seconds before her husband tells Melanie in a recorded phone call that she's still in the cabin acting crazy?"

"But she left a suicide letter."

"Well, someone left a suicide letter, didn't they? Let's check out their cabin."

They stepped into the cabin and paused to slip on protective booties and latex gloves. During the next twenty minutes, Marwah took notes while Brick methodically examined the cabin and placed several items in envelopes before slipping them into his evidence-and-chain-of-custody bag. That task completed, he sat down on a sofa near the French doors of the mini-suite. "Raju, pull up a chair. Do you have the suicide letter?"

"Right here, boss."

Morgan placed the letter on the coffee table and then scrutinized a half-dozen slips of paper that he had placed in the envelopes. "People have three types of signatures, Raju—initials, a short signature, and a formal signature. Initials are rarely used.

"When people sign a credit card slip or a room service bill, they get sloppy and use their short signature. But whenever they sign a legal document or a personal letter, for example, they use their formal signature. Look at these slips signed by Mrs. Bianchi for room service. She signs as Cris and a large letter B that's followed by a wiggly line about an inch long. Take it to the bank that she would never use her short signature for the final words of her life."

"I'm with you so far."

"Now, compare her signature from these room service slips with the suicide letter. What do you see?"

"They're all the same."

"Another thing, Raju. When we listened to the audio replay of Bianchi's call to Melanie, we could hear Cristiana's voice. The problem was there was no echo. If she had been in the background screaming, her voice would have bounced off the walls and resonated more than it did."

"Maybe the balcony door was open and it didn't resonate as much as you thought inside the cabin."

"I don't think so. If it had been open, someone in one of the other cabins almost certainly would have reported the screams. But no one did."

"People don't always report things that are none of their business. Maybe they didn't want to get involved and just ignored it or were out of their cabins in the restaurants or the bars, or dancing. We had an Eagles tribute band playing in the Luminosity Bar on deck six."

"That had me stumped for a while too. But I'd bet that he started an argument with her somewhere else—maybe at home or on an outing somewhere—and secretly recorded her responses. Wherever they were, there was no echo left on the recording. After that, he could have arranged the cruise as a way to make up with her for the argument. So eventually they board the ship."

"And he could have done that six months ago for all we know."

"Exactly."

"Sorry, Brick, the light just came on. Now I see where you're going with all this."

"It's about time, Raju. I was beginning to think a giraffe could walk in here and sit on your face and you wouldn't notice."

"Well, I'm a security officer, not an investigator."

"Which is why I'm here to help. Better include the evidence I used and the steps I've just shown you when you write your report so you won't forget it."

Still wearing his latex gloves, Morgan turned over a file folder and wrote the date and time on the back.

"Here's how I see it, Raju. Pat Bianchi boards the ship with a prepared suicide letter and a small digital voice recorder. On the recorder is the loud argument with Cristiana set at the point where her screaming will begin the moment he pushes play on the recorder. He also locates a room service slip and copies his wife's signature to the letter, something a handwriting expert could detect in five minutes. Huge mistake.

"At some point, Bianchi kills his wife—probably strangles or suffocates her. Then, he opens the balcony door, lifts her up, and drops her over the railing into the ocean. Finally, he returns to the cabin, dials nine one one, gets Melanie, and after a few words, turns on the recorder. There it is.

"Back to your office, Raju. I need to give Florida a call."

Nobility Fleet Security Director Rob Spencer was at his desk enjoying a huge salami-provolone sandwich from Fort Lauderdale's new La Sandwicheria restaurant when Morgan's call came in. Spencer had two choices: spit out an entire mouthful of the best sandwich he had ever eaten or pick up the phone. Desperate, a third option struck him. Spencer stood, pushed open his office door, and signaled his executive assistant, Angelica Morales, who laughed so hard when she saw his predicament that she was barely understandable when she answered the phone. Morgan thought he had the wrong number and was about to hang up when Angelica finally became coherent.

A full twenty-five seconds passed before Spencer picked up his extension. "Listen to me carefully, Brick. No one, and I mean no one, should be interrupted while eating a salami-provolone from La Sandwicheria. Angelica saved my life."

"And I'm about to save your bacon."

Spencer flicked on his recorder. "What have we got?"

"What we've got is Pat Bianchi by the short and curlies."

Spencer listened intently, asking only a few questions as Morgan led him through his findings, specifically the time-line anomalies between Bianchi's call for help and the time of the closed-circuit video.

The more details he explained, the angrier Morgan became. What incensed him as much as the murder itself was the possibility that Cristiana Bianchi might not have been dead when she was thrown overboard. What if she was still alive during the nearly three long seconds it took to plunge from her balcony to the water below? "We can't let the scum get away with this, Rob. It can't happen."

"I agree, but the prick's a lawyer, and as good as your evidence is, a lot of it's circumstantial. He could beat the charge and walk away with his wife's eight million."

Morgan hesitated for a moment. "Do you have some old friends with the Miami PD who would help me go one-on-one with our guy? Tomorrow is day six, and we pull into Half Moon Cay, Bahamas. I can be in Miami by afternoon."

"What do you mean by 'one-on-one'?"

"Just conversation, Spence. I'm not going to kill him."

"Call me when you get off the *Bernini*, and I'll connect you with two of Miami's finest. Just remember you won't be operating in international waters."

"Since I can't shoot him or throw him to the sharks, I reluctantly understand."

Spencer signed off and put in a call to the FBI where he would send the audio file of Bianchi's call to Special Agent Jon Moore for analysis.

After his call to Spencer, Morgan leaned back in his chair, looked at Raju, and broke out in a big grin. "Mr. Gurkha, are you ready to be a movie star?"

"A what?"

"I need you to do a couple of things. First, figure out how to adjust the direction of one starboard closed-circuit television camera so it's aimed right at Bianchi's balcony. Then, borrow a female mannequin from the ship's dress shop and meet me in A-seven-oh-nine in forty-five minutes."

The unmarked Chevrolet Tahoe rolled down Coral Gables' Miracle Mile, a pleasant, tree-lined district filled with smiles, chic specialty stores, office buildings, restaurants, theaters, cocktail lounges, trendy eateries, and ubiquitous parking meter checkers all vying for their share of the tourist dollar. Wearing a tan summer suit, blue Paul Frederick button-down shirt, and loafers, Morgan sat in a rear seat bantering with Miami homicide detectives Amando Cromar and Carl Rubio who occupied the front buckets. Rubio was behind the wheel.

Both detectives were about six two and solid. Cromar sported a small goatee, while Rubio wore a perfectly trimmed Tom Selleck mustache. Both were dressed in light sports coats and slacks, professional but well suited for the weather.

Cromar twisted in his seat to face Morgan. "We had our LT make a courtesy call to CGPD and let them know we were going to play in their sandbox for a little while."

"You guys get along with your neighbors?"

"Very well. CG has about a hundred ninety officers, and we're over twelve hundred. My guess is one out of five of their guys started in Miami but moved next door because of better potential for promotion. How come you left Seattle PD?"

"Long story, but the short version is to escape an ex-wife, and I thought the Justice Department would be cool. It wasn't. Got assigned to Interpol. A little too political for me, so I set up my business in Tacoma and have been happy ever since."

"Understand you know Spencer."

"Sure do. Good man."

"Our division knows Spence real well. Hated to see him retire. Must admit a lot of us are a little envious of his gig at that cruise line."

"I would be, too, but he's been very supportive of my maritime security company, and I scratch Nobility's back in return, which is why I'm here today. The filth we're visiting dumped his wife overboard from one of Nobility's cruise ships a few days ago like she was a piece of garbage. Figures he'll collect eight million her dad left her. He's about to have a change of plans."

"We're about five minutes out, Brick. We'll turn north on Salzedo Street and park about a block away on Aragon Avenue," said Cromar as Rubio made the turn.

"My plan is to play hardball with this jerk. Understand he considers himself a tough guy."

Rubio exchanged glances with Cromar and grinned at Brick. "Spencer said to give you as much space as you need. We'll hang back unless bullets fly. Cool?"

The trio exited the Tahoe before Morgan responded, "We won't need any bullets, gentlemen."

Bianchi's law firm stretched over the entire second floor of a two-story turquoise and white office building covering more than an acre on the south side of Aragon Avenue, directly across the busy street from Gabriella's Fine Jewelry Design. A Step Forward, a pricey shoe store featuring Weldon Excalibers on sale at just $3,100 a pair for the "well-heeled woman," was just next door. Not yet nine o'clock, both boutiques appeared to be doing brisk business already as Morgan and the two detectives entered the office building, took the stairs to the second floor, and faced a large mahogany sign reading, "Bianchi & Higgins, Attorneys at Law, Trademarks, Copyrights, & Patents."

The men entered, and Morgan approached the receptionist while noticing a door down a short hallway with Patrizio Bianchi's name on it. Bianchi's private office. "Brick Morgan to see Mr. Bianchi, please."

"Sir, he is with a client at the moment. Do you need an appointment?"

Morgan ignored her reply, smiled, and headed down the hallway as the receptionist began to rise from her chair and protest. A moment later, Morgan opened Bianchi's door and walked in. Cromar and Rubio followed but stopped just outside the now open office door.

Bianchi looked up, stunned, as the six-foot-four black man penetrated his private domain and stepped to his desk. Before the lawyer could respond, Morgan turned to face the client who had been seated in one of the two chairs across from the desk. "Sir, your meeting is over. Please leave now!"

"Who the fuck are you? You can't just barge—"

"I'm your worst-case scenario, Patrizio. Shut up, and stay seated," barked Morgan as he sized up the overweight attorney. He then noticed the framed diploma from the Syracuse University College of Law behind the desk and a large world globe opened to display several bottles of whiskey. As Morgan opened his briefcase, the two Miami detectives showed the receptionist their credentials and suggested she take a coffee break. The client needed no further encouragement and left the office suite in a rush.

"Mr. Bianchi, my name is Brick Morgan, and I represent Nobility Cruise Line."

Bianchi started to get out of his chair as he shouted, "I don't give a shit who you are! Get out of my office! You have—"

"Sit down, asshole! I'm here to save your fucking life!" Morgan knew that the best way to deal with a bully like Bianchi was to act like a bully.

"What do you want?"

"I want to throw you out that fucking window, just like you threw your wife off the balcony of the *Bernini*, but those two cops are here to keep you alive." At the mention of Cristiana, Morgan noticed a change in the lawyer's demeanor and a pronounced twitch that began below the man's left eye. Before Bianchi could reply, Morgan laid two pieces of paper and his iPad across from the attorney.

"You're a cold-blooded killer, Bianchi, and you're either going to cooperate with me today or the good state of Florida is going to fry you like a fat piece of bacon," Morgan began. "It's too bad, isn't it? I mean, it looks like you've put together a nice little gig here in the Gables. Fancy office—I love the carpeting you have in here—expensive furniture, top-of-the-line computers, fat salary, nice expense account, employees who help grow your bank account every month.

"And was that your red Mercedes parked out front, Pat? The convertible? Well, maybe after your electrocution, the pathologist can determine whether you had a brain tumor or something that caused you to put together a murder plan so pathetic that a parrot could figure it out. And for what? You had it made here. You didn't need Cristiana's money."

For the next ten minutes, Morgan walked him through the evidence that carefully boxed Bianchi into a corner, proving, said Morgan, that Bianchi was culpable in the murder of his wife. After each submission of proof, Bianchi offered the same reply, "It doesn't prove anything." Morgan then displayed a closed-circuit television photo of Cristiana Bianchi entering the water eighteen seconds before the call to the purser's office.

"This is bullshit. At best, it's circumstantial."

"No, it's not bullshit, Pat. It's proof. The only question now is whether you find yourself an attorney good enough to get you off the hook, and I'll tell you right now that attorney doesn't exist. Your life is over."

Morgan observed a remarkable change in the man's resolve. Gone was the aggressive bully, replaced by an analytical attitude.

"Mr. Bianchi, what I hear you saying is that all this proof that you killed your wife is inconclusive, right?"

"You know damn well it is. No court in the world would find me guilty. It's crap."

"Really? Well, maybe a court would like this." Morgan picked up his iPad, found his video application, touched a CCTV file, and held the iPad in front of Bianchi.

There was a noticeable silence in the office as the men watched a black-and-white video showing a large man dragging and then throwing a person over the clear glass railing of a balcony on the starboard side of the *Bernini Under the Stars*. The video automatically ran again; this time, a digital insert was included that identified the cabin as A-709 and a time stamp of 00132009112015. For the first time, Bianchi had no response.

Morgan took a seat in front of the desk, leaned forward, and studied Bianchi for a moment. "I need you to listen very carefully, Pat. We have several options." Detectives Rubio and Cromar edged farther into the office so they could hear.

"It's clear you committed a preplanned murder. That makes it premeditated, first degree. The fact that you threw your wife overboard and she might have lived for three full seconds makes it special circumstances. You'll have a choice of electrocution or lethal injection. Do you remember Ted Bundy, Mr. Bianchi? The guy who slaughtered dozens of young women across the country in the seventies and eighties? He was from my hometown—Tacoma. We even went to the same high school. They fried Bundy in the same chair you could sit in over there in Bradford County.

"It's also possible the FBI may turn you over to the Panamanians, where you would be left to rot in the Penitenciario Federal de Chitré for the rest of your life. Of course, they'll keep you entertained down there.

"You've heard of it, haven't you, Mr. Bianchi? I mean, what they do there to lard-ass scum like you for the enjoyment of the guards? I have some printed descriptions out in the car I can bring in. It's the kind of stuff you never hear about on C-SPAN because—and this is the beauty of it—it's not happening in the United States."

"That's fucking bullshit! I'm an American and an attorney who knows my business and my rights as a citizen, and they don't include being sent to prison in Panama on a trumped-up murder charge in Florida!"

"You may be an expert on copyright law, Pat, but you don't know shit about maritime law. The *Bernini* has a flag of convenience, not from the United States, but from Panama. You killed your wife in international waters, and the FBI would save a lot of money and time if they turn you over to the Panamanians.

"But I can save your life—if you let me. We both know you're nailed. There is no chance of you getting out of this. Your only chance of any kind depends on what you decide right now. The FBI owes Nobility a favor for some work I did that helped them last year. If I ask them to send you to that hellhole in Panama, they probably will. If I ask them to only charge you with first-degree murder, they probably will. Who knows, you might spend the next twenty years running the law library at a federal country club prison. So, is it going to be door number one, door number two, or door number three?"

While Bianchi was writing out a confession on one of his own legal pads, Detective Rubio made a courtesy call to the Coral Gables PD and gave them the opportunity to make the arrest. Rubio was thanked for the call and then given the go-ahead to hook up Bianchi and transport him to the Miami FBI office.

Brick placed a call to Rob Spencer while he waited for Cromar and Rubio to locate a black-and-white to transport Bianchi. "Tell me it isn't true, Brick, but there's a story making the rounds that you dressed Raju up like a fat lawyer and he threw the dress shop's favorite mannequin over the side of the *Bernini*."

"Guilty as charged, Spence. Also, I promised my computer expert, Rilee, a thousand bucks for editing Raju's Hollywood premiere."

"Give me the details tomorrow, but that was a hell of a fine job wringing a confession out of Bianchi."

"Well, he forgot a very important rule: an attorney who defends himself has a fool for a client."

Chapter Seven

The fifty-four-foot Carver yacht, diesel engines bubbling softly, slipped away from its moorings at the Tacoma Yacht Club in midafternoon carrying Gas Rizzo and two of his business associates, including attorney Larry Hickman, a man whose toys demonstrated that he liked to enjoy the pleasures offered by the fruits of his labors. He was riding in one right now.

Hickman's yacht—the *Knot Guilty*—was richly appointed, not that he would have accepted anything less, of course, for he was a man on the move who had successfully defended several high-profile racketeering suspects in Washington and California in the last four years. Since a man on the move needed something classy in which to move, Hickman purchased his yacht from a yacht-club friend who was retiring to Miami and then renamed it to fit with his professional accomplishments.

At forty-seven, the lanky, blond-haired Tacoma barrister had acquired significant lucre for his services, not to mention tidy sums of cash that didn't have to suffer the indignity of landing in a bank account. And for Hickman that meant a luxurious cruiser with full galley, electric and microwave ovens, refrigerator, dishwasher, and mahogany dining table. For the other end of the food-and-drink cycle, the *Knot Guilty* contained two heads—one in the captain's quarters and the other aft. Amidships were three other bedrooms, a centrally controlled air-conditioning system with backup, teak flooring, full bar, and cooled twenty-four-bottle wine bay. Aft was the yacht's roomy and comfortable salon now open to the afternoon sun.

Hickman eyed a seventy-five-foot Easton Galactica throttling up to follow him out into Commencement Bay.

As the boat glided easily through a light chop, Rizzo popped a beer and offered one to Hickman, who accepted, and to Carlo "CC" Conti, who declined, while studying a marine map that would guide them across the bay and into Colvos Passage between Vashon Island to starboard and mainland to port. Along the way, they would pick up two others for a group discussion about the merits of a tentative business proposition Rizzo developed after his phone conversation with a stranger a few days earlier. The caller had offered a proposal that, if planned and carried out with the most extreme caution by the proper people, could enrich each of them without the possibility of ever being linked to it.

Rizzo also understood that every planner of every major crime in history thought he had worked out every detail beforehand, only to know moments before the hangman dropped him that he was wrong. At the moment, though, Rizzo was enjoying the serene blue skies, warm afternoon sun gleaming off the bay, and the soothing sea breeze that easily washed away any thoughts of failure. He liberated another beer from the refrigerator, handed it to Hickman, and slipped on his shades. He was seated behind Hickman on the boat's command bridge while Conti reclined on a sofa just aft of the bridge area.

The two other associates would meet the yacht at a private dock near the community of Olalla on the mainland as it threaded its way through the passage toward the northern tip of Vashon Island, a thirty-seven-square-mile landmass between Tacoma and Seattle left by the ice flows that carved Puget Sound fifteen thousand years ago. Accessible only by ferry, aircraft, or personal watercraft, Vashon's residents range from wealthy loners to authors, artists, "weed" farmers, and others scraping out a living away from the throngs of nine-to-fivers schlepping to and from their jobs in Seattle and Tacoma.

Hickman advanced the Carver's throttles to eighteen knots in order to pass well ahead of the giant Hapag-Lloyd container ship *Bremen Express*, inbound from Hamburg to the Port of Tacoma with nearly nine thousand containers aboard.

DETONATION

"Better not bump into the *Titanic*," Conti advised, glancing up from his map. "We might chip some paint."

"The *Bremen* there is almost tiny compared to what's coming," Rizzo chipped in. "The *Wall Street Journal* had a great piece about it yesterday."

While the small talk continued behind him, Hickman cut his boat speed back to fifteen knots as the Carver entered Colvos, also known as West Passage by some. No marine traffic loomed in the distance, so he steered to midchannel and churned ahead. Above him on the hundred-foot bluff to port were trophy homes one after the other, and he gave them nods as his boat passed by.

Rizzo noticed Hickman's interest in the homes on the high bluff. "Still considering a big house on the hill, Larry?"

"If this plan is as lucrative as you believe, maybe."

Rizzo shook his head. "Too much money and trouble. There would be needed upgrades, landscaping improvements, and so forth. It might be easier for you to buy an existing house, have it bulldozed, and then construct a new estate there. You would need plenty of room for a fresh residence, pool house, tennis court, and perhaps a helipad for quick trips here and there."

Hickman smiled. "I will have to consider it all later. There is a dock to find now."

"Need a little help up here," Hickman said over his shoulder. "Where are we, CC?"

"About three miles. Keep peddling."

The *Knot Guilty* continued north as picturesque Vashon Island passed to starboard.

"You have any clients living on Vashon?" Conti asked.

"Hell no. I don't take dopers as clients."

"But marijuana is legal here now."

"I don't give a rat's ass if it is legal, CC. Dopers are dopers, and they make bad clients." As Larry spoke, the boat dock appeared a few degrees to port, its two occupants waving a greeting.

Five minutes later, with Mark LoNigro and Mitch Steinberg onboard, Hickman steered to the Vashon side of the passage and slowed to a crawl. He positioned the mahogany-trimmed craft in a quiet cove about a hundred feet off an eighty-foot-high embankment, set the Raymarine Autopilot to hover mode, and poured himself a Black Jack over ice before joining the others seated in the main salon.

"Since this is our first group meeting about the proposal, I'll review the basics, and then we can discuss the concerns and risks," Rizzo began. "CC and I have had three conversations with our contact and received the standard fifty thousand dollar deposit. The down and dirty is this: we've been offered one hundred twenty-five million dollars cash, plus expenses, to destroy the new third lock of the Panama Canal. That's twenty-five million dollars apiece if we succeed, gentlemen. And we *will* succeed."

Quiet settled over the group like a Northwest fog. Destroy a lock at the Panama Canal? Nearly a half minute passed before LoNigro, a custom-home developer whose family emigrated from Argentina to the states in 1961, raised his hand.

"You all know where the Tacoma Narrows Airport is, back down the channel about five miles from here," he said. "That's where I park my B-52, the *Lackanuki*. I always keep a couple of thousand pounders aboard. We could be down there in four hours or so, bomb the canal, and be back to the airport before rush hour. It's got two big-block Buicks and a six-speed box in there; runs like a bat outta hell."

"What about cruise control?" Conti wondered.

"Why, hell yes! We can sleep all the way back!"

"I'm in," proclaimed Mitch Steinberg, as all five men erupted in prolonged laughter, including Rizzo, who realized that his meeting was out of control barely a minute after it began.

Fifteen minutes passed before the men laughed themselves out, and LoNigro tried a question. "How can you be sure the people behind your contact have pockets deep enough to deliver that kind of money? And can they structure the payments so as to not trip alerts to the Feds' money-laundering regs?"

"That's a two-part question," replied Conti. "Gas, would you address the first part—their solvency—and, Larry, the money laundering?"

"Our clients are grade A," said Rizzo. "I've researched the hell out of every one of them, and they're all highly regarded businessmen and women from all along the West Coast—solid as they come—well educated, hugely successful, active in their communities—connected realists who understand the world as it is, not dreamers with their heads up their asses. They're a mix of conservatives and liberals who also are strong union supporters because they know who really gets things done in this country, the unions—the working men and women—not the blowhards in Congress."

"No argument there," added Steinberg.

"Mitch, this year the Port of Tacoma will process forty billion dollars of international trade, and that will produce a hundred thirty million in revenues. Then you have the ports of Everett, Seattle, Portland, and Frisco, and the huge port of LA / Long Beach, all of which are in the same relative situation as the POT. The funds we're interested in will come from hidden union accounts in all but two West Coast ports, from our clients' internal and external resources, from owners and prospective investors in port real estate, and from some accounting magic with port support equipment. Interests from Vancouver also have stepped forward."

"Vancouver, BC, or Vancouver, Washington?" LoNigro asked.

"Both," smiled Rizzo, taking a seat.

Hickman's money-laundering credentials came from connections made during his 2011 defense of Marcus "Marco" Basilone on federal charges that he masterminded the hijacking of a government armored truck carrying $7 million in cash from the San Francisco mint to Los Angeles in September 2008. As Basilone's attorney, Hickman had asked the man privately how he would have laundered the cash if he had "actually" been involved in the crime. With the disappearance of two key government witnesses the day trial was to begin, Basilone's case was dismissed. Sipping a brandy at a private club two hours later, Basilone provided Hickman with everything the attorney wanted to know about laundering cash.

That experience made Hickman a natural as the group's money-man. He would be assisted by Steinberg, the youngest member of the crew at forty-two. Steinberg had inherited and operated thirteen money exchanges in Washington and Oregon and had made a small fortune handling the legitimate transfer of money from immigrants back to their families in Mexico and South America. It would be an ideal fit.

"First, to Mark's question about federal money-laundering regulations. It began with the Fed's Money Laundering Control Act of 1986 and was beefed up by the 1996 Suspicious Activity Report that banks file if they think someone is trying to get around the rules. For instance, if you deposit ten thousand bucks or more, your bank will notify the Treasury Department in a heartbeat. But let's say you start playing games by depositing ninety-nine hundred, or somewhere in that vicinity, multiple times, trying to beat the system. That's called structuring, or smurfing, and the Feds are wise to it. You can end up in jail counting the bricks on your cell wall for that little scam. Virtual currencies like Bitcoin now are treated the same as dollars.

"Bottom line: stay away from banks and develop your own system of moving money. Ask the right questions like I did with Marco Basilone. In this case, I'll take care of it for all of us. But remember this: if you don't know what to do with whatever you have on a given day—cash, coins, bars, whatever—just bury it in the woods, wait until you have a concrete solution, dig it up, and move on. If you bury it in your own backyard, your next step is killing yourself for violating universal stupidity laws.

"Okay, since I'm the so-called money expert, enlighten me on port support equipment accounting magic."

Rizzo washed down a handful of cashews with his Budweiser and dove into the accounting waters for the answer. "The Port of Tacoma has capital assets in the range of $1.42 billion. Those assets, Larry, include $5.25 million in land and $1.15 million worth of machinery and equipment. Even applying depreciation, the port has assets of nearly a billion dollars. Our clients here and elsewhere have the means and methods of fine-tuning depreciation schedules to free up millions. And remember, the POT is one of several large ports our clients will draw from. One source, one means, to help pay our fee. Other prospects, other means."

Hickman's obsession with money was a benefit to the enterprise, though his drill-down questions drove Rizzo crazy. "Our clients may have the means to pay our fee, but we need specifics, Gas. We can't spend their good intentions."

"Okay, listen up, everyone. Three waterways serve the POT—Hylebos, Blair, and Sitcum. There are ten cranes on the south side of Blair, and six of those are the big hundred-gauge container cranes. They cost thirty-three million each. I'm told that by discreetly playing with the cranes' years of service, or depreciation, our clients stole five million dollars," said Rizzo.

"Crap, we're in the wrong business. We should be renting cranes to the port," cracked Hickman. "We may need a little seed money, though."

"There's more, Larry. The port has more reach stackers than they can keep track of."

LoNigro caught Rizzo's eye once more. "I've built two hundred homes and never heard of a reach stacker. What the hell are they?"

"A reach stacker is a liquid petroleum gas vehicle that picks up and stacks containers, Mark. They're four million bucks a pop, but if you can stack containers, say five high, on a ship or on port property, you'll save a ton of money because of the reduced footprint they provide. Room for product is just as important at a port terminal as on a ship.

"Mathematics wasn't exactly my best subject in school, but the older I get, the more respect I have for what it can do for people," Rizzo continued. "Take our clients, for example. The port 'purchased' a new reach stacker last year that was never delivered. That's four million dollars floating in the wind, off the books. Our clients used their pencils to set aside three million toward an expense fund for whoever ultimately was hired for our job and kept the other million for their trouble. Planning for the canal project began well before we came along."

Hickman then reopened his discussion of the money-laundering issues. He and Steinberg shared an obsession with the layers of firewalls and partitions that would shield the group if a hired contractor were caught or money questions arose.

"A preliminary examination of their finances and our need for multiple financial firewalls suggests that we bounce digital bearer certificates between our banks in Belize and the Caymans. Our first priority is insulating the business from the law. We'll continue to use the most sophisticated digital cryptocurrency and bearer certificates," Hickman said.

"Larry, are you using Bitcoins, and how do we convert the digital money to real assets?"

"I'm not comfortable with Bitcoins, CC, but eDragon is stable and accepted at most digital currency exchanges. Once we have a sizable deposit, Mitch and I will convert at least fifty percent of our money to gold, and we'll continue to do that until the project ends."

At Rizzo's suggestion, the men broke for a few minutes to stretch their legs and refill their glasses.

While LoNigro and Steinberg filled their glass tumblers with ice and choices from the boat's well-stocked liquor cabinet, Hickman checked his watch and stepped to the main cabin bridge.

"I'm going to kick off the autopilot and move the boat to a cooler spot on the mainland side, Mitch. It's gotten too hot over here. Would you pull the sandwich tray from the reefer for everyone?"

Twenty minutes later, the *Knot Guilty* was resting in a shady and deserted lagoon on the west side of the passage.

Heads visited and glasses full, the men relaxed on the special memory foam lounge chairs and cushions that Hickman had installed as replacements for the more pedestrian seat cushions that came standard with his twelve-year-old cruiser. He slid onto his chaise as Rizzo began outlining some canal history and how it related to their project.

"Let's start with the why before the how. As you know, the Panama Canal was completed in 1914—one set of locks in each direction—and was controlled by the United States until 1977 when Carter turned it over to Panama."

"That dim-witted son of a bitch!" interrupted LoNigro.

"You're not alone there," snarled Hickman.

Undeterred, Rizzo continued. "The third lock is actually two. One is on the Atlantic side and will lift the New Panamax ships up to Gatun Lake, and the second new lock will take the ships to the Pacific Ocean. To avoid confusion, please refer to this new pair as the third lock. That's singular! Be clear on that! The new lock will run parallel to the two existing locks.

"At issue are the limits placed on the size of ships that can pass through the canal. The largest ships authorized to transit right now are called Panamax. Maximum beam for these ships is about a hundred and ten feet, but the most relevant metric is the size restriction that limits cargo ships to five thousand TEUs."

"And TEUs are . . . ?" Steinberg asked.

"Containers, Mitch. That's what the hell I'm talking about!" Rizzo snapped.

"Oh, well, pardon me, Gas. I didn't know that T-E-U spells 'containers' nowadays," Steinberg shot back as Rizzo raised his eyes to the sky.

"Put 'em back in your pants, fellas, and let me explain," Conti said. "TEU stands for twenty-foot equivalent units. If a cargo container is twenty feet long, it's considered one TEU. Some containers are forty feet long and are counted as two TEUs. Because the Panama Canal can only handle a five thousand TEU ship today, it makes economic sense for the shippers in Asia to use ships of eight thousand TEUs or more to off-load at West Coast ports.

"About seventy percent of the container cargo coming into Tacoma right now is due for distribution here in the Northwest. Seattle is about the same. The other thirty percent is transferred to the Midwest by truck and rail. Tacoma and Seattle are damned efficient operations, and both are improving their infrastructures to handle the largest container ships the markets can deliver. But a huge snag is developing very quickly in Panama.

"US ports have been making millions for decades because of the size restrictions at the canal. To word it another way, Panama has been losing a fortune. The Panama Canal Authority charges eighty-two dollars per TEU per trip. The present fee for a maximum-size Panamax vessel transiting the canal is about four hundred ten thousand dollars per trip. The Canal Authority decided in 2007 to build a third lock to run parallel to the two others—a larger lock—much, much larger. The new one would allow ships as wide as a hundred eighty feet to pass through, vessels that could carry thirteen thousand TEUs and possibly more. The revenue projection for a ship that size, called a New Panamax, would be over a million bucks per trip.

"Look, Washington is the most trade-driven state in the union. Forty percent of the jobs here are trade related, so consider what would happen to our economy if the thirty percent container share we now redirect by truck and rail to the Midwest never arrives here.

Instead, it's diverted to Panama's third lock and then on to the gulf ports. Now you have a good idea why the concern is very real. A solution—at least for the short term—is badly needed, and we may be it. How are we doing so far, Larry?" Conti asked.

"You're on a roll. Don't stop."

Conti continued. "The *Marine Economist* says forty percent of existing container ships today are too large for the canal now. Forty percent! The third set of locks would change all the economic dynamics. It could become more cost effective for a ten thousand TEU ship to bypass Tacoma, Seattle, or California, continue to the canal, and then on to the Gulf Coast ports.

"New thirteen thousand unit ships are under construction now, and much bigger ones are planned. Gentlemen, the new third lock of the Panama Canal will devastate the economies of the West Coast. Our commission is to eradicate that lock."

Rizzo stood to lay out the issue of the day for his fellow conspirators. "You've heard the background and reasoning behind the proposal. It's clear that this project would be the largest and most ambitious by far of anything we've ever contemplated. What you're hearing here today is only the tip of the iceberg. CC and I have heard considerably more, and you need to hear that too.

"I can tell you this right now: our exposure will be virtually nil. We'll explain at the next meeting. But if we decide after three meetings that this is not for us, we say no as a group and look for greener pastures. We buy in or move on.

"No names or face time have been exchanged with our local contact, but he's a shaker in the shipping industry and he initiated contact, so I see no entrapment issue, and he has checked us out at least as much as we've done with him, which is why he called us in the first place. CC and I propose our next discussion in two weeks to present the second half of the plan. It's a no-brainer, so if there's no objection . . ."

Steinberg motioned to Rizzo and stood, hands deep in the pockets of his tan Dockers. "Guys, we haven't heard the strategies or operational details, but I want to be straight up with you. At this point, I'm against the project, and the why is pretty simple. Most of this mission would be conducted outside the US, particularly in Panama, meaning we have very little chance of maintaining the control necessary to pull it off. Why expose ourselves at all without holding onto the reins? I vote no."

"So noted," replied Rizzo. "I get it, Mitch, but all the cards are not on the table yet, which is why we need another meeting. Fair enough? How about two weeks from today at your place, Mark? Keep your car in the garage, and the rest of us will come in an Uber."

LoNigro offered a final question. "You haven't said a word about how we would destroy the lock. That's a pretty big piece of the puzzle for me."

"We sink a ship in there—a huge New Panamax giant."

"Nice payday for us, but it just delays the inevitable, Gas."

"Maybe not, Mark. If we sink a ship that's passing through the new lock, the section could be repaired in three months. But if we sink a New Panamax ship contaminated with radioactive material in there, that new section of the canal will be untouchable for decades."

"You're talking about a nuclear bomb?" Steinberg gasped incredulously, his drink tumbler falling from his hand and shattering on the deck. Mouth open, he gazed around slowly at the others. It was ninety-one degrees, but Steinberg was shivering.

Rizzo stood and suggested the men call it a day. "We've been at this for almost three hours. Let's wrap it up, drop Mark and Mitch off at the dock, and head back. Not a word about this meeting, everyone. I'll have assignments for each of you over the next week."

Chapter Eight

Avery Griffin pulled his sapphire-blue-metallic Porsche 911 into the driveway of his University Place home. The then undeveloped Tacoma suburb was chosen in 1890 as home to the fledgling College—later University—of Puget Sound. Organizers purchased 420 acres for its campus, but the financial depression and panic of 1893 caused the college to forfeit the land before the campus was built. The community name remained, and it ultimately became a small but upscale town whose 2015 hosting of the US Open Golf Tournament provided residents with a renewed sense of pride and accomplishment.

Glancing at his $1,500 gold-tinged Gucci wristwatch, he expected that his current love interest would already be home. The stock market had been closed for several hours, but stockbroker Griffin had used the time for marketing calls to several of his Pacific Opus Securities clients before making the rush-hour trip from downtown Tacoma to UP. His home was a standout in the plush west-end neighborhood, as was his $130,000 Carrera. The secret that he kept to himself was that his life was a thinly veiled masquerade. Every asset he possessed was leveraged to the hilt, including his rented home and the Giorgio Brutini loafers on his feet at the moment. Even his gold-plated Gucci that told him the time of day was purchased on credit. Indeed, Avery Griffin was a twenty-four-carat phony.

Before stepping out of the leased Porsche, the thirty-seven-year-old securities dealer reached over and plucked his custom-made cashmere-wool blend navy-blue blazer from the passenger seat. When Griffin ordered the $2,000 jacket, he insisted on pewter buttons instead of the customary gold. He locked the car in the driveway and entered the home through the garage, where a black Lexus 330 rested in one of the two bays, and two moving pods, filled with worn apartment furniture, were stuffed into the other bay. That second garage door was rarely opened. Neighbors looked down upon disheveled garages.

But Griffin had something most homes near him didn't have—a buxom, well-cut, twenty-five-year-old slice of heaven named Angela Wallace. They had met at the Ram Restaurant and Brewery on the Ruston Way waterfront, where she was holding court with two gentlemen, both of whom longed to meet with her in more comfortable surroundings. Griffin had sent over his business card with a note promising to buy her two shares of Microsoft in exchange for a drink with him. Five minutes later, she settled in at his table.

Angela had received her associate's degree at a local community college five years ago and was hired immediately as manager of the Aplomb Salon and Spa in the Seattle suburb of Bellevue, where her effusive personality and business sense earned dividends from day one. Those dividends benefited and created an atmosphere of camaraderie with employees and clients alike. Her personality also helped convert a chance meeting with Avery Griffin into an opportunity to invest a little of herself now with the likelihood of reaping bigger and better rewards much sooner than would her 401(k) down at the Aplomb.

As he made his way past the Lexus and around the pods, Griffin was again mulling an issue that had weighed on him for the last several months. Should he have remained a CPA instead of exchanging his accounting career for the life of a commissioned broker? The question troubled him still, and the answer would not come.

Griffin joined the accounting firm of Everson & Everson after graduating with an accounting degree from Pacific Lutheran University. During his six years with E&E, he had specialized in providing accounting support to medical and dental practices. Years of working with doctors and dentists had proven to him that the phrase, "Your strength is also your weakness," was directed at the medical profession. The same intelligence and self-confidence that got them through medical or dental school often gave doctors the false belief that they could navigate the investment world equally well when reality most often proved they could not.

After joining Pacific Opus Securities, Griffin succeeded in moving the pension plans, 401(k)s, and personal stock portfolios of many of the doctors and dentists who had been his accounting clients into new brokerage accounts with Pacific Opus. The problems his client base could not solve were Griffin's financial dilemma of declining commissions and a love interest who felt entitled to the finest in jewelry and fashions.

Before opening the door to the kitchen, he glanced in a mirror attached to a tool cabinet and double-checked that his teeth did not contain the remnants of an apple he had consumed on his way home. His two hundred pounds were a bit much for his five-eleven frame, but his pleasant disposition, disheveled light-brown hair, and near-constant grin helped make Avery Griffin likable to nearly all who knew him.

"Avery, is that you?" called Angela as she closed the cover to her latest issue of *National Enquirer*.

"No, hon, it's a serial killer from Lakewood who's about to fix himself a drink. Want one?"

Walking from the travertine-tiled kitchen to the wool-carpeted family room, he spotted Angela reclining on the room's settee with a half-filled wine goblet on the glass coffee table. She had changed from her spa working attire to jeans and a purple cotton halter that barely contained her considerable bosom.

"How about a cosmo instead, and then I need to talk to you."

Griffin changed pace entirely, offering her a concoction starring two fingers of $130 bottle of Highland Scotch smothered by four pieces of ice in a crystal tumbler. "No cranberry juice for your cosmo. Give this one a try," he suggested. She took one sip, turned up her nose, and looked him in the eye.

"Can I have a Rolex, Avery? All the ladies who come to the salon have Rolexes. I know they're expensive, but they're so beautiful, and

I would just love one." As she asked the question, she stuck out her lower lip and pretended to pout.

He had been watching a Lakers' game at the Ram Restaurant and Brewery, next to the Prawnbroker Restaurant on Ruston Way, when he met Wallace, and they had been an item ever since. Her position as manager of the Aplomb Salon and Spa gave her time to try new hairstyles and makeup all day. Centrally located in the fashionable Seattle suburb of Bellevue, the Aplomb attracted affluent residents from much of the surrounding area. Angela's spa boasted two treatment baths that were reported to use a proprietary solution of therapeutic minerals. In addition to wet body treatments, her spa developed a regular clientele who desired facials, chemical peel, and microdermabrasion treatments.

Avery and Angela had been living together for about a year. Avery had led Angela to believe that he owned the $500,000 residence, the Porsche, and all the rest, and that such trinkets as Rolexes were easily within his income range.

A five thousand dollar Rolex could be done, he thought, but he knew it would just add to the tens of thousands of dollars of debt he had already accumulated. If he was going to keep his high-maintenance girlfriend, he would need to find more money. "Tell you what, Angela. Why don't I just give you a couple of swats on the butt instead? You've got a Lexus in the garage, live in a beautiful house, and now you want a Rolex. Maybe I should trade you in for a less-expensive model."

"You don't mean that!"

"I'll have to think about it for a while."

"How long?"

"Probably six months at least. Maybe a year."

She suddenly left her seat, ran across the room, and slipped onto his lap, facing him. "You're just playing with me, aren't you?"

Avery reached behind her, quickly slipped off her halter, and pulled her toward him. "Now I'm playing with you, darlin'," he said with a chuckle.

A moment later, they were on the carpet as clothes and inhibitions flew. Angela most often was the more aggressive partner in their sexual interludes, and today was no exception. She roughly pushed him to his back on the carpet, guided herself downward with his help, and then rode him with circular and up-and-down pelvic thrusts, her head tipped back and her gasps increasing as his hands gently squeezed her breasts, teasing her nipples before moving away and then returning.

Their passion took them over the top three times in the course of an hour before he rolled her over and slowly leaned back against a sofa trying to recover. Her use of her right foot trying to interest him yet again drew an "I surrender" from Avery and a giggle from Angela before she threw her arms around his neck and hugged him tightly.

They shared their feelings about the last hour and toward one another. "Now, about that Rolex, sweetheart," she began, running her fingers across his chest.

"Okay, Angie, tomorrow I'll meet you in Bellevue, and we can look for a Rolex. You are amazing."

"Thank you, thank you, honey! You're so good to me."

"Good" and "fool" both contained four letters, but Griffin didn't know the difference. Angela Wallace most certainly did know. Her Lexus, the home in which she lived, and the Rolex she would own the following day made that very clear.

"Do you think that wanting sex every day makes me a nympho?" she asked as she played with the bead dangle nipple ring inserted in her right nipple.

"No," replied Griffin. "If you wanted sex *three* times a day *that* would classify you as a nympho. I think my insurance man is a nympho—absolute animal. He had to have it three times a day when he was in college. Worked his way through our chemistry class on a bet with ten other guys, including me. He won over two hundred bucks.

"I'm making another drink, Angela. How about you? Want one?" He pulled on his clothes while returning to the bar located between the family room and the formal living room. She waved a no, returned to the settee, still nude, slipped a blanket over her lap, and picked up her *National Enquirer* once again.

Slowly sipping his scotch, Avery contemplated "adjusting" client portfolios as the only realistic solution to his money problems. But from which clients? Whoever he selected would not be his first. In the last twelve months, he had stolen $9,000 from the securities account of Ruth Abel, the widow of Dr. Ben Abel, who had a very successful plastic surgery practice in town. When he was killed in a private plane crash, Mrs. Abel brought a $600,000 stock portfolio to Pacific Opus and broker Griffin. He altered her account statement the first month and demonstrated that he had used $9,000 of his own money to purchase put options to protect her portfolio in case of a down market. Mrs. Abel believed the scam, withdrew the money from her account, and gave it to Griffin.

He was a brazen thief, but Griffin viewed it as merely self-preservation. The brokerage companies had forced him to steal went his thinking. When he first joined Opus, he received a payout of 60 percent on sales. When a mutual fund was sold and it was not a no-load fund, his firm would receive 5.75 percent of the proceeds. That commission was called a gross dealer concession, or GDC. He would then be paid 60 percent of the gross dealer concession. The percentage had been reduced so many times since then that he now received just 30 percent of the GDC. If a client wrote a $10,000 check, the firm would receive $575, and now he would only be paid $172. Not enough; not nearly enough. Those corporate assholes were forcing him to steal, no doubt about it. If he could find a safe way to embezzle $30,000, he would buy himself at least six months.

"Angela, get dressed and let's go to the country club. Tonight is prime rib night. We can celebrate your new Rolex."

Chapter Nine

The Uber cab proceeded south on Gravelly Lake Drive, the very-old-money district of suburban Tacoma, before slowing and turning left down the long and winding driveway leading to custom home developer Mark LoNigro's Mediterranean-style residence.

The ninety-four-hundred-square-foot home, featuring a peach Tuscan stucco exterior accentuated by white trim and a red-orange tile roof, was built by Northern Pacific Railroad tycoon Charles Arbogast in 1921 and rested on five lushly landscaped acres fronting the lake. LoNigro's own company correctly remodeled and enlarged the posh three-story structure in 2008, utilizing original plans and identical materials.

The cab cleared rows of perfectly trimmed Leyland Cypress trees as it entered a magnificent circular driveway and pulled under the home's portico, allowing Mitch Steinberg and Larry Hickman to exit without payment. Their ride would be billed to Steinberg's revolving Uber account. Ignoring the company's no-tip rule, Hickman handed the driver a fifty, got out, and followed Steinberg to the elaborate fountain at the center of the circular driveway as the cab pulled away.

Three tall sections of granite, six, eight, and ten feet in height by two feet in diameter, stood on end in an enclosed circle. Water from an unseen source was continually pumped upward through each and then cascaded down into the circle to be recirculated. An outer ring around the geyser contained red geraniums, accentuating the fountain and the grand home behind it.

Steinberg pointed to the tallest group of granite rocks. "How in the hell do they drill holes all the way through those rocks end to end to create a fountain like that?" he wondered, perplexed.

"Well, Mitch, I'll bet they asked Britain and France how they drilled their tunnel under the English Channel and then just used a smaller bit."

"You're the worst smart-ass I've ever met, Hickman."

Their banter was interrupted by LoNigro standing at the massive oak front door wearing a blue-and-white striped sport shirt, light gray Dockers, socks, and flip-flops. "What are you guys waiting for, a tour guide? C'mon in; CC and Gas are already here." With that, LoNigro waved the pair to join them. "We'll hold our meeting in here, but grab a drink and join us out on the deck."

Glasses filled a minute later, Steinberg and Hickman crossed the red-tiled interior of the great room, beneath a twelve-foot archway supported by two white columns at each end, and outside to the fifteen-hundred-square-foot, two-level deck. Their Brown-Jordan Havana deck chairs were positioned around a natural-gas fire pit constructed with an inlaid granite base and a pit of Sangria Luster glass beads. A ten-inch ring of Red Dragon granite provided ample room for cocktail glasses.

The exquisite home was not the largest in the privileged neighborhood, but the property's landscaping and exterior decks were second to none. Rizzo and Conti were already relaxing when Hickman and Steinberg arrived, and LoNigro was taking a moment to adjust the height of a birdhouse hanging in the boughs of a nearby cedar tree, planted by Arbogast's daughter ninety years ago.

The fire pit and outdoor ceiling heaters made for a comfortable and picturesque setting even on cool Northwest evenings. This wasn't one of them, however. It was nearly eight o'clock, and the temperature was still seventy degrees.

While the others talked of the current pro-football season, Steinberg caught Rizzo's eye twice and tapped his watch. The second time, Rizzo stood, stretched, and started back to the house. "Okay, guys, let's go to work."

"Aren't *we* grumpy," offered Hickman.

"Not really, Larry. It's my damned knee."

"Time to get a new one, Gas. What are you waiting for?"

"Easier said than done." Rizzo's knee had been a running joke for a decade. He amused new acquaintances by saying he injured the knee while as a catcher for the New York Yankees. The reality was that he never played organized baseball, but tore his meniscus digging for geoduck—a large type of clam—on Washington's Hood Canal in 1990. It was the same knee he injured in Saigon in 1967, and after surgery, he still was left with an annoying ache that would stay with him for most of his life.

The men found seating in LoNigro's beautifully appointed family room. The open-spaced architecture provided for an adjoining dining room that led into a kitchen designed by gourmet Italian chef Giancarlo Cedroni and constructed by LoNigro's crew. The dining room's focal point was a Gino Vanni dinner table with seating for twelve. The three-pedestal table featured a feathered mahogany top with an outside band made of cherrywood. All three rooms were connected by rich burgundy-colored Brazilian cherrywood floors accented in the family room by a twelve-by-fifteen foot Oriental Persian rug, hand-knotted and displaying a palette of cerulean, Paris, and Chinese blues. LoNigro chose his upholstered armchair while the others spread out on a U-shaped sectional sofa designed for ten guests.

Rizzo nodded, and Conti picked up where he had left off two weeks earlier.

"To review a bit, we need to put the new third lock of the canal out of commission for many years. If we blow up a gate or sabotage the lock mechanically, Panama will have it operational in six months. Even sinking a cargo ship in the middle of the damned thing would only obstruct it for under a year. But if we sank a ship and it became radioactive, it might take ten years before workers could even start to clear the wreckage. What Gas and I have in mind is using a dirty bomb."

"Here we go again; an atom bomb," Steinberg groaned. "Have you guys lost your damned minds? A nuclear bomb?" He threw his hands in the air.

"Mitch, no—a *dirty* bomb, not an atomic bomb. There's a hell of a difference."

"What difference? It's a bomb. It spreads radiation, and radiation kills people. How else do you define a dirty bomb?"

LoNigro piped up. "It's a bomb that never takes a shower."

"Damn it, I'm dead serious."

Conti smiled before walking over and leaning against the stone-encased fireplace mantel. "Okay, Mitch," he began.

"I'm listening, CC!" Steinberg snapped, offering Conti an intense stare.

"First point, Mitch, is that a dirty bomb isn't an atomic bomb. There's no fission. The Hiroshima bomb had a hundred-plus pounds of uranium-235, and when it was compressed, it created a nuclear fission and released an explosion equal to about seventeen thousand tons of TNT."

"That bomb was called Little Boy," Rizzo interjected, "and almost a hundred forty thousand Japanese died either instantly or over the next ten years or so. The bomb that struck Nagasaki was more powerful than Little Boy. Most people think it was the opposite."

"Correct," added Conti. "With a dirty bomb, the objective is not to kill or injure people, but to create a denied area."

"A denied area?" Rizzo snickered. "Sounds like you're talking about my ex-wife's pussy."

While the others hooted, LoNigro stepped to a refrigerator built into the family room wall and removed three large platters of cheeses, meats, vegetable plates, cream cheeses, a fruit plate, and grilled shrimp, which he warmed in a microwave before adding to the mix.

The hors d'oeuvres hit the spot, and Conti turned technical. "Let's try again, gentlemen. A dirty bomb is a mixture of explosive and some radioactive material. You take some C-4 or dynamite and wrap it with something radioactive. When the explosive goes off, it scatters lots of radioactive dust and material into the surrounding area. This will make a large area very contaminated or, as I said before, turn it into an area of denial. Questions?"

"If the bomb contaminates a cargo ship, can't it be cleaned up?" asked Steinberg.

"No. It dissipates over time. The only product out there is a decontamination foam, but it only works against chemical and biological agents, not radioactive contamination. Again, so there is no misunderstanding, we're not blowing up the third lock; we're introducing radioactive contamination to it by exploding a small, nonnuclear device wrapped with radioactive material. The idea is to spread that contamination throughout the area surrounding the ship and making it inhospitable to work crews.

"All right, now let me explain the plan as it stands, to steal some radioactive material that would be needed to make the bomb.

"We've all been over to eastern Washington and the Tri-Cities area. The Hanford site was a major part of the Manhattan Project, which resulted in development of the atom bomb, and today its tanks hold two-thirds of the nation's high-level nuclear waste and the largest total quantity of nuclear waste in the country."

Conti explained that more than two hundred million liters of that waste was created between 1947 and 1987 while the US and the Russians competed to build the most and largest nuclear bombs for the war against each other that never came.

"During the Cold War, Hanford subjected uranium ore, which is ninety-nine percent isotope U-238 and less than one percent U-235, to a process called isotope separation, which removed the needed U-235 isotope from the ore," he said. "The U-235 was used in one type of atomic bomb. To produce plutonium, needed for another type of A-bomb, fuel rods were subjected to neutrons in what is known as a breeder reactor. The U-238, when hammered with neutrons, becomes plutonium-239. It is isotope Pu-239 that our government wanted, in very pure levels, for its nuclear arsenal. What we're interested in is the waste from the Pu-239 production process."

"Exactly how is all this waste stored at Hanford?" asked Hickman.

"In a hundred seventy-seven tanks, and the fun part is that a hundred forty-nine of them were constructed with a single wall, and by some estimates, about a third are leaking. Twenty-eight of the tanks are double-walled, but some have leaks in their first wall. There are two tanks known to be leaking at the rate of three hundred gallons a year. The shit in those tanks is what we want."

LoNigro quietly raised his hand. "I'm assuming that our people won't just sneak into Hanford and fill their pockets with this stuff. What's the thinking here—mayonnaise jars or a couple buckets from Home Depot? And another thing. What exactly is this 'shit' you're talking about? You're dancing around it a little bit."

"Let me answer your first question in a minute, Mark. As for the tank sludge, it's the worst of the worst. It contains dozens of radioactive isotopes, and some are still extremely radioactive to this day. Half-life is the controlling factor when dealing with nuclear isotopes. Some of the waste was iodine-131, very dangerous, but with a half-life of eight days. That means that after eight days, half of the I-131 is used up. After another eight days, another half is gone. Suffice it to say, after sixty years, there's nothing left of iodine-131.

"Then we have radium-226 with a half-life of sixteen hundred years. The nuclear sludge in many tanks has cesium-137, strontium-90, and radium-226. As a side note, there's plenty of uranium-238 mixed in with the sludge. U-238 has a half-life of over four billion years. Many of these long-life isotopes are big gamma emitters and would be perfect for a dirty bomb. Some of the tanks have a concentration of americium-241 and iodine-129, which are very bad dudes. Am-241 has a half-life of four hundred thirty-two years."

"Guys, I wouldn't be honest if I didn't express my extreme concern about this job," Steinberg declared. "I appreciate your medical background and the research you've done, CC, but this is way over our heads."

Conti paused before responding. "Mitch, with your permission, I'd like us to cover a few additional aspects of the job, and then we can return to all questions and concerns, beginning with yours. Fair enough?"

"Go for it. But as of now, I'm a no vote."

"Noted. Mark, why don't you talk about the man we have in mind to build the device?"

"We may have found our perfect guy. He just doesn't know it yet."

In over thirty-six years in business, LoNigro had developed a network of sources that supplied him with names of potential recruits who might be contracted to perform an assortment of nefarious but well-paid activities. As a high-end building contractor, he had met scores of people from various walks of life, some of whom were engaged in illicit business activities or casually introduced him to acquaintances who were. One of those acquaintances handled jail discharges for the Pierce County Sheriff's Office.

Each month, LoNigro received names and backgrounds of men and some women recently released from state jails and prisons, including the Washington Corrections Center for Women in Gig Harbor. Most were never needed. Some were ideal. Others needed prompting.

"The guy's a widower and a high school teacher with a master's degree in chemistry. He stole twelve hundred dollars from his high school sports fund because his teenage daughter has cancer, and when his insurance ran out, he had no more money to pay her medical bills."

Conti picked up the story from there. "The case got quite a bit of media attention, and when he came to court for sentencing, Judge Walter Stone sympathized with him and refused the prosecution's demand for prison time. He gave the guy three years probation and time served in jail—that's it. Even people in the community started donating money for his daughter's care. Now that he's out of jail, our people may be able to convince him of the importance of our project and the need for his cooperation."

"Why do we think he would help us?" Rizzo asked, arms folded.

"No guarantees, but he became friends in jail with a thug we've worked with before. Now he's lost his house, doesn't have a job, and still needs money."

"Of course he needs money. His daughter has cancer!" Hickman thundered, drawing stares from the others. "How is she?"

"She's holding her own from what I'm told, but the donations are drying up."

"Why, hell, there it is! He needs money for her treatment. My kid brother died of cancer nineteen years ago, and I hate that shit. Let's offer him some major cash upfront right now for her care plus serious money after the project for the rest of his life."

"Should know next week."

Hickman persisted. "Show him the money, CC. Put some in his hands now. He'll cooperate."

"I like that idea—a lot. Any more questions?"

"Just one," asked LoNigro. "What else do you know about him. Anything?"

"He's separated from his wife and lives in Federal Way."

"So his job, assuming he helps us, CC, is actually to build the device," Hickman said.

"That is correct."

"Let me point out," Steinberg hissed, "that there is one hell of a big difference between a high school chemistry teacher and a nuclear physicist. Chemistry teachers are rarely called upon to detonate bombs in the Panama Canal."

"Absolutely, Mitch. I'm getting there. But to answer Mark's

earlier question, let me spell out our progress with storing the sludge before it goes aboard the ship. The key is a flexible glass shell developed by a UC Santa Barbara professor. I'll give you his background in a moment. He says the shell will conform perfectly to the interior of fire extinguishers where our sludge will be retained." While Conti distributed a one-page summary, LoNigro got up and turned on three Stiffel lamps as the sun was settling down for the evening.

"Please read these pages, memorize their contents, and burn them in this fireplace before you leave tonight," Conti said, patting the stonework behind him. "Gas and I have been working with this UCSB physicist since I stumbled across him while I was playing *War Age*." He suddenly had the undivided attention of every man in the room.

"What the hell is *War Age*?" asked Rizzo

Conti took a few minutes to explain the world of computer role-playing—how a player creates a character, or avatar, and the in-game chat feature. He described chat rooms that allow role-playing gamers to make contact and dialogue with each other during a game.

"I made a connection a month or two back with a *War Age* player who turned out to be this professor. After texting with him for about a week in the chat room, I started using an encrypted email address that I use only for very special messages."

"Lots of people have believed their messages were encrypted," noted Hickman, "until the FBI knocked on their front door. Now they're making license plates in the graybar hotel."

"Relax. I selected a web-based encryption site called Infocrypt," Conti responded. "I'm confident that his communications are secure.

"Now, to your earlier question, Mark. It turns out that our professor has been censored by UCSB for plagiarism, and he's afraid of being fired even though he's tenured," Conti continued. "He's the physicist who developed the glass container that will safely hold Hanford's hot stuff. He calls the glass shell a wafer. It's made of multiple layers of graphene, silicon, and boron that have nanocrystals imbedded in the matrix. When energized by a twenty-four-volt lithium-ion battery, this modified smart-glass blocks deadly gamma and neutron radiation from escaping a closed container. To improve his finances, he's agreed to mold this glass into two fire extinguishers. Then, we'll arrange a scheduled extinguisher exchange where our people will bring 'fresh' extinguishers into the Hanford facility and exchange them for the ones doctored with the sludge by our inside asset and walk out the door."

"Who do we have in Hanford, CC?" asked Steinberg.

Conti nodded toward LoNigro. "Mark?"

"I've been reading some blogs and press releases from an activist group called Hanford Tanks that's trying to pressure the Department of Energy to clean up the leaking tanks. I found a Dr. Byron Dunbar, PhD, who works at an inside lab who claims whistleblower status. DOE managers were furious last month when he went public with a press release that said Tank AY-102's eight hundred fifty thousand gallons of nuclear stew is leaking between its inner and outer walls. Dunbar now believes he'll be fired for his activism, and he needs money. He's agreed to steal the material."

"Agreed with who, when, and how?"

"Those are details you probably don't want to know, Larry."

"How long do we have before Karen comes home?" asked Rizzo.

"She's doing a sister thing, in Seattle. Back tomorrow." LoNigro and his wife, Karen, recently celebrated their eighteenth anniversary, a second marriage for both.

For the next few minutes, Hickman reported on the group's cash flow. He had moved three blocks of money and split a new deposit into two accounts in Belize. A few months earlier, the men earned $1.4 million rigging a federal construction bid. LoNigro had discovered that a senior naval officer was involved in child pornography and that same officer was in a position to massage a bid to construct a $50 million submarine dry dock at Naval Base Kitsap near Bremerton, Washington, to service its missile-carrying Ohio-class "boomers" and

Virginia-class fast-attack subs.

After an enlightening conversation with a group representative including two lurid photos, the naval officer found it more convenient to swing the big contract to Seattle-based Benedict Construction than being imprisoned for the next decade for sexual deviancy.

Steinberg, working with Hickman, directed Benedict Construction to quietly transfer the group's finder's fee for the contract out of the country. The men used a local Belize lawyer to act as their registered agent with a Belize bank for their international business company, or IBC.

"These guys in Belize set up a phony company as our IBC," Hickman began. "We needed it to avoid paying taxes on our money and to conduct business there without using our names. This is very sophisticated stuff. They'll hold our accounts in any currencies we request.

"This stuff is amazing," he chuckled, growing more animated. "They've set up a bullshit company for us that pretends to be a deep-seas salvage operation. They even have a couple of boats, and they go through the motions of looking for old pirate ships and finding bars of gold and silver on the ocean bottom. We pay a modest fee to the workers through the IBC. It's a perfect front for moving dirty money around the world. Arrangements have been made to have a shadow courier move fifty-six pounds of our Swiss twenty franc gold coins into our hands in the next two weeks."

"You can see the value of offshore banking," Steinberg said. "We paid our Belize people eighty thousand US to transfer and transport the francs. Each of us will get two pounds, or nine hundred sixty-one gold coins. At two hundred sixty dollars a coin that's a quarter million each. Our fee is less than seven percent—a hell of a bargain."

"Damned clever, guys. I hope my knee holds out while I'm hauling my coins to a safety deposit box," said Rizzo with a half smile, rubbing his knee for dramatic effect. "CC, we need to discuss your research on backup plans."

Conti pulled a pair of three-by-five cards from his pocket and then looked at Rizzo and started to laugh. "Gas, we've been hearing about your damn knee for years. I'm the guy with the broken back. I'll give you a hundred of my francs if you'll get that damn knee replaced."

"If I got a new knee, then I'd have nothing to bitch about. Tell us about plan B."

"Listen up, everyone. I'm very confident that we'll get the nuclear sludge out of Hanford, but we do have a plan B. A pakhan, or Russian crime boss, is operating out of South Florida. His organization has associates in Russia with access to plutonium-238 and strontium-90. The federal government believes there are about a thousand radioisotope thermoelectric generators, or RTGs, scattered throughout the old USSR, and inside each one is radioactive material. Putin and the rest of Moscow have lost track of these generators."

"Putin has lost them, but you've found them? Damn nice work, CC," said LoNigro, lightly clapping.

"No, I haven't found them, but my physicist at UC Santa Barbara believes the Russian pakhan in Florida has access to them for the right price."

"Careful, CC; this guy could be a money pit. A million each time you hear his bullshit, but the product never materializes."

"We're all over that, Mark. Bullshit walks. Gas and I have a meeting with the guy Wednesday in Miami. We're bringing along our professor for his expertise.

"RTGs are very precise devices," Conti continued. "When we send a satellite into space, it contains an RTG power supply that turns heat from slowly decaying plutonium aboard the craft into electricity using an array of thermocouples, which convert thermal energy directly into electrical energy."

"Now I wish I hadn't slept through college physics. What's a thermocouple?" Hickman asked.

"Basically, it's a platform made of two kinds of metal that can both conduct electricity. They're connected to each other in a closed loop. If the two metals are at different temperatures, an electric potential will exist between them. Put heat on one side and cold on the other side, and you get volts. When an electric potential occurs, electrons will start to flow, making electric current that powers the spacecraft.

"On Earth, fission generates very large amounts of heat, but it's much more complex and not as reliable as simply using the heat produced by radioactive decay. Fission gives you a huge release of energy and uses fuel rapidly. An RTG provides a steadier and much smaller amount of energy. Many remote weather stations, navigation beacons, lighthouses, and buoys also use RTGs to provide electrical power. This is a much different technique than that used by nuclear power stations on Earth. That process is called fission, and gets very high efficiency rates by literally splitting unstable radioactive materials, such as uranium, into smaller parts."

Observing the glassy eyes around the room, Conti suddenly clapped his hands loudly. "Look, plutonium-238 has a half-life of eighty-seven-point-seven years. A twenty-year-old unit would still have seventy-eight percent of its radioactive potency left, and that's plenty for our purposes. Getting our hands on one of these is the first phase of plan B. If all goes well, we will convince our chemistry teacher to begin building the device once we purchase the RTG, probably from our contact in Florida. He's the guy with the associates in Russia. That," Conti concluded, "is our backup plan to the Hanford project."

"Any idea what kind of time line we're looking at?" asked Hickman as he kicked off his shoes.

"Not a clue. We may know more after Wednesday. Remember, if the pakhan's contacts are real, it's likely that they care about one thing only—getting the most bucks for their bang. Count on that. And the world is full of terrorists who would do anything to obtain a nuclear device. We could be looking at weeks, months, or years."

"We don't have that kind of time," said Rizzo firmly. "If necessary, I'll make our Russian associate an offer he won't refuse. Proper diplomacy often must be accompanied by bold persuasion. It worked pretty well for Al Capone."

Emily McClelland had been a housekeeper for forty-two years, ever since her husband, Navy Master Chief Jack McClelland, stepped on a mine while walking the sixty yards between his hooch and the river patrol boat he would be commanding that day on a tributary of the Mekong River.

With only a high school degree, two children to feed, and no practical work experience, McClelland opted to begin her own housecleaning business in the Tacoma suburb of Lakewood. She regularly cleaned two homes a day, earning more than a hundred dollars, plus tips. Customers often recommended her services to friends and business associates. One of those customers raved about her work often enough that her longtime neighbor on Gravelly Lake Drive, psychiatrist Joanne Bancroft, interviewed and hired McClelland herself.

Within a month, Bancroft and her husband, Puget Sound National Bank vice president and Vietnam veteran Arlen Bancroft, hired her as their full-time housekeeper. It was a new position that required many skills, but Emily McClelland had them all. She also had an annual salary of $45,000, full benefits, days off, annual bonus, and vacation. Because she often worked late whenever the Bancrofts had guests for the evening, she was even given her own upstairs room, formerly used by their daughter, Kelli, a recent graduate of the University of Washington School of Medicine.

It was an ideal arrangement for McClelland. Because of Jack's combat death, the federal government paid for her children's college educations. She had many friends in the area, some military, some not, plus her own home and a nearly new Toyota Camry. Neighbors in the area were invariably pleasant, without the snooty attitudes of the new-money owners of homes she had once cleaned.

Mark and Karen LoNigro were wonderful examples of that charm. Emily knew Mark was a custom home builder, and having been inside their home twice herself, it certainly looked the part. On the outside, a big deck extended from the house to within twenty yards of the heavy landscaping between the adjoining properties. From her room in the quiet of late evenings, Emily could often hear soft classical music and even quiet conversations emanating from the LoNigro home.

Arlen Bancroft was having a small surprise dinner party for his wife this evening, celebrating Joanne's appointment as director of adult psychiatry for Multicare Medical Center in Tacoma. Arlen was extremely proud of her, and he had worked with Emily to plan the event. She took it from there, arranging for caterers, two in-home chefs, formally dressed waitstaff, and appropriate wines for the fresh-caught lobster that was flown in by courier jet from Maine that afternoon.

The surprise, the party atmosphere, and the sumptuous meal were what Arlen Bancroft later termed "spectacular" as he quietly and privately handed Emily a $5,000 bonus check along with a bear hug to show his appreciation.

Emily was back in her room by ten o'clock, feeling euphoric over the evening's events. The room, which looked directly toward the LoNigro home, had become stuffy in the August heat, causing her to open a window and the screened sliding glass door on the side of the room facing the LoNigros. The bright deck lighting illuminated her room as well, so she left her own lights off.

Wearing a light bathrobe and seated in her comfortable recliner next to the screened door a few minutes later, Emily wasn't listening at first to the apparent angry conversation coming from the LoNigro's family room, where another screened door also was wide open. The scenario surprised her on two fronts: the volume and the vulgarity of the voices, neither of which she had heard before in her nearly six months with the Bancrofts.

But Emily McClelland's surprise was about to change to the worst shock she had felt since the naval officer and chaplain had appeared on her doorstep so many years ago to tell her that her husband, Jack, would be coming home in a box.

Hickman's suggestion for a piss break was heeded by all but Steinberg, who had all but ignored his Black Jack and water since arriving. The rest resettled, and Rizzo began outlining what he called a mission plan for the Panama Canal.

"You'll remember me saying that we need to get the package aboard one of the New Panamax ships, which are too large to fit through either of the two present locks. That's the major key to the success of our plan. A cargo ship will have about thirty crew members aboard, while a cruise ship could have five thousand passengers and crew."

Steinberg threw up his hands, causing Rizzo to stop his presentation. "I apologize; it must have gone over my head. Not only do I not favor this job, I have no interest in killing five thousand people, or even *fifty* people, to make a few million. No fucking way!"

"Don't jump to conclusions," Rizzo growled in return. "If you did this in combat, you'd be dead by now!"

Barely sixty feet away in her room, Emily McClelland's jaw dropped open, and she began to tremble. She reached for a yellow legal pad and began taking notes.

"Look, Mitch," Rizzo said, lowering his voice. "We're certain we can minimize injury. We'll use a two-punch approach. First, we detonate a couple of C-4 bricks, stopping the ship cold in the lock. Then, one of our people will telephone the canal superintendent on

DETONATION

a burner phone and say the ship will be obliterated in thirty minutes and stress the need for immediate evacuation of the area. Other calls will go to local television and radio stations and even President Juan Carlos Rodriguez's office, stressing the danger and yelling incoherently about losing a job and a pension.

"A second call will follow in ten minutes, sounding even more urgent. We, of course, will not be obliterating the ship. Instead, we'll only be scaring the crap out of people anywhere near it, causing them to panic and run for their lives. We'll then wait another ten minutes and have our man make one final call. This time, he'll sound nearly hysterical, crying alligator tears, and begging the superintendent or whoever answers to forgive him and say he was forced to call by men who took his children from their school that morning. Our man will be Panamanian and sound genuine as hell. Exactly ten minutes later, we'll do nothing. Some people will start to believe it's all a hoax. Five minutes later, a remote detonator will trigger the bomb. By then, the entire area should be vacant.

"Now for the ships. There are three types of cargo ships: auto transports, container vessels, and bulk carriers. The majority of the auto transports are still Panamax, which means a maximum beam of a hundred and six feet. These carriers are known informally as ro-ros because new vehicles from Asia, for example, are quickly rolled on the ship at the sending ports by dockworkers and rolled off the ship in the receiving ports. Some port operations can roll on or roll off nearly eight thousand cars in a twenty-hour period. It's amazing—a combination of a ballet and a Chinese fire drill.

"However, the odds that a specific ro-ro ship would be assigned the new lock are almost nil because most ro-ros will fit the original locks. That leaves bulk carriers and container ships, and since the new lock is being designed almost exclusively for container ships, we'll need to use one of those."

"Gas and I have located the owner of a large equipment company in Long Beach who frequently exports huge shipments to Europe on cargo ships," Conti interjected, peering over the top of his glasses. "It would be easy to hide a bomb inside a big dump truck or excavator."

"Have either of you looked at how we would find a specific ship and ensure our package goes aboard that ship?" Hickman wondered.

"I called a Danish line, a Japanese carrier, and a Chinese company in Los Angeles, passed myself off as a potential customer, and asked the same question," Conti replied. "The Danish and Japanese companies said they get calls like this all the time, and that they could provide that information within three to four days of sailing. The Chinese company said they could do it within forty-eight hours. After that, no promises. Then they hung up."

"The next ten days will be key," Rizzo asserted, eyeing each of the other men. "We need our Long Beach construction guy and our chemistry teacher fully onboard and the Hanford job done. If those go smoothly, we'll be rounding third and on our way home."

"Or we'll be caught in a rundown," Steinberg shot back. "Am I the only sane man in this asylum? Let's just hold everything right now!" He stood, making a "timeout" sign. "Am I the only one getting this? First, the five of us are being asked to use radioactive materials to commit a crime that not only will contaminate one lock in Panama, but probably all of them. Second, this would be viewed as an attack against world commerce—against *humanity*. Third, countless innocent people would die, sooner and later, as wind spreads the radioactivity over the entire area, making us all murderers. Twenty-five million bucks won't look like much to any of us when the hangman is slipping a rope around our necks."

"Well, now you're just being picky." Conti smiled.

Rizzo glanced at the other three members "Larry, what do—"

LoNigro jumped in instead. "Mitch isn't alone. He's just laid out some very serious concerns. I suspect the dangers can be overcome. How, I don't know yet, but I'm going with that belief at the moment.

If potential slaughter is even a possibility, I'm out.

"What bothers me now is that the five of us are tasked with popping a big cap on the Panama Canal that would save countless millions of dollars for ports up and down the Pacific Coast for the benefit of unions, their workers, railroads, and gigantic corporations everywhere you look, and our total reward is a hundred twenty-five million. That's a lot of dough, no doubt about it, but it's a drop in the bucket for any one of those organizations, not to mention all of them combined, and it's our asses in danger, not theirs. I'll continue listening to the concept, but if this is all there is, the risk is greater than the reward."

Conti appealed for calm barely a moment before hell was about to explode around him. "Relax, gentlemen. This is just a meeting to discuss the idea of shutting down the new lock and, if so, to discuss how we might do it. Mitch, your concerns were expected on all counts and are appreciated, so let's proceed with what we've got and then break it down to see if we can rebuild it to suit everyone. Fair enough?"

Led by Rizzo, the men had spent well over a decade assisting others to relinquish their money or property for causes that were carefully explained to the donors. Now and then, unfortunate methods of persuasion were required to clarify misunderstandings with property owners who originally preferred to keep their money, paintings, jewelry, and real estate themselves. These and other lucrative moneymaking projects for the group included bribery, theft, trafficking human organs, securities fraud, smuggling antiquities, arranging hijackings, intercepting jewelry couriers, bid rigging, and extorting funds from politicians, business leaders, and celebrities.

Steinberg stood, thrust his hands into his pockets, and faced the others.

"For a long time we've ducked bullets by only taking jobs in our pay grade. We made it all work because we never got our hands dirty; others did it for us. We used our heads, not our fists. We've limited the number of soldiers involved and always insulated ourselves from the people we hired to do the dirty work. This job would require three times as many soldiers as anything we've ever tried.

"We're jumping into a new realm here. Everyone in this room has serious money stashed away, and we're all too old to trip over our peckers now. This job with the canal is just too fucking complicated and dangerous as hell, period!" Steinberg turned and, without another word, stepped to LoNigro's bar to fill his glass with ice and Canadian Club.

Conti started to respond, but Rizzo gave him a look that signaled his intention to handle it. Rizzo understood that Steinberg had the most responsibility of any member of the group. His charge was to protect the members from any venture that might implode.

LoNigro, a bear of a man at six six and 310 pounds, wore a salt-and-pepper beard and often tied his shaggy black hair in a short ponytail. He used the ruse of an aging biker to fraternize with and recruit patrons for tasks requiring their unique expertise. Biker bars south of the city were his hunting grounds. Rizzo reminded the big man often of the importance of ensuring that hired thugs acquired no knowledge of the group's membership, which LoNigro complied with to the letter.

After a minute, Rizzo replied, "Mitch, you're correct. It *is* too complicated. If it weren't for your diligence, all of us would either be in jail or broke. Last week, CC and I had the same conversation. Is this job too convoluted, too much of a long shot? Then we broke it into manageable parts. We looked at how we might find a way of containing a radioactive substance. If we were hired to build a container to carry nuclear shit, would we take the gig? I said yes, so long as we maintained the layers of protection we always insist on. We then looked at the job of stealing the waste from Hanford. Again, we felt we would take the job.

"This is my recommendation, Mitch. If you feel that Long Beach is safe and Hanford has our usual firewalls, specifically that Dr. Dunbar has no idea who we are and all communication has been through encrypted emails, then let's give those operations a go and regroup at my place in ten days. If then you feel we're compromising our standards, I'll be the first to pull the plug."

Steinberg promptly agreed. "Ten days it is. I should have the Swiss francs by then. And one more thing. When we meet at Gas's, I'll need a few minutes to discuss cell phones and our use of burner phones since Tacoma is using their StingRay cell phone surveillance equipment. Until the next meeting, keep pulling your SIM card and battery when you finish doing your mischief."

"Mischief." The word hung in the air. Emily McClelland turned on her computer and began transcribing the conversation.

"What do I do now?" she wondered, her voice barely a whisper.

Chapter Ten

Morgan spent another two days in Florida after Patrizio Bianchi's arrest, meeting with federal prosecutors in Miami who were preparing first-degree murder charges against Bianchi, and then flying to Fort Lauderdale for a day with Rob Spencer, who picked him up at the airport just before three o'clock.

The men spent ninety minutes at Gold's Gymnasium on the east side before showering up and driving to Spencer's handsome tri-level home off Bayshore Drive, where Rob's wife, Gail, a Fort Lauderdale attorney, had taken the afternoon off and prepared a dinner for the ages.

Spencer parked his black Lexus in the driveway, and the men walked past an attached three-car garage to the tan stucco residence situated on a large lot with two date palm trees framing the entry and another overseeing a corner of the backyard. A maroon Spanish-tile roof and landscaping gave the residence killer curb appeal.

Two overstuffed leather chairs rested on the wide, covered porch, where a big tiger-striped cat, eyes partially open, held forth on one of them, surveying the men as they stepped to the solid walnut and plate-glass front door.

"That's Boris. He doesn't take too well to strangers," warned Spencer, opening the door and stepping inside.

"Sometimes I don't either."

The trio had become fast friends since Brick became a Nobility consultant three years earlier and often got together when he was in town. The Spencers maintained a relaxed and convivial atmosphere at home, assisted by their inherent senses of humor. Rob kept a prized baseball, signed by former Dodger great Duke Snider, on a mantel above a rarely used fireplace, while Gail's kitchen wall held a placard urging visitors to "Keep Calm, Drink Wine."

The couple met while students at Florida State University in Tallahassee, where Rob majored in criminal justice and Gail in political science. Rob joined the Miami Police Department after graduation, and Gail, a five-six bundle of energy and brains, breezed through the University of Miami law school in just two years and was hired immediately by a growing Miami law firm.

Now in their fifties and living in Fort Lauderdale, both were well-regarded professionals who lived comfortably on their high six-figure income. Their daughter, Kimberly, was a meteorologist with the National Weather Service in Miami.

After cocktails by the pool, the group moved inside. Their timing was good; the aroma emanating from the kitchen had tantalized Brick for over an hour. Gail had prepared roast grain-fed beef, slow-cooked with baby onions and mushrooms in gravy, served with miniature red potatoes, Caesar salad, and paired with a superb 2008 Benziger Merlot. After dinner, Gail served homemade lemon meringue pie using lemons from the Spencer's backyard.

Good-natured banter ruled the remainder of the evening as the men in particular
tried to digest what, for Morgan at least, had been an unforgettable dinner and warm experience all around. He shook his head.

"An evening like this makes me think of maybe settling down with the right woman one of these days and maybe even having a couple of kids," he declared with a broad smile. "Wow!"

"Well, you're not settling down with Gail. She's taken, so forget about it, Brick," chuckled Spencer, a former FSU linebacker, drawn there from his native Idaho, where his father was a state police captain.

When Morgan stood and prepared to call a cab an hour later, Gail steered him from the door to a large guest room on the first floor. "Oh no you don't, big boy. You're staying here tonight."

As he drifted off to sleep twenty minutes later, Brick found himself wondering if the "right woman and a couple of kids" would ever really invade his future.

By early afternoon the next day, Morgan was back in Tacoma, traveling south on I Street past the enormous 111-year-old Rust Mansion built for the president of what then was the city's ASARCO smelter. Someone with very serious money would restore the majestic structure someday and find the hidden spaces and untold secrets almost surely lurking among its eighteen ornate rooms and eight massive fireplaces. "Something to think about but not today," Brick told himself.

Morgan slowed several blocks later as he spotted the garish sign of the Parkway Tavern, which opened near Wright Park in 1935 as Rawling's Market and evolved into the cozy Parkway in 1971, blossoming into a trendy and popular bar and grill ever since. He parked his Beemer nearby, jaywalked across I Street, and strode into the bar, where he spotted Port Commissioner Barry Mott seated near the back, reading a newspaper.

Mott already was in a grumpy mood as the men shook hands and settled into his rear booth. The bespectacled executive was about five ten and wore a medium-brown herringbone suit, light-blue shirt, and paisley silk tie over his slender frame. His gray hair was brushed back carefully, and he wore a thin Clark Gable mustache that was absent at their first meeting.

A waitress materialized and placed coasters and menus in front of both men. Mott ordered a pint of Deschutes Inversion IPA, and Morgan nodded the same, glancing at the backbar with its more than thirty active beer taps and dozens of colorful antique taps adorning its wood rafters and beams.

"Would you like to order now?" asked the waitress.

"In a couple minutes," said Morgan.

"Look around you, Brick. What you're seeing in here is foresight."

This little bar grew into what it is today for one reason—vision. That's the key to success, and in the port's case, that foresight has worked very well. So far. But we've got to continue producing leaders who can visualize opportunities and spot potential problems, which is why I'm interested in you for our port security project. And it goes beyond that."

"You've got my full attention."

I believe our security system is as good or better right now than any other port in the world, but I've been wrong before. That's where you come in. Are you going to get that security proposal to us or not?"

"You'll have it this week, Barry. I've been in Florida on business; got in this morning."

"Good, very good," Mott replied. He signaled the waitress and ordered a jalapeno burger and another IPA. Morgan ordered a BLT but waved away a second pint.

"I understand your new name is the Northwest Seaport Alliance," Morgan said.

"Yes, it is, with regard to marketing and operations. We maintain the Port of Tacoma entity to manage our own assets, of course. Seattle does the same."

The waitress returned to their booth. "Would you fellas like fries with the sandwiches? There's no extra charge."

"No fries," said Morgan.

"We also have spinach salad. It comes with a nice honey mustard—"

"No salads," barked Mott.

The waitress departed.

A telephone camera flashed across the room, drawing a scowl from Mott and intruding on a point he was trying to make.

"Selfies—that's all the kids do today," he grumbled. "They've got their heads so far up their asses they don't even recognize how ignorant they are."

"Sometimes the gene pool needs a little chlorine, Barry."

Mott shook his head as the waitress set down their pints and sandwiches. "I call this the Gravy Train Generation—welfare and cell phones. They're going to wake up in ten years and have a million pictures, most of themselves, but they won't know anything about their own city's history."

"Budget problems. Look around the country. History courses are being dropped everywhere," Morgan said.

Mott nodded and returned Morgan's gaze. "Damned right they are, and the worst of it is that history is the key to the future—always has been. Listen, the headquarters of Frank Russell Company, the Cadillac of corporate pension fund consultants worldwide, opened downtown in 1988. Frank's nephew, George Russell, designed it. He sold the company ten years later for a billion dollars cash. A few years later, the company moved to Seattle, stuffing itself into the already overcrowded downtown. And why? Because Tacoma's political and business *leadership* couldn't figure out how to keep that company here. That was a huge failure. They didn't have a plan B."

Mott stopped talking long enough for their waitress to set down their sandwiches.

"The Port of Tacoma needs its own plan B—or plan C, if necessary—to keep it as safe as possible from the terrorist lunacy out there, Brick. The sons of bitches will get around to our ports soon enough. I just want mine to be as prepared as possible.

"In another year or two, I'll probably head for the barn, but in the meantime, I need to do whatever I can to improve the direction of this town. I can best do that at the port. If problems aren't fixed, they fester; look at what ASARCO, Hooker Chemical, and the St. Regis pulp mill did here for generations. The city still hasn't recovered from that era, so I'm determined to have the port take the lead and let city government catch up."

"You've already done your share, Barry. Why not let someone else take a turn in the barrel?"

"That's why I'm talking with you, son," Mott shot back. "You've got a perfect background for the Port Commission. You were raised in this town, you run a first-class maritime investigations company here that gives you firsthand knowledge of port operations, you're a hell of a quick study with a great education, and you're not a candy-ass beholden to anyone."

"I appreciate your confidence, but let's look at one thing at a time."

"Time is the issue, Brick. Back in 1873, the Northern Pacific Railroad chose Tacoma as its western terminus, and the city began to boom. The Tacoma Hotel opened in 1884 as the finest hotel north of San Francisco. That's over a hundred years before Russell built on the same site. The hotel was an enormous building for its day—a block long, incredibly ornate, huge rooms, largest billiards parlor in the West, and a kitchen that baked five hundred pies a day.

"Then came the fire in 1935—totally destroyed. Two Japanese-American bellboys helped get all the people out alive. Then in 1942, Roosevelt had them interned along with thousands of other citizens. How's that for gratitude?" Mott wondered.

"Progress comes from education and dedication, and the only things kids understand these days is their damn cell phones," Mott continued. "Some people give them to their kids in grade school. It's lunacy. You following me?"

"Oh yeah," said Morgan resignedly as a thirty-something near the front of the bar fired off another selfie and set about seeing how quickly her phone could get it online.

Mott glanced over at the bar, sneered, and continued.

"Remember our meeting at the car museum when I was admiring that red sixty-one Chrysler 300G and said that within ten years that same company was on the verge of bankruptcy? That was a huge leadership failure. Chrysler was a business. Cities are businesses, and so are ports. We can't afford to be behind the curve. And I believe you can help us stay on top."

"I remind you of a sixty-one 300G?" asked Morgan, straight-faced.

"Something like that. I was drawing a parallel for you. Tacoma lost Russell because it lacked the sophisticated leadership and vision to keep it here. But the Port of Tacoma isn't going to lose its momentum as long as I'm around."

Morgan settled into tapping Mott's information bank relative to port operations. Anything he could learn aboveboard that could assist his company's bid could be huge for Morgan Maritime Investigations. "What are the port's immediate priorities?"

"We have to modernize the equipment that loads and unloads the larger ships. We could lose a third of our business if we don't upgrade the cranes and support equipment to deal with the new Panamax ships that carry twelve thousand containers. We've got dozens of huge cranes now, but we need even bigger ones to reach containers piled at the tops of these huge ships."

"Can't you just use one of the cranes you have now on each side of the ship to lift off all the containers?"

"There's more to it than that, Brick. The devil is in the details, as they say."

"Has the new canal expansion started impacting your traffic?"

"Not yet, but that's why we're modernizing now. Up north, the Port of Vancouver is running at seventy-seven percent of capacity, and Tacoma and Seattle are at fifty percent. But together, we're also bigger than Vancouver. The ports of Tacoma and Seattle support fifty thousand jobs here. We're riding high with our container traffic. We can't afford to go backward."

Discussing contract specifics was off limits legally, but Morgan offered a question that skirted the boundaries. "Stop me if you need to here, but how would you grade the POT's emergency response now?"

Mott set down his burger and took another sip of beer. "Shoot— nothing confidential about emergency preparedness."

"What happens if there's a fire at one of the port terminals or on a cargo ship?"

"Well, we've got three high-speed fireboats here for any scenario. They didn't exist back in sixty-three when pier seven went up. It was a hell of a fire; you could see it from Seattle. The fire department lost a battalion chief in that one, and the damage was in the millions. But more to your question, it depends on the trains."

"Trains?"

"As a port commissioner, this issue sends me over the edge. Some fools in city government decided in 2013 to close the only fire department near the port. We have to rely on a few departments that ring the area, but their response time is over ten minutes, unless the trains get in the way."

"But *what* trains?"

"We have three commercial rail lines linked to the port, and we have cameras monitoring every inch of those lines, not to mention all the cameras covering our terminals, docks, structures, and everywhere else around our operations. We've also got our own line, Tacoma Rail, that moves cars brought in by the railroads. We never allow trains to block emergency access points to our terminals. It happened by accident sometime back, and there was hell to pay, believe me. Today, we can clear any rail crossing in the port within five minutes. Unfortunately, the city geniuses are at it again, having okayed a plant near the port that compresses methane to its liquid form, LNG. The battle never ends."

Morgan smiled and then asked, "How do you sleep at night?"

"Only after a bucket of good Kentucky Bourbon."

When the check arrived, Mott nodded to Morgan. "You mind covering this, Brick? All I've got is a hundred-dollar bill."

Morgan's mouth dropped open. One of his contacts had told him days earlier that Mott was so cheap that he would attend garage sales, buy old Craftsman tools, and then return them to Sears and demand they honor their lifetime replacement policy.

"One more thing," Mott said, turning his head as they ventured out into a midafternoon breeze. "Remember, back in thirty-five, the Parkway was a food market. Today, it's a bar and grill making money hand over fist. The future belongs to those who appreciate history."

Before Morgan could respond, Mott already had popped the door on his Caddy parked out front, gotten in, and fired the engine. But the man was right about history. Mott had invited Brick to two meetings and never once picked up the check.

Chapter Eleven

The volume on Mott's television was low, and he occasionally glanced at the infomercial selling romantic songs of the sixties. Sleep was elusive tonight; twice he had picked up a book on the history of the American bison. Mott had always been infatuated with history, and he hoped that reading about buffalo would take his mind off the canal project. But it was inescapable.

How would history treat the attack on the canal? swirled around in his head.

Restless and frustrated, he tossed the bison book aside and reached for the TV remote. Within a few moments, Mott had located an on-demand program titled *Panama Canal: A History of Challenges*.

This could be an omen, he thought. After adjusting his pillow, he turned up the volume, pushed the watch button, and soon heard the narrator state, "The year was 1901.

"Located in Buffalo, New York, the Temple of Music Concert Hall was designed in an Italian Renaissance style for the 1901 Pan-American Exposition, a world-class fair designed to bring together the people of the Americas in the wake of the 1898 Spanish-American War.

"Buildings of the great fair spread over nearly 350 acres, and the design and architectural style of its many structures emphasized what its designers called a uniquely American style. The Temple of Music was an exception to the rule."

Images flickered across the screen of the vast array of structures built in this so-called unusual architectural style.

"Stretching from the four-hundred-ten-foot Electric Tower at the north to the Triumphal Bridge at the south, the fair's central plaza incorporated the spacious Court of Fountains and the vast Esplanade, capable of accommodating a quarter-million people for concerts and assemblies," the narrator continued. "To the northeast was a twelve-thousand-seat stadium. A system of lagoons and interconnecting canals encircled the exhibit area. Electric light throughout was powered by hydroelectric power from Niagara Falls barely twenty miles away."

Streaming footage of the masses appeared. "More than eight million people visited the exposition during its run from May to November. Leon Czolgosz was one of them." A grainy photo of a young man with thick, dark hair and a slight smile shot across the screen. "The unemployed and self-proclaimed anarchist believed he had been denied his share of America's economic prosperity and held President William McKinley personally responsible.

"Czolgosz entered the Temple of Music shortly before four o'clock on the afternoon of September 6 with his cheap Ivar Johnson revolver carefully hidden in his suit coat. He joined a line of fairgoers awaiting a chance to shake hands with a jovial President McKinley, who had labeled the exposition 'my fair' in a speech in the building a day earlier. A few minutes later, as McKinley reached to shake his hand, the twenty-eight-year-old anarchist pulled the gun and fired two .32-caliber bullets, one glancing off the president's breastbone and the other burying itself deep in his abdomen. McKinley's death from gangrene a week later catapulted Theodore Roosevelt into the White House, becoming at forty-two the youngest man ever sworn in to the presidency." The bespectacled Roosevelt with slicked-back, side-parted dark hair glowered from the screen.

"January 9, 1902" in white block letters then appeared at the bottom of Mott's television screen. Intrigued, he sat upright, leaned forward, and stared unblinking at the unfolding scene.

The reenactment showed President Roosevelt sitting at his desk, reviewing a report.

"The Walker Commission, appointed by Congress to debate construction of a canal that would allow commercial shipping to pass between the Atlantic and Pacific oceans using either the Isthmus of Panama or through Nicaragua, presented President Roosevelt with a report outlining the details of such a project," the narrator explained. "It was a job that needed doing, and President Roosevelt had openly declared his wish for America to do it after a costly French failure in Panama three years earlier and a new attempt by France that already appeared hopeless."

On the right side of Roosevelt's mahogany desk rested a Chinese rose porcelain bowl containing five hard-boiled eggs. The stout chief executive reached for a sugar bowl and added several more lumps to his enormous coffee cup. Next to the egg bowl was a linen napkin he used to dab drips of coffee from his thick mustache.

"Roosevelt's first act as president four months earlier had been to change the name of the Executive Mansion to the White House," the narrator stated. "Today, he was faced with a final recommendation of the Walker Commission for location of an American-built canal in the Panama-Nicaragua region."

Mott's ears perked up as he leaned closer to the television.

Roosevelt leaned back in his comfortable leather armchair, withdrew a cigar from an inside pocket, and set it afire.

The narrator intoned, "Roosevelt had closely followed France's attempt to build a canal across Panama and knew it was doomed from the start. The private French corporation that first undertook the project was led by overconfident engineer Ferdinand de Lesseps, builder of the sea-level Suez Canal in Egypt that joined the Red Sea and the Mediterranean in 1869." An image appeared of the white-haired de Lesseps with a thick handlebar mustache. "De Lesseps was venerated throughout Europe and the Middle East as an engineer without peer.

"A decade after the Suez success and armed with funds from Paris, de Lesseps began development of a canal that would cut across Colombia's Panama Province and connect the Atlantic and Pacific via the Caribbean Sea.

"The French began excavation in January 1882, and seven years later, over twenty thousand workers had died, most due to malaria and yellow fever." A montage of black-and-white photos of lifeless bodies spread across Mott's sixty-two-inch screen, making the scene appear even more gruesome. "More than one and a half billion gold francs were gone, and completion of the project was nowhere in sight. De Lesseps's magic touch in the sands of Egypt had been lost in the jungles of Panama."

"Death by mosquito," the president reflected aloud as he slowly folded the report and set it atop his desk. He examined a pocket watch lifted from his vest and checked the time.

"The president knew that if America were to take over France's crumbling second try in Panama, workers would require now-available vaccinations against yellow fever. That was a clear imperative," the narrator said, as images of masses of beleaguered workers flickered across the screen. "With that problem harnessed and American engineers in charge, Roosevelt believed that a US-led operation could succeed where France had failed.

"The only other serious issue would be cost," the narrator continued. "Even now, French officials were busy floating a trial balloon. For only a hundred and nine million dollars, went the Washington rumor mill, their entire project, including all equipment and buildings, was for sale."

Roosevelt chuckled as he read the report that lay before him. "Who is the French kidding? America is the only possible customer." He laughed louder as he continued to read. "An 'adjustment' in the French price tag will be required, if needed. If the Walker Commission selects Nicaragua, France will receive nothing. Just as it should be."

The narrator broke in. "Those in the know believed that Admiral John Grimes Walker's commission would recommend building the canal in Nicaragua instead of picking up the pieces of the French debacle in Panama. But that was before the yellow fever vaccine became available in quantity and ahead of France's decision to fold its tent in Panama."

The president's reading was interrupted with the announcement from his secretary that Secretary of State John Hay had arrived.

Secretary Hay entered the president's office with a smile and placed his hat and overcoat on a coatrack near one of the two windows of Roosevelt's office. The president arose and walked around his desk to give the secretary one of his trademark vigorous handshakes while his left hand grasped Hay's right shoulder.

"Mr. Hay, please have a seat. Today we're faced with a little challenge."

"I assume that we're talking about the Walker report, Mr. President."

Roosevelt returned to his chair. "John, talk to me about the change of events. Even considering bailing out the French on their fiasco in Panama makes me angry.""Sir, when the Senate ratified the Hay-Pauncefort Treaty, everyone, including the French, was certain we would build the canal through Nicaragua."

The chief executive removed his round, steel-rimmed glasses and gave them a quick polish with a linen handkerchief. "Look at the logic," he replied. "The French said they wanted over a hundred million dollars to transfer the authority to us—a ridiculous price for their junk pile of disease and rust. Old Man Morgan will have a stroke if the American route doesn't go through Nicaragua."

Secretary Hay nodded. "Senator Morgan has been the nation's strongest advocate of a Nicaragua canal—not counting you, of course, Mr. President."

"Well, events have changed my thinking, John. Have you heard from the senator since the commission's report was changed?"

"No, sir, not yet."

The narrator interrupted, saying, "The powerful and feisty John Tyler Morgan of Tennessee was a former general in the Confederate

Army, Grand Dragon of the Ku Klux Klan, and the current chairman of the Senate Committee on Interoceanic Canals. His championing of a Nicaragua canal was driven by his conviction that it would provide greater economic stimulus for the southern Gulf states. Also a factor was that Nicaragua was a stable country compared to Colombia and its province of Panama."

Hay referred to his notes while stroking his bushy, light-gray handlebar mustache that contrasted his black beard and hair that was parted down the middle. "It's my opinion that the majority of our countrymen have read about the thousands of workers who died in France's Panama venture. Many have the opinion that Nicaragua does not have the problems of disease, sir."

"But there are some who say that once we start digging in Nicaragua and disrupt the soil we'll have the same malaria issues as Panama. One of the problems, John, is that most of Congress has not read the original commission report. If you throw out the original report, there are many engineering factors that favor Panama."

"Mr. President, some of our top civil engineers feel that de Lesseps started his project with a false premise, and that was to copy the sea-level method he used with the Suez."

"I'll let the engineers decide that, but . . ." The president paused as he spotted his wife, Edith, near his open door. "Edie, are you meeting with Mr. McKim today?"

Mrs. Roosevelt stepped into her husband's office with one of their children in hand as Hay rose to his feet. "Mr. Hay, I'm sorry to interrupt. Mr. McKim will be arriving in an hour and has new blueprints for the first floor."

"Before his assassination," the narrator stated, "President McKinley had received authorization from Congress to remodel the White House—the Executive Mansion, as it was known during his administration. The president and his offices shared the second floor of the White House with the First Family's residence. President Roosevelt had commissioned renowned architect Charles McKim to move his offices to the newly constructed Executive Office Building on the west side of the White House. Roosevelt hoped that the construction would begin in the spring and would not last more than ninety days."

"Edie, please tell Mr. McKim that I plan to stay here during the construction," the president said as she exited the room with a wave. He then resumed his conversation with the secretary of state. "As I was saying, I'm not an engineer, but we need to learn from the French mistakes. Walker tells me the turning point in his thinking came when the French dropped the asking price by over sixty percent."

"Yes, sir. They wanted a hundred nine million dollars, but with the collapse of the second canal company, Compagnie Nouvelle, and their inability to issue more bonds, they were forced to reduce the price to forty million dollars."

The president rose from his chair and walked over to an office window. "The key to getting an agreement to shift the project from the Nicaragua route to the Panama route rests with the influence of George Morison and his ability to bring Senator Hanna to his way of thinking."

Hay nodded and then added, "Walker has committed to Panama. But Morgan never will. We need Morison to get Hanna to understand the engineering advantage to a Panama route, and then we have a chance to get favorable legislation."

"A lawyer and a civil engineer, George S. Morison was considered one of the nation's most brilliant engineers, and his genius made it possible for the design and construction of many steel truss bridges that now span the Mississippi and Missouri rivers," the narrator stated as a sepia photo of a rotund George S. Morison appeared on the screen. "Morison studied dozens of the French blueprints and reports and was certain that the success of an isthmus canal required the use of locks instead of the sea-level Suez approach."

"John, we have an uphill battle with those committed to Nicaragua.

We need to leave the engineering to the engineers."

"Yes, sir."

"And one more thing. The best executive is the one who has sense enough to pick good men to do what he wants done and the self-restraint to keep from meddling with them while they do it."

As Hay stood and prepared to retrieve his coat and hat, the president walked over and gave him a hearty pat on the back.

"If you hang around until dinner, Mr. Hay, I'll buy you a mint julep."

"Make that two mint juleps, and you've got a deal."

"Be in my anteroom at six o'clock, and we'll head for the library," Roosevelt said with a laugh. "The White House bartender is the best in town. I've already tried the rest."

Fueled by this unexpected treasure trove on the canal's history, Mott clicked off the television. He sat in the deepening darkness as he mulled over his decision to contract with Tacoma's corrupt underbelly.

This just might work . . .

Chapter Twelve

The client file of Dr. Phillip Kezer stared back at Avery Griffin as he wrestled with his latest financial crisis. American Express had just notified him that his credit card payment was late. Last month, Griffin had taken a maximum loan on his only whole life insurance policy, and he had exhausted every other source of cash. Being a registered financial services representative placed him in a precarious position. If Pacific Opus Securities learned he was financially underwater, the compliance department would be on him like moths to a flame.

Griffin refocused on Kezer's file. It was more than a folder of accumulated papers, notes, and statements; it was a testament to a man's forty-three-year medical practice. The doctor graduated in 1963 from Tubingen University in Germany. A year later, he emigrated to the United States and settled in Tacoma, where he opened a specialty practice in anesthesiology with which his skills and dedication would serve both his patients and himself well for decades. By the time Avery took over the doctor's securities portfolio, Kezer, now eighty-two, had an account with Pacific Opus valued at $3 million.

Griffin could feel the moisture forming on his upper lip as his financial dilemma pushed aside his other thoughts. His anger toward Opus's continuing reduction of his commissions burned in his gut like molten lava. "Screw 'em," he said out loud, picking up the doctor's file. During the next hour, he wrote himself a $30,000 check from Kezer's cash management account, created a phony set of security account balances, and using a color copier and the firm's watermark paper, inserted the new balances on an Opus monthly account activity statement. He then phoned Kezer and proposed a meeting to discuss a rebalancing of his portfolio due to changes in energy-stock valuations.

Just after one o'clock the next afternoon, Griffin turned west on Bristol Street and navigated his Porsche into the large circular driveway of the sprawling twenty-acre Franke Tobey Jones retirement community adjacent to the city's 760-acre Point Defiance Park.

Dressed in his trademark turtleneck, slacks, and no socks, he parked and exited the car, walked past brightly blooming flower gardens and a sign with a deer painted on it, and headed toward the main building.

Dr. Kezer had his own apartment next to the main facility, but because Griffin believed most of the residents of Tobey Jones were well heeled, he wandered through the full center when he visited, hoping to meet prospective clients.

Kezer, who stood about five nine and wore a small white meticulously trimmed goatee, greeted Avery warmly minutes later and ushered his guest to an expensive dark-oak dining table while he entered his small kitchenette to make coffee. Griffin noticed three months of account statements still unopened on the table and took the opportunity to open them and replace their contents with his fictitious new statements. He made a mental note to return in a month and retrieve the next statement that would list the forged check. The legitimate reports were discreetly slipped into his briefcase. When the coffee arrived, he offered to organize the replacements for his client.

"That would be fine," replied the doctor. "How have my stocks been doing? I know the market has been up this year."

"I was expecting you to have a roughly three-percent gain this quarter, Phillip, but when the price of oil tanked, it pulled down your energy stocks, causing a thirty thousand dollar offset. The good news is you didn't lose money in the quarter, but missed out on about thirty thousand of stock appreciation."

"It's the damned Arabs. They flood the market with oil so they can bankrupt our shale business. International bullshit."

"You nailed it, Doctor."

"You said on the phone you had some recommendations."

"Yes. There's a question whether oil will return to a hundred dollars a barrel soon, so I think you should trim your energy stocks and rebalance your transportations." He spent the next thirty minutes using financial doubletalk to explain the proposals and gain his client's approval for them, his verbal chicanery easily deceiving the elderly physician about his actual $30,000 loss.

Satisfied that Kezer was none the wiser, Griffin returned the files to his briefcase and thanked him for being a good client of Pacific Opus. The men shook hands, and Avery left feeling pleased with himself. He was at least temporarily solvent and still driving his Porsche.

A glance at his Gucci wristwatch told him it was nearing four o'clock, time for a Black Jack and soda. Perhaps more than one. He headed home to celebrate.

Most of the POS brokers were in the office by six fifteen the next morning, loaded up with coffee and waiting for the opening bell. Griffin logged in and used his business computer to input the market sell orders for a few of Kezer's energy stocks and then changed screens to read a half-dozen emails. He was deep in thought when he heard a light knock on his already open door. Looking up, he recognized the firm's compliance officer and waved her in. Shit. The last thing he needed now was the Opus SWAT people snooping around his practice.

Every brokerage house or financial institution has a department dedicated to registered representative supervision and compliance. The Securities and Exchange Commission and Financial Industry Regulatory Authority required a minimum of one person in every principal office, or Office of Supervisory Jurisdiction, to be dedicated to ensuring their stockbrokers followed the rules. The compliance officer at the Tacoma OSJ was Helen McClosky. She had been the firm's top cop for five years.

"No complaints, I hope" was Griffin's greeting as McClosky approached his desk.

"Better than that, Avery. Time for your unannounced review."

What fucking timing. The day after he stole thousands, they want to inspect his files. "I'm all yours. What do you need?" Every brokerage office in America is required by law to have their files inspected annually. The file-and-practice review was always done on an unannounced basis and included an inspection of randomly selected files.

"Here's a list of ten of your clients. Pull these files, and I'll get out of your hair."

Avery took the list and approached his bank of file cabinets, turning weak-kneed when he noticed that requested file number seven was Phillip Kezer's. McClosky took the ten files in her arms, walked down the paneled hall to her office, and set them on a circular worktable that served as her desk.

Griffin closed his eyes and rubbed them in exasperation. *I'm so perfectly screwed. I steal from a client, and the next day, McClosky chooses me for an inspection. And out of five hundred clients, the bitch selects Kezer.*

Griffin endured the next forty-five minutes feeling like he had just spent all day strapped to an electric chair waiting for the warden to flip the switch. He had a fleeting thought of pulling the building fire alarm, or maybe running to his car and escaping to Canada. One approach might be to contact his attorney and plan some kind of plea deal. Just as he reached for the phone, he spotted McClosky approaching his door.

He started to get up, but she passed his door and continued down the hall. *She's taking a piss break!* he thought. The only offices to his right were a stockroom and women's restroom.

In seconds, he formulated a plan, left his office, and quickly walked to McClosky's office and worktable. If he could find Kezer's file, he would steal its contents and just play stupid. He knew it was a weak play, but it might buy him time to cover up his one-day embezzlement fiasco.

Griffin figured he had maybe sixty seconds as he looked down at his ten client files, six of which had been reviewed. He removed Kezer's file from the smaller stack and slipped it into the pile of completed audits. *Just maybe she will be preoccupied and not notice.*

He was sweating and felt light-headed as he left McClosky's office and started back to his own. He had covered only a few steps down the hallway when he nearly collided with McClosky.

"Oh. Were you looking for me?"

"No, well, yes. I'm making a coffee run. Want me to grab you a hot one?"

"Shouldn't, but sure."

Five minutes later, he was doing the doorknob juggle—holding two coffees in one hand while opening a door with the other.

"I'm just about done with your files; ten more minutes, Avery. But first I want to ask you a favor."

Looking at the two stacks of files, he noticed that she had only one left to review, and her yellow pad did not contain any notations referencing Kezer. *What is bitch cop trying to pull? A favor?*

For the next fifteen minutes, McClosky complimented him on the CPA approach that he applied to his files. She said 70 percent of the files she reviews are out of balance concerning clients' risk tolerance and the products in their portfolios. Each year, Pacific Opus asked its clients to fill out questionnaires declaring their tolerance to risk from conservative to aggressive. McClosky explained that she found too many files in which clients had declared they were conservative but their portfolios were composed of speculative and volatile stocks. The meeting ended with Griffin agreeing to be part of a firm competence meeting next month to share with other associates his background as a CPA and how that experience helped him maintain his clients' records.

Griffin drove through downtown traffic later that afternoon and felt a twinge of anxiety as he passed the county courthouse. The bullet he had ducked that day could have killed him professionally, and he needed something to calm his nerves. *No coffee this time.* When he reached Wright Park, he turned west on Sixth Avenue and headed for the Cloverleaf Tavern.

The Tacoma thirst quencher opened on the city's west side in 1950 and remained as much a part of T-Town's history as the Narrows Bridge and Almond Roca.

Two beers later and armed with two pizzas, he turned south on Bridgeport Way and drove toward University Place, his thoughts bouncing between the Kezer embezzlement and his own need for still more cash. The idea of slashing expenses never entered his mind.

Screw it—let the pizzas get cold. Griffin passed the town library, eased into the right lane, and entered the Green Firs Shopping Center, anchored by a Safeway store and also home to a Trader Joe's specialty grocer and other smaller retailers. He maneuvered his German wheels across the lot to a safe spot next to his destination. Almost hidden in a corner of the Green Firs next to a sports card shop was the quaint and discrete Jade Palace Chinese restaurant and lounge.

Before he could deal with Angela's antics at home, he needed a couple drinks and some quiet time to devise a plan to stop his financial hemorrhaging. Griffin walked through the first set of doors, grabbed one of the free weekly trash papers filled with boring news briefs, corny riddles, and escort service ads, and continued through the second set of doors into the restaurant. Still hours before the dinner rush, the aroma of garlic, hoisin sauce, and Mandarin beef greeted him as he passed the desk and walked into the empty bar. Quiet time was at hand.

Griffin recognized the bartender, and though he couldn't recall her name, he remembered she was a Mariner's fan and one of few who was not a Seahawks groupie.

"My first customer. A double on me," she proclaimed after spotting him entering the lounge.

Glancing at the backbar, he knew the Scotch selection was light. "Chivas on the rocks, please."

"Chivas. You got it. Do you want ESPN turned on? I think that—"

"No, not unless your next patron wants it." He took his double, thanked the barkeep, and found a table in a far corner.

Griffin flipped through the weekly news rag unconsciously while searching his mind for a solution to his predicament. He knew for sure that he had stolen the last of client monies, not because of any moral quandary but the reality of risk. He felt no pangs of guilt or responsibility for appropriating his clients' money. Some might call him sociopathic or even psychopathic, of course, but they wouldn't have understood the obvious—that he was the victim here. He was merely returning money to himself that corporate greed had stolen. In recent years, Opus had made systematic cuts to commissions he had earned by making sales that had benefited clients and the company. His reward had dwindled to chump change. Griffin felt at ease recovering money that in truth was already his.

By the time he drained his second double, a plan had begun forming in Griffin's mind for permanently solving his cash flow problem. He like that word: "permanently."

He stared across the room, unseeing.

His father had divorced Avery's mother four years earlier and quickly married a selfish trophy wife twenty-five years his junior. Avery had begged his dad not to do it, but his father had persisted, even trying to cut Avery's mother's settlement to the bone.

Two years later, the jerk refused to help Avery with a paltry $5,000 loan. Griffin was underwater on a rental property and needed the money to avoid losing his investment. But he had turned him down flat, explaining disdainfully that Avery himself set the decision in motion by siding with his mother during their divorce. It wasn't his fault, his father had said. It was Avery's. "How could he turn down his only child?" Avery wondered.

His dad had constructed an impenetrable wall between Avery and himself. There would be no change of heart, no reconciliation, Avery knew. His selfish father had cast him aside just as he had done with Avery's mother—like trash. Instead, the bastard doted on his new wife, a woman Avery dismissed from the start as nothing more than a snippy, gold-digging little bitch.

Taking the last sip of his Chivas, Griffin decided he would kill both his father and his whore stepmother and then assume control of his dad's estate, worth more than $5 million. Setting up a home-invasion robbery scenario should be fairly simple, he reasoned, and eliminating two objects of his hatred would be frosting on the cake.

Griffin left the bar and walked out into the warm late-afternoon sunshine, holding the restaurant door for an elderly couple on their way inside. For the first time in a long time, he felt relieved, jovial even, for now he had a solution that had eluded him for too long. He smiled broadly as he fired the Porsche and headed home.

Chapter Thirteen

Nobility Cruise Line's ten ships were dispersed among many of the world's twenty-four time zones, making communications a challenge for Fleet Security Director Rob Spencer. It was 9:58 a.m. in Fort Lauderdale, and the fifty-eight-year-old former detective was reviewing each ship's threat-assessment training schedule when his cell phone demanded immediate attention.

"Hiya, big brother!"

"You're moving early," replied Spencer with a grin, recognizing the voice of his younger brother, Terry, from Tacoma.

"I figured if I waited till midmorning back there, you'd have cleaned up all the problems on the high seas and have time to chat."

"Let me take a look at my busy schedule. You're in luck; my astronaut-training interview at Cape Canaveral was postponed until this afternoon. What's new?"

"Something came up last night that I thought would interest you."

Terry Spencer had spent the past thirty-one years as a probation officer for the Pierce County Probation and Parole offices, a division of the state Department of Corrections. Over the years, he had shared tales of the parolees under his supervision— stories that often rang bells for Rob. Terry's workload was evenly split between pretrial supervision and probation oversight.

"What have you got?"

"Last night I got a call from a parolee who was assigned to me two months ago. The guy has a master's degree in chemistry and, before his arrest, was a high school teacher in Federal Way, a suburb outside of town. Name's Daniel Pearce. Last year, his teenage daughter was diagnosed with cancer. The medical bills went through the roof, so he sold his house, cashed in his retirement and other investments, and still was sixty thousand in debt. Now besides being the school's chemistry teacher, he also was a varsity football coach and was caught embezzling twelve hundred bucks from his school's sports program. But he had been a model citizen all his life and had such a clean record that the judge gave him probation and time served in jail."

"Is that when you picked him up?"

"Yep. The guy's so clean he squeaks. Here's where it gets interesting. Last night, two guys visited him, one he met when he was in county. They want him to use his chemistry knowledge to build C-4 bombs and a dirty nuclear bomb."

"You've gotta be shitting me!"

"It gets better. The visitors said they plan to sink either a cargo ship or a cruise ship."

"Oh shit, Terry! Who does this Pearce guy think they represent? ISIS, al-Qaeda?"

"Not a clue. Both these guys are Caucasian; that's all he knows. This is way above my pay grade, Rob. I wanted to get your thoughts before I called the FBI."

"Give me the contact info on the guy, and I'll call them for you. I'm on a first-name basis with a couple of high-level suits in the bureau."

"That sounds peachy, bro. Ask them to send my reward in used fifties and hundreds by armored car, will you?" Terry deadpanned.

"Consider it done—the request, not the cash."

Spencer recorded the address and phone number of Terry's parolee, and the brothers signed off. Rob leaned back in his chair and considered what he had just heard. Reaching behind his desk, he pulled a Diet Pepsi from his mini-fridge and took a long swig. He and the FBI had developed a good relationship concerning shipboard security and criminal issues since the Lashkar-e-Aalam attack on Nobility's *Matisse Under the Stars* last year. Spencer had developed particular respect for Herb Wallace, assistant director of the FBI's Counterterrorism Division within the agency's National Security branch, during that investigation.

"C-4 and nukes; now it's come to this." Spencer dialed Wallace's Washington, DC, office, and a secretary put him through. For the next fifteen minutes, he shared his brother's concerns. Wallace listened silently to the gist of it before questioning why terrorists would want to sink a cargo ship carrying perhaps thirty-five crewmen.

"If this is a terrorism play, sinking a passenger liner carrying thousands of people seems a more likely target if there's any truth behind the story."

"That's what I'm thinking, Herb. We stopped the bastards on the *Matisse* last year, but no cruise line could hope to prevent thermite or nuclear attacks. One successful attack and the cruise industry dies worldwide."

"I'll take this upstairs, Rob. The bureau usually wants actionable signals or events to open up what we call a predicated investigation. My guess is we'll initiate a preliminary inquiry because of the possible national security threat. From there, we'll just have to see what develops."

"Better put a rush on this one. My brother has been a probation officer over thirty years, and he doesn't get riled up easily. Something's up, Herb, I can feel it."

Spencer's phone rang just before lunch with Herb Wallace on the line.

"We're opening the prelim now," said Wallace, "and we'll have a couple agents from our Seattle office interview Pearce in the next few days."

"Interviewing him in the next few days isn't exactly the kind of rush I had in mind, Herb."

"I can't go beyond protocol yet, Rob. I've got a boss too. Everyone's got a boss."

"Not Brick Morgan, Herb. He's his own boss."

"And a damn good one, Spence. Wish I had him right here at the bureau. I wonder if he's been in town to visit Liz Monroe since she was confirmed as head of Homeland Security?"

The political firestorm that was precipitated by the near-disastrous Lashkar-e-Aalam attack on the *Matisse* resulted in Elizabeth Monroe being promoted from assistant director of the FBI to secretary of Homeland Security. It was no secret that the former colleagues got along "well."

"Can't help you there, Herb. Brick doesn't often contact me about his social life, but I think I'll call him to see what he can find out about our Daniel Pearce while the bureau is waiting on 'protocol.' He's right in Brick's backyard."

"Let me know right away if he comes up with anything, Rob."

"Count on it."

The men signed off, and Spencer texted Morgan to ascertain his schedule for an urgent phone call, catching him in the middle of a morning workout. Morgan ignored the request but called back immediately.

"Morning, Spence. Where's the fire?" Brick asked, wiping his face with a towel then leaving it hanging around his neck.

"It may be nothing, Brick, but it may be something pretty damn serious, and I'd like you to look at it since it's right in your neck of the woods." Spencer laid out the story over the next ten minutes, but was unable to field any questions. "I know it's thin, Brick, but that's all I've got."

"Thin? It's almost invisible."

"Yes, it is, but if it's real, these guys could be looking at frying ships in the ports of Tacoma or Seattle. Alaska cruise lines use Seattle. Picture a liner lighting up the Port of Seattle or maybe Anchorage. It's a hell of a thought, but we're living in an age of crazies, Brick. I'd feel a lot better if you would interview this guy Pearce and tell me what you think. Just don't mention my brother. If something looks fishy that appears to involve our industry, I'd like you to investigate further, and I'll reach out to Royal and Carnival and ask them to join in the hunt. The word 'nuclear' should get them to pry open their wallets."

"You might want to add Diamond Cruise Line to your list. I've had a contract with them for two months," said Morgan.

"How soon can you interview Pearce?"

"I'll try this afternoon. Consider me in with both feet now, Rob. If this turns out as hot as it sounds, I don't want to get a call from another client and be on a plane elsewhere tomorrow."

"Good. I'll call my brother and set it up. He said the guy is scared shitless of anything that would screw up his probation. One more thing, Brick. Don't trip on the blue suits. Wallace will have the Seattle bureau on this in the next day or so."

Shaved and showered thirty minutes later, Morgan was cooking a cheese and pepper omelet for breakfast when a text message from Spencer informed him that Pearce would be at his Federal Way apartment at three. After inhaling his breakfast and rescheduling a previously planned afternoon appointment into the next week, Morgan contemplated the facts and questions he had at the moment. Why would two strangers pick a suburban schoolteacher to construct two potentially devastating bombs for the apparent purpose of incapacitating or sinking one or more ships? A chemistry teacher is one thing, a nuclear physicist quite another.

Were ships the real target, or was some other use the actual plan? Or was the teacher given to drug use and hallucinations? Answers to these and other questions should come this afternoon.

Morgan spent the rest of his morning dealing with personal business issues and returning calls and messages. Now dressed in brown slacks and a lightweight blue sport coat, he adjusted the high-ride hip holster holding his nine-millimeter Kimber Solo sidearm and left home at 1:30.

He turned right on Narrows Drive and passed rows of Madrona

and Alder trees along the street that had been trimmed to create a partial arbor effect. A soft beep and visual signal on the Beemer's iDrive display indicated an incoming text message, and the big German sedan's smartphone displayed the first ten words. "Not again, not now," Brick muttered.

Slowing to enter an SR-16 on-ramp, he stole a quick glance at the message.

> From: Desiree Morgan Kellogg
> To: Brick Morgan
> "Sorry to bug you, but I have a little problem . . ."

"No, Desiree," he muttered again to himself. "Your problems are never 'little.'" Unless he wanted new texts every five minutes, he needed to reply to his ex-wife soon.

Morgan prided himself on his ability to keep his cool under the most stressful circumstances. The exceptions were those rare occasions when he had to deal with Desiree. While he was studying for the Washington State bar exam, he also explored a law enforcement career. After passing the bar, and with his Stanford JD in hand, he accepted a job with the Seattle Police Department, where he was introduced a year later to Desiree Kellogg, a caseworker with King County Children's Protective Services. *How could I have been so damned stupid?* Morgan and Desiree were married five months later, and within six months, he knew he had made the biggest mistake of his life. A month later, he started the process of pulling the plug on the debacle, and the divorce was finalized the following year.

He would return her call after arriving in Federal Way. While waiting for a green left turn light at the on-ramp, he returned her text with two words: "In meeting."

Traffic cooperated, and Morgan soon left Highway 16 and entered northbound Interstate 5, quickly traveling through the Puyallup Indian reservation and the small community of Fife. He passed the

DETONATION

Highway 18 cutoff to eastbound Interstate 90, glancing to his right at the 430-acre Weyerhaeuser Timber Company campus, and took the Federal Way exit just ahead. "Big W" opened in Tacoma in 1905 and now owned or controlled more than eighteen million acres of timber in eleven countries.

Morgan was running ahead of schedule, and after leaving I-5, he pulled into a handy Starbucks, where an energy boost from a Tiramisu Frappuccino could prepare him for the dreaded call to Desiree.

Only six other customers were inside, and he had no problem snagging his coffee and a corner table. He wondered what drama his ex-wife had for him, certain that whatever it was, it would involve her latest need for more money. "Sorry, Desiree. The bank is closed."

Though it had been five years, he remained cynical about his relationships with women. What ate at Morgan most was how he had misread Desiree's personality. The woman totally lacked empathy and could spend an hour with a new acquaintance without ever asking his or her name and remain oblivious to their occupations or families. The world was all about Desiree and her career. His aversion to making a second mistake had left him wary of future romantic entanglements with the many women who weaved in and out of his busy life.

He left Starbucks, coffee in hand, deciding the parking area would afford him a little more privacy. Brick stood in the shade of a huge maple tree, took another sip, and dialed Desiree's number.

She answered on the first ring. Within five minutes, Morgan learned that she was fed up with her King County job and wished to "borrow" $20,000 to open her own child counseling center. *That's all kids need these days*, he thought ruefully. *Life counseling from Desiree, the personification of bad ideas.* "What is it you want exactly? A gift, a loan, or my investment in your business?" he asked her.

After a long pause, she replied simply, "I don't know what you mean. I just need twenty thousand to open my counseling business."

"Look, five years ago, I gave you fifteen grand to buy you out of my Seattle PD pension plan. A year later, I loaned you six thousand for a car—money you haven't even tried to repay—and I'm not interested in an equity investment in a psychology store."

"Counseling center, not a psychology—"

"No, I'll pass. I hope you—"

"If I end up on welfare or have to live on the streets, it will be your fault!"

"I feel badly already, Desiree."

Morgan disconnected the call, entered his car, and dialed Daniel Pearce's number at Club Nebbiolo Apartments on South Star Lake Road. Pearce sounded game but shaky as they spoke briefly. Brick estimated his arrival in ten minutes.

Three stoplights later, Morgan spotted a small marquee sign and turned into a narrow road that split with two very large purple rocks that were painted with the word "Club" on the left rock and "Nebbiolo" on the right. A light westerly breeze fluttering through the parking lot was separating a few leaves from an assortment of cottonwood, Japanese maple, and Pacific dogwood trees that were displaying their early fall colors as Morgan pulled into a visitor's area and locked the Beemer. It appeared that the complex was designed around four separate three-story buildings, each containing at least thirty units. Pearce had given his unit number as B-38. Building B lay just ahead, and Morgan took the wooden stairs to the second floor.

Unit B-38 was just to his left, and as he approached it, he noticed the drapes were pulled closed. He did a triple tap on the door and stepped back. Spencer had painted a bleak picture of this former teacher—his daughter's cancer, fired from the school district, and now on probation for a two-bit felony beef.

"Okay, Pearce, where are you? Sitting on the can? We just spoke." He gave the door another knock, waited a few moments, and pulled out his cell phone. Moments later, he could hear the ringing of a cell phone inside. What the hell?

Instinctively, he touched his right hip and felt his nine-mil Kimber. Morgan's left hand tried the doorknob and found it unlocked. The apartment door appeared to be a heavy one-hour, fire-rated type, and he used his right shoe to hold it open as he again called Pearce's name. No answer. His threat radar now on high, he pushed open the door and stepped into Pearce's apartment.

"Pearce, you here?" he asked again. Silence. Morgan pulled his sidearm and swept it side to side as he slowly entered the apartment and began moving through. He eyed a small kitchen table to his right and noticed that one of its four chairs was tipped over and lying on its side at an odd angle. Whirling to his left toward the living room, he spotted a sandy-haired man slouched in a recliner. The bullet hole above the man's left eye and blood spatters on the adjacent wall told him his interview with Daniel Pearce had been permanently canceled. The rest of the afternoon was about to become a three-ringer.

Morgan approached the brown suede recliner and pressed a finger against the victim's carotid artery. Feeling no pulse, he decided to clear the rest of the residence and then call it in. The apartment's only other doors were the bathroom and the bedroom. He chose the bedroom.

Right hand gripping his pistol, Morgan pushed open the bedroom door with his right foot and followed the movement with his eyes, too late to spot the long-haired man on his left holding a silenced Ruger automatic aimed at Morgan's head.

"Drop your gun!" came the command. It was cold, clear, direct. "Do it now or I blow your brains out!"

Caught off stride, Morgan already had stopped moving, cursing himself for making what might well be the last dumb-ass mistake of his life. All his years of judo and self-defense training would do him no good at the moment, unless . . .

"It's yours. It's yours. I'm dropping it now!" Morgan replied, lowering his arm and allowing the Kimber to slide from his hand in a manner that caused it to land atop the thug's left foot. Still holding his .380 in Morgan's face, the ski-masked man allowed his eyes to glance down for a fraction of a second, just long enough for Morgan to bring his left arm across his body and deflect the gun arm away. *Don't attack the weapon—attack the arm that's holding the weapon.*

Morgan's right hand came forward, grabbed the man by the face, and slammed his head backward into the doorjamb. Five seconds later, Morgan had the bloodied killer on the floor screaming in pain from an arm bar. He was using his foot to recover his Kimber when a second ski-masked intruder emerged from the bathroom and swung an expandable baton at Morgan, striking him in the head. He felt like the right side of his head had just been blown off. Then a dark, mysterious void opened and engulfed him.

Chapter Fourteen

Byron Dunbar, PhD, performed exemplary work for a national contractor at the Hanford nuclear waste site in Washington State. That was expected of him. As an institutional fellow at the University of California, Berkeley, his postgraduate research into recombinant interleukin-12 treatment of acute radiation sickness won him national acclaim and a prestigious position at Hanford in 1999.

Eighteen years later, Dunbar now was deeply involved in another complex radiation-related project in the analytical laboratories section onsite, which tested and stored nuclear waste samples from Hanford's 177 underground storage tanks. His knowledge that a half dozen of those tanks were leaking their radioactive isotopes within two hundred feet of the groundwater below infuriated him for what he considered good reason. The federal government was ignoring the problem.

The US Nuclear Regulatory Commission and the Department of Energy had routinely pigeonholed his reports detailing threats posed by leakage of the toxic cocktails underground into the streams, rivers, aquifers, and drinking water of eastern Washington. Dairy milk in the region had for years shown signs of contamination that the Feds dismissed as inconclusive. As far back as the 1960s, an entire senior high school class east of Hanford—male and female—had been rendered sterile by something, and although that something was hushed up at the time, Dunbar had no doubt about the cause. A catastrophe of epoch proportions was coming.

After three years of getting nowhere with the Feds, Dunbar joined the nonprofit activist group Hanford Tanks. His employer frowned upon his membership in the group, but he had been assured Dunbar's involvement would not impact his employment. That had changed during the last four months.

Dunbar had discovered that tank AY-102 had a serious leak and the radioactive muck would soon contaminate the Columbia River, whose huge water flow was vital to irrigating the otherwise arid farmlands of eastern Washington. When he first presented the tank-leak data to his employer, Tennessee-based Ionic Mass Data LLC, he received the shock of his life. Upper management told him his radiation analytics were wrong and that he needed to recalibrate his equipment, which he already had done three times and gotten the same results. The manager then informed Dunbar that he was not to retest AY-102 because budget restrictions limited only one analysis per tank.

The next two weeks were pure hell for Dunbar, whose conscience rejected his participation in cover-ups. If Ionic Mass Data had its way, hundreds of gallons of deadly slime would soon ooze into the fourth-largest river in the United States, creating an environmental catastrophe.

People consuming contaminated river water or eating fish taken from it would surely die by the hundreds, perhaps far more. Farmlands feeding national and world markets using Columbia River irrigation systems would dry up overnight, resulting in a mass exodus of people from the region and an economic disaster for the state. The state's wine industry—second largest in America behind California—would disappear along with most dairies, their products unusable. Many fish caught in the lower Columbia already appeared to be mutants by their enormous sizes and grotesque, misshapen features.

Dunbar's personal dilemma was compounded by the reality that he had two daughters in college, and losing his job would wreak havoc with his family finances. It was a no-brainer that if he participated in the cover-up and the truth surfaced, he would face decades in prison. Byron Dunbar was out of options.

Two days later, he laid out the full story for fellow members of Hanford Tanks, met with the editorial board of the *Tri-City Herald* newspaper with the same shocking information, and consulted an attorney about whistleblower protection status.

Once news that AY-102 was leaking near groundwater hit the newspapers and wire services nationwide, Ionic Mass was besieged by NRC and DOE investigators and national and international print and electronic media inquiries. All four major US television networks and their foreign counterparts descended on Hanford like locusts. This wasn't just a story; it was an international revelation—the initial throes of what appeared to be a scandal of unprecedented magnitude.

Agriculture is far and away the largest industry in the state, dwarfing the ubiquitous dot-coms and everything else. Its more than three hundred crops—fruits and vegetables of all kinds—flourish in eastern Washington's hot and dry seven-month growing season, making consumers from around the country and much of the world stakeholders in the state's agricultural health. They ate the foods and drank the wines, and they wanted answers.

Dunbar's laboratory assignments continued through late summer as investigations of his claims droned on. Although some colleagues had whispered encouragement from the beginning, most still avoided him. Invitations to weekend barbecues dried up entirely. Dunbar had painted a big target on his back; aside from his family, he was alone.

By early October, two months after his revelations to the media, Dunbar was still employed by Ionic but believed his chances of staying with the company were slim to none. With that in mind, he agreed to a confidential meeting with an unidentified caller that he was sure would pertain to some form of industrial espionage.

On Tuesday and Saturday evenings of the next week, he drove to the nearby city of Richland, where he left his car in the back of a Denny's parking lot and entered the front seat of a black Escalade without making eye contact with the two occupants of the rear seats.

One seemed to have overall charge of the conversation, while the other filled in details. Together, they explained that a powerful lobbying group needed a large sample of radioactive sludge from one or more of the leaking Hanford tanks to bring pressure on the NRC and the DOE to accelerate the site's cleanup project.

Dunbar was assured that no one would be hurt and that his efforts, although illegal, would save lives by expediting government efforts to mitigate the dangers of contaminated soil and groundwater. In exchange for two liters of extracted tank fluids, he would be paid $250,000 in cash or gold bullion—his choice—and his name would never be mentioned. *My girls won't have to drop out of college!* he thought. Science had created the problem by splitting the atom. Now science would solve it.

Elation had suddenly replaced the nagging fear that had consumed him since his lengthy meeting with the *Tri-City Herald*. The worry that had gripped him then had been replaced with complete confidence in his ability to remove two liters of Hanford's Cold War legacy. Dunbar left the meeting impressed with the two strangers in the black SUV and confirmed that impression during the second meeting when they explained the science behind the modified fire extinguishers.

He had read articles in the *American Journal of Physics* about advancements in electrochromism—a method of altering light transmission in glass by introducing electrical voltage, light, or heat. The process is commonly used in industry to alter glass from transparent to translucent as in bathroom window and shower applications, but Dunbar was amazed to learn that the same process could be modified for use in blocking the escape of gamma rays from common containers. His handlers explained that two altered fire extinguishers would be discreetly switched with regulation units and placed inside one of the analytic laboratories adjacent to his Hanford office.

Two days after his second meeting, Dunbar received a message to drive to the La Quinta Inn in nearby Kennewick, where he would receive the time line and an incentive payment. He drove to the location three hours later, parked his car, and entered the inn's restaurant for lunch. When he returned, a bag emblazoned with "Zip's Burgers" rested on the front seat. Inside were 250 Benjamin Franklins that had replaced Richland's best burger. *This is the most cash I've seen in my life!*

Dunbar had passed the point of no return. The theft would take place the day after tomorrow.

From the outside, Hanford's Ionic Mass Data facility looked more like a federal prison than a state-of-the-art laboratory. The ninety-thousand-square-foot structure was constructed of concrete masonry units with no visible windows. Inside, Dr. Dunbar's two-hundred-square-foot office was located near three large laboratories. Doors to each lab were constructed of two-inch-thick, sixteen-gauge steel. Fingerprint biometric door locks with RFID card readers insured that only authorized personnel could access the secure labs. Next to them was a vast changing area that resembled a locker room at a major league baseball stadium.

At precisely 10:00 a.m., Dr. Dunbar entered the changing room and approached his locker. Next to a cabinet and lockbox was an open closet that contained two sets of protective gear. He stripped down to his skivvies and climbed into an orange Gammatex encapsulated suit. He covered his face with a double-canister respirator and zipped up the hood.

With one hand not yet secured in a bright yellow glove, he pressed a button on a biometric sensor and listened for the three beeps that signaled his admission to Lab 2. The far wall inside was configured with support rows of reinforced stainless-steel shelves that held dozens of lead casks and smaller lead-lined containers known in the industry as pigs. The adjacent wall contained several radiation protection cabinets, the kind equipped with two large radiation-shielding gloves.

In a far corner was a wash station designed to provide an emergency shower in case of a radiation leak. Another cabinet containing three twenty-pound, bright-red Acorn fire extinguishers was located to the right of the wash station.

The doctor waddled across the laboratory covered completely in his orange-hooded safety garb. He knew that one of the large casks, labeled C-109, contained more than three liters of liquefied radioactive isotopes. Dunbar used an overhead lift system to move the lead container to a protection cabinet. He then retrieved one of the modified and pre-positioned fire extinguishers from a lead-lined box also accessible from an outside hallway and placed it on the same cabinet. Slipping his gloved hands into the cabinet's work arms, he carefully removed the container's lead top. Next, he unscrewed the extinguisher's lid, examined the lithium battery module, and noted the on-off switch. Dunbar then selected a graduated glass pipette and used it to transfer one liter of tank C-109's sludge into the first extinguisher.

A wave of anxiety washed over him, and he began trembling as he started filling the second extinguisher. Beads of sweat formed on his forehead and dripped into his eyes. One drop, another, a third . . . Hands and arms inserted in the protection cabinet, he was helpless to wipe away the stinging perspiration and finally set down the pipette on the cabinet's bottom. He took a deep breath, exhaled, and squeezed his eyes shut as he thought about his daughters and the security the money would bring.

The panic attack subsided five minutes later, and Dunbar finished transferring the second liter of sludge into the second extinguisher, activated the lithium battery inside, and screwed the top back on the twenty-pound red cylinder. He returned the near-empty lead cask, replaced the fire extinguishers in their storage location, and made a false entry on the laboratory log before returning to the changing room. He then stood beneath the automatic shower for two minutes, returned his protection gear to his locker, and retrieved his street clothes.

Dunbar returned to his desk, ate a sandwich and piece of coffee cake brought from home, and absently pushed paper around and pretended to be consulting online journals for the next three hours, half expecting to be confronted and arrested for the crime he had just committed. Sweat was returning to his forehead once again when he observed a man wearing a Tri-Cities Extinguisher Company uniform pushing a handcart loaded with a dozen fire extinguishers down the access hallway outside his office while escorted by an Ionic employee.

By the time Dunbar wrapped up his workday, a gray van with "Tri-Cities Extinguisher Company" emblazoned on its sides was clearing the last security gate onsite and turning left onto Hanford Route 10.

Chapter Fifteen

Dick Zigler pushed a button on a key fob and fired up his new Dodge pickup through an office window, activating the truck's air conditioner at the same time. The high clouds that cooled much of Southern California earlier in the day had burned off by early evening, bumping the temperature to eighty-five degrees as he prepared to leave for the day.

Zigler straightened up some project paperwork for the next morning, selected a bottle of cold water from the office refrigerator, and activated the company security system covering the buildings and grounds. He double-checked the $38,000 check and deposit slip in his wallet and locked the heavy-gauge steel door behind him.

Zigler seemed born to success, a man with an innate flair for business whose instincts had enabled him to turn sound ideas into solid profits over time through hard work and sheer determination without him ever having set foot in a college classroom. A decade earlier, he had spent his nights stocking canned goods at a local supermarket to live and by day used most of an inheritance from his grandfather to buy discounted heavy equipment at state and federal auctions. His business acumen impressed his banker, enabling Zigler to leverage what he had to purchase more and newer equipment and the land on which to keep it. He hired three former military mechanics within two years to keep the machines in working order, cross-trained them as operators and drivers, and convinced them to stay with him.

Now forty-three, his Long Beach Truck and Equipment Company was one of Southern California's most successful specialists in commercial trucks and equipment, with an inventory including dump trucks, cranes, and even some tugs, the large-wheeled tractors that push airplanes around airports. Today's check was for the sale of two

2004 Ford 750 fifty-five-foot Altec bucket rigs.

Zigler also was a self-described gym rat. He stood five ten, weighed 215, and commanded respect in a tough profession. His traditional attire of jeans and a white T-shirt provided testimony to his four workouts a week in the nearby YMCA weight room. Kicking yard dirt off his work boots, he climbed into his truck, smiled at its frosty temperature, and drove through the equipment yard's gate, headed to his local Bank of America branch.

Maneuvering his truck through afternoon traffic on East Livingston Drive, he calculated today's net profit. His cost basis for the two bucket trucks was $26,000, and they were parked for just five months, leaving him an after-tax gain of nearly two grand a month. "Easy money," he chuckled to himself.

Bank deposit completed, he headed to Shannon's Bayshore bar, home of the signature "Shoot the Root"—a pint of house craft beer cut with an ounce of root beer schnapps. Zigler had made Shannon's his home away from home in recent months. The very long backbar and creative cocktails were to his liking, as was the fact that every bartender knew his name.

He nodded to a few regulars as he entered the narrow lounge and snagged a stool near the end of the bar. Rodger, the afternoon bartender, made a beeline for him.

"What'll it be, Dick?"

"A Shoot the Root. I'm celebrating."

"Sell a steam shovel today?"

"Close; a couple of bucket trucks."

"Comin' right up."

Zigler sipped his drink, slowly enjoying the warm aftertaste it offered, and scanned the hundreds of liquor bottles making up the imposing backbar. A large blackboard was hung from a brown beam displaying today's featured shooters. The selections hadn't changed in weeks, which was fine with him. He gazed briefly at a silenced television to his left displaying a Dodger's game and lifted his glass to take another sip when he noticed a sudden lull in the bar's chatter level. A quick glance to his right and the reason became crystal clear.

Zigler's mouth fell open as his eyes feasted on the most beautiful woman he had ever seen. She walked into the neighborhood bar as if she owned it, her bright yellow spandex dress clinging to her dusky complexion like a second skin. A model or an actress meeting someone perhaps, she carried herself effortlessly, shoulders back, eyes straight ahead—a confident beauty who might have just left the stage at an Armani fashion show. For however long she planned to stay, this smoking-hot vision of loveliness had gained the full attention of every human soul in the room.

She was about five six and slender with blood-red lips and piercing black eyes set below arching, expressive eyebrows, a dainty nose, and a slender tan face that looked to have been carved from granite. Her ebony hair fell to just below her shoulders, curling just enough to cover a portion of her left eye and face. From every angle in the room, she elevated the word "stunning" to an entire new level of meaning.

Zigler guessed her age at about thirty. She had left behind the cute stage of her early twenties and had arrived at fully blossomed womanhood—that point in time when, for women such as her, time should stand still forever.

Zigler motioned to Rodger for another shooter. "And somewhere," he thought ruefully, "there's a guy out there who's tired of screwing her." He stole a subtle glance as she headed his way and locked her eyes on him like lasers. Zigler met her gaze and nodded as she pulled up a seat just two stools away from him. He accepted his second shooter as Rodger turned to the center of attention.

"What can I get you this evening?" the bartender asked as he placed a cocktail napkin in front of the woman.

"I'm new in town. Let me look," she whispered, looking up at the blackboard. "How about the ... Mexican Lollipop?"

"Lollipop shooter coming up."

While the bartender prepared her drink, carefully combining tequila, watermelon juice, and a few drops of Tabasco sauce, Zigler thought he noticed her glance his way. A second glimpse moments later left no doubt. He focused on the backbar, deciding to sip his shooter and see how this little drama played out. His wait was brief. A moment after receiving her drink, she stood and moved to the stool next to him.

"If you're looking to meet a producer here today, you've got the wrong guy," he said with a grin as the glow from his beer and root beer schnapps shooters began kicking in.

"Hola. I'm Jorine Souza," she replied with a sexy accent, extending her hand.

"Sorry, did you say Jolene?" Zigler asked, returning her handshake. Her voice was soft, and he couldn't help but lean in to her.

"No. My name is Jorine. *Sinto muito.* Please excuse my accent; English is not my first language."

By now, all eyes in the bar were on the pair.

This chick a hooker or what? The Long Beach area of LA had its share of working girls, but he had never run into one that was this classy or smooth. He had been divorced for six months and had no objections to making a new best friend tonight.

"I'm Dick. Nice to meet you, Jorine."

"We have lots of Gabriels and Pedros in Brazil, but not many Dicks. It's nice to find one."

He tried not to chuckle at her bravado. "So . . . Brazil. You're a long way from home. What brings you to our little bar?"

"Does a girl need a reason to want a drink with an American . . . Dick?"

Her aggressiveness needs taming, he thought, but he couldn't help but get pulled into the game. "One more time . . . what brought you to California?"

"In São Paulo, I am a model. Several agencies here wanted to discuss modeling opportunities, so this week I have go-sees. They are like interviews."

As the bar banter flowed, Rodger returned and inquired about more drinks. Two shooters were enough, and Zigler switched to a margarita. Just in case things worked out tonight, he decided to pace himself. Jorine doubled down on her Mexican Lollipops. "So tell me, what's your life like as a model in Brazil?"

"The pay is good, but it's only about a third of what modeling in Europe or your country pays. If you have a good photographer, it's fun, but some are very rude and think I should go to bed with them if they take a good cover shot."

"Maybe I should have become a photographer instead of a truck salesman," he snickered.

She tossed back, "És um brincalhão e um querido." She had called him a tease and flirt, but her quiet smile told him that she was in the role of seducer. The bar banter continued for another hour before Jorine made her move.

"Mr. Dick, have you ever had a Caipirinha?"

"Is that anything like the cha-cha?"

"You are so funny. No, it is the national drink of Brazil. We make it with cachaça and lime."

"And cachaça is what?"

"Our rum. Made from sugarcane juice. Much better than Puerto Rican rum."

Zigler sensed an opening and took the money shot. "Where do we get a Caipirinha?"

"Either we drive to a Brazilian bar in North LA or to my hotel down the street."

"How did you get here today?"

"I went for a walk this afternoon and stopped here on my way back. Then I saw you, and here we are, yes?"

DETONATION

Zigler knew nothing worthwhile was this easy, but after three drinks on a nearly empty stomach, her answer was good enough for him.

As they drove to her hotel, she caressed the leather seats, almost luxuriating in the textures of his truck. They turned a corner a moment later and pulled into a vacant parking space at the eight-story Rialto Hotel, an upscale hostelry catering mainly to commercial interests doing business at the Port of Los Angeles / Long Beach. The classic eighty-year-old inn had reopened after a two-year renovation that included a build-out for a modern first-floor sports bar now equipped with eight cable television sets. Zigler had never expected to visit the finished product, especially dressed as he was in a white T-shirt and jeans, but he gazed approvingly about the structure, which from all appearances had been superbly redone.

After navigating the lobby, he turned toward the bar entrance, but was overruled by Jorine, who tugged him toward an elevator. This one was for guests on floors five through eight. A second lift carried riders to floors two through four. Moments later, they stood outside Room 532.

Her room said high class all the way with its ornate windows rising nine feet to the ceiling, large private deck with hot tub, generous sitting area, forty-two-inch cable television, and separate bedroom. It reminded Zigler of an upscale Embassy Suite—a similar layout but much bigger and furnished in rich dark oak. A black granite bar that reached into the room from a corner offered a small refrigerator and a variety of liquors, including Brazilian cachaça. Jorine removed a bowl of limes and placed them on the counter before excusing herself and visiting a bathroom down a short hallway, leaving Zigler to wonder whose money paid for all this. He blurted out the question when she returned a minute later.

"I thought you said Brazilian models don't make much money. How did you afford a palace like this?"

"Oh, I didn't pay for it; my clients did. My plane fare too—first class. America is treating me well so far."

"If you don't mind me asking, who are you modeling for up here?"

"I am not modeling yet, but my interviews and trial photos are with three magazines—*Vogue, Cosmopolitan,* and *Vanity Fair*. I've done the first two, and *Vanity Fair* is tomorrow morning. They send limousines for me."

After a quick visit down the hall himself, Zigler took a seat on the living room sofa and tool stock of the situation. They came from completely different planets—he from industrial-vehicle sales and she from the world of high fashion. Yet here they were. He stood and walked to her behind the bar, put his hands around her tiny waist, then turned her around and lifted her to the granite counter. He left his hands where they were and looked into her dark eyes, searching for an answer.

"Why me, Jorine? Why would you enter a strange bar filled with people you don't know, walk up to a man you've never seen before, and in a very short time invite that man to your hotel room? What's this about?"

"It's about nothing. You think I am—how do you say—a girl of the night, a prostitute, yes? It's not true. It is as I said. I'm a model. I left my hotel for a walk after I returned from a photography studio and stopped for a drink. The others stared at me. I know what they are thinking. But you did not stare. You were by yourself, and at first, I wanted to be by myself too. Then I greeted you, and you were a gentleman to me. Most men I meet think I am a thing, not a person. What do you think now, Mr. Dick?"

He looked at her intently for a long moment. "I think I was wrong."

She wrapped her arms around his neck and kissed him deeply. Their tongues touched and then explored. He pulled her to him and kissed her neck, her cheek, her closed eyes . . . until she slowly disengaged herself, laughing. "We cannot forget the Caipirinha. I must explain this."

Zigler set her down, and Jorine approached the bedroom door and kicked off her shoes. She reached into her small leather purse, located her iPhone, and plugged it into a Bose music device that sat on an end table in the sitting area.

"Brazil is a very romantic country, and we have many traditions that need to be followed, especially when drinking the Caipirinha. It is legend that one will have bad luck if they do not follow two such customs."

"And they are . . . ?"

"First, you must only drink the Caipirinha when listening to the romantic music of Cateano Veloso." She made a few entries on her iPhone, and the room filled with the warmth of Veloso's acoustic guitar and mellow baritone. She swayed in subtle ecstasy as she filled two old-fashioned glasses with ice from the refrigerator and mixed the lime and cachaça together. She handed him his glass and raised her own for a toast. "*Saúde!*"

Veloso's music had a hypnotic effect on Zigler. What had seemed like twenty minutes in the room had been nearly an hour. Jorine's sensuous voice against the music was arousing, and he was certain she noticed how she affected him. She held up her hand as he started to reach for her.

"Senor Dick, aren't you going to ask me about the second ritual required when you drink a Caipirinha?"

"I was hoping you would tell me," he replied, taking a long sip of the dark liquid.

"The second tradition is a Portuguese proverb. I will spare you the Portuguese and translate to English: 'A Caipirinha cocktail without sex is a meaningless experience.'"

Zigler was caught under her spell, facing an uncharacteristic loss for words. He didn't resist as Jorine placed her drink on the coffee table, reached for his hand, and silently guided him into the bedroom. She escorted him to the California King bed, locked eyes with him, and wordlessly unzipped her dress and let it slide to the floor. Clad only in a yellow G-string thong and matching lace half-cup bra, the bright color glowed against her dark skin. She reached down and unbuckled his belt. Almost accidentally, she touched his erection as she dropped his pants before removing his shirt. Only when she had Zigler naked did she slowly unclasp her lace bra.

"Because you are on my bed, we will do things my way . . ."

"Okay with me."

She gently but firmly pushed him back onto the bed. After removing her thong, she stuffed it in his mouth. She wasn't rough, but her confident determination was enticing as she climbed onto the bed and rested on his chest. For the next few minutes, she alternated caressing her breasts, rubbing her clitoris, and reaching back and stroking Zigler, whose own hands seemed to be everywhere at once. He loved how she allowed herself to get lost in her own pleasure and still took him with her. Rolling to his back, he lifted her easily, positioned her, and pulled her onto him, eliciting an instant and prolonged gasp as her head arched back and her fingernails found the back of his shoulders.

Their interlude continued for over an hour. The coup de grâce came when she tied him to the bed with long charmeuse scarves from beneath her pillows, repositioned herself so her face lined up with his manhood, and buried his face between her legs. They came together and without restraint.

Zigler lay back, spent, yet still somehow aroused by the self-satisfaction beaming from her. He tried to open his mouth to break the spell, but she beat him to it and took the air from his lips.

"*Me da um beijinho!* Kiss me again, Mr. Dick, here and here . . . that's it, yes; please do not stop!" Her lips were still slightly wet. They laid back in each other's arms, kissing lightly and caressing, as their erotic evening wound slowly to a close.

"Dick, *eu sinto muito*, I'm sorry, I could enjoy this all night, but I must be, how do you say, prepared for my close-ups at the agency in the morning." By now, her words were a drug. Even in sending him away, she had captivated his soul.

A half hour later, Zigler was back in his truck and heading home. Selling a couple of trucks was the hit of the day, but his erotic evening with this brazen Brazilian beauty was the homerun of a lifetime.

Chapter Sixteen

Morgan began to stir, still caught in a mysterious limbo somewhere between darkness and the perception that he still existed. His eyes flicked open for a moment before closing as the room spun around him. A deep breath, then another. A third breath held off a threatened wave of nausea. His right hand found the knot near the top of his skull where the gunman had clubbed him, and head throbbing, he rolled carefully to his back to evaluate himself for other injuries. He was alone and he was alive, two important pieces of information at the moment.

Morgan rested for a full minute and then held up two fingers, pleased that his vision now seemed almost normal. Another half minute passed before he stood using a doorjamb for support and began evaluating his circumstances. He wasn't quite alone after all. The body of Daniel Pearce slouched in the recliner across the living room answered the questions his mind had begun asking. A glance found his gun, wallet, and cell phone resting on the kitchen table.

Professionals. They didn't steal my gun. Amateurs wouldn't hesitate to steal an $800 pistol, but a pro would take nothing that could connect him to the crime. That also was why he was still alive. The hit men had one job—dispense with Daniel Pearce. They weren't paid to kill visitors.

Morgan moved to the table, sat down, and dialed 911. He gave the operator his name and occupation, the address and apartment number, and the fact that he was staring at a man with a bullet in his head. He told her his gun, wallet, and cell phone were in the apartment, and that he would wait outside for the police. Despite her protests, he disconnected and placed a second call to the FBI field office in Seattle, alerting them of his situation. He replaced the phone next to his wallet and gun and made his way out the door. Morgan wasn't interested in a rookie cop mistaking his cell phone for a gun.

Within fifteen minutes, unit B-38 was filled with four uniforms, two homicide detectives, one captain, and the unfortunate Mr. Pearce. Ballistics technicians arrived to tend the scene while Morgan responded outside to preliminary questions from the detectives. An overweight type A uniform listening to the exchange concluded that Morgan was a suspect and reached to his belt for a set of handcuffs. A withering glance from Morgan changed the man's mind.

The captain, one Rosalie Cummings, had been with the Federal Way PD for twenty-two years after a three-year stint as a military police officer that included service in Operation Desert Storm. Cummings, five four in her stocking feet and 180 pounds, had heard enough from the blond, twenty-something patrolman and pulled him aside.

"Officer Mitchell, why don't you make your way into the kitchen and retrieve Mr. Morgan's belongings for me. Make sure the techs are done with them, and don't touch anything else!" Fifteen seconds later, type A was back and handed the three items to the captain, who rarely let a teaching moment pass. "Officer Mitchell, does it appear to you that Mr. Morgan's piece has been fired?" Mitchell, turning red, sniffed the Kimber's barrel and acknowledged that it had not. "Mr. Morgan, would you clear your pistol and show Officer Mitchell here your six nine-millimeter cartridges?"

That little task completed, the gun, phone, and wallet were returned, and Mitchell assumed parking lot duty, shielding the scene from neighbors. A paramedic put Morgan through a concussion protocol, washed the knot with alcohol, decided against a bandage, and nodded an okay to both Morgan and the captain. From there, Morgan drove first to a nearby Walgreens for a large bottle of Tylenol and then to Federal Way Police Headquarters on South 333rd Street, where he wrote a detailed statement and discussed the case further with detectives. A conference call ensued with the FBI in Seattle in which the detectives were urged to clamp a tight lid on background details of the homicide.

Nuclear electronics technician, Kelly Cobb, entered the Hanford laboratory a few ticks past fourteen hundred hours. Six years in the navy were enough for Cobb to earn her second-class petty-officer rank and attain a working knowledge of the A1B nuclear reactor nearly equal to that of most nuclear engineers. When she was assigned to the nuclear aircraft carrier USS *Gerald R. Ford*, she had been determined to learn as much as possible and use that wisdom and experience later in the private sector.

Today, two years into her civilian career at Ionic Mass Data's Hanford lab, she was garbed in protective clothing and taking routine readings of radioactive tank waste samples drawn from the site's underground storage tanks and kept in a progression of lead-lined vessels within the lab itself. Largest of these vessels were more than a dozen fourteen- by thirty-six-inch casks. Inside the casks were smaller lead-lined containers known as "pigs," and within the pigs were the lead-lined, high-density glass vials in which the waste samples resided. Testing the radioactivity level within each cask enabled Cobb to determine the amount of waste material inside. The samples replicated results that could otherwise be obtained with much more difficulty from the underground storage units themselves.

Cobb's protocol called for her to use a Model 3007A Geiger counter equipped with a 360 Pancake Probe to compare today's readings with those taken the prior week. Her Geiger counter provided measurements of alpha, beta, gamma, and X-rays. The casks were organized in sets of five, and she would measure a set, make her comparison, and move to the next set.

What should have been a normal afternoon turned sour when

Cobb checked the fourth set. The readings were below normal. Startled, she double-checked the previous week's test to ensure the Geiger counter was working properly and then rechecked the cask labeled C-109 to confirm that the three deviations she had found occurred in nuclear waste generated from underground tank C-109. She then carried one of the ten-inch square containers to a workbench and placed the pig inside a shield cabinet. After inserting her gloved arms and hands into the cabinet, she lifted the lead-lined lid. Two high-density, lead glass vials were missing.

An hour later and a mile away in the Department of Energy's Richland Operations Center, Ramona Vicente received a call that sent shivers down her spine. The slender, forty-eight-year-old brunette had managed Hanford's Office of Audit Services and Investigations for two years. Routine supervision of field audits usually took up 90 percent of her workday. But her routine on this day had just taken a detour. The MUF call —material unaccounted for—came from DOE Inspector General Ward Noe, director of the agency's national audit and law-enforcement programs in Washington, DC, who relayed a report from the director of Ionic Mass Data that two liters of nuclear sludge had just been reported missing from its Richland lab.

A MUF call was a drop-everything, all-hands-on-deck crisis. Noe demanded immediate answers and "a full report on my desk yesterday" before slamming down the phone. A no-nonsense, round-faced man with a receding red hairline, Noe regarded the world from a wheelchair thanks to a mortar that found him near the Vietnamese town of Xuan Loc in April 1975. He wanted hourly updates, and it would be Vicente's job to provide them.

The department's history of missing nuclear material was well documented. Prior audits had verified that as much as five tons of weapons-grade material had somehow disappeared from its facilities over the last four decades. No one at DOE over the years seemed to know where ten thousand pounds of radioactive material had gone. Perhaps someone had carried it out in his lunch box when no one was looking. Possibly a stealthy visitor had slipped it into her purse during a power failure. Could antigovernment hippies have loaded it into their Volkswagen buses decades ago while armed guards were smoking marijuana? Nobody knew.

Then came 2009, when the department established a zero-tolerance policy for any inventory deviations. It had seemed like the right thing to do, what with all those tons of radiated waste having been misplaced already. Eventually, it was decided that a history of loss, random variations of measurements, and recording mistakes did not justify spending anymore resources trying to reconcile old inventories. The suits in DC had decided that nothing really was missing; nuclear engineers and regulators all had merely made simple mathematics errors about five tons of radioactive material. It could happen to anyone.

The problem went away. After that, Vicente's audit department developed a new electronic material reporting system that could now spot the smallest of inventory aberrations. There would be no rest, however, until the issue of Ionic Mass Data's missing two liters was resolved.

Noe ordered Vicente to contact the Dallas office of Nicole Cofield, special agent in charge of FBI Region IV, and get a criminal investigator up to Hanford to assist with the on-site investigation. His next call to the FBI alerted the bureau to enter the report in its new Sentinel case management system that replaced former paper processes with purely digital workflows during investigations.

Vicente's phone call to Dallas was answered by a secretary who put it through to Cofield.

"It's been awhile, Ramona. Are you calling to wish me a happy birthday, or am I about to visit the beautiful Columbia River?

DETONATION

"I wish I had a better birthday present, Nicole, but we've got a MUF alert up here. I just spoke with Ward Noe. We need your help."

"How about a quick rundown?"

"Two liters of radioactive sludge is missing from one of our storage casks. C-109."

"Is it weapons grade?"

"No, but it's the worst-of-the-worst tank waste, Nicole. C-109 is a thick concoction of cobalt-60, technetium-99, cesium-137, and the bad boy, radium-226."

"Shit! Are you on lockdown?"

"Began ten minutes ago."

"Keep everyone there. I'm on my way."

FBI Assistant Counterterrorism Director Herb Wallace prided himself on his ability to connect the dots. It wasn't always that way at the bureau. After the death of FBI founder J. Edgar Hoover in 1972, some critics began viewing the connection of dots as an old-school flatfoot technique that took too much time and manpower in the new whiz-bang computer age. Worse, the bureau and the CIA began operating more at cross-purposes rather than as teams working for the common good. That fierce interagency rivalry ultimately led to the horrific September 11, 2001, Islamic terror attack on New York City.

Now, Wallace's methodology was standard practice in his division, where every opinion was encouraged and considered. The trim six-footer with dark graying hair and hazel eyes was well respected across the board by his staff who appreciated the common-sense approach he brought to complex investigations.

Wallace had been insistent that the counterterrorism division be dedicated to the new Sentinel application, and it had proved its value in spades ever since. Today, his Sentinel dashboard flagged a new entry from the bureau's Seattle office that updated him on results of his information request based on the call he had received from Rob Spencer at Nobility Cruise Line. Wallace's brow furrowed the moment he read that Brick Morgan had walked in on the homicide of Daniel Pearce, who had told his probation officer about being approached to build a radioactive bomb. That information alone was cause for concern, but a second flag from the DOE that radioactive waste had gone missing from the Hanford nuclear reservation, also in Washington State, caused his mouth to fall open.

Wallace picked up his phone and dialed the FBI's Seattle regional office.

Chapter Seventeen

To many, it is the "hoot owl" shift; for others, it's simply "graveyard"—that time of night when all that matters on the docks of industrial America is the jobs that need getting done. Thousands of men and women sweat through night shifts in ports across the nation, doing the work that puts products on store shelves while their countrymen sleep. One of those men was Ralph Sprague.

Sprague enjoyed his five-hour, 3:00 a.m. to 8:00 a.m. work shift in part because it paid him well and in part because it offered a certain inner solitude that day shifts couldn't match. While the rest of the world pretty much ran on eight-to-five schedules, he lived life on his own terms. Graveyard suited him in ways most jobs never could.

Its name alone was intriguing, having been derived eons ago from suspicions that laborers who worked excessive night shifts and ran on fumes during the day also wound up in earlier graves than people working day jobs. Well, that was one storyline behind the "graveyard" sobriquet. There were others as well, he knew.

The forty-three-year-old former junior high school history teacher found more job satisfaction as a longshoreman than he ever had trying to transmit knowledge to the brains of dimwitted inner-city students whose attitudes needed adjustment more with bullwhips than anything he could do for them. It was unfortunate, of course, because he liked teaching. Well, he *once* liked teaching. That was more accurate.

Sprague had been an idealist when he walked out of Seattle University with his teaching degree in 1995. Back then, he was certain he could make a difference in the lives of central-area youths who merely needed teachers who understood their plight and could lead them to futures of economic prosperity and life fulfillment. At least that was what his professors had preached.

Understanding problems was one thing, but Sprague never could dissolve his students' disconnect between doing the schoolwork needed to move from where they were at the moment to lives of economic success down the road. That would take effort, and after all, when you're a teenager, there are other things to do. Year in and year out, it was the same. A few showed potential over the years, but not potential as educators or entrepreneurs. Rather, these students viewed their futures as sports stars that would reap staggering fortunes while exhibiting their skills to cheering fans who would worship the ground upon which they walked. Fantasy bred fantasy in the inner cities of America, and Tacoma was no different.

After seven years as a history teacher, trying to expand the mindsets of bonehead students, Sprague concluded he never would make a difference regardless of how hard he tried. It was time to punt. Gray already was making inroads at his temples, and at age twenty-nine, he left the school district to try his hand as a longshoreman in the Port of Tacoma, where hard work was rewarded and the headaches were fewer. At five eleven and 175, he was a nonsmoker in top physical condition and valued the chance to prove himself. He began as a casual laborer landing single-day jobs. Over time, multiday jobs came his way as his reputation for hard work and reliability grew. Two years after bidding goodbye to teaching school, the POT offered him a full-time longshoreman position.

Sprague was proud to have secured a good job at the port, which had turned around the fortunes of Tacoma, or "T-Town," as it was widely known since the early 1970s when a strong wind might have blown away its business future. Now, fourteen years into his port career, he was a journeyman stevedore and signalman assigned to work hoot owl at the Husky Terminal on three-mile-long Blair Waterway.

But tonight would be different than most, for there was another side to Ralph Sprague that no one knew; a twist in his persona that he kept to himself. Opportunity existed in the port that could skyrocket his income without anyone ever suspecting. And what good was opportunity if one didn't take it? He had planned it in his mind many times, and as his plan came together, he detailed each step on his home computer for reference. Those carefully developed details could soon make Sprague a handsome side income, of that he was certain. And it would be so bloody easy.

An hour earlier, he had crossed the Eleventh Street Bridge into the port from downtown, passed PCC Logistics, and turned right on St. Paul Avenue to Stewart Street, and then made his way to Marshall Avenue, two miles long with businesses within the port, where at this early hour longshoremen were shuttling new KIA automobiles around the tip of Blair Waterway to hundred-acre fenced parking lots of AWC Warehousing Company for temporary storage where they would be readied for rail transport to the Midwest.

He eased his black Ford F-150 unnoticed into a dark AWC employee parking lot just down the street from a big US Oil Refining Company depot, where two twin-trailer gasoline tanker trucks were filling up for their deliveries in the hours ahead. He locked the truck, but did not use his key fob to chirp the alarm. Personnel at the well-lit fuel terminal didn't notice him move past AWC and between buildings and vehicles to one of the several hundred-acre parking lots enclosed within chain-link fences topped with multiple rows of concertina wire. Within the enclosures were hundreds of shiny new Mazda automobiles, light trucks, and SUVs, recent arrivals from the company's chief manufacturing plant in Hiroshima.

Sprague observed just six "gotcha" cameras as he circled the lot's exterior while trying to appear only as an interested auto aficionado. Before him was an auto parts store that could offer handsome pickings to the right people. He tucked that information into his memory bank for later review, returned to his truck, and drove to the Blair, one of seven waterways serving the nearly three-thousand-acre Port of Tacoma.

There was a bite in the air this November morning as the lanky father of two left his truck off East Eleventh Street and strode onto the Pierce County Terminal at the east end of Blair Waterway just before 2:00 a.m., his arrival hardly noticed by a security guard stationed there. That scant notice was fine with Sprague, whose plans for the next hour before his assigned work shift at three o'clock had everything to do with security—or lack of it.

An after-midnight squall had been replaced by a bone-chilling breeze, reminding Sprague to unpack his long underwear once he got home. For now, he was dressed in blue water-repellent work jeans, a heavy black wool sweater, wool-lined cap, steel-toed boots with wool socks, and a worn brown bomber jacket. It wasn't enough, but it would do.

Lunch bucket in hand, Sprague walked a quarter mile out onto the county terminal while looking for any changes to its security camera locations. Seeing none but wondering about those he couldn't see, he reached a position on the wharf almost directly across from where longshoremen were unloading the thirteen-hundred-foot *Emma Maersk* that had arrived from Melbourne in midafternoon with mixed container cargo and was tied fast to bollards alongside the pier. His plans made, he slipped between two stacks of containers on his side of the dock to where a short mound of wooden pallets rested and hoisted himself atop the pile, facing the ship.

Behind him, four snarling tugs were moving the Hyundai auto carrier *Asian Dynasty,* inbound from Ulsan, South Korea, to a berth from which stevedores would begin unloading its five thousand Hyundai sedans. The vessel was a ro-ro, whose cargo is rolled on in the Port of Ulsan, south of Seoul, and rolled off by longshoremen in the POT at the rate of nearly five hundred cars an hour and stored in lots similar to the one Sprague had visited an hour earlier.

At the moment, however, Sprague was interested in the smuggling business, and smugglers were nothing if not ingenious in trying to pass drugs and other contraband through the nation's ports. For them, darkness was an ally. Ports worldwide countered with powerful lighting and the often-inconspicuous cameras that sought out people, materials, and activities that didn't belong. Smuggled booty ranged from electronic equipment and prized autos to narcotics, jewels, treasured artworks, "and everything in-between," he chuckled to himself.

Sprague opened his lunch box and withdrew two Cabela's deer cameras of the type used by hunters to observe pathways of game animals. The cameras were small but efficient, ideal for his needs. He eased to the ground and secreted one between two pallets below him pointing toward the off-loading operation at the *Emma Maersk*, and placed the second several feet away partially hidden beneath a different pallet and aimed farther down the dock to the west, away from the container activity. The former was to look for magnetized packages attached to the undersides of containers as they were lifted from the giant ship. The latter would allow him to study patterns and dock coverage zones used by security personnel and their German shepherds. Both cameras now hidden from view, Sprague regained his perch atop the pallets. He would retrieve the cameras after his shift to see if anything interesting turned up.

His project set in motion, Sprague selected an apple from his lunch box, took a bite, and watched a mammoth port gantry crane reach across eighteen containers and pluck a forty-footer from the 165,000-ton vessel. The spreader bar attached to the crane's hook was equipped with clamps that automatically locked onto the corners of the twenty-ton steel containers, enabling crane operators to lift them directly to the beds of long-haul trucks lined up from the dock to Interstate 5, three miles away. Blair Waterway utilized seven of the cranes that drank nearly fifteen thousand volts while moving containers from ships to the trucks that would transport them either directly to local destinations or to the three rail lines serving the port for movement across the country.

Sprague still marveled at the efficiency involved in the operation and in particular at the sheer sizes of the instruments at play before him. To most, a commercial semi-trailer truck rig was *huge*, but the word took on new meaning when comparing it to a seventy-foot-tall crane lifting multi-ton containers across the 130-foot beams of cargo ships that were themselves larger than the biggest US Navy aircraft carriers. Everything was relative.

Container handling systems are fully mechanized across the industry worldwide so that all handling is done with cranes and special forklift trucks. All containers are numbered and tracked using computerized systems. One day, Sprague knew, robots might reduce or even eliminate the need for longshoremen. But by then, he could be a retired man of leisure, perhaps enjoying Cuban cigars and cognac after sumptuous meals in some tropical locale where gentle sea breezes would stir the fragrance of tropical flowers across his veranda. Best of all, the port would help him do that, but with much more than its own retirement package.

Sprague turned his attention to his bank account, which was doing quite well at the moment. Once his shift began, he would use his first break to request a follow-up day shift. If that could be arranged, he would take a few days off to handle some pressing personal issues, including overdue dental surgery for an abscessed tooth.

Contract negotiations early in the year had cut into his hours, but he believed his earnings this year still would top $140,000. Not bad for a man who once tried to inspire the uninterested for a measly forty K. Yes, life was good now. Very good indeed.

Sprague's reverie was interrupted by the man who quietly approached from one side and lit him up with a black tactical LED flashlight. Covering his eyes, Sprague jumped down from the stack of pallets and faced the stranger wearing a badge. "If you shine that fucking light in my eyes one more time, one of us won't be able to work our next shift!" He took a step closer.

The German shepherd next to the stranger began showing its teeth as a low rumble escaped its throat and its eyes locked onto Sprague's crotch.

"Easy does it. Port security. Better stop right there, bud, before Cujo here turns you into a soprano. May I see your identification please?"

Chapter Eighteen

According to the eBay listing, the tugs were resting in an auction yard in southern Oregon, where they would be sold to the highest bidder. But California businessman Dick Zigler wouldn't be waiting for a bidding process to play out. He was satisfied that the Harlan A650 tow tugs could be had much sooner at a price he was willing to pay, and even with shipping costs to his heavy equipment center in Long Beach, the potential for a respectable profit was clear. It would be a good deal all around.

The general public knew these vehicles as the squat, truck-like machines used at the nation's airports to push back airliners from terminals, enabling pilots to then taxi to runways for takeoff. Although most jetliners are capable of moving themselves backward on the ground using reverse thrust, known in airport lingo as a powerback, it is rarely done since the resulting exhaust wash could damage terminals and assorted equipment. The tow tractors for sale on eBay were used, but if the owners were to be believed about their condition, they would be ideal for resale to regional airports in Southern California.

Zigler cut through the eBay online bid system, located the equipment owners at a regional airport south of Roseburg, and made plans to visit their offices the following weekend. That done, he leaned back in his overstuffed office chair, raised his arms over his head and stretched, his focus interrupted as he recalled his bizarre romp the previous evening with Jorine. It had been a one-night stand for the ages, an event his memory bank would maintain—and possibly even embellish—until his last breath. Then again, how could one embellish perfection? The smile on his face widened. Zigler likely would never see her again, but he planned to stop at Shannon's again after work today, knowing the other regulars would quiz him without mercy.

DETONATION

He made a quick call to a supplier at three ten and had just resumed his paperwork when a black Ford Explorer carrying two strangers pulled into his equipment yard. He smelled trouble even before the men left their vehicle and approached his office door. Both were of medium height and dressed in jeans; one wore a black leather jacket and the other a tan raincoat, which seemed odd for a comfortable Long Beach afternoon. Zigler double-checked his desk drawer for his loaded .357 Magnum and clicked off the safety.

"May I help you?" he asked warily as they came in. He doubted they planned to shoplift a steam shovel; maybe they were serving him with legal papers. The gaunt, rat-faced one with the day-old stubble wearing the raincoat was the first to speak.

"Here's a video you'll want to watch," the expressionless man declared. He handed Zigler an iPad Pro and told him to push play.

"First, I don't take orders from you, asshole, and second, if I want to watch a movie, I'll go to a theater. Now scram before I bounce your asses out of here like a couple of basketballs."

"Your girlfriend last night thinks you'll want to see this," replied rat-face evenly. He then reached for the iPad and pushed play.

For the next twenty seconds, Zigler watched a replay of his previous night's performance in Jorine's hotel room. The two yokels before him were pulling a shakedown. Zigler nodded slowly, suppressing a belly laugh. Since he was now divorced, he really didn't care who had a copy of the video.

"So are you here to offer me a role in a porn movie, or did you just get lost trying to find a sewer for the night?"

"This isn't complicated, Mr. Zigler," said rat-face. "You help us, we give you fifty thousand plus expenses and delete the sex video. You don't help us, we put the sex video on YouTube."

"And why would I care if you put it on YouTube, other than you're a couple of dirtbags trying to tarnish my reputation?"

"You might want to stop and think that over, Mr. Zigler," said the man with wiry black hair in the leather jacket. The man was about forty, stood a bit under six foot, was of average build, and wore aviation-style sunglasses balanced on a nose that appeared to have been tweaked by someone's fist. "We know your clients, your business acquaintances, your neighbors, your daughter, Ericka, attending UCLA. There are others—club memberships and such—where your stardom here could cause, let's say, concerns."

"Anything happens to my daughter, and I mean anything at all, I'll find each one of you and personally rip your balls off. There's a concern you better take seriously."

"Relax, Mr. Zigler," leather-jacket man responded softly. "Please understand that we are merely businessmen offering to pay you for cooperation on a business matter of our own. You collect fifty thousand in cash, and we shit-can the video. It's a very simple proposition."

Feigning concern, Zigler eased back in his chair, pushed a button that would send incoming calls to his office answering machine, and looked quietly at the speaker, who slid into a chair in front of his desk.

"We have a package that needs to reach a stevedore who works at the new southwestern lock of the Panama Canal. For reasons that don't concern you, he needs to remove it from a freighter transiting the canal from west to east for further disposition within the country. Your role is small but important, and for that we will pay the fifty thousand in cash—half when the package leaves your yard here, and the other half when the package is received. No strings.

"You soon will receive a medium-size excavator—one large enough to conceal a box about two by three by five feet for shipment to a government facility in the City of Chitré in southwestern Panama. The excavator will be delivered to you erroneously. Your job will be to resend it to an address we will provide. The package will already be welded in place and painted and will be removed by crane before the ship enters the lock's second chamber. That's all you need to know."

"You're sending drugs *into* Panama?" Zigler responded, astonished.

"The contents of the box do not concern you. As I said, we will have the excavator delivered here. Your role is to act as though it was incorrectly sent to you and to reroute it to Panama, nothing more. Agreed?"

Zigler assumed an anxious look, gazed back and forth between the men, and folded his hands in front of him.

"Listen to me. You can't use that video; it could ruin me. There are things you don't know about me, personal plans that I have. I need to think about this, and I've got a couple of guys meeting me here any minute about a dump truck I have for sale."

"There isn't time for you to think about it, Mr. Zigler. Either you agree or you don't. Which is it?"

"Look, I've got to talk with these guys. I set this up a week ago, and I don't think you'll want to discuss this with them. Please!" He looked back and forth at them anxiously as a vehicle pulled into the parking lot outside his office. "There they are now!"

The two strangers glared at him.

"You know Shannon's Bayshore bar, two miles from here, down near the beach? I'll be there at six thirty."

"Six thirty!" responded the rat-faced man with a scowl as the men abruptly headed for the door.

Zigler opened his desk drawer and secured the safety on his pistol. He glanced at his watch while his two clients left their vehicle and walked past the two strangers toward the building. He had two hours and more questions than answers.

Half expecting to see his sizzling Brazilian partner of the previous night, Zigler ambled into Shannon's at 6:20, nodded at Rodger the bartender, and headed to a rear table, a grin crossing his features as three regulars smiled and raised their glasses in a toast. No Jorine in sight. It was either good news or bad, depending on how one looked at it. Right now, it was good.

"Will your lady friend be joining you, Dick?" asked Rodger with a tight smile as he approached and set a down a coaster.

"Now don't start with me, Rodger."

"I didn't say a thing."

"Okay, now listen to me. First, I'll have a Bombay Sapphire martini straight up. Second, I expect two guys to meet me here any minute. Keep your eyes and ears open. If I ask you for a Singapore Sling, that means I need you to call nine one one and tell them two men are threatening a customer and you need cops right away."

"You expecting trouble?"

"Maybe. I just want to be prepared. Later I'll fill you in about last night."

"You got it, bud," Rodger replied, turning back toward the bar.

Zigler removed two envelopes and a pen from the inside pocket of his leather jacket and jotted down a few notes. His game plan was to continue feigning concern over the video and see what the two thugs really had up their sleeves. He discarded narcotics as nonsense, but curiosity was killing him. He knew two things: they wanted to smuggle a thirty-square-foot box through the Panama Canal and were willing to spend serious money to do it. And then there was the third thing: they needed a pawn, and he was it.

Five minutes went by, then ten. Zigler drained his martini just as leather-jacket man entered the bar, made eye contact, and walked toward the table, carrying a worn Nike gym bag. Rat-face, still wearing the tan raincoat, trailed behind his partner, gazing around the room as he moved.

Zigler ordered beer for all three and tried focusing on the men's appearances—facial features, eye colors, complexions—details that might later help authorities identify them. As before, rat-face spoke first.

"We're pleased you decided to work with us. What equipment will work for—"

"I haven't decided anything! What assurance do I have that you'll give me the video if I help you?"

"Trust is what holds humanity together, Mr. Zigler. We have your video only to persuade you to assist us. Once you do so, it will be deleted. We also have twenty-five thousand cash right now, and you'll receive the second payment by courier when the package arrives in Panama. This is a one-time opportunity. Take it!"

Zigler shifted his gaze to the other man with the light-blue eyes, a two-day growth, and the frizzled black hair who held the Nike gym bag in his lap. On his right hand, leather-man wore a 1950s gold-plated Benrus watch, similar to one Zigler's grandfather had received when he retired as a locomotive engineer.

"If you want to smuggle something like a large box, I recommend a Caterpillar six thirteen elevating scraper."

"Why is that?" asked rat-face.

"Do you have a name?"

"How about Bob. My friend is George. Now, why a Caterpillar rig?"

"A Cat scraper is about thirty-two feet long and is used to scape up dirt during land development and road construction. It has a big internal compartment, or bowl, that can hold twenty-six thousand pounds of dirt. It would hide the box and not be visible. What will be in the box?"

"Never mind that."

"I need to know where it's going if I'm going to ship it."

"The package must be on a cargo ship heading eastbound through the Panama Canal—and most important, it must be on a ship traversing the new third lock."

"Why the third lock?"

"Look at a map, Mr. Zigler. This shipment is going to Chitré, southwest of the canal, and the third lock is the only one with an emergency crane station on it for adding or removing cargo quickly before the ship steams halfway to the Caribbean Sea. You ask too many questions for a simple deal like this, pal."

"Well, I've got one more."

"Make it quick."

"What's the time line for the delivery to me?"

"Three weeks from tomorrow."

"Here's the deal," said Zigler. "I have a Cat scraper in my yard, but before—"

"You're not in a position to deal," George said again. "The video goes viral unless you do as you're told, buddy."

"You listen to me for a change, whatever your name is," Zigler replied, banging his fist on the table and drawing a glance from Rodger behind the bar. "That video could ruin me, but more important, my kid brother died of drug addiction. I'd rather die myself than participate in drug smuggling. I hate dope dealers. If your box is drugs, shove it up your ass and put the video on *60 Minutes*."

Incensed, George appeared ready to stand, but Bob's glance changed his mind.

"Relax, Dick," said Bob. "No drugs, no human trafficking, no weapons. We have a client who needs some chemicals that can't be shipped on the open market. That's it."

"Chemicals? Sounds like Ecstasy, Spice, or Krokodil to me. I want no part of drugs." Zigler wasn't sure what he was talking about, but he wanted to find out what would be in the box.

"Look, no drugs!" George shot back under his breath. "Here's all we know. The chemicals contain a little radiation and can't be trucked. The client needs the stuff for medical research and the US Government won't let it be exported. It's ridiculous, but that's why we need to ship it ourselves."

"What about the cash?"

George lifted the Nike gym bag and set it on the table. "The other half when the equipment is delivered in Panama. Now, are you in?"

Zigler gazed at each man briefly before slowly nodding and silently applauding his own performance.

Chapter Nineteen

Brick angled his BMW into the Point Ruston development and took an extra spin around its two traffic circles before settling into a parking area, shutting down the engine, exiting the car, and coming face-to-face with condo resident Dolphus Quinn.

"Does this parking lot look like a racetrack to you, mister?" the diminutive old-timer barked through his snow-white beard. "People live here, and we don't need the likes of you practically burning rubber around the parking lot."

"Well, I may have——"

"I don't want to hear it, buster!" Quinn growled. "I run this development. Do that again, and I'll have that kraut-meat wagon of yours towed out of here and left on the beach at low tide." He turned on his heel and strode toward the office labeled "Management Center."

Thoroughly chastened, Morgan tried in vain to avoid the stares of two well-dressed forty-something women standing next to their own cars and watching him cross the slate-gray lot of pavers and red brick and head for Rilee's penthouse condo. *Well, I can't go anywhere but up after that*, Brick thought to himself.

Rilee was the most complex woman Morgan had ever encountered. If she wasn't grinding on him for a good toss in the sack, she was hacking into the servers of corporate giants or even drawing down on unsuspecting visitors. Two years earlier, she had climbed out a basement window with her twelve-gauge Mossberg 500, confronted a suspected prowler, and offered to end his day on the spot. The shaken man turned out to be an FBI agent who had her under protective surveillance.

Brick waved at her condo's security camera and rattled the door-knocker to announce his arrival.

Dressed in leopard embellished jeans and a light-blue, three-quarter-sleeve Gucci blouse with plunging neckline, Rilee greeted Brick with an over-the-top "I've missed you" hug. Her auburn hair was pulled back in a ponytail, and an emerald silk sash encircling her waist complemented the sparkling green eyes through which she surveyed the world. "Hola! I've dug out some great material for your port security proposal."

"That's my girl. Let's get started," Morgan replied, stepping into the condo's spacious foyer. "I see you've made a few additions," he added, admiring two new bamboo Chippendale chairs placed beside a pair of matched twenty-four-inch Oriental ginger jars. Above them on an inlaid mahogany shelf was a framed color photo of Rilee and her mother taken in 1993 when Rilee was ten.

"I was mucking around in the Alibaba site. I think the jars came from Ningbo, in northeast China."

"Garden spot of the Far East," Morgan responded with a sigh. "Beautiful area; flowers everywhere."

"You've been to Ningbo?"

"No. I read *National Geographic*."

Rilee's rolled her eyes.. "Come over here and get comfortable," she said with a bemused expression. "Can I get you a drink? I'm going retro."

"You're what?"

"I'm having an old-fashioned. It's from a 1950's recipe, and it's yummy."

"Just an ice water for me, babe."

Rilee liberated her premixed old-fashioned from her refrigerator, clinked three ice cubes into her glass, and removed a cold water bottle for Brick while he took in the assortment of marine activity on Commencement Bay from the condo's 180-degree view. A jumbo ro-ro auto carrier, afternoon sun glistening off its crimson stack, slid its way along the south side of Vashon Island and eased to starboard, preparing to transit East Passage and churn its way north toward the Strait of Juan de Fuca and the Pacific Ocean. Morgan counted seven container ships in queue for port berths on Sitcum and Blair waterways in the distance, and the Chinese bulk carrier *Good Hope* riding high at anchor awaiting its turn at a Continental Grain terminal three miles away.

"My favorite time is at night," said Rilee softly, slipping up next to him in her stocking feet, a transient, wistful smile crossing her features. "The yellow hue from the port's sodium lights and the ships' navigation lights is mesmerizing." So was she—a delicate combination of tantalizing beauty and lavish intellect. He resisted an urge to reach for her, and the moment passed. She tugged gently at his arm. "Grab a seat. I think you'll like my report."

They settled into a baroque leather love seat, and Rilee produced an iPad and two file folders and set them on a long coffee table before them. "Between public records and maritime port's servers with UNIX operating systems, I believe I've got what you need."

Morgan withdrew a hand-held tape recorder from an inside pocket and flicked the on button. "What's the deal with UNIX?"

"To hack into a system, I first have to assess its vulnerabilities. Most of the time, I exploit applications that are already installed, and the rest of the time I get in through operating systems, such as Apple Mac, Linux Kernel, or Windows. Networks used by municipalities are more vulnerable, and many of those systems are based on the old UNIX design, so getting into them is fairly simple. Others are a different story."

Morgan made a quick T with his right hand and left palm. "Better keep the hacking details to yourself and just lead me to the bottom line."

"Because you need—"

"Plausible deniability. Exactly." He grinned.

She returned it and continued. "The majority of proposals and contracts I've examined divide port security into three components: cargo transported on ships—mostly in containers; the actual ship itself—both cargo and cruise ships; and the assets of the local port. On paper, the big security gorilla out there is the Department of Homeland Security, but it's a mirage. What you see is not what you get, Brick. It's a bloated, disorganized bureaucracy that eats tax dollars but doesn't do the job its name implies."

"We haven't had another nine-eleven, Rilee."

"Not yet, but ignoring problems doesn't make them go away."

Morgan grimaced. "I wouldn't argue with that. Bush forty-three overdid it when he created that department; even rolled the Secret Service into it. Then he appointed an inspector general who began laying out its problems publicly and fired the guy a year later for doing it."

"Clark Kent Ervin. He was saying a dozen years ago that our ports are wide open to terrorists, and nothing I've found changes that position."

"You *have* been doing your homework."

"It's gotten much worse, Brick; the evidence is everywhere. On paper, DHS is concerned about the ports and so is Congress, but that's as far as it goes. I've been combing through government databases, including those you don't want to know about, for two weeks, and the real news is in what I haven't found: security. You want a bottom line, well here it is: for all intents and purposes, the federal government all but ignores port security. That's the constant I'm seeing."

Morgan sucked in his breath and frowned. "That's a stretch, Rilee."

"Is it?"

"Port security was one of the driving forces behind DHS in the first place."

"Sure it was, with emphasis on *was*."

"So what are you driving at?" Morgan asked, a quizzical expression creasing his features.

"I'm not driving at anything, Brick. I'm just laying out facts for my client; you'll have to draw your own conclusions. Look, the initial concept was sound enough. Tuck a couple dozen semirelated agencies and departments under one roof, and everyone keeps the bad guys from hitting us again. Fine, but now it's got a quarter million employees, and its own mission statement about border security was overruled by President Obama. What does that tell you?

"Let me answer my own question: it tells me that Homeland is a sham. The federal government creates a huge agency that includes protection of our ports, and then, under specific direction of the president of the United States—and with Congress offering hardly a whimper—our borders were left wide open to terrorists."

"That begs the question, doesn't it?"

"Uh-huh, but which question? Are we really that well protected, or do the Feds *want* us to be hit so we can hammer another country like we did Iraq, rev up the economy again, and kill a few thousand more people for the common good? Interesting comparison, isn't it? With some exceptions, Homeland doesn't know who is coming in, where they come from, or what their intentions are. The deeper I've looked, the more I'm convinced that its primary job is for show more than anything else—shaking down old ladies at airports, looking for machine guns in their girdles."

"You're looking at a systemic problem. I'm working in a specific environment with this proposal."

"But they're directly related."

"Absolutely. They're different angles on the same problem. Your research is taking us to a place neither of us really expected. Now that we're there, it's time to share those conclusions with the good folks at the Port of Tacoma. Your handiwork is going to wreak havoc when I lay the proposal on the table, Rilee. And I've got to do it without mentioning your name, which goes totally against my grain."

"Not mine. I work behind the scenes—more intrigue, less sweat. You haven't even heard the details yet."

"Lead on."

"I've scoured Homeland's individual departments, Brick. I've researched them through the media and slipped into government files so deep they're almost invisible. Put it all together, and what I see is a Chinese fire drill—vast duplication of effort with only modest results. I even checked MARAD, the federal Maritime Administration under the Department of Transportation, which refers inquiries to the coast guard. MARAD's job is assisting the merchant marine, and their chances of protecting the country's port security are next to none.

"Our ports are sitting ducks. Besides the coast guard, there's little serious effort by the Feds to protect them. That job is being left to the ports themselves, which is where you come in."

"I may not want in. This whole RFP might be a can of worms I can do without."

Rilee nodded. "Make that a bucket of worms, that's the problem. Let me finish, and then we can hit that RFP."

"Rock on."

"The coast guard has its own port security units. That's government-speak for patrol boats. They've designated PSU 313 to provide protection for ships entering and departing the Port of Tacoma. Those boats are built a few miles from here near the Bremerton navy shipyard. They're fast, they're armed, and they're lethal. The coast guard also performs port vulnerability assessments.

"Then, we have Customs and Border Protection—the border patrol. This unit has over sixty thousand employees, but its mission statement doesn't even mention ports. That said, they do input freight exporters, forwarders, customs brokers, and even importer excise inspectors into their software to identify high-risk containers and other threats. Sounds good, but I took it upon myself to visit the CBP server that manages the analytics, and I came away uninspired."

"No details," said Morgan, holding his hands out palms down. "I understand there are gray areas with internet searches, but keep me buffered from your methods."

"Plausible deniability again?"

"You bet your keister. How do they define a 'high-risk' container?"

"No idea, but I can't fault them for that. No point in letting terrorists know our methods."

"See what you can dig up on the high-risk containers, how they're defined. I'd like to bring that into my proposal. It just takes one to carry a nuke."

"Will do. For now, I've examined eleven security proposals presented in the last three years to ports across the country from Savannah, Georgia, to Valdez, Alaska, and New York to Los Angeles, and all of them aligned along four separate subdivisions: screening of incoming containers, security of port assets like cranes and piers, coordination of government agencies and local public safety, including technology systems to detect WMDs, and threatening activities by personnel. Those four take in a lot of territory, Brick." She excused herself and disappeared down a hallway.

Morgan clicked off his digital recorder, stood, and stepped out onto Rilee's deck for a breath of salt air. His security proposal stood to gain a sizable competitive lead over others thanks to Rilee's research. Her work was her life, and he marveled at her ability. Cautious wording to POT leaders would be required. Morgan Maritime Investigations was a one-man operation—him—and he would be squaring off against big security agencies from across the country. What he lacked in manpower, he would have to make up for in cunning. That's why he had Rilee, who joined him on the deck a minute later.

"Sorry to throw you a curve about DHS, Brick."

"Don't be. You fired a fastball right down the middle, and that should give me an edge I didn't have before. Then again, if I can't dazzle them with your detail, I'll try baffling them with my bullshit."

The comment drew an elbow in his side from Rilee.

"When I read the POT's proposal," Morgan continued, rubbing his rib cage, "it was apparent in Section C, the statement of work, that they're not sure what they want."

"Their lack of clarity is very clear," she replied with a smile, turning back inside toward the bar. "That part struck me as a desire to complement DHS, but complement what? It even provides the option to replace some security features that are already in place. Why do you suppose they would do that?"

"I don't have an answer for that one. Not yet."

She joined Morgan at her picture window and handed him an old-fashioned. "You just went retro," she said.

"Retro it is," he replied, taking a sip and nodding his approval. "Here's what I have in mind. My reply to the RFP will be very narrow. What I won't do is try to replace any of the overlapping processes now provided by the coast guard and Homeland."

"That would receive huge pushback from the hierarchy at Homeland."

"Homeland won't like a word I say, Rilee. I'll design the proposal into just two sections. Section one will be counterintelligence. MMI will provide ongoing threat analysis by exposing the Port of Tacoma's existing security apparatus to hypothetical attacks. Section two will zero in on technology. The port has a zillion surveillance cameras, but its video monitoring and analysis are only first generation. We'll coordinate the upgrading of closed-circuit cameras and include software with advanced facial-recognition features and algorithms that are threat predictive.

"First, I'll hit 'em between the eyes with the severity of the danger, maybe using a single Power Point slide with a target over a photo of the POT at a time when terrorists are looking for easy prey. Then I'll lay out the advanced technology defense I propose, emphasizing its effectiveness and reasonable cost, and, one two, there it is. The port commission will either see the problems and jump at it or face the music publicly if they opt for something cheap. I doubt Barry Mott will let that happen."

"When that turns into a public presentation, you'll knock it out of the park. I'll prepare a fact sheet you can give the commissioners and the media when the commission hears the proposals publicly. You'll have reporters lining up for interviews."

"Good idea. I'll create a detailed draft, and then you can add the sizzle and fireworks to section two. Give me about three days."

"Deal!" Rilee stretched and took several steps before turning, arms folded, eyes on her feet, a clear sense of uneasiness having replaced her cheerful demeanor. "That's settled, but before you go, I've got a little mystery going on with one of my neighbors here in the complex." Her facial expression turned blank, and her hands dropped to her sides as she spoke.

"Which neighbor is it? I'll go over and explain things to him right now."

"No, no. It's nothing like that. It's just, well, I've got a strange feeling about him. Please stay for a minute and let me explain."

"Only if you promise I won't be indicted by a grand jury."

"Never worry; I keep bail money handy for emergencies."

"Good. Now what have you gotten yourself into?"

"Nothing. At least I don't think so."

"Your neighbor?"

"Let's move into my computer room."

"You sure all these wires won't make me sterile?"

"If you stick around tonight, we can find out."

"I walked into that one, didn't I? Now tell me about the neighbor?"

Rilee slipped into an office chair in the Faraday cage surrounding the front of two Eizo twenty-four-inch backlit color monitors, while Morgan settled into a comfortable Italian leather lounge chair. "It all started when I discovered a black hole here at the complex. Bear with me."

"You've got my full attention."

"When the navy tries to detect submarines and other objects underwater, they use passive sonar equipment to listen for radiated noise from the other submarine to measure distances. Some countries, especially the US, have subs so sophisticated that they are ultraquiet and make little or no noise at all. The Chinese have stolen our technology and now also have a few submarines that do this."

"And the black holes . . .?"

"Coming up. The ocean is a natural orchestra. Modern subs and their advanced sonar can hear and analyze these natural sources of ocean noises. We also can detect subs blocking the ocean's natural sounds, which create what we call a black hole in the ocean. So now our navy not only listens for noisy subs but also for areas of the ocean that are absent of noise.

"With that said, I've discovered a black hole here in my condo. I've learned that about half of the condo owners have landlines, and all of them also have cell phones. Of the owners who don't have landlines, all but one have cell phones. I used the condo directory and other tools to discover that the man in two-forty-three only uses burner phones."

"Sounds like a drug dealer or maybe someone with bad credit who can't qualify for a normal cell."

"Someone with bad credit wouldn't be living in a Point Ruston condo, Brick. The other thing that disturbs me is that the man in two-forty-three changes phones once a week."

"How do you know that?"

"In the old days, cell phones were analog and operated in the eight hundred megahertz range. They could be easily intercepted. Today's cells, including disposables, use digital technology. I have a Wolfhound-PRO cell phone detector. Yes, it's legal to own. The Wolfhound has a frequency discretion feature that will pick up and detect a cell phone even if it's in standby mode. I just walk around the building and can locate all the cells.

"I also have a Bandit Catcher II that enables me to intercept the international mobile subscriber identity, or IMSI, from each phone. I've got each condo owner's phones listed, which is how I know that Mr. Two-forty-three changes phones each week."

"Your Bandit Catcher II can't be legal."

"It's legal in Belarus."

Chapter Twenty

Gas Rizzo's two-story brick residence was set back from North Yakima Avenue and nearly obscured by a grove of native cedar and fir trees towering more than a hundred feet in a neighborhood of majestic homes, most built in the early twentieth century.

Scarlet and yellow roses set against a backdrop of delicate blue delphiniums greeted guests approaching the three-inch-thick dark walnut front door. Nearby, a dazzling twirl of pink Omoshiro clematis rose through a webbed trellis eight feet high. To its right, a hummingbird flitted among the large blossoms of a Painted Lady spiraea shrub that had taken color to a new level, its hot-pink flower clusters set against yellow-and-green variegated foliage. Completing the ensemble, two dozen purple lavender fronds reached toward the afternoon sun from beneath a neatly trimmed magnolia tree left of the front walk.

Rizzo had summoned Carlo "CC" Conti and Mark LoNigro forty-five minutes early for the group's scheduled six-thirty meeting in the home's handsome lower-level recreation area. Mitch Steinberg and Larry Hickman would join them shortly. For now, the three were huddled in Rizzo's main floor office, where he held forth behind a burled mahogany desk. A grim look wrinkled his features.

"The last two weeks have been a combination of one victory and one complete fiasco!" he snarled, hands gripping the sides of his desk.

With the volcano starting to rumble, Conti tried to hold it back. "I agree, Gas, but don't overreact. The success of the Hanford operation far exceeded the misstep in Federal Way, and in Long Beach—"

"Misstep?" roared Rizzo, his face a portrait of incredulity. "Is that what you call it—a misstep?? Killing the very guy we needed to make the bomb was a bloody disaster!" Rizzo appeared ready to rip his desk from the floor and fling it at them.

Conti held out his hands in a calming gesture. "Wait until you hear the full report," he said. "We have no conclusions yet on Long Beach."

Rizzo looked back and forth at both men, fire in his eyes. "Listen to me, both of you," he growled, jabbing a finger at them. "It's pivotal for the three of us to be on the same page with this project. Obviously we're not, and now we have a dead schoolteacher right out of the gate. Explain that to me, Mark."

"Well, they arrived at his apartment house in Federal Way and determined in about five minutes that all Pearce wanted was details of our plan; that was it. They called me, and I gave the go-ahead to eliminate the guy; it was my decision. I was concerned he was trying to set *us* up. About that time, they saw a big black guy walking toward the apartment. He knocked on the door and then pulled a gun and walked in. That's when they clubbed him and got out of there after checking his identity. Seems he's a high-profile private investigator who specializes in marine crime. Name is Brick Morgan. Works out of Tacoma."

Rizzo looked up. "High profile?"

"Morgan is an ex-cop who now owns Morgan Maritime Investigations. Here's the kicker—he's the guy who helped the Feds stop the terrorists who tried to poison the passengers on a cruise ship a couple years ago."

Rizzo's left eyelid began twitching. "Well, isn't that just peachy," he replied, his blood pressure heading for orbit. He reached across his desk and selected a Padron Family Reserve 50 Years cigar from a colorful humidor, passed it under his nose, and then walked around the desk to face LoNigro.

"Listen to me carefully, Mark. No more wild-ass calls, got that? Cops have a habit of investigating murders, and you just opened the fucking door for them. I don't give a personal shit about our dead science teacher, but a hotshot private—"

"Here's how I see it, Gas," LoNigro interrupted. "The problem isn't the Federal Way science guy or that jerk who owns the California equipment yard either. Our biggest challenge is how to keep Mitch Steinberg from going ballistic."

This time the volcano erupted.

"Interesting you should say that, Mark," thundered Rizzo, throwing his hands in the air, "because at this very moment, I'm personally trying to keep from going ballistic myself. Forget Mitch for now. You've created a *mess,* Mark, a mess we need to clean up. That cruise ship terrorist plot involved the FBI, which means your Mr. Morgan has contacts there. And now he's sticking his nose into our plans. If we hit him too the Feds will swarm around here like flies to shit. It's the law of unintended consequences, and it could kill us all."

"To be clear," LoNigro responded, "the usual firewalls between us and the two guys who took out Pearce haven't been compromised. One other thing, Gas: your mouthwash ain't makin' it."

The comment broke the ice, and all three men snickered. Rizzo took a deep breath, exhaled loudly, and returned to his chair. "All right, it is what it is. From now on, we keep Mitch and Larry in the dark about Federal Way and Long Beach. We'll tell them the science guy broke parole and fled the state and that the idea of putting a dirty bomb inside heavy equipment wouldn't have guaranteed a transit through the new larger lock."

Conti removed his reading glasses and motioned to Rizzo. "Let me handle the Hanford end for the others, and Mark can feed them a line about Federal Way and downplay the situation in Long Beach."

Rizzo nodded, looked at his watch, and glanced at a closed-circuit monitor that displayed the home's driveway. He turned to face LoNigro. "You've earned an assignment, Mark. After the meeting, I want you and your network to dig up everything you can about our friend Morgan and find out what he's up to. Do it quietly, do it carefully, and do it immediately."

Steinberg and Hickman arrived, and the five men descended to the home's recreation area on a broad walnut staircase that featured an elaborate Persian patterned stair runner and white-framed movie posters adorning the walls. One of them, from the movie *Tin Cup* and autographed by its star, Kevin Costner, was prominently displayed at the entrance to the combined bar, arcade, and home theater.

Steinberg headed to a *Pirates of the Caribbean* pinball machine while Hickman poured himself a tall gin and tonic, settled into one of the high-backed barstools, turned it outward, and scanned the scene before him.

Ten minutes later, after big Mark LoNigro drilled the eight ball into a corner pocket, ending a brief game of pool with Conti, the group settled in the alcove. Hickman opened the meeting with a report on the group's financial position that was music to their ears.

"We've received a third of our fee—forty-two million—and a couple of bucks to cover expenses. You'll remember that I recommended avoiding Bitcoin because of traceability concerns. I stand by that decision. Most of the cybercurrencies don't have invisible block chains; that's the ledger currency transactions. I've diversified, and currently we're moving money using eDragon and Purplewallet. The cybercurrency geeks are optimistic about the future of Zcash, but it's much too early for us to consider."

"What's our transaction ratio?" asked Rizzo

"We're spending twenty-six percent moving the money from our client to cash and gold. Mitch and I are moving deposits that come into our eDragon account to an eDragon broker, who buys our digital money and sends us cash via MoneyGrams. Not a nickel goes through Mitch's check-cashing business or anywhere near it.

"Maximum MoneyGram transactions usually are three grand, so it takes us a hundred transactions to convert a third of a million. The facilitator we use has a slick team of illegals who go to different retail outlets to convert the MoneyGrams to cash. Counting Purplewallet and eDragon fees, cybercurrency brokers, and MoneyGram runners, we've spent ten million six hundred sixty thousand dollars as of one hour ago. It was money well spent. We're now sitting on thirty million three hundred forty thousand dollars in gold and cash. Next Monday, I'll distribute five million bucks to each of us. That will leave us fifty-three pounds of gold and forty thousand Ben Franklins, or about five million dollars to work with."

Rizzo stood and looked each man in the eye one at a time. "Before any of us sees one thin dime, let me be very clear. No one—and I mean no one—spends anything whatsoever. This is retirement money. No large purchases of any kind—none. By now, each of you should have a small safe. If you don't have one, drive to another city and buy one. Put your share into it, find the right spot, make sure you're alone, and bury it. Tell no one. If you don't do this, and your stupidity gets the rest of us caught, you'll receive one final present. There will be no escape and no mercy. Do you understand me?" Each man locked eyes with him and responded clearly in the affirmative. "Any questions?" Again, he looked at each man. All four shook their heads. Rizzo returned to his seat and asked Conti for an update on the Hanford theft.

"We now possess two liters of highly potent radioactive material, perfect for our needs. Our Hanford scientist has been paid and the material is stored in Boise, Idaho. More good news—a Geiger counter that was passed within eighteen inches of the containers displayed no abnormal readings of gamma or X-rays. The Hanford project was a major success." Conti noticed Hickman was rubbing his forehead. "Question, Larry?"

"Have there been any missing juice reports out of Hanford?"

"No. Once we paid off Dunbar, the nuclear scientist, we cut ties and made sure all the firewalls were in place. I'm following the media reports and scanner traffic, and all is quiet so far. How about the high school science guy, Mark, the one with the chemistry degree? What's his status?"

LoNigro reached back and adjusted the rubber band that held his small ponytail in place. His massive physical size, salt-and-pepper beard, and slicked-back hair enabled him to blend in with the lowlifes that comprised his network. It was from those fringe groups that he found enforcers to eliminate loose ends, such as schoolteacher Daniel Pearce. But for now, Pearce still lived in LoNigro's report. "You'll recall we had a solid lead on an ex-con with a chemistry degree who we hoped would help us design the dirty bomb."

"Is this the guy who stole the money from the high school athletic fund? The one whose daughter has cancer?" asked Hickman.

"That's him. Turns out he violated his probation and apparently skipped town. Left the girl and vanished. I've got people with their ears to the ground, but there's been no news, nothing. It's too bad because on the surface he looked like a good prospect. Hitting the road is his problem, not ours. We'll make other arrangements."

Hickman merely nodded; Steinberg offered no expression. *Hook, line, and sinker*, thought Rizzo.

LoNigro sipped his bourbon and turned to the Long Beach equipment-yard scenario. "At first, we considered hiding the bomb inside a large piece of construction equipment like a bulldozer or excavator and then shipping the equipment through the canal. We had arranged a deal with a heavy equipment company in Long Beach through a guy named Zigler, only to find out later that using a cargo ship wasn't the ideal solution for our needs. That little ripple cost us twenty-five K in seed money."

"I liked the cargo ship idea—only having to worry about a crew of thirty. What moved us away from using cargo ships?" asked Steinberg.

LoNigro looked up from his notes and spoke directly to him. "I liked it, too, Mitch. We tried every which way, but when you ship cargo, you lose control, and we couldn't guarantee that our package would load on any specific cargo ship, let alone one that would transit the third lock. Zigler contacted three heavy equipment transporters—the ones that coordinate with shipping lines that select cargo ships. It was no dice. If they choose a Panamax ship, it would use the original locks through the canal.

"Only if the shipping broker happened to select a line that uses the larger New Panamax ships would there be a chance it could slip through the new third lock—our target. But it's only a chance, and we have no way of controlling it. Zero. Bribing Zigler was one thing, but trying to bribe our way through a maze of transportation companies, shipping lines, dock foremen, and all the rest is out of the question and off the table."

"What happened to Zigler? Did we tip our hand to him?" asked Steinberg.

"Zigler thinks we're drug dealers who need his help to move a fortune in narcotics to the East Coast. We gave him the twenty-five K upfront for following our instructions and made him happier when we handed over his sex video and told him our plans had changed. He has no clue who our guys were, and his equipment yard and the bar didn't have video surveillance. That's it on Zigler."

"Wait a second . . . what sex video?"

"We paid a hooker to seduce him and taped it. Then we used the tape as encouragement for Zigler to work with us. It's immaterial now. Check to you, Gas, for our plan B."

Steinberg could be a prick at times, but this time he said nothing as Rizzo began with a twist. "There's another factor out there about cargo shipments that we hadn't considered. Homeland Security has ginned up its focus on cargo ships far beyond what they have with passenger liners. They've installed radiation portal monitors everywhere. The cranes that lift containers off the ships have RPMs on their spreader bars, and all cars off-loaded from ro-ro ships now pass through radiation monitors that are calibrated to pick up any aberrations in gamma or neutron radiation. We believe our radiation-mitigation technology can defeat these monitors, but we may be wrong. If we tried it and were wrong, the whole operation would be toast."

Rizzo stood without a word and stepped up to the pinball machine, setting his tumbler of Blanton's Single Barrel bourbon on the glass top, where it stayed for a moment before slowly sliding down the sloped top and stopping at the edge. "I tried this ten times before you all got here. Same conditions. Six times, the glass didn't move after I set it down. Four times it did what you just saw. That's forty percent. We won't test the radiation monitors, gentlemen. We're going to use a cruise ship to blow that third lock."

Hickman frowned and shook his head. "Whether we're detonating a nuclear device aboard a cruise ship filled with five thousand people or a freighter carrying thirty-five, the principle is the same—we're risking mass casualties, probably mass murder. There's no other way to look at it. I was expecting to hear a solution today. Where is it?"

Rizzo was sure CC and Mark were thinking the same thing he was: first Steinberg and now Hickman looks shaky. "We're committed to fulfilling our contract without any injury or deaths, Larry. Just listen, please.

"For our plan B, I'm looking at Diamond Cruise Lines. Several of their ships have beams of at least a hundred twenty-nine feet, requiring use of the new lock. We'll have Mark embark in San Diego carrying the hot sludge inside the types of oxygen containers used by passengers with chronic lung issues like emphysema. These containers will be similar to the fire extinguishers we used to steal the juice from Hanford.

"We'll also smuggle some C-4 inside a couple magnums of wine. The one-and-a-half-liter size would be perfect to hide several demolition charges. To minimize casualties—"

Steinberg leaped to his feet, waving his arms. "You must be shitting me! C-4 and a dirty bomb and nobody gets killed? During our last meeting, Mark, I expressed my reservations. Today, I'm convinced this plan is not only dangerous, it's also bizarre, reckless, and every other negative I can think of. I'm out."

"Calm down, Mitch. Let me explain the details," Rizzo responded. "If you're out after that, fine, but let me finish before you have a coronary." He paused as Steinberg closed his eyes and resumed sitting, his head down.

"We have multiple packages of C-4 roughly two inches by eleven inches each. Mark will mold two of them into each bottle—a piece of cake. Once the ship enters the lock, he'll detonate half of the C-4 in a vacant niche below the waterline. Nobody gets hurt, Mitch, but the explosion will cause the ship to stop and evacuate everyone. When the passengers abandon ship, he'll set off the remaining C-4 next to containers of our nuke package. No one is harmed unless some idiot returns to the ship and rolls around in the bomb fragments."

"Well, if no one is harmed, then what's the point of using a nuke in the first place? All along, the story has been that this device would close down the lock for months at least because of the radiation. In other words, the bomb has to be deadly or potentially deadly to do the job we're being paid for, and now you're telling me it won't be. Which is it?"

The men looked at one another. Rizzo finally sighed, withdrew his Padron Family cigar from a coat pocket, and set it afire. Conti dragged a barstool to Steinberg's chair and looked him in the eye. "Mitch, if you break this up into its manageable parts, it's very doable. If things start to go FUBAR, we pull the plug and walk away."

"It's already FUBAR," Steinberg declared. "I'll help Larry wind up the money matters, but after that, I'm gone."

Tick-tock . . .

Chapter Twenty-One

FBI Special Agent Nicole Cofield pulled her paddle holster from her hip and settled into a borrowed desk in a borrowed office in the Richmond, Washington, Department of Energy complex. Agent Cofield was dispatched three days earlier to help the DOE determine what happened to two liters of radioactive waste missing from the nearby Hanford nuclear reservation. She and Ramona Vicente had spent much of the last seventy-two hours reviewing surveillance video, interviewing Ionic Mass Data employees, and looking for aberrations in the lab's history of storage-tank sample readings.

While awaiting Vicente's arrival this morning, Cofield logged into her FBI dashboard and reviewed indexed events in the bureau's Sentinel case management software. She focused on an annotated comment from Assistant Counterterrorism Director Herb Wallace, who had provided a link to a case involving the murder of Daniel Pearce and another case just opened in Long Beach, California. She read the attached complaint form, FD-71, and virtual case file describing Dick Zigler's phone call to the FBI after meeting with two possible terrorists. *Two reports of dirty bombs plus this case of missing nuclear material could be a prescription for disaster.*

"Better take a look at Sentinel this morning," said Vicente as she breezed into the room, pulled up a chair, and set down her iPad next to Cofield's laptop.

"It's on my screen now. Our missing sludge case has jumped to the big leagues. We need to catch up in a hurry."

Cofield's reputation as a quick study had earned her a place on the FBI's fast track upstairs. She came highly recommended to the bureau eight years earlier from the Austin PD, where her instincts paid big dividends in several high-profile cases—her last one in particular.

A discarded ladder had caught her eye while she was on a night patrol in the ritzy Walnut Forest neighborhood. The ladder seemed out of place on a resident's manicured front lawn. As she stopped to have a look, a department BOLO, or be on the lookout alert, reported the kidnapping of the five-year-old daughter of an NFL quarterback from her second-story bedroom in the family's nearby home. In what became a career-making move, Cofield linked that information to the abandoned ladder and requested a CSI unit to dust for fingerprints on the possibility that it might be connected to the kidnapping. The prints led her and fellow officers to a home six miles away where the child was recovered safely and the kidnappers apprehended. The kidnapping, a federal crime, involved the FBI, whose agents were struck by Cofield's intellect and field savvy. Four weeks later, she was invited to an interview in the bureau's Dallas field office and hired two weeks after. Three promotions later, she now is the special agent assigned to the Investigations and Operations Section of the Weapons of Mass Destruction Directorate in Dallas.

"The first thing they teach at Quantico, Ramona, is there are few coincidences in criminal investigations. There's got to be a connection between Hanford, the narrative from Long Beach, and the reference to the Panama Canal."

Vicente shrugged. "My first thought was a terrorist plot of some kind here—ports of Seattle, Tacoma, Portland, or somewhere else on the West Coast—but the canal notation threw me."

"I don't know about the DOE, but the bureau hesitates to make the leap to terrorism until they have a signed confession from the Prophet himself."

"Don't worry, I won't mention 'radical Islamists' around your fellow blue suits," snickered Vicente as she opened a new email. "Well, it looks like we're not the only ones connecting the dots. Our bosses have scheduled a big powwow for this afternoon."

Cofield punched up the same message and took note of the

attendees who would join her and Vicente at three o'clock—Terry Carver, supervisory special agent of the Seattle field office, Special Agent Seth Early from the tri-city resident office, and private investigator Brick Morgan from Tacoma. She lingered at seeing Morgan's name and then Googled it for more background. Cofield had been assigned to the FBI's WMDD a short time when she read about Morgan's role in neutralizing an attack by Islamic terrorists against Nobility Cruise Line. Her interest intensified when she learned he was black, eligible, well connected with the bureau, and, most important, very good-looking. "Well, my goodness," she mused to herself as his photo popped up.

Vicente stood and stretched her long legs. At a bit under six foot with stylish short hair, the dark-eyed beauty always caught the eye of the opposite sex. Truth be told, she was gay and had recently married her long-time partner. "I understand having several FBI agents at the table, Nicole, but who's this Morgan guy from Tacoma?"

"He's a former Seattle cop who was with the Justice Department and Interpol and now has his own maritime investigations company in Tacoma. I've heard he's on first-name basis with the directors of the CIA and FBI."

"That still doesn't explain why a marine security investigator is invited to a meeting about missing nuclear waste."

"Well, you just said your first thought was some sort of terrorist activity in one of the ports up here. Maybe that's it. Bide your time, Ramona. He's not coming to play the piano for us."

The Beemer's navigation system indicated a travel time of three hours and twenty minutes to the tri-cities of Richland, Kennewick, and Pasco as Morgan eased northeast from Interstate 5 onto state Highway 18 and headed for I-90 and Snoqualmie Pass. He was glad to be making the trip in October, less than a month before late-fall snow would begin blanketing the pass and turning a trip from Tacoma into a five-hour marathon. October also was prime apple harvest time in eastern Washington, and Brick reminded himself to pick up a case or two before returning home.

Before leaving, Morgan had received a call from Agent Carver, who briefed him on the calls from Long Beach and headquarters, believing they might be connected to his own investigation into the slain science teacher. He suspected Carver wanted to work with him about as much as a sailor wants a dose of clap. *Had to have come from Herb Wallace*, he thought.

Morgan and Wallace had many mutual friends, attributed to Morgan's time with the Justice Department, assigned to Interpol. His Interpol team included a half-dozen FBI agents who later rose in the hierarchy of bureau leadership. The reality that he was not constrained by the bureau's rules of engagement was an added benefit. Brick's own rules, which included Rilee, his cybersleuth, would not have fit into the FBI profile. It worked equally well for the bureau, whose leadership accepted the fact that she was part of Morgan Maritime Investigations.

Special Agent Early was cranky. He hadn't slept well the previous night, and office coffee wasn't much help this morning. His frumpy blue suit wasn't much help either. Much like Ramona Vicente, Early was antsy about working with a private investigator.

"I don't need some amateur looking over my shoulder," he whined to Agent Carver.

"Amateur? Read my lips, Seth. Unless you want to be a special agent in Barrow, Alaska, don't fuck with this guy. Morgan's more than connected. Remember our former deputy director, Elizabeth Monroe—now secretary of Homeland? They worked together with Interpol, and rumor has it they're more than good friends."

Early nodded in acceptance, took another sip of cold coffee, and found a chair at the conference table. Morgan arrived at 10:04 a.m., and ten minutes later, the group of five was seated and formal introductions made.

As senior agent, Carver opened the meeting. "NCTC wants DOE to quarterback this adventure. That works for us; the president of China will be visiting the state next week and we'll be spread pretty thin."

The announcement shocked Morgan. He said nothing, but the sudden wrinkles across his forehead spoke for him. He had walked in the front door barely ten minutes earlier, and the FBI already was backing out of the case. Abandoning ship wasn't how the bureau had made its reputation.

NCTC, the National Counterterrorism Center, is the primary government organization for integrating and analyzing information pertaining to terrorism. President Bush created the organization in August 2004 with the understanding that the FBI would handle a threat deemed as domestic terrorism. But the bureau had just bailed out with that question still unanswered.

Morgan held his tongue as Carver and then Vicente laid out what they had on each prong of the three-point investigation. It was bare bones, and all of them knew it. Morgan took stock of what they did have—missing nuclear waste, murdered chemist Daniel Pearce, and California business owner Dick Zigler propositioned to transport a nuclear device to the Panama Canal. The pieces were there, but the Feds seemed reluctant to pick them up. Things took a better turn when Nicole Cofield began her report about the missing waste.

My God, she's beautiful, Morgan thought. He liked everything he saw and heard from her. He took notes while she spoke, but found her natural beauty captivated him. He noticed her twinkling eyes, long lashes, and arching eyebrows. Her raven hair created a setting for her flawless dark skin. Morgan was determined to make her his new best friend.

"We've cross-checked the lab's samples using both quantitative and qualitative analyses. All other samples correlated with prior tests and the lab's logs. What's interesting here is there was no attempt to substitute the material with something inert to delay detection. Specifically, we're missing two liters of hot waste from tank C-109." She then led a dialogue of methods that could have been used to steal the material. The consensus was that all forty-seven employees with lab access at Ionic Mass Data needed to undergo polygraph exams.

Vicente thanked Cofield and asked Morgan to give the group a firsthand account of the Daniel Pearce case.

"I'm a former agent with the Justice Department, assigned to Interpol, and now a private investigator and owner of Morgan Maritime Investigations in Tacoma. A friend of mine, Rob Spencer, is the head of security for Nobility Cruise Line in Fort Lauderdale. His brother, Terry, is a parole officer in Pierce County. Terry was assigned to a former high school chemistry teacher named Daniel Pearce, who stole twelve hundred dollars from his school's athletic fund trying to pay medical bills for his daughter who has cancer. A sympathetic judge sentenced him to probation. Then, two men who learned he had a master's degree in chemistry visited his residence unannounced and proposed that he build two bombs—a C-4 bomb and a nuclear bomb for the purpose of sinking a cruise or cargo ship. Pearce told Terry about it, Terry told Rob, and Rob called me. I made an appointment with Pearce, but found him shot in the head when I arrived. Two men were in the apartment, and one clubbed me over the head, knocking me unconscious. The bureau became involved because of the bombs issue, and here I am."

Carver added to Morgan's report. "I had one of our Seattle agents interview Terry Spencer, and the case file agrees exactly with Brick's chronicle. The key words are C-4, dirty nuclear bomb, cruise ship, and cargo ship."

"Let me shed more light on my presence here today," added

Morgan. "Last year the cruise industry estimated it lost about three percent of its projected forty billion in revenues because of the attack on Nobility Cruise line—that's over a billion dollars. A successful nuclear attack on a cruise ship would financially set the industry back a decade. The leadership at the DOE and FBI knew my firm would be investigating the threat and felt it would be better if I didn't trip over your investigation—and you over mine. We're each better off working separately but together."

Carver then passed out copies of the report involving Long Beach heavy-equipment company owner Dick Zigler. "He called us after he was approached by two strangers. Zigler appears to be a legitimate businessman whose company resells large industrial equipment. He was the victim of a badger game, a classic sex-extortion scheme. He said he was offered fifty thousand, twenty-five upfront, to facilitate the smuggling of a thirty-cubic-foot box through the new third lock of the Panama Canal.

"Zigler was adamant that the container was not for drugs or weapons, but something radioactive. The cash he received was picked up by our agents in Los Angeles and is being processed for the usual—prints, fibers, hair—anything we can find."

"Any idea when the strangers may contact Zigler again?" asked Agent Early.

"Best guess is within the next three or four days," said Carver. "Which is why you, Ramona, might consider sending your own team down to Long Beach to reinterview Zigler."

"Nicole's already planning to interview him, Terry; no point in me going, too," replied Vicente curtly before turning to Morgan. "We have three issues on the table, Brick. Cruise ships or cargo ships have come up twice. Add in the Panama Canal and radiation. What do you think?"

Morgan looked at the others. Except for Early, the lightweight agent from Richland, he found the rest to be competent and professional but surprisingly feeble in their responses. They seemed to accept his involvement, so he decided to lay it out for them. "I'm thinking what seems obvious—that we have a person or persons out there who may be plotting a nuclear attack at the Panama Canal and that, right now, the American government isn't taking the threat very seriously."

Carver's mouth flopped open, but no words came out.

"My initial reaction was to focus on radical Islamic groups based in part on my own challenges with Lashkar-e-Aalam. But I no longer believe this fits a jihad group; it doesn't feel right. The guys who attacked me and the two guys who approached Zigler were Caucasian. I believe that if radicals got their hands on a dirty bomb, they would shoot for a homerun, and that likely is New York City or DC. Zigler's report about the third lock suggests a money motive to me, so who would benefit from closure of the new third lock? Maybe the Chinese; they have a huge investment in the Nicaragua Grand Canal. If the third lock was knocked out, the biggest cargo ships would have no choice but to use Nicaragua."

Vicente abruptly announced that the goals of the meeting had been met and that any future gatherings would have to await more information. This time Morgan's mouth fell open.

"That's it?" he asked in disbelief, looking at each of the others. "Are you kidding me? We've barely skimmed the surface of an action plan, and you're ending the meeting? I could have done this by phone."

"Look, Brick, it was important to get our players together for some face time," said Carver. "From here we can each pursue pieces of this thing. We can't all be going the same direction at the same time."

"How about all of us going in the same direction one time?"

"We're all facing time crunches at the moment, Brick," said Vicente. "I have to stay put and work with Seth to locate the missing material. Terry, you said you needed to return to Seattle and deal with the Chinese president's visit."

"Yeah. Could be a career-ending event if the Chinese president was abducted by

Greenpeace during my watch."

"Am I hearing this right? You're kissing off a potential nuclear disaster to babysit the president of China?"

"We don't have much actionable intelligence yet, Brick. My people are still looking at the Pearce murder, Ramona is investigating the missing hot sauce, and we need Nicole to follow-up with Zigler in Long Beach. You're welcome to join her if you wish."

"Fine, but this isn't a time to protect our career assets. For all we know, whoever stole the juice from Hanford may be putting it together with radioactive material from other sources and planning the biggest bang since Nagasaki. If that nuke blows, you'll have your career-ending event on a silver platter."

"I understand your concern, Brick, but until we have more facts to work with, there's no action to take. We need answers first and then we'll determine what to do. Ramona and Seth will supervise the polygraph exams beginning tomorrow, and Nicole, I'd like a call from you and a follow-up email as soon as you and Brick interview Zigler."

"Got it," Cofield responded. "If you're game, Brick, we'll fly down in the morning."

"If the bureau has a business jet available, we could fly down tonight and see Zigler first thing," Morgan suggested.

"No can do, Brick. I've got VIPs swirling in and out of the state right now," said

Carver. "I'll have my secretary arrange a Delta flight from Sea-Tac for both of you tomorrow. She'll call you with the details."

Morgan glanced at Cofield. "Deal?"

"Deal," she said with a playful wink. "I could use some sunshine."

Flight reservations, a room near the airport for Nicole, and an appointment with Zigler were made within the hour, and Morgan agreed to pick her up at a nearby FBI guest house for the long drive back across the state. Alone in the meeting room for the moment, he sipped ice water and wondered grimly whether they already were too late to avert the disaster that he knew was coming like a freight train. But from where?

A more pleasant thought—that of Nicole and her flirty wink—also invaded Morgan's consciousness. *Maybe I'm about to get lucky,"* he mused. He dropped the plastic water bottle into a recycle bin and headed out the front door to his car.

Tick-tock . . .

Chapter Twenty-Two

The navigation system on the big German sedan displayed 113 miles to Seattle-Tacoma International Airport as Morgan's dark-green BMW flashed past the Ellensburg exit on I-90 toward the waning afternoon sun.

"I hope you don't mind my questions, Brick, but you're a very interesting man."

The car's black leather upholstery enveloped Nicole Cofield's petite five-foot-four frame as she sat nearly facing him, left leg curled under her, a mischievous smile crossing her features.

"I'm serious, Brick," she said playfully. "I've never met anyone who worked for Interpol."

Morgan grinned. He liked her. She smiled easily and often, and her relaxed banter was for more than just occupying time. Nicole was genuine—a vibrant and accomplished woman who felt no need to prove herself at every encounter. At just thirty-five, her position with the FBI spoke volumes about her professional life, but there was much more to her than that, and as Brick's Beemer blasted westward into the Cascades, he was gaining a look inside her persona that he doubted many other men had seen.

"And you're a very interesting lady, Nicole. I know that much already, and I haven't even asked a question yet."

"Why not?"

"I rarely interrupt a lady, especially one as charming as you are."

"Am I making you nervous?"

"Do I look nervous?"

"You haven't said much."

"No sense rushing things."

"What does that mean?"

"It means I find you beautiful, intelligent, and unpretentious. But I could be wrong."

They both laughed out loud. They had been together less than an hour yet they shared a chemistry neither had felt in months.

"Let me know when you want me to spell you at the wheel. I received a top-of-the-class score in the bureau's driver-training course."

"Were you driving a BMW?"

"No, a Chevy."

"Nuff said. My Beemer and I have an understanding. I take care of it, and it only lets me drive."

Nicole punched him on the arm. She was referring to the FBI's pursuit and defensive driver course at the Quantico, Virginia, one-point-one-mile training track. Brick had tried it out once. He was certain her score outshined his. Morgan looked at her for a moment, nodded slowly, and eased the car off the highway onto a forested secondary road leading into the quaint little village of Cle Elum.

"Do you like cinnamon rolls, Nicole?"

"Till I die and go to heaven."

"Well, don't look now, but we've arrived at the nearest thing to heaven. No one, and I mean no one, bypasses the Cle Elum Bakery on I-90." He parked the car out front and led her inside. They each ordered one roll and coffee, plus a bag each for the road.

Nicole devoured her roll and plucked another out of her bag. "These are incredible."

"Washington has three wonders of the world—Mount Rainier, the Grand Coulee Dam, and the cinnamon rolls at the Cle Elum Bakery."

"You convinced me on the rolls." After a second cup of coffee, she had a clerk refill her carryout bag, and as the clocked ticked to 6:20, the pair returned to the car.

Morgan opened the trunk and placed their rolls next to her small travel case, his go bag, and the two boxes of Red Delicious apples he had purchased as they passed through Yakima. He abruptly tossed her the car keys with a smile. "Okay, let's see what you can do."

The two traded seats and were off. Morgan made a show of carefully fastening his safety belt and was rewarded when she burned rubber on the town's main street.

Back on I-90, Nicole accelerated to seventy-five, set the cruise control, and slid into a passing lane.

"What made you leave the DOJ?"

"It's never one reason, but an accumulation of events, Nicole. About six months after I was assigned to Interpol, we started seeing an increase in Red Notices that were clearly in violation of Interpol's constitution."

"You mean the international arrest notices?"

"Yep. A member country would send Interpol a request to locate a fugitive. We reviewed the requests, and if the petition didn't violate Interpol's rules, we would issue a Red Notice. On paper, Interpol is forbidden from issuing Red Notices if the request pursues any agenda that's political, military, religious, or racial. I started to create waves when Iran requested a Red Notice for a guy who was accused of insulting Islam. I turned it down because it obviously was against Interpol policy. But some jerk overruled me—said we needed to show the Muslim people we were sensitive to their world. He was a suck-up who wanted to move up the ladder by impressing certain people."

"And the weasel got his way?"

"Someone else up the food chain told me in no uncertain terms to ignore the violation and just keep my head down if I wanted to continue doing what I did."

"No shit?"

"It gets better. A month later an editor of a Spanish newspaper published an article that said Islam couldn't coexist with democracy. Interpol issued another Red Notice at the request of the Iranian government. That editor was arrested, extradited, and is presumed dead. That's when I set up my DOJ exit strategy."

"How'd that bring you all the way to me?"

"While I was still working a few cases involving the cruise industry, I discovered a potential niche market. There are about a hundred eighty-five cruise ships in the North American market. I noticed a big gap between the work of small onboard security teams and the point where cruise-line operators needed to request coast guard or FBI assistance. Bad publicity is the major concern of cruise-line owners, so with that in mind, I immersed myself in every case of maritime crime that hit our Interpol office. Nine months later, I formed MMI in Tacoma to fill that niche, and here we are."

"A self-made man," she replied, tilting her head and smiling broadly. "I'm very impressed. Most men I work with are cookie-cutter bureau types. Nice guys, but . . . well, you're quite different." They stared into each other's eyes for a long moment before she returned her gaze to the road.

"Okay, my turn," she said, opening with a statement that she was divorced with no children. By the time they reached Snoqualmie Pass summit a half hour later, Nicole had laid out the twists and turns of life that had brought her from her home in Waco, Texas, to the University of Texas in Austin for her criminal justice degree and on to the Austin PD for five years before being plucked from that department by the FBI at the tender age of twenty-seven. She clearly had a bright future, and Morgan suspected she'd soon have her pick of assignments.

"I was still in college when nine-eleven happened, and I knew from then on I wanted to do something important for the country. Joining the police force in Austin was a great opportunity, and when I got the chance to move to the bureau, I jumped at it, Brick. It was an incredible piece of luck, and once I got there, I took every course and seminar I could find about terrorists' backgrounds, tactics, weapons of choice, WMDs—you name it—and landed with the WMDD in Dallas, barely a hundred miles from my hometown. Now here I am actually looking for a WMD. To be honest, maybe it was too much too soon. I have to admit I'm a little frightened."

Morgan reached over and squeezed her right hand. They drove into the night in silence for the next several miles.

An hour later, with Nicole checked into the Red Lion at Sea-Tac and their flight reservations confirmed for the next morning, Brick drove back to Tacoma, his mind awash with thoughts of her. At dinner in Fort Lauderdale with Rob and Gail Spencer days earlier, he had mused openly about maybe settling down with the right woman. Had he found her? Could Nicole be the right woman? Or was she right about her own life moving too fast? It was a conundrum for which he had no answer.

He rolled over and fell into a fitful sleep.

Morgan was shaved, showered, and back on I-5 north by six fifteen the next morning. As he wound through the crowded Sea-Tac terminal an hour later, he spotted Nicole waiting for Delta's Flight 128 at Gate A-3 in the airport's south satellite.

Other passengers were queuing up behind her, and in that moment, he stopped walking just to absorb the sheer beauty of her. Nicole was radiant in tan slacks and a navy blue sweater with the small, gold FBI initials over a light-blue blouse. A pair of white Keds canvas shoes completed her travel ensemble. They hugged as he stepped up to her and then handed their boarding passes to an airline employee before he steered her up the ramp toward their waiting 737-800's first-class cabin.

"Are you trying to get me fired?" she laughed as she settled into the plane's roomy first-class window seat. "Some of us still work for the government. The bureau frowns on perceived extravagance."

"Don't blame me; it's Delta's fault. I'm a frequent flyer with them, and they upgrade me and my companion anytime I get within a hundred feet of a plane."

"Oh, so I'm a companion now?"

"Think of it this way—you can pretend you're a federal air

marshal." Morgan held her gaze for a moment as she smiled and then removed a copy of *EARTH Magazine* from his briefcase, turning to an article on developing seafloor-mapping technology.

Nicole glanced over at the article, made a face, and then tapped Morgan lightly on the arm. "Would you rather read about rocks than talk with me?"

"It's a habit, or maybe an addiction. I buy and read magazines about obscure topics every time I fly. At the end of a year, I've learned fifty or sixty new things. Last month, for instance, I read about Clara Foods. They make chicken egg whites without the chicken by using genetically modified yeast. No cholesterol to worry about."

"They make chicken eggs without chickens? Do you have extended blackouts, Brick?" she asked as the plane completed its takeoff roll and began its turn to the south. "Ever hear voices?"

"Okay, okay, I surrender," he chuckled, tucking the magazine back in his briefcase. "So, where are we meeting Zigler?"

"O'Kelly's bar on Main Street in Seal Beach. Zigler believes the suspects are looking for him. He's avoiding his business and usual bar." She handed Brick her iPad. "Here's a Googled street view of O'Kelly's. Typical two-story."

"Seal Beach is also the home to a naval weapons station and has lots of ammunition storage space buried next to a wildlife refuge."

"You don't say. Did you read that in one of your magazines?"

Morgan laughed and looked over at Nicole. "No. I think it was a question on *Jeopardy*."

After Delta 128 landed at LAX, they walked to baggage claim, where Morgan retrieved his Pelican gun case from the circling carousel. As a federal agent, Nicole kept her firearm at all times. Twenty-five minutes later, they were in their rented Ford Fusion and exiting Interstate 405 leading to Seal Beach.

1:55 p.m. They were right on time. "There's a parking spot right in front of that coin shop," said Nicole before pulling her sweater loosely over her standard-issue Glock 19.

Once inside O'Kelly's, Brick noted the Irish décor, including an ancient, prominently displayed Old Shamrock Stout advertising sign that he guessed had cost the owner serious money. They passed the long wooden bar that a framed sign said had been reclaimed from a San Francisco bistro destroyed in the 1906 earthquake and settled into a corner booth. The regulars hadn't arrived, and the room was about half full. Morgan made eye contact with a husky man wearing a leather jacket and black T-shirt seated nearby who got up and approached their table. They had their man.

Morgan extended his hand. "Dick Zigler, I presume? I'm Brick Morgan. Please have a seat."

"You guys mind showing me some ID?"

Both displayed their credentials, and Zigler examined them carefully before sitting down.

"Mr. Zigler, I'm Special Agent Cofield with the FBI, and Mr. Morgan here is a private investigator who is assisting the bureau with this case. First, let me thank you for meeting us on such short notice." Zigler sat with his back against the wall, offering him an easy view of the front door. He signaled the barmaid for drinks.

"Hope I can help. Look, yesterday I gave the money to another agent. I have his card somewhere."

"No need for the card, Mr. Zigler. We know about the meeting."

The barmaid, who Morgan suspected was also the owner, greeted them wearing a blue polo shirt displaying a Bushmills Irish Whiskey logo. She placed Guinness Stout beer coasters on the table and took their orders—Murphy's Irish Stout for Zigler, Pepsi for Cofield, and black coffee for Morgan.

"When I called you yesterday, y'know, I thought I had a few days, but those guys have phoned at least ten times since I met them. They know

I'm not cooperating and that I have—had—their twenty-five thousand. My regular bartender in Long Beach alerted me that they twice came looking for information about my whereabouts. They know I'm up to something. I came to the FBI, and you haven't protected me at all."

Cofield kept her tone even as she tried to keep Zigler focused. "We know you described your contact with them to our agents already, but I need you to take us through it one more time. This is very important, Mr. Zigler. Please don't leave out anything."

Nearly an hour and another beer later, he had answered most of their questions while Morgan took notes to be entered into the bureau's Sentinel database. The FBI's onerous note-taking protocol, little changed from Hoover's era, hadn't sped up things a bit.

This place is really filling up, thought Brick. Zigler had chosen one of the busiest bars in Seal Beach, and the more patrons who entered, the louder it became. Morgan and Cofield exchanged glances while Zigler reached into his pocket.

"Here are the envelopes I used to take notes." Zigler paused before continuing. "The container was to be a thirty-square-foot box. They liked my idea of a Caterpillar six thirteen."

"Why a six thirteen?" Morgan asked, glancing up.

"It's an elevating scraper used in road construction. It'll hold thirteen tons of dirt—a perfect place to hide their fucking box. And here's my note about the third lock. They were adamant that the shipment *had* to go through the canal's new third lock."

Brick's eyebrow arched as if he caught the scent of something in Zigler's words, but Cofield seemed more interested in what they were moving.

"Tell us everything about the contents of the shipment."

"They only gave me general information. They said it was chemicals, slightly radioactive, that were used in medical research. Yeah, that's why I drew the atom symbol on this envelope. I didn't feel like it was the place to take a lot of notes, y'know, but we did spend some time discussing their time line—specifically when the shipment was to transit the third canal lock." Zigler interrupted his own thoughts and stood up. "My bladder's floating. Let's pick up their time line after a head call."

The two watched Zigler maneuver through the crowd toward the back of the pub. He turned back to them before disappearing among the throng.

"What are you thinking?" asked Morgan as Cofield examined the two envelopes.

"He's consistent. Today's narrative is a perfect match to what he said when he called yesterday."

"Exactly. Here we sit with the same information we had even before that ridiculous meeting in Richland yesterday. I've never been more sure of anything in my life. Someone is planning a nuclear attack, and every clue we have points toward West Coast involvement—Pearce, Zigler's contacts, and, further south, vessels—possibly within the Panama Canal. There's got to be a connection. Meanwhile, Carver's babysitting the president of China, the DOE is busy polygraphing forty-seven Hanford employees, and we're getting the same story today that Zigler provided to the Los Angeles agents three days ago. We're all wasting time."

"Are you going to put Zigler in front of a forensic artist? He said he studied their faces. Maybe we could ID these guys."

"Definitely." Nicole looked at her watch and glanced toward the men's room. "Why don't you give him a shout? We'll head downtown and get that done. I'd like to fax it up the line today."

Morgan navigated between groups of Irish wannabes and spotted the door to the men's room with a sloppily written "Out of Service" sign taped to it. The odor of coppery wet metal was unmistakable. He opened it a few inches, felt resistance, and then kicked it open. On the floor was Dick Zigler, blood pooling from a gaping slash across his throat.

Tick-tock . . .

Chapter Twenty-Three

Emily McClelland stared quietly down at the grave of her husband, Navy Master Chief Jack McClelland, for the second time in three weeks. Her red jacket, black slacks, and multicolored paisley scarf warded off the early morning breeze sweeping across the veterans' section of Mountain View Memorial Park, carrying with it a rain squall that peppered her briefly before moving on to the south. It had been over forty years since Jack's combat death, yet she found his grave a tranquil and solemn place to gather strength for life's difficult decisions.

Nearly a month had passed since she overheard the frightening conversation coming from the home of Mark LoNigro, a neighbor of her employers, Arlen and Joanne Bancroft. Her euphoria from orchestrating a dinner party that evening celebrating a major workplace promotion for Joanne had vanished when she overheard several men discussing what sounded like a plot to attack the Panama Canal.

It had made no sense, and she had wanted so badly for it all to go away. Emily had been relaxing in her upstairs room after Dr. Bancroft's party when the loud conversation drifted on a warm late-evening breeze across sixty feet of landscaping. She didn't get everything, but each time she reread her notes, snippets from their sentences seemed to almost jump from the pages: "Panama Canal," "shutting down the new lock," "attack against humanity," "radiation," "nuclear sludge," "atom bomb," "killing five thousand people . . ."

There had to be a rational explanation for what she heard, and she had tried hard to put it out of her mind, but could not. Now, as out of place as it all seemed, coming from a lavish residence in suburban Tacoma where multimillionaires abounded, Emily knew what she had to do. Her visit to the wind-swept cemetery this morning was to explain things to Jack and ask for his blessing.

"But what about the Bancrofts? I can't bear for them to think I was spying on their neighbors. What if I'm wrong?" Emily wondered aloud. At sixty-four, her job was all she had, personally and professionally. Her two children were grown and gone with careers of their own, having never known their father. She stood alone, contemplating the oxidation slowly claiming her husband's brass tombstone. Tears slowly trickled down her cheeks, and she began to weep. "Help me, Jack. Please help me."

She pulled a lone, wilted dahlia from the hydrangea and zinnia arrangement she had brought for her husband. At the same time, she resolved to speak with Dr. Bancroft that evening.

Housekeeping was Emily's primary responsibility at the Bancrofts' home, though she also purchased most of the groceries. She volunteered to make dinner for Arlen and Joanne this evening and also asked Dr. Bancroft if she would have time after dinner to help her with a "personal challenge." The doctor seemed amenable, if somewhat distracted, before she left for work. This did little to assuage Emily's nervousness that grew over the course of the day.

Mr. Bancroft arrived home from the bank before Joanne, and Emily prepared him a plate of Camembert and aged cheddar cheese accompanied by crackers, apple slices, and Genoa salami. She then returned to the home's gourmet kitchen and put the final touches on a dinner of venison-stuffed sweet mini-peppers. By preparing one of the doctor's favorites, she hoped to set the right tone for the difficult conversation.

While the Bancrofts finished their dinner, Emily hastily tidied up the kitchen and reviewed her meeting notes for the fifth time that day.

"Emily, please come here. You've just been a ball of stress tonight. Arlen has volunteered to put the dinner plates in the dishwasher, okay? Why don't you and I move to the game room?"

"Oh, Dr. Bancroft, no, please. It's fine, really. I could—"

"Would you be comfortable if Arlen joined us?"

"I don't want to be a bother."

"Don't be silly—you're family. We want to help any way we can."

The game room was an intimate setting off the large den that once seemed to serve no purpose. After much back and forth, Mr. Bancroft had christened it a game room by purchasing a forty-eight-inch Lux interchangeable game table and custom shelving. Amid the colorful boxes of games was Emily's favorite décor item in the house—a vintage bone and bamboo mahjong set that the couple brought home from a trip to Beijing four years earlier.

"How can we help you, dear?" Joanne asked as Arlen sat down opposite them.

For a moment Emily thought she might cry, but she looked up, steeled herself, and laid it out. "The evening of your surprise party ... I overheard a conversation that has made me a nervous wreck. I just haven't been able to . . ."

Mr. Bancroft set down his wine glass and looked startled. Emily reacted to the *clink* with a little flinch. The Bancrofts exchanged nervous glances at her obvious distress. "Was it something one of our guests said?" asked Mr. Bancroft, concern creeping across his features.

"No, sir. It was—please excuse me. After I retired to my room, I overheard a loud conversation coming from outside my window. From the LoNigro home."

"From Karen and Mark's?"

"Mr. LoNigro and several other men, yes."

Dr. Bancroft leaned back in her club chair. "Okay, Emily, tell us what happened."

Emily reached into a pocket and produced several sheets from a yellow pad she had used that night to make a record of what she had heard plus a follow-up transcript she had written on her computer that included further details. She glanced down at her notes as she recounted the specifics and the tone of the conversation and repeatedly assured the Bancrofts that she wasn't snooping on their neighbors.

"Don't worry about that for a second, Emily," responded Mr. Bancroft. "We know you much better than that."

Emily punctuated her story with apologies before reiterating what she thought were the key points. "I'm so sorry. I know the LoNigros are your friends, but there's no question that I heard Mr. LoNigro and the others speak of stolen radioactive material from Hanford, about the Panama Canal, and something about equipment from Long Beach. I heard the words 'nuclear bomb' and 'innocent people would die.' They mentioned 'radiation,' too, more than once." She handed her notes to Joanne, who sucked in her breath as she read the entries.

"My God, Arlen, listen to this. 'I have in mind using a dirty bomb,' 'it spreads radiation, and radiation kills people,' 'a nuclear bomb'—and some material from the periodic table—uranium-235, radium-226—multiple references to Hanford, and one other reference."

"What is it, Joanne?"

"Little Boy!"

"God Almighty!"

"One of the men was louder than the others and sounded like he disagreed," Emily added.

"Did that man sound like Mark LoNigro?" asked Bancroft.

"Well, I've met him twice before and have been in their home once when he was there. No, it didn't sound anything like his voice."

"Did you get any sense that they were just talking about nuclear warfare, or movies they had seen, college class topics—anything even remotely like that?"

"Nothing like that. I listened to them clearly for over a half hour. It sounded like they were planning something. I hope I'm wrong, but I don't think so. I'm not an educated woman, as you know, but I'm not a fool either. I know what I heard. I believe I must speak with the police, but it was important that I speak with you first."

The Bancrofts were stunned. Finally, Arlen stood and leaned

against a wall unit that displayed several antique games. As Emily hung on his response, he picked up a candlestick from a classic 1952 edition of "Clue" and rolled it between his fingers.

"She needs to report this situation, Joanne. I'm a big believer in the philosophy that small problems never go away. They just get bigger. I don't think it's a call to the Lakewood PD, though, Emily. I think you need to speak with the FBI."

Joanne had spent twenty-six years as a psychiatrist, and tonight she was certain her housekeeper was telling the truth. "You made the right decision confiding in us, Emily. There's an FBI office downtown. We'll call them first thing in the morning."

Emily went to bed at eleven o'clock, but sleep wouldn't come. She tossed and turned all night, finally arising shortly before six.

Two hours later, with renewed strength from her late husband and with Dr. Bancroft at her side, Emily picked up the telephone and dialed the Tacoma field office of the Federal Bureau of Investigation. Emotions in check, she was filled with resolve as she waited for someone to pick up the phone.

Transfers? Emily hadn't expected her call to bounce among three agents. She hoped they wouldn't think she was a crank caller or some lonely woman needing attention.

After five minutes on hold, she finally was able to share her story with Special Agent Dexter Copeland, who sounded intrigued. She explained that she did not want the FBI to visit the Bancroft home but preferred to meet at their office.

Copeland, already swamped with the coming arrival of the Chinese president, was more than happy to schedule the meeting with Emily for the end of the week. He would wait until then before filling out Form 302 and making an entry into the bureau's Sentinel database.

Tick-tock . . .

Chapter Twenty-Four

Morgan deactivated his security system, walked in the front door, and headed for the kitchen and a cold Heineken. He was relieved to be home but far from happy. The last forty-eight hours had taken him and Agent Nicole Cofield near a major break in their investigation of Hanford's missing radioactive waste only to have their key witness butchered beneath their noses. Now they were back to square one, and he hated it.

They were so close.

Morgan took a long pull on his beer, held the cold bottle against his forehead for a full ten seconds, and reviewed it all in his mind yet again—the conversation in O'Kelly's bar, the relief he had felt at finally making progress in the frustrating case, and the sickening sight of Dick Zigler sprawled in a crimson pool on a restroom floor, his throat slashed, a shocked expression frozen on his face. Brick knew it was his fault. He had dropped his guard and allowed himself to relax. He had let a key witness walk out of his sight in a room full of strangers, knowing the man could be in mortal danger. He had been stupid and unprofessional, and Zigler was dead because of it.

Morgan extracted a second beer from his refrigerator, tapped a button on his stereo, and slumped in a recliner as the mournful sounds of blues great Etta James quietly filled the room. If there had been one positive, it had been the way Nicole held her ground through a jurisdictional power play that had ensued in O'Kelly's between herself and arriving Seal Beach police. The standoff continued for forty minutes until five more FBI agents arrived along with the Seal Beach police chief, who finally directed his officers to begin questioning bar patrons and a crowd that had gathered outside as a CSI unit processed the crime scene.

Once his credentials were cleared and Cofield's reports were submitted, it was too late for a flight back to Tacoma, which admittedly had its advantages. Spending the evening with Nicole at the Renaissance Airport Hotel had relieved some of the frustration they shared, a workout he still felt today.

But it wasn't nearly enough, and they both knew it. Dick Zigler had a twenty-year-old daughter in college.

They had virtually nothing to go on. During the return flight to Sea-Tac, he and Cofield concluded only the obvious—schoolteacher Daniel Pearce and now businessman Dick Zigler had been slain to ensure silence in a plot they had yet to uncover but which seemed to involve Panama. The possible motivations seemed to be a radical Islamist plot or a crime for economic profit. Morgan suspected the latter, but proof may as well have been in another galaxy.

Morgan's last conversation with POT Commissioner Barry Mott had been troubling, prompting him to analyze current financial positions of Northwest ports and compare them with Panama's post-third-lock projections. The news wasn't good. All would be impacted, but the heaviest hammer seemed likely to fall first on the ports of Tacoma and Seattle, also known as Northwest Seaport Alliance, with Portland not far behind. Now seemed a good time to probe Mott's thoughts and possibly refocus his investigation. It couldn't hurt; the case was going nowhere at the moment. If the deaths and the ports were as tied together as Morgan imagined, he might be able to kill two birds with one stone.

Mott entered Morgan's North Tacoma home at 3:02 p.m., pausing to scrutinize a wall of three Yurly Shevchuk original oil paintings of jazz-music legends. "I see Miles Davis, Muddy Waters, and B.B. King. What happened to Coltrane?"

"Trane is downstairs where we can start the day together. Can I get you a beer?" A nod later, Morgan handed him a Sea Otter Red Ale and led him past the kitchen to his spacious family room. Morgan cut the volume of a Steve Tyrell album to a whisper so the men could talk, only to have Mott strain to hear the final notes of Tyrell's "That Lovin' Feeling" before looking up.

"Anything earthshaking happening down at the port, Barry? I've been a little out of touch."

"A *little* out of touch? We still don't have your security proposal, and you're running out of time fast. What are you waiting for? Christmas?"

"It will be in your hands shortly. I'm tidying up a few details. Any relevant news while I was gone?"

"Not really. We're updating our five-year capital-improvement plan. Once we get a handle on our upcoming capitalized projects, the cargo ships get bigger, and we have to change the size of the cranes we buy. It's the nature of the beast. You'd be surprised by the variance in crane sizes and how that affects shipping. In fact, since the nineties, the shippers—"

Morgan saw the history lesson coming and ducked under it. "Let me share some news that may hit you in your pocketbook, Barry. A client has asked me to investigate several incidents that appear to be related and may involve the Panama Canal. At least two murders seem to be connected."

Mott appeared startled at the mention of Panama and sharply averted his gaze for a moment before taking a sip of beer. He listened in silence for the next few minutes, nodding briefly twice as Brick disclosed the missing Hanford radioactive waste, the dirty-bomb threat, and the possibility of the canal as a target. His mention of the murders drew no visible reaction.

"Who or what would be the prime beneficiary if Panama's new lock is put out of commission?"

"You should listen to the news more often, Brick. Hell, if you had asked about the whole canal, I would have guessed Islamic militants are at it again. But a threat specific to the third lock, well, that's another story. My money would be on the Chinese. They're years away from completing their Nicaraguan canal, and their yuan are getting caught up in the delays."

Morgan picked up two small stacks of papers from his coffee table and handed one to Mott. "I was copied on this report by a state senator—Ron Coffee, of South Tacoma—that's very critical of what he claims is a lack of preparedness by the Tacoma-Seattle Alliance for the impact of Panama's new lock."

"I read it yesterday, Brick. It's bullshit, pure fucking bullshit," Mott shot back. "Coffee doesn't know what he's talking about. He never even spoke with me, and I'm the president of the Tacoma Port Commission. He's trying to score political points, nothing more."

Mott's raw response raised Brick's eyebrow. "Okay, I get you, but I need your help to understand because he claims the new lock accommodates ships that are twenty-five percent longer, fifty percent wider, and with deeper drafts. He claims the larger ships will bypass the Northwest, pass through the canal, and use ports in Texas, Georgia, and South Carolina. True or not true?"

"It doesn't matter whether it's true or not, Brick. Every cargo ship in the Pacific Ocean can't use Panama's third lock at once. While they're at anchor waiting their turns, they could be off-loading in Tacoma or Seattle."

"But if Coffee is right, and those shipping lines do opt for Panama, won't that cause a big financial hit here? That's Coffee's main point; 'ifs' do happen now and then, Barry."

"And what's his source, a bunch of part-time aides paid by lobbyists? Remember, if ifs and buts were candy and nuts, we'd all have a merry Christmas. Damn it, Coffee's premise is flawed and based on inaccurate information." Mott abruptly pointed to a guitar on a wall across the room. "Hey, what's the history behind that little beauty?"

"A gift. Built by premier guitar-maker Stephen Marchione for Mark Whitfield." Morgan wasn't about to let Mott off topic now when his instincts were screaming for more. "Maybe I'm confused, Barry. Help me understand why Coffee is so wrong. Looking at his numbers, the reasoning seems pretty solid."

"Easy, Brick. This is my business, so trust me to set you straight. Prior to the third lock, the maximum number of containers that could be carried by a ship was five thousand. Those were just called Panamax, one word. The new lock allows for the larger New Panamax ships to transit with up to thirteen thousand TEUs. For the last ten years, foreign shipyards have been building a new class called Ultra Large Cargo Ships. Maersk built six of them in 2006 and 2007 that carry fifteen thousand five hundred containers. "In 2015, MSC built several ultra-large ships that can carry more than nineteen thousand containers, and Maersk now has a class called Triple E. Those big boys can carry over twenty thousand containers. We saw it coming, and we've been replacing our cranes on Blair Waterway to handle them. Piers three and four at Husky Terminal will soon have cranes capable of unloading the Triple E models, which are too large even for the canal's third lock. So damage to the Panama Canal wouldn't have much, if any, impact on us. We're already on top of any supposed 'threat' from Panama. Trust me."

"The last time I heard the words 'trust me' from someone, my ex-wife ran off with the carved ivory chess set my grandfather gave me when I turned twelve."

Mott snorted. "Were you any good at it?"

"I was until I met Raymond Berle in eighth grade. I never did beat him."

"Berle? Any relation to Milton Berle?"

"Who's that?"

"Doesn't matter. Just so you're clear, the POT and the alliance with Seattle are in great shape for the foreseeable future. But I'm a realist. Maybe in fifty years Amazon will be delivering containers by drone."

Morgan nodded. He had done his homework and knew he had just been fed a shovel full of numbers buried in bullshit. Far more New Panamax ships would bypass Northwest ports for the canal than there were ultralarge ships to make up the difference. "I appreciate your insight, Barry. Any additional ideas on this canal cabal?"

"Maybe," Mott said, glancing at his cell phone as if itching to dial. "You didn't hear it from me, but one of our stevedores has been acting suspiciously—sneaking around during his hoot-owl shifts. It's not every night, but once in a while. No apparent schedule to it."

"Think he might be involved in drug drops or pickups?"

"Not likely. Name's Ralph Sprague, a former schoolteacher, married, two kids, spotless record. Our security people have stopped him a few times walking or sitting in areas where he didn't belong, but he always turns up clean. We haven't alerted Homeland Security because we don't really have anything, and once we do call them, well, you can imagine our union issues. What a headache! We're keeping an eye on him, but you might check him out from your end."

"Appreciate the information, Barry. I'll pass it along."

"As far as the canal is concerned, I'm sure it's all Chinese shenanigans. When their Nicaraguan canal opens, you're going to see a lot of competitive mischief going on. That's why we have plan B, Brick. Buying those new cranes was our protection against this canal business. I honestly can't see how this new ditch down south should be worthy of any attention up here."

Hamlet, Act 3 Scene 2: The lady doth protest too much, methinks, Brick thought to himself. Before he could ask another question, Mott abruptly stood, thanked him for the beer, and said he had some office work that needed attention. The men shook hands, and Mott walked briskly to his car while Morgan watched him through the lens of his home's security system.

DETONATION

Mott struggled to juggle his keys in his right hand while his left hastily dialed a cell phone number. Was he just protecting his turf? As his guest sped away, a curious and inexplicable uneasiness settled over Morgan. The answers to his real questions seemed as elusive as ever.

Tick-tock . . .

Chapter Twenty-Five

"Wow! How do you get any work done with a view like this?" asked Nicole almost reverently, beholding the expansive view of the Narrows Bridge from Morgan's high-bank home above Puget Sound. She watched a pair of sailboats tacking south beneath the bridge toward McNeil Island, while a hundred feet away, a lone seagull seemed to float in the breeze, framed against the snow-dusted Olympic Mountains far to the west.

"It's not easy sometimes, Nicole." Morgan grinned, slipping on a sport coat and picking up his car keys. "I just tough it out." The pair had a three o'clock meeting with Port of Tacoma longshoreman Ralph Sprague at his suburban home, and Morgan planned to be on time.

Nodding toward the mammoth bridge, Brick recounted how the original structure—"Galloping Gertie" to the locals—had collapsed in a howling windstorm four months after opening in July 1940. "It just tore itself apart. Its four-lane replacement was completed in 1950, and the new parallel bridge opened in 2007. Together, they're the Narrows Bridge."

"I've read that it gets its fair share of jumpers."

"True. Three somersaults and a *splat*," Morgan replied bluntly. "Saltwater doesn't forgive from two hundred feet. It's like hitting concrete. The local newspaper stopped printing the stories long ago to avoid encouraging jumpers. But they still come."

Nicole turned away and shivered involuntarily. "There must be a better way to check out than jumping. I'd prefer getting shot by a jealous wife."

Morgan glanced at his watch and ushered her out the front door to his car for the twenty-five-minute drive to Lakewood, a sixty-thousand-plus suburb bordered on the south by the adjoined Fort Lewis and McChord air force base. Nicole had flown to Tacoma that morning after learning of Brick's appointment with Sprague and his concerns about Barry Mott.

Brick avoided Interstate 5's afternoon congestion and wound his way past the manicured lawns of the city's west side, through University Place, home of the 2015 US Open Golf Tournament, and into Lakewood, a community seemingly always in transition from one identity to another but never quite pulling it off. One thing it did have was traffic and lots of it. Luckily, Morgan had timed the traffic signals perfectly all the way. "I scheduled the meeting for three because Sprague works from three to eight o'clock on what Mott calls the hoot-owl shift."

Nicole reacted with a subtle laugh. "Hoot owl or graveyard. I knew a lot of cops who used that shift to catch up on their sleep."

"That's reassuring news, Nicole. My guess is that a longshoreman who slept on his shift down at the port might end up in a container bound for China."

They passed Eighty-Third Avenue Southwest and made two more turns on side streets before slowing and stopping before a two-story, white-trimmed gray house with gables jutting above its three-car garage, second-story bedroom, and above a wide and covered front porch supported by twin white columns. The home was set back on a slight hill about seventy feet from the road. A man-made stream gurgled its way from a circular flower bed below a porch through a neatly trimmed patchwork of multicolored shrubs, western ferns, and gold forsythia to a small waterfall and pond in the center of the front yard.

"Looks like the Spragues have done very well. I'd say about three thousand square feet. Value over four hundred thousand," admired Brick as he and Nicole left the car and walked up the brick-paved driveway past a black Mazda SUV and on toward a small brass staircase leading to the home's deep-mahogany-paneled front door.

"Nice garage," offered Nicole as they passed. "I smell a sixty-three

Corvette Split Window hiding behind those doors," she said nonchalantly, drawing a glance from Morgan.

Before they reached the staircase, an electric motor hummed, and both looked toward the garage door, which lifted to their right. A man emerged from the home's interior and turned toward what appeared to be a workbench without seeing them. A radio came on a moment later and music filled the space. Morgan quickly noticed, for resting on the garage floor was a red 1963 Corvette Stingray. Brick and Nicole stared without a word. Finally, Morgan turned toward her.

"Are you clairvoyant? You knew about this guy, didn't you, but how? How could you possibly have known?"

"I'm just smarter than you about cars. It's that simple."

"Listen, Nicole, nobody is sharper than me about Corvettes."

"Well, I am," she replied calmly, head cocked to the right, smile steady as a rock.

"No, you're not."

"I'm totally sharper than you about cars—especially Stingrays."

Morgan was speechless. Finally, he said, "Well, since you appreciate classics so much, why don't we visit the LeMay auto museum downtown? It's full of them. How about it?"

"You're on."

At that moment, the man in the garage thirty feet away spotted them, walked past the 'Vette, and approached. "I'm Ralph Sprague," he said evenly, extending a hand to each of them in turn.

Cofield took the lead and introduced herself and Morgan. His broad smile, chestnut brown hair, and deep amber eyes didn't appear to hide the personality of a criminal as he readily led them into the residence. A moment later, Sprague's wife, Arlene, entered the home's foyer and greeted them with equal warmth. She was blond, about forty, perhaps five two, and observed the world with sparkling brown eyes that peered from behind wire-rimmed glasses resting on her mildly freckled little nose.

The pair led them to a kitchen table that was positioned between a French door and the kitchen. "Can we get you some coffee or a soft drink?"

"I'm fine," replied Cofield.

"Thanks just the same," added Morgan.

Sprague selected a Gatorade from the refrigerator and asked if Arlene could join the conversation.

"That would be fine, and thank you for seeing us on short notice."

"It's not every day that the FBI comes a-calling. You said it was a matter of port security. How can I help you?"

Morgan had interrogated numerous suspects over the years, and he honed in on Sprague's demeanor as Cofield began the interview. Morgan was looking for signs of nervousness or anxiety as much as indicators of deception. A suspect who lies often needs to concentrate or consider his responses more than a person who is speaking truthfully.

Cofield first asked general questions about Sprague's longshoreman duties and began taking notes on a yellow legal pad. A few minutes into the session, she turned her questioning to Sprague's habit of arriving at work early. "Our records indicate that you have arrived at the port as many as two hours before your designated shift time."

"Is that what this is about?" asked Sprague, appearing astonished. Neither Cofield nor Morgan responded, creating a conversational vacuum that kept the pressure on Sprague. "I could just shut up and send you guys packing and call my union rep, but I won't," he said, looking across the table at Arlene. "Are you really here because I come to work a couple hours early?"

"Yes, Ralph. Tell us why," responded Cofield evenly.

Sprague smirked before answering the question. "I come to work early because of hashish, cocaine, and marijuana. I'm interested in the area of Laos, Myanmar, and Thailand along the Mekong River that became known as the Golden Triangle because of the enormous production of opium there in the twentieth century."

"We're aware of it," replied Nicole without skipping a beat.

Morgan was a little confused. *The guy appears not to have a worry in the world. Where's he going with all this?* he wondered to himself. Cofield pressed on with her narcotics-trafficking questions as Arlene leaned her elbows on the table and covered her eyes with her palms.

Sprague paused for a moment and shook his head incredulously. Cofield bored in.

"Mr. Sprague, do I understand that you are involved in the trafficking of illicit drugs. Is that your statement?"

"For heaven's sake, tell them, Ralph!" barked Arlene, whose attempt at stifling laughter failed completely as her shoulders shook and tears began rolling down her face.

"Hell no! I'm not involved in drugs!" Ralph answered sharply. "I'm just screwing with you. The Golden Triangle stuff is true, but it's not what you think. About six months ago, I began writing a screenplay about dope smuggling from Asia into the ports of Canada and the Pacific Northwest. It's a period piece, set in the 1970s when that region produced most of the world's opium, which was refined into heroin and spread everywhere on Earth. China has cracked down hard on opium sales there since the midnineties, basically ceding that revenue to places like Afghanistan. But Afghanistan doesn't have the romantic mysticism to it that the Orient does, which is why I've centered my play there.

"A screenplay is much different than a novel," he continued blandly. "It's an outline of my story in a visual format. As a screenwriter, I need to create a story as it will appear on the screen. I include pictures, sound, and dialogue, and the filmmakers add the rest."

Morgan had heard enough. "What's the title, and what software do you use?"

"Arlene, would you grab my laptop? The working title is *The*

Golden Triangle, but I also like *The Voyage of Bernice.* I write it in Word and save it to two external hard drives that protect the product against a home burglary."

Morgan perked up at hearing "Bernice," which, along with others, such as "dust," "flake," "blow," "line," and "nose candy," has been a popular nickname used by cocaine dealers since his years with the Seattle PD. Arlene returned and handed the laptop to Ralph, who placed it in front of Morgan. Cofield was around the table in a moment, eyes glued to the screen as Sprague pressed an icon bringing his Final Draft 9 screenwriting software to life.

"But why all the sneaking around the port before your shift?" Morgan asked, his eyes following the text as Sprague scrolled down from Act 1, Scene 1, through page thirty-three, where that scene ended and another began.

"Best time to do research and maintain secrecy. The big money guys are always stealing ideas—you know, industrial espionage."

Ten minutes later, Morgan was satisfied that they had treed the wrong cat. He and Cofield thanked the Spragues for their time, wished Ralph good luck on his production, and headed back down the stairs toward the driveway. It was then that Morgan spotted the small decal on a garage window that portrayed a 1963 Corvette that read, "'63 Stingray Club of Washington." He stopped and glared at Cofield, whose attempt at looking innocent failed as she convulsed and stamped her foot for emphasis.

"I carved you up like a Christmas turkey on that one," she declared playfully.

"No, you didn't."

"Yes I did. Totally."

Morgan started to reply when he noticed three goons leaning against his Beemer at the curb. "We've got company. Looks like some heavyweights from the docks. Let me deal with these guys; we'll have less paperwork."

"Okay with me."

Morgan was right about heavyweights. Each of them appeared close to three hundred pounds. All three wore blue jeans and brown work boots and stood motionless with their arms crossed. Two defied the October chill by wearing T-shirts without coats, biceps bulging.

As Morgan and Cofield reached the car, Morgan decided to let the fun begin. "I didn't know the Seahawks were in town this week," he said. "I assume you guys aren't here to make me an offer on my car."

All three took steps toward Morgan and Cofield. The one wearing a Boston Red Sox sweatshirt was the first to speak. "If you got business with one longshoreman, you got business with the whole dock, asshole!"

"Actually, you're wrong about that, bud," said Morgan. "I don't have any business with you or your pals. I am a private detective, though, and the lady here is an FBI agent. We'll be on our way now if you'll just move away from the car."

Tick-tock . . .

Chapter Twenty-Six

Morgan was having no luck diffusing the situation. It wasn't that he hadn't tried, but the three goons standing in a semicircle next to his car were having none of it. He tried another tack, smiling and extending his right hand toward Red Sox Man. "I'm Brick Morgan, and this is FBI Special Agent Nicole Cofield. Who are you, and how can we help you?"

"Name's J.T. Lassiter—T-Bone for short—because I take apart jerks like you and feed 'em to my dog," he growled, arms folded. "We don't take kindly to one of our family being hassled by a couple of Nazis."

"Really? Well, you may enjoy boning other men, but that has nothing to do with why Agent Cofield and I are here today."

Red Sox Man took a menacing step forward, stopping two feet in front of Brick, who didn't move an inch.

"Our business with Mr. Sprague is between him and us. It's none of your business, the longshoremen union's business, or the Girl Scouts' business. Now if you'll move away from my car, we'll be on our way."

"What if we don't feel like moving?"

"Let me explain it, assuming your IQs are greater than pumpkins." Morgan turned slightly toward the second man wearing a light rust-colored T-shirt with greasy, short brown hair and the third man with a graying black beard, graphite eyes, and a toothpick protruding from his mouth. "Agent Cofield has already uploaded your pictures to the bureau, so your options are few. If you don't move away from my car, we will have no choice but to move you. There's a small chance you'll win the fight, which won't be easy with bullets in your knees and hips, but regardless, each of you will sustain broken bones and then be charged with assault and battery. In Agent Cofield's case, you'll be charged—and convicted—in federal court because, as I just told you, she's a special agent of the FBI."

Cofield, eyes blazing with fire, held up her credentials as each man glanced her way nervously.

"Because Agent Cofield will be injured, each of you will face prison terms up to twenty-five years. But you're all tough cookies; you'll survive federal prison and those long, lonely nights, no problem. Now, if there's nothing else, let me open the door for you, Agent Cofield. It's time for these gentlemen to prepare for their shift at the port."

"Hold on, buddy," hissed Red Sox Man between clenched teeth. "She won't get hurt if we don't touch her."

"You're forgetting something," Morgan responded as Cofield began rubbing her arm briskly as if in pain. "She'll be writing the report."

Still seething, the men moved ever so slightly away from the car as Morgan opened the passenger door for Cofield and then entered on the driver's side. He started the car and put it in gear. Then he rolled down the driver's side window and looked back at Red Sox Man. "By the way, sport," he said acidly, "your fly's open." Morgan glanced in the rearview mirror as they drove away in time to see the stunned bully grappling furiously with his stuck zipper. While one of his friends extended both middle fingers toward Morgan's departing sedan, the other pointed toward Lassiter's dilemma.

"Need a hand, T-Bone? Catch your pecker in there, and you'll need stitches."

"You touch me, Carl, and I'll rip your throat out!"

Dexter Copeland, "Dex" to his friends, had joined the FBI straight out of Arizona State University in 1984, recruited for his brilliance in mathematics, accounting, and computer technology. His leadership as captain of the ASU Sun Devils basketball team had also caught the agency's eye. Copeland's first posting had been to the bureau's Denver office, where he worked on several major cases relating to industrial accounting fraud before moving on to San Francisco in a similar capacity in 1992 and to Salt Lake City in 2001. Originally from Portland, Oregon, he jumped at the chance in 2010 to become Special Agent in Charge of the smaller, but key office in Tacoma, which borders on Washington's two largest military installations and the burgeoning Port of Tacoma.

Copeland and his three agents had been assigned to oversee security for Chinese president Xi Jinping's upcoming visit to Tacoma's Lincoln High School as part of the president's goodwill tour of the US. But the timing for Dex Copeland could hardly have been worse. The runny nose had begun on Tuesday; a day later came the cough and sore throat, and by Thursday, he was personally elevating the stock of Theraflu Multi-Symptom, popping the caplets like candy to ward off a 103-degree fever and associated aches he hadn't felt since his basketball days at ASU.

By the time President Jinping departed Tacoma late Thursday afternoon, Special Agent Copeland was nearly out on his feet and sure the Grim Reaper couldn't be far away. He contacted his secretary, Evelyn Simmons, and asked her to call Emily McClelland to postpone her visit to his office until ten o'clock Monday morning.

Five minutes after arriving home, Copeland was in a hot shower, and ten minutes after that he took another round of medication supplied by his wife and slid into bed, electric blanket pegged on high. Dex Copeland wouldn't be thinking about Emily McClelland for more than three days.

Tick-tock . . .

Chapter Twenty-Seven

The dark and thick cumulonimbus clouds rolled menacingly across the sky, bringing with them another round of the heavy rain and wind that had battered the city for the last four days. The autumn storms sweep down from the Gulf of Alaska or spin northeast from the Pacific Ocean. Either way, they mark the Pacific Northwest as the rainfall capital of America.

A storm of another sort was brewing in the North Tacoma home of Gaston Rizzo—one with far different implications.

Seated on a pair of brown leather sofas arranged around a first-floor stone fireplace were he and fellow business partners Larry Hickman, Mark LoNigro, and Carlo Conti. There were final decisions to make today.

Rizzo held the floor, wearing a gray wool sweater and jeans over brown loafers and a no-nonsense expression. His slightly disheveled appearance was that of a man who had already been awake for several hours this Saturday morning.

"In less than two weeks this job will be over. Before we delve into the details, we need to look at security a final time and lock it down tight. Two specific vulnerabilities have brought down many businesses like ours. The first is sloppy communication." Rizzo let the last word hang in the air for a moment, glancing at each of the others before adding, "And the second is a lack of firewalls between us and the soldiers we hire."

"Don't forget stupidity and spending money like drunken sailors," offered Hickman. "I've represented those geniuses, Gas."

"Yes, and we don't want to end up where they did, Larry. Now listen up. Once this begins, pull the SIM card on your cell phones and remove the batteries. Don't forget! These are different times, gentlemen. Electronic gadgets out there today can trick your phone and enable cops and the NSA to read every text message you send or receive."

"And put this tape over your phone's camera eye," said Conti, handing each man a small roll of black electrical tape. "Malware out there can activate them automatically. Not a good thing!"

"All right, let's look at this job from thirty thousand feet," Rizzo continued. "The Carbone organization collapsed here in seventy-eight because they had no firewalls. Once the Feds found a loose thread, the whole ball began to unravel. The FBI started cutting deals with their street soldiers, and soon they had the names of the crooked sheriff and John Carbone. The rest is history.

"We haven't gone down that road because we've kept a tight ship. All our job inquiries have filtered through Irv Kelso at the Dolphin's Whistle. Until this moment, there have been no leaks. Now I'm asking each of you: Is there anything whatsoever that you know, or even suspect, that changes that assessment, because if there is, we all need to hear it right now."

"No way. Kelso knows none of us," said Hickman. "We're clean."

"As clean as it gets," agreed LoNigro, attired in jeans, black work boots, and red sweatshirt. "Depending on our future, we should keep paying him for a while after we retire."

"A conversation for another day, Mark. Right now, we're discussing risk assessment, and your piece of this pie is now the riskiest. Lay out your plans so everyone is crystal clear."

"We've hashed this over for months, Gas."

"Humor us again, Mark!" growled Rizzo.

"I arrange our 'associates' through an ex-con named Perez at a biker bar near Olympia. He thinks my name is Doyle and that I'm part of an Irish independence gang. The pukes he finds never have contact with me. There've been no breeches. We're ready, Gas; let's go. I'm tired of waiting."

Rizzo was apoplectic. "You're tired of waiting?" he snarled. "Damn it, Mark, that's what the first wave of GIs was saying about Omaha Beach before D-Day—'We're tired of waiting'—and look what happened to them! We already know about your Olympia connections! Take us to the damned cruise ship. What you do there is the crux of the entire bloody operation. Spit it out, man!"

LoNigro casually flipped a passport at Rizzo. "Meet the new Bart M. Stevenson. I have medical documents supporting my lung disease, and Diamond Cruise Lines has approved my use of oxygen cylinders. At noon Tuesday, I'll head for San Diego in a Ford Transit van that will be left for me near the University of Puget Sound. Karen thinks I'm going to a homebuilder's convention in Houston. Along the way, I'll find all-night grocery stores, park in their lots, and sleep in the van. That pace should get me into San Diego Thursday evening, and I'll remove the oxygen tanks from a storage unit that's been rented for me at Seaport Village near the pier where the ship will be moored."

"Hold on," sputtered Conti, raising a hand. "We're getting ahead of ourselves. The cylinders were retrofitted last weekend. Our Santa Barbara physicist utilized the same electrified translucent glass process that we used to steal the sludge from Hanford. He then drove to Boise, Idaho, where the extinguishers were stored for us in a rented lab, and transferred the juice to the cylinders. He says this was done without incident, and he's had a Geiger counter with him the entire time."

"So the professor now drives to San Diego and leaves the tanks in a storage unit for Mark?" asked Hickman.

"Negative. The professor will remain in Boise until Tuesday morning to check the Geiger counter twice a day. That's where our mule, an ex-con named Cody Dettering, enters the picture. Cody and the professor each will have a burner phone for the sole purpose of communicating Tuesday. If the Geiger counter detects any problems, the professor will contact Cody and warn him away from the laboratory.

Otherwise, Cody will use his key to enter the lab at seven, remove the cylinders and the Geiger counter, and depart for San Diego where he'll store the package for Mark and leave. The men will never meet, and we'll have no further contact with the professor."

"Cody is one tight dude," LoNigro chimed in. "I hired him through Perez in Olympia last June to burn four fireworks stands on the Colville Indian Reservation that were interfering with our client's profit margin. He's handled a few other things since then, and I like him for this job. It's ironic; the guy actually has a lung disease—COPD from smoking all his life—which makes him ideal to transport the oxygen cylinders. Cody's got his own medical documentation for having oxygen tanks with him. He doesn't do drugs, and he cleans up well. He's perfect."

"Okay, my legal background is getting the better of me," Hickman said. "Why was he in prison?"

"Felony battery. He got into a bar fight in Centralia and ground a broken whiskey bottle into a man's face."

"Okay—enough information." Hickman shook his head slowly and asked nothing more.

"Friday morning, I'll pack both tanks and the two magnums of C-4 into two suitcases along with two changes of clothes and drop it off at the cruise ship terminal, where I'll check in. I've got a two-wheeled walker and a real oxygen tank, air tubing, and nose inhalator as props. From there, I'll park the van in a lot near the USS Midway Museum and make my way back to the pier. Later that day, the van will be driven to Oregon, where it will disappear.

"I'll board the *Rose Diamond* before noon with my walker and a carry-on bag containing my passport, laptop, medical papers, medications, toothbrush, and shaving gear. A few gasps at the right moments as I walk up the gangway with my oxygen gear, and I should be on my way to my cabin. I've also got a shoulder bag that holds one oxygen cylinder, making it easier for me to move around once I'm aboard.

"I found a schematic of the *Rose* online, and I've studied it for days. The ship's a big sucker—fifteen decks, over a thousand feet long, a hundred twenty-five-foot beam, and more than a hundred twenty-four thousand tons. She weighs anchor at one o'clock Friday and is due to arrive in the third lock the following Tuesday. I'll rest up for a day after I board and start snooping around Saturday night when the partying begins."

Rest up! You're not the only one who's tired, Rizzo thought. He let his mind wander. He'd been brooding all morning. Something was missing, but what? He couldn't quite put his finger on it, and the feeling ate at him. His zest for adventure and making money had ebbed over the last year, and he had considered retiring to a less exhilarating and less-lucrative life. Then came the anonymous call and the job proposal of a lifetime. Not jumping at it would have been like Admiral Nimitz sitting out World War II. Still, he was past his prime, and in his heart he felt the Panama job might be the grand finale of the business that had brought him so much satisfaction and wealth. And some of that money had even been earned honestly . . . well, almost. Rizzo snickered to himself.

A sudden, bright flash outside lit up the room and was followed instantly by a thunderclap that seemed to explode right above the house. Driven by a persistent heavy wind, the rain came in sheets, pounding on the roof and overwhelming the gutters. Rizzo glanced outside, grimaced, and then set another cedar log in the fireplace. On the other hand, Arizona *was* nice this time of year . . .

But first things first. Conti interrupted LoNigro again.

"Mark can use the walker's tank carrier depending on the circumstances, and the dummy tank will maintain his cover after he places the charges in the ship. The tanks themselves are twenty-six inches tall, perfect to hold the hot sauce."

"Fine, but are you satisfied they were properly retrofitted and that Mark can get them on the ship?"

"As satisfied as I can be from here, Gas. More importantly, our professor is confident with the retrofit. Remember, the glass is made with layers of polymer-dispersed boron crystals, and when electric current is applied, the crystals all align along several parallel axes—"

"Enough bullshit! Will the damn thing work or not?"

"Yes, it will work. As long as our batteries keep energizing the glass, we won't trigger any radiation monitors. The batteries the professor used are brand-new, and we have spares. As Mark said earlier, we're ready. Any other questions?"

Hickman turned to LoNigro. "Explain how you'll use the C-4."

"As I said, the C-4 will be within the wine bottles that will board with me. I'll use two kinds of blasting caps that will be hidden inside a MacBook Pro in my carry-on bag. The primary will be an M-6 military cap setoff with an electrical charge initiated by a call to a cell phone."

"Like the IEDs used by the Taliban," murmured Hickman.

"Similar, but not nearly as powerful," LoNigro replied. "The backup plan will be a nonelectric blasting cap setoff with a timed fuse. The first blast will occur in the crew bar on the starboard side near the bow once the ship enters the middle chamber of the Pacific lock. This charge will blow a hole roughly sixteen inches in diameter below the waterline, flooding the compartment. The watertight doors will close, limiting damage to the bar."

"What about damage to people *in* the bar?" asked Hickman incredulously.

"No crew members are allowed in cruise-ship bars during canal transits, Larry.

"Since you mentioned the crew, how do you expect to be wandering around down belowdecks without being challenged?"

"There will be more than eleven hundred crewmen on that ship. I'll be wearing a blue jumpsuit over my clothes, identical to those of crew members working in engineering spaces. If anyone questions me, I'll respond with gibberish and be arrogant about it. My grandparents were Portuguese; I'll use a few words of it if necessary. It's all in attitudes. I'll just act like I belong there and keep moving."

"I don't like it, Mark. You're courting disaster with this cockamamie idea. A dozen things could go wrong, and if just one of them does, it all falls apart."

"Listen to me, Larry. I'll have no problem getting to the crew bar to set that charge. I've even obtained a set of skeleton keys from a Diamond Cruise Line source that should get me through any door on the ship, including the crew bar. We paid handsomely for those keys. If they don't work and we have to scrub the mission, my source will receive an unexpected visitor."

Hickman opened his mouth to speak, but nothing came out.

"Stay with me. I'll be in my cabin when I call the cell phone, setting off the first bomb. The crew will head to their emergency stations and assist with evacuation of the passengers. Meanwhile, I'll locate a cart or hand truck, wrap the dirty-bomb cylinders in a blanket, and just wheel them down the passageway to a service elevator near my suite that I can take to deck four. I'll plant that bomb in a refrigeration room there. Then I'll take an elevator up several flights, remove my jumpsuit in a restroom stall, and discard it.

"Once passengers and most of the crew are off the *Rose*, I'll dial the burner phone from my cabin to trigger the dirty bomb and then join the crew leaving the ship. The blast will blow a second hole in the ship, flooding deck four. With the bar already flooded, that will be enough to slowly ease the ship to the bottom, blocking the channel. The radiation will spread throughout the blast area as planned. That completes our mission."

"How can you possibly know if everyone is off the ship?" demanded Hickman, his voice rising. "And what exactly is your 'backup plan'?"

"It's not an exact science, Larry, but once the second blast occurs, radiation monitors aboard would warn the captain and any lingering crewmen to disembark. If the second bomb doesn't explode, I'll return to the freezer and reset the charge with an Abrams nonelectric blasting cap and timed fuse. By the time that blows, I'll be disembarking with my oxygen gear and the final crewmen."

"Is this Abrams fuse what's referred to as det cord?"

"No. Detonation cord is not a fuse; it's an explosive used to wrap around doors to blow openings for SWAT teams. A timed fuse burns slowly according to its setting. Any more questions?" asked LoNigro. The others shook their heads. "In that case, Gas, I'd like to hear details of your plan for getting us out of Panama once we terminate the cruise."

"My plan is very simple. I'll fly to Tocumen Airport near Panama City the day before the ship arrives at the canal and stay at the Gamboa Rainforest Resort about an hour east of Panama City and located next to the Chagres River, which is after the Pacific third lock. That locale will give me a perfect view of the canal.

"When the first charge goes off, I'll use a burner phone to send a prerecorded message in Spanish to the Panama Canal Authority and an English message to Diamond Cruise Lines. The purpose is to motivate them both to evacuate the cruise ship. From that point, I'll wait another twenty minutes at the hotel. If I see the *Rose* pass, I'll know the second package failed. Either way, I'll head back to the airport. Your next job, Mark, is to slip out of the canal zone after the second blast and meet me at Tocumen, where we'll use fresh passports and aliases and fly to Houston. From there, we return home."

"Slip out of the canal zone along with the other three thousand passengers?"

"Find a civilian and offer him a pocket full of hundred-dollar bills for the ride. Serious American green still works wonders in Panama."

Rizzo took a moment as the others assimilated his report in what likely was the last meeting of the criminal organization he had founded in the 1980s. *Enough is enough. Know when to fold 'em*, he thought. His occasional flashes of smoking cigars on a beach in Aruba seemed closer to reality.

"One more thing," said Rizzo as Hickman started to stand. "You were the last one to talk with Steinberg, Larry. What's your read on his frame of mind?"

"His ass is tighter than a banjo string. He hardly said a word. Most of my time with him was spent closing out his share of our funds. As we agreed, he was happy to receive sixty-five percent of his original projected share."

"Are you comfortable that he's now a nonissue? Be honest. Is he going to be a problem? We've never had a member go sideways; it could be new territory."

"All I can speak to is what I saw—and didn't hear. He wants nothing to do with this operation. He's very conscientious, and I respect that. Besides, he's made a ton of money with his currency-exchange business. He could retire tomorrow with a fortune."

Hickman stopped, wrinkled his nose, and looked at the others.

"What's the problem, Larry?" asked Conti.

"Simple. Detonating C-4 is serious business. You worked with it in 'Nam and should know that better than any of us. My stomach has been doing flips for months over this, and it's not going away. The money isn't worth the aggravation."

"Why?"

"Because we've been dancing on the edge of a black hole for thirty years, Gas. This job is right on the edge; our luck might be running out. Our only saving grace has been that we've done our business without anyone getting killed. When I think about explosions on a cruise ship, I think we've crossed a very big line."

If he only knew the truth, Rizzo thought. He knew Larry would go ballistic if he learned about the hits on Pearce and Zigler. No telling what he'd do.

"Damn it, we just went through this with Mitch," said Rizzo. "You've got to trust Mark. He won't pull the trigger on the C-4 until the area is clear of passengers and crew and the *Rose* is sitting empty in the middle chamber of the Pacific lock. It's a piece of cake."

"Well, I don't know. It seems so—"

"I *do* know! Mark will deal with the ship; you just move the money so the Feds can't find us. Okay?"

Hickman nodded quietly and stared into the crackling fire. Outside, the gale was picking up steam, whipping the rain almost sideways against the house. Hickman started to say something but remained silent, his eyes back on the fire.

"It will all work out, Larry," grinned LoNigro before turning to another topic. "I've done some legwork into this Brick Morgan character you mentioned, Gas."

"Who's Brick Morgan?" asked Hickman, looking up quickly.

"He's a private investigator who specializes in maritime crimes," LoNigro responded. "God only knows how he stumbled onto the missing Hanford material. Morgan was with the Justice Department several years ago."

"This is the first I've heard of him," said Hickman, clearly shocked, as he looked first at LoNigro and then Rizzo. "How does he figure into this?"

LoNigro shrugged. "It's not that big a deal, Larry. He apparently learned of the Hanford theft and has been fishing around, but no matter where he looks, he won't find us because there's no connection."

"If a good PI knows something, the FBI also knows it, Mark. That's an absolute."

"There's no trail for them to follow. It's that simple."

Rizzo turned to an end table and selected an AVO No. 2 from a humidor. The room was silent while he cut the cigar, set it afire, and returned to his recliner. "Larry, you and I are the only ones who have had recent contact with our money conduit behind this mission. While Mark and I are gone, I'd like you to grind on the guy for more cash. Tell him our expenses have doubled—whatever it takes. And CC, have someone put a tail on Morgan. I don't like loose ends, and

Morgan's a fucking loose end."

As the men prepared to depart, the ringing of one of Rizzo's burner phones interrupted them.

"There's only one person who has that phone number," said Rizzo. Tick-tock . . .

Chapter Twenty-Eight

Morgan dropped off Nicole at the Hotel Murano late Friday and drove home to reply to a dozen messages and give them both some downtime.

A cold-weather front moving in from the north encouraged him to ignite his gas fireplace a moment after entering. Five minutes later, his Keurig coffee maker produced another needed antidote for the chill, and he settled into an overstuffed chair to think things over. The information he and Nicole had gathered was almost nil, and he knew time was running out.

There were notes to compare and theories to discuss in a case that had more sinister twists than a Wenatchee rattler. He needed Nicole, and she needed him. Besides, he missed her already. Morgan picked up his cell phone and dialed. She answered on the first ring.

"Hi there, stranger," she laughed.

"Hi right back, Nicole. How about this: I'll pick you up at nine in the morning and take you to a great place for a late breakfast where we can pick apart this case. I'll even sweeten the deal with something I haven't mentioned yet."

"You're on, cowboy! I figured you would be sitting around your fireplace by now."

"I *am* sitting in front of my fireplace, but I figured since both of us is thinking over this case by ourselves, we ought to be doing it together. Plus, I'd hate to see you miss a great breakfast."

"How thoughtful of you."

"I'm just that kinda guy."

Nicole was wearing a hooded parka over jeans and a heavy orange sweatshirt when Morgan ushered her into his car outside the Murano at two minutes past nine on Saturday. The drive to Marcia's Silver Spoon Café on South Tacoma Way took less than ten minutes, time enough for Nicole to share the latest information from Hanford.

"Remember Ramona from DOE and Agent Early?"

"Sure. Ramona was fine; Early needed an attitude adjustment."

"Maybe. I've never worked with him before. They found video that suggests the stolen material was smuggled out of Hanford in two fire extinguishers."

"No way!"

"That's the way it looks, Brick."

"Hold onto that thought," he said, pulling into a parking spot beneath a large sign reading "Café" resting atop a red-and-white Coca-Cola logo. The eatery was located in an industrial area far from the city's trendy restaurant row. Three cars and an old green pickup truck were parked outside.

"Really, Brick?" asked Nicole, looking over the vintage building's exterior with a raised eyebrow.

"Don't let the location fool you. Trust me on this one."

The restaurant was nearly full as they entered. Brick requested a spot in back being vacated by two seventy-something men wearing military veterans caps and satisfied smiles. A cheerful waitress wiped off the red table with the "Silver Spoon" logo in the center, handed the new arrivals menus, and poured coffee for both before departing.

"Now what's this about fire extinguishers?"

Nicole spoke softly, describing how security cameras had captured video of two fire extinguishers being removed from the Hanford lab a few days before the two liters of nuclear waste turned up missing. "The name on the truck and the uniforms of the employees were bogus. Ramona believes a lab tech devised a way to put the muck into the extinguishers and the accomplices just walked out the door with it. What has everyone stumped is why the building's radioisotope identification alarms didn't react."

They ordered a minute later and resumed their discussion.

"With radiation, Nicole, the only thing that stops gamma rays is lead. A lead fire extinguisher would weigh a ton."

"Ramona said the same thing, but these guys carried them out easily." She spread her hands, palms up. "Another conundrum."

"There's an answer; we just have to figure it out. Meanwhile, let me run something else by you."

"Some*thing* or some*one*?"

"Barry Mott, president of the Tacoma Port Commission. I mentioned him on the phone."

"You mentioned having *concerns*. What are they?"

"Let me elaborate a bit and offer a suggestion for testing a theory I have. He approached me in September about submitting a proposal to upgrade the port's security to complement protection provided by DHS and the coast guard. We've had several conversations since then, and he's lied to me every time."

"So don't submit a proposal."

"There's more to it than that. When I mentioned the stolen Hanford material and that authorities also were focusing on the Panama Canal and two murders, you would have thought I'd set his hair on fire. He denied proof that Panama's third lock would have any economic impact on West Coast ports and was adamant that the Chinese would be the prime suspects if harm came to the canal, which I don't believe for a second. Then he fed me Ralph Sprague, which was more bullshit. The man is clearly deceptive, and I've got a gut feeling that he's also corrupt."

"So he's another political animal spouting BS. How does that make him corrupt?"

"Remember, he contacted *me* about the port security proposal, so why would he blatantly lie when I asked questions about the canal's potential effect on future port business? He clammed up completely when I mentioned the murders."

"You think the security proposal was a red herring?"

"No, I believe that was legitimate. The red herring was his Ralph Sprague story. But why send me on a wild-goose chase? The only reason that makes sense is that he seriously regrets contacting me in the first place. I've been an investigator for a long time, Nicole. Something's up with this guy, I can feel it. And I'd bet my Beemer that it involves the canal."

"Your gut feeling and five bucks may get you a cup of coffee at Starbucks, but you'll have to do much better than that to get serious attention from the FBI. I'm a big believer in instincts, but the bureau needs actionable evidence before it puts Mott under surveillance."

"I'm getting to that."

"Wait a second, Brick. I went out on a limb and requested an assessment on Mr. Mott to see if he's had any irregular financial transactions. It's not much, but it's something. The Hanford theft is a full-blown investigation, and the National Terrorism Task Force is on red alert. It seems you still have friends in high places."

"Don't give me that much credit. If memory serves, that means we have thirty days to firm up probable cause."

"Yep."

"The problem is we don't have thirty days, Nicole. We may not have thirty *hours*."

"I know that," she growled softly. "But we need more than your *gut feeling*!"

Just then, their breakfast platters arrived, drawing wide-eyed approval from Nicole and a satisfied grin from Morgan. Coffee cups were refilled, and he leaned closer.

"Listen carefully, Nicole. I've got a plan."

"I'm glad one of us does," she said, pointing her fork at him. "Let's have it, buster."

"Help me set up Barry Mott."

"I'm listening," she said, digging into a plate of country fried steak and eggs.

"We carefully feed him—only him—some information and watch him act on it. If he takes the bait, we've got him."

"Got him for what exactly?"

"It's too soon to tell."

"Your breakfast is getting cold, Brick," she said skeptically.

"Let me finish. I'll call him and report that Sprague is not a suspect. Then I'll say the bureau shared some confidential information that a Portland pimp arranged for a Brazilian prostitute to set up Dick Zigler in Long Beach, and that after learning her client was later killed, he wants to clarify that he only arranged the meeting—nothing more. I'll say the guy just bailed out of jail on a drug charge and hopes to avoid a prison sentence in Oregon by telling what he knows about Zigler. Finally, I'll tell him the pimp saw my name in a news story about Zigler and asked to meet me in Portland because he doesn't trust federal agents."

"Your scenario doesn't wash, Brick. The pimp would have nothing to sell and nothing to gain from meeting with you. Zigler was killed in Long Beach, which is a California state crime. The pimp would be facing prison on another state crime in Oregon. The FBI wouldn't get involved unless—"

"Exactly. *Unless* the pimp's story could help the bureau solve a major federal case."

"A case that doesn't exist right now."

"All we would do is feed Mott the story and see if we get a reaction."

"Sounds like a long shot."

"It's better than no shot at all." Morgan speared a slice of sausage and avoided Nicole's bemused expression.

"You remind me of a bulldog we had when I was a kid. Once

he got hold of something, he wouldn't let go until he was good and ready."

"It's all in the feisty company I keep, Nicole."

"Could Mott be the head of the snake? You don't expect him to actually show up, do you?"

"Very unlikely on both counts; it's too sophisticated. He's not a hands-on guy, but behind the scenes, he could be involved right up to his hundred-dollar ties. The heist from Hanford, killing of the science teacher, and the butchery in Seal Beach required an organization. If he is connected at some level, I'm counting on him getting worried and passing the story to the dudes doing the heavy lifting."

Nicole set down her fork, dabbed her mouth with her napkin, and looked at him almost as if seeing him for the first time. Her expression softened. "You do have the courage of your convictions, Mr. Morgan."

He looked directly into her eyes. "There's something else I believe, Nicole. Right here, right now, it's up to us."

They ate in silence for several minutes before Brick retrieved his iPhone and began searching for a suitable Portland location for an FBI sting, finally settling on the historic Sentinel Hotel in city center.

"We set up shop tomorrow after I tell Mott the pimp will meet me for a drink there that night. Can you get a federal agent to play along?"

"You mean ask him if he's willing to become a target to support your theory?"

"The whole idea is to draw out someone related to the conspiracy and see where that leads us. We'll both be there, and all of us will wear Kevlar just in case."

She nodded. "I'll arrange it, but if this goes badly, my next job posting may be a night shift in Alaska."

Morgan pressed a button on his key fob and started his sedan remotely, its heater running. "Look, if this doesn't draw someone out, we'll leave the bar, go up to my room, and wait another half hour. If nothing materializes, we go home. Fair enough?"

"I hope so, Brick. I really do."

Morgan took his last bite of home fries a few minutes later, dropped three twenties on the glass-topped table, and they headed outside, where they were greeted by pouring rain and an icy north wind that nearly stopped Nicole in her tracks. A streetlight a block away seemed to dance in the wind a moment before its lights went out, nearly causing collisions in both directions.

They got in the car, and Morgan checked the National Weather Service website on his iPhone. "Let me make a suggestion," he began, a frown creasing his features.

"I read you loud and clear. Let me grab a bag at my hotel, and we'll flesh out the details on our way."

Their early departure due to weather concerns would get them into Portland by late afternoon, leaving them a day to iron out details before Morgan and a local agent would act out a meeting Sunday night.

Morgan found a parking spot near the Murano's front door. His go bag was already in the car. While Nicole went upstairs, he phoned Mott from the lobby, thanking him for the Ralph Sprague tip and saying the man had checked out okay.

"I'm not sure this is relevant to your port, Barry, but we have a lead the FBI thinks is worth a look. A Portland pimp apparently arranged a hooker to set up a honey trap."

"What's a honey trap?"

"A woman seduces a target to a hotel room where he's videotaped having sex with her and then blackmailed. The pimp has agreed to have a drink with me at the Sentinel tomorrow night in Portland. It may be nothing, but he claims to have the name of whoever hired him to trap a guy named Dick Zigler in Long Beach. Zigler was later murdered, possibly in connection with a plot against the Panama Canal. It may be a waste of time, Barry, but if not, I might have our first good lead on the missing nuclear waste and the canal plot."

"Why in the hell would he contact *you?*"

"I was there moments after Zigler was killed. My name and company was mentioned in a news story, and he called me."

"Let me get this straight; you're going to meet a Portland pimp who you believe might be a key player in the theft of radioactive waste from Hanford and a plan to harm the Panama Canal. Is that what I'm hearing? And you're serious?"

"It's thin as a gnat's ass, Barry, I know that, but the guy seems convincing. Says he'll tell what he knows if it will help him reduce a drug charge he's looking at in Oregon. Wants to talk with me because he doesn't trust the Feds."

"I don't trust the bastards either, Brick. Anyway, thanks for the call and good luck."

Forty minutes later, with reservations made at the Sentinel and FBI approvals and meeting times set, Morgan and Cofield detoured around a freeway fender bender, entered I-5 at South Fifty-Sixth Street, and eased into the passing lane, where they remained for the next three hours.

Portland's Sentinel Hotel began life in 1909 as the Seward Hotel, a boutique facility designed by Oregon architect William Knighton. It was renamed the Governor Hotel in 1932, a name it kept after reopening in 1992 following an extensive multiyear remodel that doubled its size by blending in an adjacent Italian Renaissance-style building that formerly housed the Portland's Elks Lodge. A second major remodel was completed in 2014, and the sumptuous structure was rechristened the Sentinel. Morgan had stayed there twice during business visits to the Port of Portland. It was ideal for the plan he and Nicole had devised on their way south.

Moderate rain was falling when they arrived late afternoon on Saturday, the temperature a relatively balmy forty-six degrees, more than twenty degrees warmer than the cold front moving into Tacoma 150 miles north. They entered the hotel fifteen minutes apart to avoid being seen together while also arranging nearby rooms on the third floor. They had a day to kill.

Damn it, Mott. Take the bait, Morgan thought to himself. He checked in at the reception counter and took an elevator to the third floor, admiring the large black-and-white period photographs decorating the hallway as he walked to his parlor suite. He entered the suite's bedroom, laid his bag on the king-size bed, and sent Nicole a text message. "In 385. Come on up,"

Nicole had just entered the hotel when she texted a reply. "Have met Portland agent. He will be up a few minutes after me."

Morgan placed a yellow legal pad and his iPhone and iPad on a desk facing a floor-to-ceiling window overlooking city center and scanned a brochure describing the inspiration behind the hotel's art collection. A striking photo of jazz saxophonist John Coltrane working in studio on his classic 1958 *Blue Train* album caught his eye. Morgan nodded and made a mental note to find a copy of the photo online when time allowed.

Which wasn't right now. Nicole was at the door.

Three minutes later, another knock signaled the arrival of FBI Special Agent Noah McDowell. Before Nicole could make introductions, Morgan's face lit up. "McD, where the hell have you been for the last ten years?" Both men smiled broadly and joined in a momentary bear hug.

"Big Brick, my friend, you look great!" McDowell was about six two, weighed 215 pounds, and wore a bushy red beard and shoulder-length light-brown hair, befitting his role as an undercover agent. He was attired in dirty jeans, old Pendleton work shirt, and used brown work boots. An ancient blue bomber jacket completed his ensemble.

Nicole's face went blank. "What am I missing?"

"Noah and I were law school classmates at Stanford. We studied together and spent many an evening at the Oasis Pub. He's a whiskey sour man." With that, Morgan popped ice cubes into glasses and withdrew two whiskeys from the room bar for himself and McDowell and a small bottle of Chardonnay and a chilled glass for Nicole. Morgan sat in the desk chair and motioned for McDowell to take a seat next to Nicole on the parlor's long dark green sofa.

"Brick's tutoring got me across the finish line in a hellish contracts law course during our first year, Nicole. If it hadn't been for him, I'd probably be in the lawn-maintenance industry somewhere today."

Morgan had moved to Washington after law school and lost track of McDowell for a time before learning he had joined the bureau. "Looks like you dressed the part for tomorrow night's gig, Noah."

"My wife says I'm a fashion plate."

"Back to business, gentlemen," said Nicole picking up a notepad. "What time did you give Mott for the meeting, Brick?"

"I didn't. I said I'd be having a drink with the pimp at the Sentinel Sunday night. To most people that's a clear reference to the cocktail lounge."

"The Jackknife should give us plenty of defensive options. It's roomy, has subdued lighting, plenty of cover. My only concern is customers," said McDowell. "A shooter would have both of us and a clean getaway to consider."

"Unless there are multiple shooters," said Nicole, warily.

"I think it's too public for that. If it were me—"

"But it's *not* you, Noah. You're thinking like a good guy," Nicole argued. "That friendly bar could become a kill zone in seconds."

"That's where you come in, Nicole," said Brick innocently. "You're a crack shot. I checked with a friend at the bureau before I got you involved in this."

Nicole's stare back at him could have melted Iceland.

"I've done this before," McDowell volunteered. "Shooting up a crowded bar is too public. I would try to separate us and either propose a payoff or try intimidation."

Nicole shook her head. "We can prepare for that, but I think they'll wait and follow you two when you leave the bar. My money's on a confrontation in Brick's room."

"I agree, but they don't know my room number," replied Morgan.

"A hundred-dollar bill to the right check-in staff could take care of that," she said.

Twenty minutes later, Morgan left the two agents to update their bosses and went downstairs to recon the Jackknife located off the lobby in the hotel's west wing, which formerly housed the Elks Temple. The bar was added during the 2013–2014 renovation to replace a portion of the lobby, offices, and storage space. He hadn't visited since the reopening and stopped at the entry to take stock.

Nice! Move this to Tacoma and it could be my regular watering hole, he mused to himself. Designers had made extensive use of dark woods for walls, moldings, and seating areas throughout, including tables, booths, and the two-dozen wood- and leather-trimmed barstools surrounding the bar itself, nine of which were occupied at the moment. Subdued schoolhouse-style lighting gave the place a sophisticated ambience Morgan found inviting. He admired a large black-and-white photograph of a boy and his Schwinn bike taken at least a half century ago and mounted above a centrally located granite- and wood-framed fireplace. Emerald-green club chairs and dark paneling complemented the random maple spice floor. The prodigious and mirrored L-shaped bar reflected multiple shelves of domestic and imported liquors and a lineup of craft-beer spigots.

From a tactical perspective, the lounge presented challenges, mainly in the form of patrons. Brick had lost Dick Zigler in a bar just days ago, and though he tried telling himself the Sunday night setup would be perfect, he knew it really wasn't. Few things were. Hands thrust deep into his pockets, he turned and headed for the elevator and Room 385.

Morgan had spent a restless night. He awoke as dawn was breaking, his mind already in high gear. The team needed better odds. He donned gym garb from his go bag and proceeded downstairs and outside for a run, giving him time to shake out the cobwebs and contemplate options.

The rain had let up, and he had the sidewalks to himself as he jogged south on Eleventh Avenue, turned east on Morrison Street past the Persian House restaurant and a Starbucks before cutting north on Ninth Avenue, passing a pharmacy and a cooking school, and smiling at a wrinkled, elderly man who lifted his weather-beaten gray fedora in silent greeting as he passed.

Morgan crossed Washington Street and passed O'Bryant Square to Stark Street before slowing to a trot and then a walk for the final five blocks back to the Sentinel. Nicole and McDowell probably were right—if trouble erupted, it wasn't likely to be in the bar. Then again, they all could be wrong.

Shaved and showered forty minutes later, Morgan donned tan khakis and a heavy brown sweater and took the stairs down to Jake's Grill, arriving just as the doors were opened at 7:00. He special-ordered French toast, hash browns, sausage, and a fruit bowl, sent Nicole a text, and settled in to read a story in the sports section of the *Oregonian* about a professional football player arrested for dealing narcotics. *The names change, but the story's the same*, Morgan thought to himself.

He finished his meal and his newspaper and was back in his room at 8:30. A return text from Nicole read, "D/T Nordstrom's 4 blks away. Must investigate. Back mid-pm."

Morgan chuckled and sent the only reply necessary: "k."

At seven forty-five Sunday evening, Nicole sat down at a table for two about ten feet from the west side of the Jackknife and ordered a vodka gimlet. Morgan had diagrammed the room for her and McDowell, and the three had selected optimum spots for viewable strategic advantage.

Morgan slowed as he entered the lounge at eight o'clock pleased it was only a third full—probably normal for a Sunday. He selected a barstool near Nicole's table but away from other patrons.

"Welcome to the Jackknife! What's your pleasure tonight?" The bartender was slim, about fifty, medium height, and dressed in a black shirt and clean jeans with a navy-blue bib apron. While Morgan examined the backbar, the bartender wiped the granite and placed a cocktail napkin in front of him.

"Johnny Walker Black. On the rocks please."

"Black on the rocks coming up."

Morgan's relationship with FBI Assistant Counterterrorism Director Herb Wallace had helped Nicole gain the bureau's okay for the scheme. He wondered if Liz Monroe still kept a bottle of his favorite bourbon at her home now that she was secretary of Homeland Security. DHS would be working with the bureau on the missing material. Morgan took a small sip of his scotch and said a little prayer that his idea wouldn't be a bust. It wasn't every day that the FBI agreed to work with a private investigator. *Please don't make it the last*, he thought.

McDowell arrived right on time at 8:10. "You Morgan?"

"Yep, sit down."

McDowell ordered a local IPA and began the charade, talking tough, looking around the room, and feigning suspicion. The song and dance went on for ten minutes while Nicole sent McDowell and

Morgan text messages of her observations. Her latest text brought Morgan to red alert: "bar is clear—guy in navy-blue raincoat hanging around elevators."

McDowell reached up and twice pulled on his earlobe, a signal that he had received her text. "Let's go to plan B," whispered the agent to Morgan.

The men dropped cash on the bar and started toward the hotel lobby. They entered a waiting elevator and noticed a man in his forties wearing a pulled-down Cubs ball cap and a dark blue raincoat. Morgan pushed the third-floor button and briefly looked at his iPhone while the gold door closed.

Nicole also left payment on her table and repositioned herself near the door where she had a clear view of raincoat man, who watched the elevator status lights blink on and off before it stopped on the third floor. The stranger made a quick call, prompting Nicole to send a short text to Morgan: "danger, think threat on 3rd floor."

Her phone indicated that the text message was not delivered.

"The concrete elevator shaft is blocking the cell tower transmission." She snapped a quick photo of raincoat man, reached for her Glock, and headed for the nearest stairway.

Morgan and McDowell left the elevator and headed for Morgan's room. Brick glanced at his phone hoping for a status report from Nicole about the stranger, but found nothing.

Just as McDowell's cell beeped, Morgan reacted to a shadow on his left, but not before being felled by a fifty-thousand-volt electrical charge from a law-enforcement-grade Taser applied directly to his neck, dropping him to his knees and then the floor, causing muscles throughout his body to spasm uncontrollably. McDowell absorbed a blast of pepper spray, blinding him temporarily and allowing a big, bald attacker to gain the upper hand, shoving the agent farther down the hallway.

A sudden *click* attracted the assailant's immediate attention.

DETONATION

"FBI! Party's over, asshole!" shouted Nicole as her finger steadied on the trigger guard of her nine-millimeter Glock aimed directly at the thug's heart.

Then came the snow—a massive ivory juggernaut racing southeast from the Gulf of Alaska into Vancouver Island and the Pacific Northwest. It had begun days earlier as a heavy rain, coupled with battering winds that continued unabated through Saturday. With the barometer in near free fall, the temperature in downtown Tacoma plummeted from thirty-four degrees at midnight to sixteen degrees by 8:00 a.m. Sunday. To those who would recall it to their grandchildren decades later, the swirling onslaught seemed a living thing as it intensified over Puget Sound and shot eastward into the state's mountain passes, enveloping cars, buses, truck-trailer rigs, state patrol vehicles, and snowplows in less than an hour, their occupants left helpless to await rescue before they froze.

Cody Dettering might have been among those trapped in the mountains if he had left home on time at 5:00 a.m. for his planned drive across the Cascades on Interstate 90 before trailing southeast into Oregon and on to Boise. There, he would pick up the package Tuesday morning that he would deliver in San Diego Thursday afternoon. But a chance encounter with a saucy blonde named Joanie in a South Tacoma lounge Saturday evening had turned into, well, a long night at his apartment, and by the time he awoke at 7:00 a.m. Sunday, snow was flying, Joanie was gone, and all the state's mountain passes were closed. He needed extra-strength Tylenol and a new plan.

Dettering threw on his clothes, inhaled three acetaminophen tablets, and ran outside to start and scrape snow from his seven-year-old Impala. Just getting the door open took ten minutes and several bottles of warm water. It was get out now or not at all.

He tossed his prepacked travel bag in the back seat, sat two boxes of granola bars and three water bottles in the passenger's seat next to him, and left his locked apartment for the dicey two-mile drive to Interstate 5, where he eased into relatively light traffic making its way southbound.

Most drivers had heeded the advice of state troopers and weather forecasters and waited out the snow, but to Cody's good fortune, those who *had* ventured onto I-5 were moving along at a moderate clip thanks to the tons of sand laid down before dawn by state highways department dump trucks. The snowstorm was continuing to move east rather than south, and by the time Cody reached Chehalis, sixty miles south of Tacoma, the snow began turning to rain.

Dettering refueled near the town of Napavine a few minutes later, wolfed down a burger and fries at a local Carl's Jr., and was back on the road in forty minutes. Four hours after leaving Tacoma, he turned east on Oregon Interstate 84 that would take him along the Columbia River from Portland before bypassing Hermiston and dipping southeast toward Boise. He stopped at a rest area and used the burner phone provided by his anonymous employer to arrange for motel rooms in Hermiston that night and in Boise Monday. The day that had begun tenuously for Cody had turned out well after all.

Tick-tock . . .

Chapter Twenty-Nine

Attired in a red Stanford sweatshirt and chino shorts, Morgan was slouched in his brown Eames lounge chair, his sockless feet propped on a matching ottoman and his gloomy mood matched by the blustery weather outside. He picked up a tan decorator pillow and threw it against a far wall, his pent-up anger threatening to envelop him. Failure was no option, but today the unknown taunted him like never before.

Two hours earlier, he had sent a report on the FBI sting in Portland to Security Director Rob Spencer of Nobility Cruise Line in Fort Lauderdale. The account mentioned that a suspect had been captured, but Morgan withheld for now his certainty of Barry Mott's involvement in a plot against the Panama Canal.

The sting had been dicey after all. The two small spots behind his left ear were still tender where an attacker using a stun gun had zapped him with fifty thousand volts during the Sunday night operation. McDowell had wiped pepper spray from his eyes before handcuffing the beefy assailant that Nicole held at gunpoint on the Sentinel Hotel's third floor.

Morgan took some solace in knowing his instincts had been right about Mott. But it was more than just Mott; organized muscle had to be behind the cabal. Morgan would attend a bureau video conference today that could connect more dots in the disjointed case.

The man in the hotel lobby was still at large, but Nicole learned that the captured thug had been identified as Ulian Vasilev, a local ex-con active in the Russian gang scene. Three hours of paperwork later, Nicole and Morgan had driven back to his home where he spent most of the morning preparing for today's meeting. Nicole slept in his guest room and caught a six a.m. flight back to her Tri-Cities office, phoning him from the plane with the latest on Vasilev.

"He's already lawyered up, Brick; won't even speak to our agents. His attorney is well-known in Oregon for representing the Russian Mafia. Last year he was managing the Club Dobre, a sleazy Portland strip bar, but lately he's been taking odd jobs out of another strip joint called the Lemon Tiger."

"What sort of odd jobs?"

"My question too. We may have more at the video conference. That's all I've got for the moment." They concluded the call.

Morgan spent a few minutes glancing at the morning paper, but his thoughts quickly returned to the same question: *Who or what is the head of this damn snake?* Armed with a fresh cup of coffee, he selected a Simon and Garfunkel album from the music system on his iPad and reviewed what they had.

Which was very little.

Two men were dead, both seemingly executed. Barry Mott's involvement now seemed clear. But what exactly was his role, and what exactly was the plot? The motivation had to be economic. Smuggling? Drugs? Weapons? With the volume of narcotics already flowing into the states across the country's southern border, he had to discount drugs. He had to! But he couldn't. Not yet, anyway. But what's the hook in Panama? Whatever it was, Mott was a small but important cog in the machine.

The ringing phone startled him. On the line was Rob Spencer with a proposal for Morgan to investigate the case on Nobility's behalf. "Your report was superb, Brick. I've passed along the gist of it to three other lines without violating any confidences. They know only that there's a serious threat to the canal out there and that you're on it. All three promised to get back to me today."

"I hope your judgment isn't misplaced, Rob. This case is a nut-buster."

"Understood, but the pucker factor is in play now. Some cruise line operators got a little too confident about being targeted after what happened aboard the *Matisse Under the Stars* last year. They're waking up now that we have a credible new threat."

"I'm fine with it as long as they don't get in my way."

"That won't be an issue. I've designated myself as point man. Nothing goes out unless it goes through me."

"Well, there's only one threat and only one me, so I guess that makes it even," said Morgan, drawing a laugh from his colleague. Morgan enjoyed working with Spencer, whose take-no-prisoners approach was welcomed. His years with the Miami PD had gained him a network of contacts throughout the Florida cruise industry. "Can you provide me a list of cruise ships due to make a canal transit in the next couple weeks that will require the larger lock?"

"You'll have it within the hour. I'll also try to list cargo ships in queue for the third lock, but that will take a little longer because about forty of them use the canal for every cruise liner doing so. The big cruise lines have a few ships with beams over a hundred and ten feet, but most still fit in the original locks."

"Concentrate on those big boys, Rob. It's got to be one of them."

"Will do. The industry reps I've spoken with will keep a lid on the situation, Brick. They have to. Perceived threats play havoc with cruise-line revenues."

"Got it, Spence. Norovirus is one thing; nuclear terrorism is unthinkable."

The drive downtown took Morgan down the North Thirtieth Street hill and its merger into Schuster Parkway. Before entering Pacific Avenue, he glanced at the dozen or more container ships from around the world waiting their turns at various port terminals. Together, those ships carried more than a 150,000 containers. *No one really knows what's inside those containers*, Morgan mused to himself.

The Tacoma FBI office is a resident facility under the supervision of Seattle's FBI field office. Morgan was directed to a conference room and told that Special Agent Dexter Copeland would join him shortly. Morgan's tenure with the Justice Department and Interpol had placed him in many cookie-cutter conference rooms over time. This one was above average with two eight-foot Steelcase tables, a wall of whiteboards, and another wall covered with a ninety-eight-inch LED ultra-high-definition video screen. A third wall featured the bureau's ten most-wanted fugitives.

Agent Copeland entered the room through a side door and welcomed Brick. "Mr. Morgan, Dexter Copeland," he said pleasantly, extending his hand in greeting. "We haven't met before, but I feel like I already know you."

"I hope that's good," replied Morgan with a smile, noting that the agent must be at least six five. "Basketball or baseball, Mr. Copeland?"

"Please call me Dex, and basketball. Arizona State. Last year I had the pleasure of meeting your cybersleuth, Miss Titus."

"I'm sure she kept your team on its toes."

"She's amazing!"

Morgan felt no need to update the agent on Rilee's new name and location. He guessed they still kept an eye on her after placing her in protective custody during the terrorist event he foiled aboard the liner *Matisse Under the Stars* in the Pacific Ocean.

Just then an assistant entered, announced that the videoconference would start shortly, and handed Agent Copeland a list of expected participants.

"Thanks, Evelyn. Looks like this case is getting top billing." Copeland handed the list to Morgan and then connected a USB cable from a laptop to the side of the digital wall display.

Morgan expected the bureau's Seattle and Tri-Cities offices to be involved but was surprised to find FBI headquarters in Washington, DC, represented, including Assistant Counterterrorism Director

Herb Wallace and Special Agent Kryss Mitchell. Director of National Intelligence Karl Sarrazin, and DHS Secretary Liz Monroe were seated with the bureau contingent. *Today we're playing hardball*, Morgan thought.

Copeland tapped a few keys on his laptop, and the video display split into four quadrants. Supervisory Special Agent Terry Carver of the Seattle office was on the upper left; Ramona Vincent and Nicole, representing the Tri-Cities, were in the top right of the screen; the bureau group was displayed in the lower left; and the Tacoma office was framed in the lower right.

Assistant Director Wallace opened the meeting and introduced Monroe and Sarrazin. "As you know, the DNI is responsible for preparing the president's daily brief, so I asked Director Sarrazin and Secretary Monroe to join us. Suffice it to say, this investigation has developed its own momentum, and once POTUS gets his PDB tomorrow, it will be on the White House radar. Special Agent Carver will take the lead today. In addition to your team's reports, Terry, let me know if you need more resources.

As Agent Carver began outlining his agenda items, Morgan recalled his time spent with Agent Mitchell and the man's misfortune at receiving a nine-millimeter slug in the thigh during a gunfire exchange with a terrorist aboard the *Matisse*. He had heard Mitchell was now leading a fly team, a highly trained force of FBI agents and intelligence analysts who conduct counterterrorism deployments on short notice. Carver then requested Copeland's report about his interview a day earlier with housekeeper Emily McClelland.

Copeland introduced Morgan, seated to his right, and then referred to a notepad with occasional glances at the room's camera as he detailed the interview, including his assessment of McClelland's veracity. "This morning I entered an FD-302 in Sentinel regarding the following. Emily McClelland is a housekeeper for Arlen and Joanne Bancroft who live on Gravelly Lake Drive here, an area of very expensive homes.

"The Bancroft home is next door to that of Mark and Karen LoNigro. Approximately five weeks ago, Ms. McClelland overheard a conversation emanating from the LoNigro's home involving several men. She was alarmed enough that she used a yellow pad to record fragments of the discussion and then entered her notes on her computer. At yesterday's interview, I obtained her original notes and a printed a copy from her computer. The words or phrases she captured that evening appear to be actionable. She recorded the following: 'Panama Canal, C-4 to stop the ship in new lock, dirty bomb, radiation, Hanford nuclear sludge, and radium 226.'"

"What do we have on the LoNigros, and where are they now?" interrupted Wallace.

"Mr. LoNigro is a contractor who builds upscale new homes; Mrs. LoNigro does not work outside the home. This morning I sent two agents to their residence. Only Mrs. LoNigro was home. She informed us that her husband had left this morning to attend a homebuilder's convention in Houston. As of an hour ago, there was no builder's convention underway in Houston this week, and no one using the name LoNigro has made hotel reservations or checked into flights. One more thing: his car is at home and Yellow, Uber, and Lift don't have records of a pickup. Finally, I was very impressed by Ms. McClelland, who volunteered for a lie detector test if we wish to conduct one. She seems very humble and patriotic. Her husband was killed in action in Vietnam."

If Morgan had harbored any doubt of a Northwest relationship to the case, it was erased by the stunning McClelland revelation. *There it is; Mott and LoNigro are connected!* he thought.

Agent Cofield then began her own report at Carver's request.

"Mr. Brick Morgan, seated next to Agent Copeland, became suspicious of Mr. Barry Mott last week," said Cofield, looking into her office camera. "Mr. Mott is a retired commercial real estate agent who is now president of the five-member Tacoma Port Commission." She then presented details, including the Portland sting and the fact that Mott was the only person who had been fed the bogus information.

Secretary Monroe of Homeland Security looked into the camera at FBI headquarters and raised her hand to interrupt.

"Madam Secretary, you have a point?" asked Cofield.

"Actually a question about the meeting at LoNigro's house. Do we have any knowledge that Mott attended that gathering? Also, I'd like to ask Mr. Morgan for his thoughts on Mott's role in this scenario."

Copeland addressed Monroe's question. "We didn't engage Mrs. LoNigro this morning, other than to imply that we needed her husband's help with a gang that was stealing copper wire from construction sites. As we speak, my people are approaching a federal magistrate in Tacoma for warrants to search LoNigro's house and business office. When we execute the warrant, we will also learn if Karen LoNigro knows the names of the meeting attendees. Specifically, Secretary Monroe, we have not connected LoNigro and Mott. Mr. Morgan, please respond about Mott's possible role."

"Mott is not the alpha dog in this pack of suspects, ladies and gentlemen," Morgan began. "The scope of this cabal requires a well-funded criminal organization that I believe has hit men in at least three states and the talent to steal cold war radioactive waste from a DOE facility."

"Do you believe Mott was directly involved in the radioactive waste theft at Hanford?" asked Monroe.

"Not directly, Madam Secretary, but perhaps indirectly. Mott is an expert on port management. I believe he represents people who would benefit economically if Panama's new lock were put out of commission. My conjecture is that Mott is connected to a group that has contracted with a syndicate to do the dirty work."

Wallace was quick to follow up. "This case is an interagency investigation, everyone. Agent Carver, don't be shy about requesting more assets. I'm certain DOE and Homeland will join us to provide all the agents and materiel we need if we make the request. With that said, what's the game plan for Mr. Mott?"

"Once we received knowledge of Portland and Mott's possible role, Agent Copeland and I put Mott under twenty-four-seven surveillance, Herb," said Carver. "We agree with Mr. Morgan that Mott might not be the nucleus of the criminality but could lead us to the organization that is pulling the strings. Yesterday, we also requested and received a search-and-seizure warrant for Mott's property. That warrant has not yet been executed. We've activated Title III electronic surveillance for possible money laundering and financing terrorism."

Morgan was pleased with the bureau's reaction time in targeting Mott. He remembered the Title III manual from his own years at the Justice Department and the detailed procedures it required for conducting electronic surveillance. He also knew the frustration law enforcement often faced with judges who limit certain types of generic felonies for which wiretaps could be granted. *Granting a wiretap warrant for a suspected dirty bomb should have been a no-brainer*, he thought.

FBI Assistant Director Wallace could be seen writing a note on what appeared to be a three-by-five card and passing it to Monroe. A few seconds later, Wallace took control of the conference call. "This location needs to go off-line for about five minutes. Don't go anywhere, people; we'll be right back."

Once the bureau's screen went dark, Copeland entered a few keystrokes and turned to Morgan. "When Herb says five minutes, he doesn't mean five minutes and ten seconds."

"So what are you thinking, Dex?" asked Morgan as he got out of his chair and stretched.

"I've learned that what *is* said is not as important as what is *not* said, Brick. Did you notice that no one mentioned the screwup at DOE and how Hanford lost a couple liters of nuclear material? That means Homeland and the FBI are beyond pissed; hell, the Secretary of

Energy wasn't even invited to the conference."

"Never have been a fan of DOE having nuclear security under its umbrella."

"Depending on how this case shakes out, that might be something Congress should look at," replied Copeland. He reactivated the DC group's audio when their screen relit a minute later.

"Let's see if we can wind this up," said Wallace. "Agent Carver, for now we need to keep this issue off the media radar. The last thing we need is tying up assets entertaining the press. Secretary Monroe and I feel this case doesn't have the feel or wrappings of a radical Islamic plot. Let's find LoNigro and keep Mott under our thumb." Wallace then nodded to DNI Director Sarrazin, who moved his chair closer to the table and looked at the camera.

"This matter will certainly be included in tomorrow's PDB. When POTUS learns that DOE lost material on his watch, he'll want the bureau to move mountains. I'm not sure how I'm going to explain that a civilian is part of this interagency task force. It certainly isn't my call to ask Mr. Morgan to recuse himself, but I don't look forward to explaining to a congressional oversight committee why American law enforcement agencies can't accomplish their mission without Mr. Morgan. With that said, I wish your team a fast resolution to the task at hand."

It took all of Morgan's self control not to respond to the DNI, but sometimes action and results are the best reply.

As the conference drew to a close, Copeland was alerted to an incoming text. He read it and turned to the video screen. "Ladies and gentlemen, I'm pleased to announce that the federal magistrate here has just issued the LoNigro search-and-seizure warrant."

Tick-tock . . .

Chapter Thirty

Mark LoNigro stepped out his front door at five o'clock this drizzly Tuesday morning wearing a leather jacket over a deep wine turtleneck and jeans. He pressed the keypad to reactivate his home security system, opened his umbrella, and proceeded down his private road to Gravelly Lake Drive, where Gas Rizzo waited in an idling Mercury Electric pickup.

LoNigro was exuberant. Today he would take the first step in a plan that would create international news and enrich him and his business partners beyond their wildest dreams.

The burly custom home contractor had planned a noon departure for his drive to San Diego, but morning offered less traffic and, more importantly, fewer eyes. His goodbye note to Karen had said he was catching an Uber cab to Sea-Tac for his flight to Houston. He put his small suitcase behind the passenger seat and got in the truck.

"Top of the mornin', Gas. Let's roll."

"Fasten your safety belt, Mark," Rizzo growled. "We can't afford you getting killed in a traffic accident."

"What do you mean, 'we'?"

Rizzo ignored the question. "Perfect timing, I just pulled up. You have any problem escaping from Karen?"

"No. She's still asleep; thinks I'm taking Uber to the airport."

"You'll like your new wheels."

"If you rented me a damn Prius, you're a dead man!"

"Relax. It's a two-year-old Ford Transit van, three-point-five-liter EcoBoost. Nice pair of buckets and three rows of seats."

"Maybe I can drive the church choir to San Diego."

"All your stuff is packed in the van, including your walker for boarding and two real oxygen tanks for your disguise. Do you have a supply of burner phones?"

"I have five. Cleaned out the local CVS and Walgreens." LoNigro handed him a list of the five phone numbers. "I've also brought plenty of cash. No credit cards this trip."

"The van is parked behind the University of Puget Sound Field House. Your map and ticket for next Tuesday's flight from Panama to Houston are inside your disguise case. Remember, when the second bomb goes off, get out of the canal area and find me at the Gamboa Resort."

Forty-five minutes later, the two men had double-checked the van's supplies, familiarized LoNigro with the Ford's features, and said their goodbyes. Rizzo drove away, and LoNigro pulled onto Union Avenue, heading south toward Interstate 5.

Today's seven-hour drive would take him to Medford, Oregon, less than an hour from the California border. He would contact the business's deliveryman, Cody Dettering, to confirm his retrieval in Boise of the cylinders containing the nuclear blast material he would detonate aboard the cruise liner *Rose Diamond*. If all is on schedule, Cody will leave the cylinders in a storage unit for him in San Diego Thursday.

LoNigro exited I-5 north of Castle Rock, found a secondary road heading toward Spirit Lake, and drove east into the dense forest before turning onto an isolated logging road. The road was covered with about two inches of heavy wet snow, its lack of tracks showing no evidence of recent vehicle use. It would be a safe place to turn himself into Bart Stevenson, whose physical presence would match his counterfeit identification documents, preventing cameras and facial recognition software from tracking his movements. Today marked the second time LoNigro applied the makeup, the first having been for a passport photo taken by Rizzo.

The four levers holding the van's middle seat gave way easily, and LoNigro lifted it off its tracks and set it aside, creating a work space between the other two seats where he got started on his disguise. Over the next hour, he colored his beard from salt and pepper to white, attached a nose prosthesis to widen it, and used mastic to affix a white handlebar mustache. He then removed the rubber band holding his ponytail, parted his hair in the middle, and let it fall over his ears. A red *Make America Great Again* ball cap completed the transformation. He used a mirror to compare his passport photo with his new Bart Stevenson persona. *Not bad at all!*

Twenty minutes later, LoNigro gassed up in Castle Rock, paid cash for three jumbo bags of Peanut M&M's and a cup of coffee at a nearby Circle K, and reentered southbound I-5.

LoNigro skirted most of Portland's morning traffic. Two hours later, he was halfway between Eugene and Roseburg in the heart of Oregon's wine country when one of his burner phones rang.

"Cooper," he answered, using a prearranged code name.

"Mr. Cooper, I'm calling you as instruct—"

"No names; just answer yes or no."

"Okay!"

"Did you take possession of the package?"

"Yes."

"How many packages did you receive?"

"Two."

"Are the packages with you now, and are you driving to your next stop?"

"Yes."

"Good. Call this number when you've made the delivery."

"Okay."

LoNigro disconnected the call and gave a sigh of relief. Damn, that was good news. He wanted to call Rizzo but thought better of it, hoping only that his conversation with Dettering hadn't triggered any local or federal intercepts despite his use of a burner phone. He reasoned that there was no reason for him to be targeted and shrugged off the concerns that had dogged him all day.

Screw the blood sugar. LoNigro took another handful of M&Ms. His weight and craving for sweets had resulted in him developing type 2 diabetes when he was in high school in the sixties. He had often promised Karen that he would take his health issues more seriously and drop at least forty pounds. Easy to promise; tougher to do. Maybe after this job. His thoughts of Karen led him to reflect on the consequences of failure.

Financially, she would be wealthy. Their home was paid for, and their joint accounts held $350,000 dollars. Any more could trigger an IRS flag. They had another $75,000 cash in their home safe, and he had hidden over $10 million in gold and coins in secret locations known only to them both.

LoNigro rolled into Medford at two fifteen and located a McDonald's on Biddle Road, where he used the men's room before loading up on a sack of cheeseburgers and a double order of McNuggets and fries, washed down by a giant diet Coke. The large, well-lit parking lot at the Motel 6 two blocks away would be ideal for parking the van overnight.

He parked in front of a busy supermarket and went for a walk to stretch his legs and clear his head. The temperature was in the mid-sixties, average in Medford for an October day, and the walk was invigorating. He passed a forest-green, split-level home on Mount Echo Drive where two couples—apparently retirees—were playing a game of horseshoes and clearly having a good time at it. A few yards away, a freckle-faced boy about ten was trying with limited success to train a puppy of questionable lineage. "No, Lucky, stay. No, stay. Lucky, staay!"

Bear Creek Park was active today, at least some of it was. Six college-age students were playing with Frisbees, something LoNigro hadn't done in thirty years. When one landed near him, he picked it up and fired it back, surprised that it flew on a line to one of the grateful players. All four waved, and he waved back.

Back in the van later, he entered the Motel 6 lot, locked the van's doors, and spread out his sleeping bag and got relatively comfortable, or as comfortable as a man his size could get in the back of a three-seat cargo van. A twinge of guilt crossed his mind for preparing to spend the night at a Motel 6 and paying nothing for the privilege. He snickered to himself, pulled out a Burr Anderson novel, and began reading.

The 585-mile drive from Medford to Bakersfield was uneventful, except that LoNigro was tired of McNuggets. He needed at least two days beyond the three he'd told Karen about, and he debated calling her. If he used a burner phone, there was a chance she wouldn't pick up, but that was still a better option than using his personal cell that could be tracked.

It took three rings before she picked up. "Hi, babe!"

"I thought you would call me last night. How is Houston?"

"Weather is midseventies. It's a typical meeting of home builders. The good news is the big boys hold lots of free receptions. Say, I ran into a guy who has fifteen acres of undeveloped land near Brown's Point. I'm going to meet him in New York Sunday and try to buy all fifteen acres. It would be perfect for us to add streets and sewers and then build forty or more homes."

"You're going where?"

"Watertown, New York. It's north of Syracuse. The guy is a contractor there. He and his wife bought it as an investment years ago and never did anything with it. I think he'll let it go for three and a half million. It would be a great investment, hon. We could triple our money."

"When will you be home?"

"My guess is Wednesday."

"Okay. By the way, two government types came by looking for

you yesterday. Not sure what agency, but they wanted your help with some crooks who are stealing copper wire from construction sites."

"Weird. Did they leave any cards?"

"No, but they said they would leave a message on your office phone."

The couple spent a few more minutes discussing the potential of the Brown's Point land and then ended the call. LoNigro was sure Karen believed his New York ruse. Regardless, he needed to focus on Dettering and San Diego.

The big man was tired of driving. He had made good time, and with less than 250 miles to San Diego, he decided to relax. A Ben Affleck and Morgan Freeman movie was playing at the Regency East Hill Mall, and he pulled into a parking space up front and went inside.

Three hours later, the lights of the Red Pepper Cocktail Lounge on Oswell Street beckoned, and he soon found their margaritas to his liking. His third went down nicely as did the rack of lamb that followed. Early evening had set in, and by the time LoNigro finished the lamb, he was about finished himself. He found a parking spot between two old hangars near the city's Meadows Field Airport and slept until eight o'clock the next morning.

LoNigro tilted the rearview mirror in the van and took a long look, almost scaring himself. *I look like I've been dead for a year.* He gassed up a final time, picked up a sandwich at an In-N-Out Burger shop on Panama Lane—Bakersfield's answer to Tacoma's Frisko-Freeze—and then stopped at a vacant rest area on I-5 just south of the city, where he brushed his teeth, shaved, changed clothes, and freshened his disguise.

With a large bag of French fries on the passenger seat and a burger on his lap, LoNigro merged back onto I-5 south for the final leg of the trip. *A man needs to eat right when he's escorting a nuke.*

LoNigro parked the van in San Diego's Seaport Village lot and walked to a Starbucks on Pacific Highway. He would have enjoyed an outdoor table and the seventy-one-degree temperature much better if he weren't anxious about the expected call from Cody. The man's major responsibility was to transfer the two radioactive cylinders from his car to the storage unit in nearby Santa Fe Depot and leave. *What could go wrong?*

A piano riff signaled an incoming call. He canceled his coffee order with a barista and stepped outside before answering.

"Cooper."

"Mr. Cooper, the package has been delivered."

"Door locked?"

"Yep."

"Good. Pick up the van at one o'clock tomorrow at the Navy Pier lot in front of the USS Midway Museum and leave town quietly. You know where and how to make the van disappear. Perez will have the rest of your due at the Oly bar."

"Got it, boss. I'll leave my car in a parking garage here and come back for it in a couple days."

"Fine. There's one more thing, Cody," said LoNigro, slowly and gruffly. "Do not, repeat, *do not*, screw up!"

"No problem."

LoNigro hung up. It would be impossible to clean the Ford to the degree needed to eliminate all traces of his DNA. Dettering would simply drive to an isolated area in Oregon and torch it. Then he could make his way to Eugene, take Amtrak back to San Diego, and pick up his car.

Time to become Bart Stevenson. Assuming it would be customary for a *Rose Diamond* passenger to check into a hotel the day before a cruise, LoNigro made reservations at the Hilton Gaslight Quarter on K Street.

The registration and check-in went smoothly, and twenty minutes later, Stevenson was in the shower removing three days of road grime and sweat. On the bed were two large powder-green Nautica suitcases that would soon hold cylinders containing some of the nation's most deadly radioactive isotopes.

After a quick refresh of his Bart Stevenson makeup, LoNigro exited the hotel via a side door and walked to the silver-and-gold van. In his mind, he checked off his and Dettering's arrivals in San Diego and the apparent arrival of his equipment. *So far, so good.* Once he had the nuclear-blast components, the success of the assignment would be in his hands alone. *Control the things that you can control.*

He entered Harbor Marine Storage, drove down Row A, and turned left to Row D and storage unit D-141 located inside a structure housing four other six-by-ten-foot units. He pulled an entry card with its five-digit access code from his wallet and opened a gate leading to locker D-141.

LoNigro inserted the unit key from his key ring and tried the lock. It didn't open. *What? You son of a bitch!* He turned the key around and tried again. No change. Sweat began beading his forehead. The key fit, but the large boron carbide Master padlock wouldn't budge. LoNigro shook the lock and banged on it with the butt of his pocketknife, all to no avail.

Then he looked closer and realized the key was to another Master lock on a storage building at his business location; the keys were nearly identical. *Damn it, Mark, wake up!* He found the right key on his key ring, and the lock opened easily.

Sitting inside on an olive-colored moving blanket were the two green cylinders. Next to them was the Geiger counter used by Cody to ensure against possible radiation leakage. It was turned on and quiet to LoNigro's relief.

He spent ten more minutes scrubbing the interior light dimmer, doorknob, and padlock with Clorox bathroom cleaner and a sponge before wrapping the cylinders in the heavy blanket and placing them on the van's third passenger seat, secured by a bungee cord. The Geiger counter was stuffed beneath the van's upturned middle seat.

It took nearly an hour to package the cylinders in his suitcases and smuggle them to his hotel room. The tanks were larger than anticipated, but by placing them diagonally he was able to fit a cylinder and one wine magnum containing C-4 into each case. He attached personalized luggage tags printed with his predesignated cabin number, H-463, to the suitcase handles. *Don't need these cases going to the wrong cabin*, he thought.

Once the contraband was safely secured, he left the room and took an elevator down to the hotel's New Leaf Bar.

LoNigro gave a sigh of relief as he paid the ten-dollar parking fee and saw that the three-hundred-car Navy Pier lot was only half full at mid-morning Friday. The 972-foot *Midway* was clearly in view as he located a parking stall for the large transit van. While off-loading his luggage, carry-on, and walker, he contemplated the *Midway*'s forty-seven-year naval record. Built with a beam of 121 feet, CV-41 was never able to transit the Panama Canal, yet she fought in the Vietnam War and served as a flagship during Operation Desert Storm.

He moved his luggage to a nearby walkway, attached his seven-foot oxygen tube to an over-the-ear nasal cannula, and slung his portable cylinder pack over his shoulder. Then, knowing Dettering had the five-number door code, he left the keys beneath the driver's seat, locked the door, and called Uber on a burner phone. LoNigro had to laugh at his appearance: wearing a baseball cap while leaning on a walker and breathing from a tank of compressed oxygen.

Ten minutes later, Bart Stevenson was delivered to the B Street Cruise Terminal from which he eyed the stunning 124,000-ton *Rose Diamond*. Painted a gleaming white with sky-blue trim, she was a beautiful sight to behold with her fifteen decks towering far above the water. Technical jargon aside, LoNigro still marveled that a massive iron-and-steel object like the *Rose* could float on water. It would be a shame to sink her.

"Sir, I'm gonna get you right close to where the longshoremen will check in your luggage. Then you just go through those orange doors and follow the embarkation signs."

"Thank you. Here's a little extra. It was a short trip."

The Uber driver helped him open his walker and even signaled to a longshoreman to bring his luggage cart to the old man with lung issues. Twenty dollars later, Bart Stevenson watched as his two suitcases were piled on a cart and disappeared inside the terminal. Once he cleared the blue doors, he moved from registration to a special security line reserved for passengers with health needs and disabilities.

A Hispanic woman from Guest's Services helped him place his carry-on bag on a belt that moved items through the X-ray machine. It seemed to LoNigro that the bald man assigned to the Autoclear X-ray inspection system was more interested in watching him struggle through a personal pat-down resulting from beeps emitted from a security wand. As a result, LoNigro's laptop and case, filled with blasting caps and an electronic detonator, sailed through the scanner and rolled down a track to a stainless-steel catch table. Once the obese wand lady cleared him, he repacked his computer in his carry-on, reslung the portable oxygen unit over his shoulder, and followed the signs toward the embarkation area.

An elevator carried him to the terminal's second floor, where signs pointed toward the gangway leading to the *Rose Diamond*. A swarthy man who appeared to be East Asian took his cruise card and inserted it in a slot attached to an elaborate security camera.

"Sir, if you would remove your hat and look into the camera, we can process you for ship access."

That done and cruise card back in his pocket, LoNigro exaggerated the difficulty of pushing his walker up a slight incline that took him to the ship's deck five, where yet another camera crew awaited.

"If you will stand here, we can take a souvenir photo of the first day of your Panama Canal adventure," said a smiling blond crewman with steel-gray eyes.

"I'll pass, but thank you." *The last thing I need are photos of Mark LoNigro showing up on Instagram or Facebook.* He squeezed his bulk and walker into another elevator heading upward with several other riders.

Each deck on the *Rose* was named for a cut of diamond. The elevator stopped at the Oval deck—number eight—and two passengers eased past him and turned left toward the port side. When the elevator opened at the Heart deck, a middle-aged man wearing a Hawaiian shirt stepped out and held the door. LoNigro thanked him profusely and then slowly pushed his walker across the brass door tracks, turning right toward the ship's bow until he located H-463. He inserted his cruise card into the card key lock and entered his cabin.

LoNigro wondered if he had created a monster using the walker as part of his disguise. He folded it and decided to tell anyone who inquired that it was to help him walk during shore excursions. After unpacking his carry-on, he sat down at a little desk and looked over the room service menu. A note from a Catalina Carmona introduced her as his cabin steward and included her phone number. LoNigro tuned the cabin's television to a music channel and opened the sliding doors to explore his personal balcony.

"Mr. Stevenson."

Startled, he turned and was greeted by a dark-haired woman about thirty who confirmed that she was Catalina and that her job was to assist passengers to ensure they enjoyed their time to the fullest aboard ship. She certainly looked the part. Her uniform was conservative, a white cotton blouse and a silver-and-black diamond vest that held a gold nametag with the word "housekeeping" beneath her name.

"It's very nice to meet you, Catalina," he replied, telling her he had just come aboard and promising to call her with any questions.

She smiled easily and often over the next ten minutes as she explained her duties and told him that there would be a mandatory muster drill at four o'clock, for which he would need to take his life jacket with him.

"The elevators are not available during the drill, but because of your medical condition, there will be a special elevator that will take you down to your muster station on deck six."

"I'll leave a little early and try to avoid the crowds."

Catalina then said she would return about six thirty to turn down his bed and refresh his towels. "You can expect your luggage any time, Mr. Stevenson. If you need help, please call my number. Would you like me to fill your ice bucket?"

"That would be fine. I don't have the lungs for long walks," he added, pointing to his walker leaning against a wall.

LoNigro removed an orange life jacket from his closet in anticipation of the required drill. A tap on the door announced the arrival of his luggage, and Catalina returned with his ice bucket just as he opened the door. He shook his head at her offer to help with his baggage and wheeled the suitcases into the cabin.

He locked the door, removed his clothing, toiletries, and wine bottles from the baggage, and then slid the luggage containing the radioactive cylinders under the bed. Fifteen minutes later, Bart Stevenson attached his oxygen tube to his nose, put on his life jacket, and headed to his muster station for the required drill.

"Mission accomplished!" said Cody Dettering to himself, smiling as he left Carnita's Snack Shack on Harbor Drive after a large rib eye steak sandwich and salad that his perky waitress had said was "to die for." He ordered a second sandwich for the road, left her a ten-dollar tip, and departed, walking south on the boulevard. It was eleven o'clock Friday morning, and a brief stroll along the waterfront seemed in order before he picked up the van at the *Midway* parking lot and began a long drive up to Oregon, where he would dispose of the vehicle.

Cody's expense money for his trip to San Diego had been paid upfront two days before he departed. Another $14,000 awaited him when he returned home. The utter simplicity of the job left him in a jovial mood as he walked casually along the busy sidewalk, even saying hello to passersby, something he hadn't done in years. But he felt good and happy, and now seemed a perfect time to share those feelings. His waitress had recommended a sightseeing visit to nearby Dead Man's Point on the waterfront near the intersection of Harbor Drive and Pacific Coast Highway. He headed in that direction, bought a magazine at a newsstand, and left a five-dollar tip for the clerk, who smiled back.

Cody was a veteran of the 1991 Persian Gulf War, and a magazine article relating to the conflict beginning on page thirty-six showed promise. He scanned its photos as he stepped into the crosswalk and headed across the road to the Point, wondering briefly how the site got its name. Cody turned to his left toward a loud noise, a moment before the Freightliner truck-trailer rig entering the intersection crushed him to pulp.

Tick-tock . . .

Chapter Thirty-One

Rilee never considered herself a computer hacker. The word was, well, wearisome and certainly unrefined. Semitalented geeks and North Koreans were hackers; Rilee felt the term "investigative computer analyst" fit the refined mastery of her own skills. From her condo on the Commencement Bay waterfront, she also enjoyed peeking into the phone systems of her neighbors from time to time to see what types of lives they led. She did this by first gaining entry to the computer system used by the on-site condo managers and then peeling open the email addresses and phone links given to management by the condo owners. She considered learning the backgrounds and predilections of neighbors a form of self-protection.

Over time, Rilee had linked herself to the systems of all but two of her condo neighbors—one an elderly woman who had proclaimed loudly and proudly to her neighbors that she would fight the need for computers and cell phones "until hell freezes over." But then there was condo 243. A single, sixtyish man lived there, but though he was tied in to the condo system, his personal computer and cell phone had resisted all her efforts to explore them.

This morning a breakfast of tossed spinach, fresh blueberries, and eight large strawberries accompanied by raw walnuts rich in healthy omegas boosted her energy level and motivation to give the situation another look. She was the best in the business at solving cyber dramas, she often told herself, having delved deeply into classified government and business files numerous times, and she wasn't about to be outfoxed by a cunning, four-eyed geezer in her own condominium complex.

The mystery of condo 243 had become an obsession, and Rilee began her day ecstatic at having finally discovered the identity of the condo's owner. She had used her Wolfhound passive receiver to detect active text, data, and voice transmissions from nearby residents, and by using the equipment's frequency discriminator mode, she was able to ascertain that the owner of condo 243 changed cell phones several times a week. A further check of county tax records showed that the condominium's owner was a corporation, Incisor LLC, and an even further check into the secretary of state's filing records revealed that the governing person of Incisor LLC was Carlo Conti.

Now that Rilee had a name, her one-track mind went into overdrive. *Tacoma News Tribune* archives showed that thirty years earlier, dentist Carlo Conti was severely injured in a fall while performing home maintenance. The article went on to say that his disability necessitated early retirement from his successful oral surgery practice. *How can a man who hasn't worked in thirty years drive a new Corvette and own an upscale condo?*

More determined than ever, she ratcheted up her quest. Rilee knew that technologies now available to law enforcement can enable agencies to listen in on cell phone conversations. Among the brands are Harpoon, Kingfish, and Stingay, the latter employed by the Tacoma PD. A lesser-known product, Bandit Catcher II, sat on Rilee's desk. Her new toy, also known as an IMSI-catcher, worked by sending out a signal stronger than a cell tower to trick localized cell phones to connect to it instead of a tower. She had set the system to track calls going to or from condo 243, though it occasionally trapped calls from condos near Conti's as well. Once the Bandit Catcher snared calls, it released the signals to cell towers while keeping participants unaware that she was listening in on the conversations or observing their texted data.

The biggest challenge was that Conti only turned on his phone when he needed to make a call. But once he did, the Wolfhound device would beep and she would activate the Bandit Catcher and capture the conversation. Most of the dialogue she heard was short, cryptic, and used coded language. Until three days ago, she suspected Conti was involved in narcotics trafficking or some other nefarious avocation.

Then her equipment picked up an outgoing call that began with vague generalities until one speaker made a critical slip. The captured conversation was almost too good to be true; a lead falling from the heavens. Stranger things had happened, but not to Rilee, and she punched the speed dial on her own cell phone. Morgan answered immediately.

"How secure is your phone, Brick?"

"It should be fine as long as you're still scrambling our calls on your end. I'm in my car. What's new?"

"I may have struck gold."

"The floor is yours."

Rilee related her story about Conti's call. "I clearly heard one of them say, 'Portland was a screwup, but he has it contained,' and then, 'the big guy has the hot stuff and should be going through the canal in a few days.'

"It was out of the blue, Brick. First time I picked up anything significant from him. I listen to his calls for my own reasons, and this one just popped out of nowhere. You figured there was a local angle to your canal case, and I think it just fell into your lap."

"Nothing just falls into *my* lap, Rilee."

"This one did."

"No way."

"Look, this guy is a retired dentist loaded with money, drives a new Corvette, and avoids electronic detection like the plague. Add that to the conversation I just heard, and there has to be a connection. It's just too good *not* to be true."

"It's a felony to wiretap a telephone, Rilee. You're officially on cybertech probation."

"In the state of Washington it's legal to record a conversation if you're a part of it, Brick. Let's just say I was on a conference call with Conti and the other rascal."

"You said the guy was a former dentist. Maybe he's talking about a patient with a wisdom tooth sensitive to hot and cold and needs a root canal."

"Morgan, don't screw with me. This Conti character is a bad hombre, and he's connected with your canal plot. I can feel it!"

"It seems way too convenient on its face."

"All I can do is provide you with information, Brick," said Rilee, exasperated. "What you do with it is up to you."

"Well, stay on it if you can do it legally, but if you can't—"

"Got it."

After helping Morgan with his proposal for Tacoma's port security, Rilee had been tasked with digging deep into the internet for activity that in any way seemed to reference nuclear materials, specifically hot waste. Morgan also had briefed her about the Portland sting and that Barry Mott was now a suspect.

"On a one-to-ten scale, Brick, what's your knowledge of the dark web?"

"I'd be exaggerating if I said a three, but it's higher than a one. Why?"

"The dark web, or as some call it, the *deep* web, is part of the internet that's unknown to most people. Just getting in there requires a much deeper knowledge of computer usage than most people have, and that makes it an ideal playground for lowlife activities ranging from terrorism to pedophiles, drug smuggling, and illegal trade practices. I've learned over time that more than ninety percent of all websites are so deeply hidden in the cloud that the general public isn't aware of them."

"That part I knew," replied Morgan. "That's where they should stay. Buried."

"But they won't; that's the reality. Listen up. I found a forum that was holding discussions about theft and storage of nuclear weapons material."

"You're going to have either terrorists or the FBI knocking on your door one day soon."

"I'm so deep in the cloud myself, the bureau would need a ladder just to find my basement. Don't forget, they offered me a job awhile back."

"I haven't forgotten, but terrorists wouldn't be offering you a job, Rilee."

"Don't sweat it. All I do is listen; I don't participate. People who go to the dark web don't want to be discovered; that's why they're there. The same thing applies to me. I use software with multiple layers of encryption, like the layers of an onion. It's called TOR, short for 'the onion router.'"

"May I be excused, Rilee? My brain is full."

"Not a chance. I found a chat room within a forum called Black Science. What got my interest was a discussion involving a Florida glass manufacturer who was furious at the federal government for trying to prevent him from selling a commercial glass product that blocked gamma rays from—"

"Blocked gamma rays?"

"Yes. He claimed to have developed a method of energizing layered crystals in silicon dioxide products that, when electrified, would block gamma rays from radioactive materials. A product like this could be behind the radioactive waste theft from Hanford. The radiation alarms would have detected nothing."

"Any mention of names, cities, universities—*anything* more?"

"No names were mentioned, only that the speaker was a glassmaker at Pratt Florida Glass in Boca Raton who was furious because the Feds claimed terrorists could use the invention to transfer nuclear weapons around the country. He believed the ruling would cost him millions in royalties."

The word "nuclear" got Morgan's full attention. "Why wouldn't he just sell his discovery to the Feds and make everyone happy?"

"My thoughts exactly, but the discussion didn't go there. It just stopped abruptly. He was clearly upset."

"Nice work, Rilee. I'll run your research by the Feds—except the part about your Bandit Catcher. Now this time *you* listen up. From now until I get this information sorted out, you need to back off on Conti. And I mean way off. This probably is just a bizarre coincidence, but until I know that for certain, it's imperative that you stay completely away from him. The dirtbags I'm looking for have killed two people and may be planning to kill hundreds more with a dirty bomb. If Conti is involved, they could swat you like a bug. I need your word, Rilee."

"I promise."

Morgan's admonishment to Rilee to stop investigating Conti was akin to asking a lascivious fraternity housemother to leave the boys alone.

Ten minutes later, while making a cup of Tieguanyin Tea, named after a Buddhist deity, she contemplated how she would break into Conti's Wi-Fi network for a peek inside the façade he presented to the world. And then there were his personal computer files and any external hard drives that needed examination. Well, as long as she was in the neighborhood . . .

The more Rilee dug, the more she found. Her first step was to use a Blackboard Wi-Fi inspector to detect Conti's network and identify his router's access point, the section that conveys radio frequencies between 2.4 and 2.5 gigahertz. Conti had been unplugging and disconnecting his router whenever he was away from his computer.

Nobody sets up that much security unless . . .

Fortunately, his router used an RC4 encryption algorithm—ancient history in Rilee's world. She captured the data stream and found the password within ten minutes. She then set up an evil-twin fraudulent Wi-Fi access point, enabling her to eavesdrop at a moment's notice.

DETONATION

If Conti would just cooperate by turning on his Wi-Fi, she might learn some serious information about condo 243. And what was wrong with that? Bad actors need to be stopped, and whether it took hours, days, or weeks, she wouldn't give up, promise or no promise.

Twenty-two hours later, her moment came to pass. Conti turned on his router, and five minutes later, Rilee slipped into the middle of his bizarre little world.

Tick-tock . . .

Chapter Thirty-Two

Twenty minutes had elapsed since the last group of trick-or-treaters rang the doorbell of Avery Griffin's University Place home. "My guess is we've seen the last of the little goblins this year, Angela."

"Some of them aren't so little anymore, and they don't stop in one neighborhood. They canvas half the city. How many did we have tonight?"

"I put fifty Hershey bars in the baskets. Looks like about fifteen left." He turned off the home's porch light and walked to the bar in a corner of the great room. "Can I make you another drink?"

"I never say no to gin," Angela replied, flicking a remote that turned on the room's gas fireplace.

Griffin splashed an ample amount of Tanqueray over ice in a tall glass, added Sweet-N-Sour mix, and filled it with 7Up. He had crushed several sleep aids earlier in the evening and now discreetly poured them into Angela's drink and stirred it with a plastic swizzle stick. It had been less than a month since he embezzled $30,000 from his octogenarian client Dr. Philip Kezer and his close call with Pacific Opus Securities' compliance officer, Helen McClosky. The embezzled money bought him a little time, but his plan for tonight would solve his money problems for good. And it would right a wrong that was long overdue.

The coming action was triggered years ago when Avery's father left his mother heartbroken and married a beautiful young secretary—a gold digger to be sure. In defiance of his father, Avery changed his last name to his mother's maiden name, Griffin, and with that walked out of his dad's life.

Tacoma is a medium-size city, and Griffin was often reminded of his father's success and wealth. After tonight, Griffin would tell

Pacific Opus to take a hike and start living the life *he* deserved. He added another ounce of gin to the cocktail before handing the glass to Angela, who took a long pull on the concoction and curled up on the davenport. His plan required that she be in a deep sleep when he slipped out of the house at midnight.

After Friday's stock market closed, Griffin embarked on the most dangerous aspect of his treachery. He needed another car to drive to his father's home. It wouldn't do to commit murder driving a Porsche 911.

He left the house at midnight driving Angela's black Lexus 330 and drove to the territory of a gang calling itself 56 Crime Fam at South Fifty-Sixth Street and Lakewood Drive, where he spotted three sinister-looking men seated on a school-route bench, each drinking a forty-ounce Colt 45. *As good a place as any*, he thought. He motioned, and all three approached. None appeared older than twenty-five.

"I need a car delivered to a local street corner Sunday night. For that service I'll pay serious money. Are any of you interested in the job?"

The tallest of the group, wearing a yellow-green checkered flannel shirt, jeans, and Michael Jordan tennis shoes, took a small step forward and appeared to be the spokesman. "Is you trazy? Boy, you got heart come dancin' in our hood."

"I want no trouble. I just need a car driven to a location in University Place at midnight Sunday with keys in it. My offer is two thousand dollars now and four thousand more when you bring me the car." Griffin figured if he had lived this long, maybe he could pull this off. "Guys, it's your call. You can roust me now for being in your hood, or you can help me steal a car and make six thousand dollars cash."

"Talk new, jack. You for sure no popo?"

"I'm not a cop. I have business to take care of using another vehicle. If you're not interested, I'll find someone who is."

"You want us to boost a whip and you will pay six large?"

"That's it. Two now and four Sunday night."

The short, scrawny hoodlum on the left still seemed suspicious. He seemed to speak to checkered flannel more than to Griffin. "If you popo, you have to tell us. It's the law."

By now Griffin figured "popo" meant police. "No police. All I need is a car delivered Sunday night for reasons of my own," he replied with a touch of irritation.

"You got the cheese now, white boy?" asked the third punk, taking a pull on his Colt 45. Like the others, he apparently preferred ghetto jive to simple conversation.

"For the fourth time, I'll give you two thousand now and four thousand more when the car is delivered. That's the deal. Take it or leave it."

The spokesman decided for the trio. He took the envelope from Griffin, counted out the twenty hundred-dollar bills inside, and wrote down Griffin's directions for where to deliver the car Sunday. With that, the three men walked off into the night, and Griffin breathed a sigh of relief that he hadn't been shot. There was a good chance he had just burned two grand, but he told himself, "Never gamble, never prosper."

In less than two days, Avery Griffin would know if he had been ripped off. If so, his father and stepmother would live another day.

The weekend flew by. Avery played a round of golf Saturday afternoon before taking Angela out to dinner that night. On Sunday, the pair attended the annual Holiday Food and Gift Festival in the Tacoma Dome. By late Sunday night, another of Griffin's doctored cocktails had put Angela into a deep slumber.

He slipped out a sliding glass door and walked to Fortieth Street West, waiting for traffic to clear before crossing the usually busy Bridgeport Way arterial. He carried a plastic bag containing an empty

Coke can, a two-liter bottle stuffed with cotton balls, and several cigarette butts he had picked up in downtown Tacoma. It was his hope that some stray DNA might convince police that the killings were the result of a burglary gone bad. He was also packing a Taurus nine-millimeter pistol purchased three weeks earlier at a Seattle gun show, plus the $4,000 cash payment for the expected stolen car and a house key.

The handoff was to take place on Robin Road West within the jumble of streets, drives, roads, lanes, and courts comprising the often-confusing University Place street system. Avery turned west on Fortieth, a well-traveled thoroughfare through the community, and continued for a half mile to Robin Road, where he turned south and had the surprise of his life: the stolen car actually was there. Two of the brothers stood next to a maroon three- or four-year-old Ford Fusion.

"There's no key; just twist these two wires together and it starts," said one.

Griffin looked in to see part of the dash had been ripped open exposing the ignition assembly. He then handed the spokesman, who now wore a black hoodie, the $4,000, put on gloves, and departed with the car. The three car thieves drove off in an old Chevrolet sedan a moment later.

Griffin's father lived in a pricey home in the nearby town of Steilacoom with a large front deck, lush landscaping, and a splendid view of Puget Sound. While making the ten-minute trip, Griffin rolled over in his mind how often his father had humiliated him. Two years earlier, he had approached him for a small loan to cover a cash flow gap for a rental property he owned, and his dad's response was to lecture him for not making a career in commercial real estate. It was always like that, no matter the issue. His father hated him. Tonight Griffin would return that sentiment permanently.

The drive down Lafayette Street was without incident, and when he spotted Sunnyside Heights Drive, he pulled the Ford off to the side into a brushy area. He reached down near his knees and disengaged the car's ignition wires, stopping the engine. Griffin then adjusted the pistol in his belt, double-checked that he had the house key, and picked up the plastic bag.

The walk up Sunnyside took about five minutes, and pudgy Avery Griffin found himself a little winded. The aqua home with royal purple accents was twenty feet away.

Avery walked quietly along the north side of the home, as the master bedroom was on the south side. He crossed a thirty-foot grass strip to the glass French doors, saw no evidence of an alarm system, and inserted his key, which twisted easily, unlocking the door. Now inside, it was critical that the murder look like Barry Mott, Griffin's father, walked in during a home burglary.

Still wearing his gloves, Griffin felt only hatred as he attached the homemade silencer to the Taurus 809. Standing near the dishwasher, he threw the Coke can against the refrigerator and used both hands to steady the gun.

The hall light flicked on, and Griffin heard steps approaching the kitchen. His plan was a chest shot and then a finishing bullet in the head. Once his father entered the kitchen, Griffin started the trigger pull.

Before the gun barked, Barry Mott was able to speak his last three words. "Avery, is that—"

A little surprised by the cotton balls that burst out of the two-liter homemade silencer, Griffin still managed to fire a second shot into his father's forehead.

He stepped over Mott and headed down the hall to the master bedroom. He didn't travel far because Mott's wife now entered the hallway. Just as he took aim, the plastic two-liter fell off the end of the gun. It took Griffin less than a second to re-aim and fire three Black Hill 115-grain hollow points into the bitch who broke up his family. He then rushed into the bedroom and scooped up some jewelry and watches and then pulled a wad of money from Mott's wallet. Quickly returning to the kitchen, he scattered the cigarette butts near the door, placed the broken two-liter in the bag, and headed out the French doors.

Avery Griffin Mott didn't know what hit him as he was body-slammed to the ground by a two-hundred-pound, crew-cut FBI agent, one of two special agents who were on the detail to keep Port Commissioner Barry Mott under twenty-four-hour surveillance.

The agents monitoring the residence had been slow to react from their position in a seven-year-old Honda parked next to a neighbor's home. By the time one did react, it was much too late for Barry Mott. His death by his own son also killed any hope of investigators finding his connection to the most shocking criminal plot in the bureau's more than one-hundred-year history.

Gaston Rizzo entered the mammoth parking garage at Seattle-Tacoma International Airport and slipped his Cadillac CT6 into a spot being vacated by occupants of a new Mercedes CLS sedan. The shiny, floating living room oozed class as it slid quietly away and down a ramp toward a cashier's booth. Rizzo's year-old ride wasn't quite as shiny, its owner having failed to wax its rather pedestrian exterior this month. *Damned monsoons.* There was another reason as well: the Mercedes owner *had* his car waxed regularly; Rizzo still waxed his Caddy himself.

But all that was about to change. After his current—and final—business deal concluded in Panama, he, too, would upgrade into the ranks of Mercedes ownership. And why not? He certainly could afford it after carving out a life with grit, long hours, and his own two hands. He had survived a war, gotten his college degree, and formed a successful electrical contracting business along the way, not to mention his side venture that lesser men might deem as criminal. That's why they were *lesser* men; they lacked perspective. He preferred the word "craft."

Rizzo and his partners were practical men who understood that few eight-to-five jobs brought in real money. They were jobs for losers. But by working together, selecting the right projects, and pushing the right buttons at the correct times, his team had stepped up all their lifestyles for the last thirty-five years.

Rizzo's entrepreneurial spirit also was the driving force behind the adventure upon which he was embarking today. The business's previous after-hours projects had been completed with scarcely a hitch, and this one would be no different. Today, he felt the pride Patton must have felt as he liberated Bastogne. He and his partners were simply stepping up a grade. Their past projects had been simple, clean, and tidy—moneymakers all. But this one would be the pièce de résistance.

At 5:15 a.m., Rizzo was checked through airport security and headed for Concourse D, where he would stop at a Seattle's Best coffee shop for a cup and perhaps a bagel before boarding a 7:10 a.m. Delta Air Lines first-class flight to Houston. He avoided large meals when he flew thanks to a lesson learned on his flight from Vietnam back to the world in 1967. The toilets on his World Airways 707 stopped working two hours west of San Francisco with two hundred servicemen aboard. A man either learns life lessons along the way, or he doesn't, Rizzo believed. There is no in-between.

He would have a forty-minute layover in Houston before catching an afternoon American Airlines nonstop flight to Tocumen International Airport in Panama City. A forty-five-minute cab ride would take him from the airport to the lush Gamboa Resort, where he would spend the next two nights until the *Rose Diamond* was on the bottom of the Panama Canal. Rizzo rechecked his hotel reservations on his cell phone for the fourth time.

Confirmed.

He smiled to himself. Now time for that bagel and a cup of coffee.

Tick-tock . . .

Chapter Thirty-Three

At five minutes past midnight, Rilee got the break she needed. During the last twenty-four hours, she had briefly connected to Carlo Conti's Wi-Fi several times to observe his Google searches but had so far only been able to determine that he was searching for cargo ship activity at the Panama Canal.

At best it was a clue, but armed with her suspicions, it was time to pry open Conti's secret world using what legal scholars call the "fruit of the poisonous tree"—a metaphor for evidence obtained illegally that cannot be used at trial. Let black-robed judges pontificate about illegalities; someone needed the balls to unravel Conti's plans now—before the Panama Canal was incinerated—and given the circumstances, she decided to develop a pair of her own. She was confident her malware could ferret out whatever nefarious schemes he had up his sleeve, and once she had the goods on him, she would figure out a way to make it legal. Morgan and the bureau knew her cyber-surveillance methods were illegal, but they looked the other way for one fundamental reason: they couldn't do it themselves.

For her mission, Rilee chose Recon-baby malware—a spy tool developed using polymorphic packers—software that bundles multiple types of malware in an email attachment. The bundles then transform within the recipient's computer system where they remain undetected by traditional security methods indefinitely. Recon-baby was 20 percent malicious code, allowing her to access Conti's search engines. The remaining 80 percent was a morphing engine code with features that caused the malware to continually change its appearance, thwarting detection.

Rilee was considering a second glass of Chateau Landonnet Bordeaux Blanc when her computer chirped, signifying that Conti's

Wi-Fi was active. In less than two minutes, Recon-baby had entered the access point of his router and was silently parked in a hidden user directory on his computer. Now she just needed to be patient while the malware began its work.

Money, money, money. It's always about the money. What a splendid day for the good guys, Rilee thought, sipping coffee early Monday morning in front of her computer screen. Recon-baby had been busy during the night, moving from file to file and copying and pasting Conti's documents to a special temporary file in Rilee's own computer system. The first file was a document outlining a scheme to move large amounts of money among six banks in Belize using digital bearer certificates. The file also identified several transactions involving digital money exchanges using eDragon digital currency. The second file was labeled "Bone-augmentation procedure." She read briefly about oral surgery techniques called sinus lifts or sinus augmentation until the file detailed a procedure labeled the "Split ridge technique." Rilee rolled her eyes. Time to move on.

The third hacked file detailed the affairs of a bogus international business registered in Belize as a deep-sea salvage operation. The phony company had outfitted several ships whose crews faked treasure finds from sunken ships around Belize and Honduras, claiming to have brought tens of millions of dollars of gold and silver to the surface. Conti had himself an ideal money-laundering contrivance, Rilee told herself, but all it proved so far was that he was a crook, which may help explain where his new Corvette and high-living style came from, but so far there was nothing tying him to the missing nuclear waste or to a Panama Canal plot. That might take a personal visit to his condo. It was risky, but if she could do it, she could dump his entire computer contents on a thumb drive. *All I need is five minutes*, she thought.

A practice run was in order, using the door to her own penthouse condo, the entrance of which was set back, blocking its view from other residents and passersby.

With her Anderson Government Steel Pro-Plus pick by her knees, Rilee got to work on her six-pin lock, which appeared identical to that of condo 243 and others within the complex. Two minutes into her task, she inserted a tension tool—known to thieves as a "torque wrench"—into the bottom of the keyhole, using her left hand. After determining the direction of the cylinder's rotation, she applied light tension while inserting a pick with her right hand. She first got the feel of each pin and its respective spring and then kept a slight tension with the torque wrench as she pushed up all six pins. She applied a little more torque, and the cylinder turned and the door opened. She would now wait for Conti to leave and then slip into condo 243.

It was twenty minutes past three when Rilee observed Conti's Corvette leave Point Ruston and drive toward the nearby Tacoma Yacht Club. A tan knapsack over her shoulder, she descended the condominium's side stairs to the second floor and knelt in front of Conti's door. She withdrew the lock pick set and also a Phthalo Seven security system bypass tool that would block the frequency of the door sensor as it sends a signal to the condo's home security panel.

Same lock as mine. While maintaining tension with the torque device, she carefully pushed up the final pin. As expected, the cylinder turned and Conti's door opened.

As Rilee stood up and slipped her knapsack over her shoulder, her peripheral vision picked up an unexpected motion to her right, but too late. Before she could defend herself, her right arm was grabbed, and she was shoved roughly into condo 243. Her foot caught on a throw rug, causing her to stumble before she regained her balance and spun around. Rilee considered her limited options as Conti slammed the door.

After a short pause, Conti blocked the door and waved a finger at her. "Who the hell are you, and why did you break into my home?"

"You're a dentist, right? I knew you'd have a stash of Oxy."

"Bullshit! You're the lady who lives in the penthouse."

Rilee knew she was stuck between a rock and a hard place, but she had a feeling Conti wasn't sure what to do. "Why don't you move away from that door, doc. I'll leave and we can forget about this nasty little adventure."

"Not going to happen. Why did you break in?"

"Well, I didn't exactly *break* in."

"Answer the question."

"I told you. I thought you would have some OxyContin, and I took a chance."

"Don't screw with me, bitch. Tell me the truth and you can leave."

Need to try another approach. "Mr. Conti, we know about your plan to set off a dirty bomb in the Panama Canal, and all the money-laundry shenanigans in Belize. Hell, my people even know about that phony shipwreck salvage trick. We've got you nailed! Now open the fucking door!"

Rilee had never seen such a quick transformation. Conti's demeanor instantly changed from confidence to angry confusion. She had figuratively kicked him in the balls. Morgan had warned that he could be extremely dangerous, and Rilee jump-started her offense. Estimating the weight of the bag containing the Phthalo signal generator and lock pick at seven or eight pounds, she spun around and hurled the bag at the room's large plate-glass window facing Commencement Bay. The window bowed and cracked loudly but didn't break. Conti, shocked by the turn of events, moved away from the entry and, with his head down, walked over and quietly sat at what appeared to be his computer desk. A loud knock at the door stunned them both.

"FBI! Open the door! FBI!"

Since Conti made no move to respond, Rilee dropped a large ashtray she had planned to throw and opened the door instead. After displaying their credentials, special agents Justin Patten and Thaddeus

(Dusty) Rhodes stepped into the room and made eye contact with Conti who was still seated at his desk. Agent Rhodes was the first to speak.

"Who owns this condo?"

After a look of confusion, Conti finally acknowledged that he was the owner. "This woman just broke into my home. I want her arrested."

It dawned on Rilee that Morgan must have told the FBI about her discovery that Conti was involved with the Portland sting.

Rhodes stole a quick look at his partner and turned back to Conti. "Tell us more."

"When I returned home, this woman had just picked the lock of my door."

Agent Patten saw an opening and jumped at it. "Sir, if you found her outside your door, how did she get inside your home?"

"She was picking the lock on my door; her picking device is right there on the floor by the cracked window. The door had just opened when I grabbed her and moved her inside for an explanation. That's what happened. I'm the victim here, unless you're blind."

"Mr. Conti, when we heard the window break and knocked at your door, this lady was inside your condo. How did she get inside?"

"I just explained that, you bumbling idiot!"

Rilee couldn't remain silent anymore. "The bastard grabbed my arm and threw me inside. Then he stood by the door and wouldn't let me leave."

Patten smiled at Conti and patiently waited for a reply.

"What was I to do? She was breaking into my condo to steal drugs. She said so herself." Conti sat down in his swivel desk chair, ran his hands through his hair, and stared at the floor, his face now wearing what combat soldiers call a thousand-yard stare.

"Is that statement true, lady?"

"Semi-true, but it's not what it looks like."

Patten motioned for Agent Rhodes to join him away from the ears of Conti. "Dusty, we have nothing on Conti. Catching someone in the act of breaking into one's residence and giving them a push inside to elicit an explanation are not federal or—most likely—local offenses. Conti appeared to have been protecting his property. But if this little squabble leads to a break in the Panama Canal case, it would be worth the bureau's time to let it play out a bit longer. Keep an eye on them while I call Dex."

Patten stepped into the next room, dialed Special Agent Dex Copeland, and laid out what he and Rhodes had, which was, at best, a broken window, an infraction for which J. Edgar's finest rarely arrest people. "Dex, this guy appears to have no clue that Mott was killed last night. You recovered two burner phones. My bet is there are a couple numbers stored on them."

"Got it. Give me five minutes," replied Copeland.

Conti continued to sit at his desk, now resting his head on his arms while Rilee and the agents whispered by the fractured window. A ringtone suddenly emanated from a briefcase sitting on a sofa. Rhodes walked to the sofa and lifted up the case.

"Mr. Conti, it seems that Barry Mott wants to tell you he has just cut a deal."

Patten reached to his belt for a pair of handcuffs. Before he could take a step toward the retired dentist, Conti reached under his chair, pulled out a Beretta M9 pistol, shoved it in his mouth, and pulled the trigger.

Tick-tock . . .

Chapter Thirty-Four

Morgan made two quick phone calls and then considered driving to Point Ruston and strangling Rilee. Exasperated by the turn of events, she had phoned him at 5:00 with news he didn't want to hear: she had broken her word and been caught trying to burglarize Carlo Conti's condo. Now, just a day after Port Commissioner Barry Mott was murdered in his home, Conti had joined the list of dead men who might have shed light on a hazy plot to explode a nuclear device at the Panama Canal. Schoolteacher Daniel Pearce, California businessman Dick Zigler, Mott, and now Carlo Conti all had met violent deaths just when it seemed they might cast light on the scheme.

But was there really a plot at all? That question appeared to have been answered by Rilee's Recon-baby malware that she used to copy Conti's files. The gist of it was that a large cargo ship containing a dirty bomb would be used to close down the canal—and soon.

Rilee's instincts were right in trying to find and copy Conti's hard drive, but her timing had been terrible. The FBI's influence deflected any local burglary charges; Rilee's case being helped by the fact that the dead condo owner wouldn't be pressing charges.

For Morgan, Conti's suicide told a story of its own. The canal plan was active. It had to be for a man obviously involved to suddenly and gruesomely end his own life rather than face criminal charges. It was a death-before-dishonor move, but who was Conti protecting—and why?

Brick was already packing his go bag when a text from Rob Spencer arrived from Fort Lauderdale at six fifteen requesting him to fly to Panama immediately on behalf of his cruise-industry clients. Morgan's second call had been to Nicole in Richland, who informed him that the FBI wanted her to meet the legal attaché assigned to the American

Embassy in Panama City ASAP.

"We need to fly to Panama tonight, Brick. We're out of time."

"I'm on it. There are no commercial flights available, but I've hired a charter out of Boeing Field in Seattle. Try to get there by one a.m., and we can be in Panama by one p.m. Wednesday."

"Done deal. I'll take a commuter flight to Sea-Tac and meet you at Boeing Field by twelve thirty. Special Agent Marcos Soler will meet us when we land at Tocumen Airport."

"No wool suits, Nicole. It's rainy season and a hot eighty-five."

9:00 p.m. Morgan checked the Ship Finder application on his iPad and was surprised to find sixty-eight ships in queue on the Atlantic and Caribbean side of the canal and eight on the Pacific side. All large vessels were required to register with the canal's Automatic Identification System (AIS), and after dialing up the AIS on his phone, he began evaluating which ships fit the threat profile for the third lock based on their dimensions. It would take awhile. He had been assured that their plane, a Hawker 900XP, would have internet capabilities. *This project can wait.*

A security monitor alerted him to a vehicle arriving in his north driveway, specifically a Rolls-Royce Phantom, and he knew only one person who drove one. Rilee's expression as she stepped from the car made him think better of chewing her out for going in harm's way.

"Are you okay?" he asked, wrapping an arm around her shoulder.

She waited until Morgan closed the door before replying to his question. "I'm fine, but now the FBI has me back on their radar."

"You were never off their radar. They just scratched out 'Titus' and replaced her with 'Rilee.'"

"Maybe you're right. Anyway, I brought you some stuff for your trip." Rilee withdrew a file folder from her jade-green Tory Burch shoulder bag and handed it to him. "I filtered all the ships with beams larger than a hundred ten feet that are in the queue for a canal transit."

"That just saved me a couple hours. Thank you."

She then presented him with a leather case that Morgan at first believed held a long-barreled handgun.

"I want you to have my Wolfhound cell phone detector," she said. "If the bomb has a cell phone trigger, it will sniff out the phone's location. It's designed to locate nearby cell phones in either standby mode or during active voice, text, or data transmissions. You can't listen to conversations, but it will help in locating an activated line."

Twenty minutes later, Morgan had a working knowledge of the cell detector. Over a quick cup of coffee, he gently scolded her daring attempt to scavenge information from Conti's computer.

"I admire your chutzpah, Rilee, I really do, but you could have been killed."

"I wasn't, Brick."

"No, but Conti is now dead, and dead men tell no tales. We've lost him as a source of information."

"I'm so sorry, Brick. All I needed was five minutes. When I saw him drive away, I thought I could be in and out long before he got back. He must have forgotten something and returned; I just don't know. I've really messed things up."

"Well, it is what it is, Rilee. The good news is that you've gotten us important information we wouldn't have otherwise."

The Rolls slowly left his driveway while Morgan placed the Wolfhound back in its carrying case and set it next to his Rush Moab go bag by the front door. He set an alarm for 11:00 p.m. and laid down on his bed. Sleep came in barely a moment.

Morgan exited I-5 north, drove down Exit 161, and then turned onto Airport Way. At this late hour, there were plenty of numbered parking spots behind the terminal building. The proper name for Boeing Field is King County International Airport, and its distinctive two-story brick office building serves as the passenger terminal. A handsome young man, perhaps in his late twenties, stood behind a small counter under the TopFlight Luxury Charter's blue-and-gold marquee.

"My guess is you might be Mr. Morgan."

"Yep, I'm Morgan."

"Please give me the number of your parking stall, and I'll make sure your car is ready for you when you return."

"Sounds like a deal. Spot number thirty-eight."

"Thank you. Agent Cofield has checked in and should be onboard. Here's a copy of your flight plan. You'll be making a fuel stop in Houston at eight a.m."

"Good. Where do I find the plane?"

"Go out the green door and follow the yellow line. The Hawker has a blue-and-white checkered tail."

Five minutes later, Morgan ducked about seven inches to clear the executive jet's cabin ceiling. He placed his go bag in a spacious closet forward and turned to take in the beautifully appointed interior of the jet. On his right was an upscale galley that appeared fully stocked. Nicole was seated in one of the five executive chairs.

"You're in my favorite seat," he joked as he chose an almond Spinneybeck Italian leather seat opposite her. A large three-seat davenport, known as a divine, also of Italian leather, balanced the cabin. Morgan rubbed his hand over a highly glossed English oak table positioned between their chairs. "Very nice."

"You're going to need a chiropractor by the time we hit Panama."

Morgan knew she was referring to his six-four frame dealing with a cabin height of five nine. "I've got it covered. Two hot chicks are on standby to give me a massage once we hit Houston."

"Listen, buddy. If anyone is going to mess with your body, it will be me."

Morgan smiled, then pulled out his iPad and looked over at her. His expression changed. "This is it, Nicole. By this time tomorrow, we should have some answers. If we don't . . . the canal may be history."

At that moment, a lanky, uniformed man about forty stepped up to them and introduced himself.

"Welcome. I'm Captain Kory Bowgren, your pilot," he said, taking a seat opposite them. "Our copilot is Captain Rich Paleo. He's finishing the plane's external inspection."

"I'm Agent Nicole Cofield, and my partner here is maritime investigator Brick Morgan."

Introductions and cordialities continued for a few minutes until the pilot glanced at his aviator watch.

"Weather is in our favor. Our flight plan has us leaving at one a.m. We lose two hours with time zones, but we should arrive in Houston at eight a.m. to refuel. We will then fly to Tocumen Airport. Our plane is a Hawker 900XP that will drink two-hundred-fifty-seven gallons of fuel an hour on this flight. I hope to fly at forty thousand feet and keep our speed at four hundred knots, depending on the winds."

Morgan pointed to the closet in the front of the plane. "Can we keep our bags in the cabin?"

"We have seats for eight and there are just you two, so keep your bags anywhere you like. After we reach altitude, I'll open the cockpit door and you'll be free to move around. The galley is filled with sandwiches, water, and good wine. The Hawker has a nice lavatory; no seat belt though." Bowgren chuckled. "We should be wheels up in about ten minutes. Please look under the small compartment near the drink holder for the control for the Hawker's dual airshow." He pointed to the two large screens that displayed flight info. "Thank you for flying with TopFlight Luxury Charters. Enjoy the flight."

The Hawker was a solid aircraft designed by British Aerospace and upgraded later after the company joined with America's Beechcraft Corporation in 2012. Despite its strong reputation as a corporate and charter aircraft, the company ceased production of the Hawker in 2013. TopFlight was one of its many loyal customers continuing to operate the plane.

The Hawker eased into the sky at precisely one o'clock this cloudless Tuesday morning, and Morgan and Nicole spent the next forty-five minutes catching up on emails and text messages. Rilee had given Brick a list of fourteen cargo ships with beams over 110 feet that would require the new third lock. Because of the approach made to the late Dick Zigler, FBI analysts believed a cargo ship would be targeted for the attack. At Morgan's request, Nobility's Rob Spencer had emailed him a list of five cruise ships scheduled to use the new lock this week: two from Carnival, one from Princess, one from Diamond, and one from Norwegian."

"Counting the five cruise liners and information from the canal's AIS system, we have nineteen ships in queue for the new lock. It gets more complicated," added Morgan. "Depending on traffic flow, the Marine Traffic Control can assign smaller ships to the new lock as well."

Nicole was half listening as she concentrated on an incoming message from Special Agent Dex Copeland's Tacoma office. Morgan returned to the plane's galley for cups of coffee for them both. This would be a long night. Captain Bowgren pushed his right headphone up and turned to provide a flight update.

"We're on time. Weather is still favorable. We should be in Houston in two hours."

"Thanks. It's been a smooth flight."

Morgan dropped off the coffees and made a quick pit stop in the plane's lavatory. The fine wood details and accents of planes and yachts always caught his eye. This Hawker executive jet was no exception.

"Dex Copeland's office is still processing the Mott crime scene, Brick. The suspect in custody is Mott's son, who said before lawyering up that his motive was financial," said Nicole.

"My first reaction was that Conti or LoNigro killed Mott to cover any loose ends."

"Mine too. Turns out the son, whose name is Avery, is deep in debt and had hoped to inherit his dad's wealth. Here's the irony: Copeland found a journal entry that provides a motive for the Panama Canal plot. He says Mott's journal documents indicate that he was racked by guilt because of his failed relationship with Avery. He had bought a large amount of real estate in key areas of the Port of Tacoma that he expected to appreciate dramatically and hoped to leave the land to Avery. According to the journal, the Panama Canal's third lock had seriously impacted the port's economic picture, and as a result, the value of Mott's real estate tanked."

Morgan shook his head. "Barry hires the mob to put the canal out of commission so he can leave his alienated son valuable land in the port. But the son kills him because he wants money now that he would have received later from Barry's estate. He didn't know or expect that money because they had a bad relationship. A vicious cycle destroyed them both. This whole case is a complete mess, Nicole. Every time we develop a lead we end up with a dead man."

Morgan thought for a moment before continuing. "Let's forget Mott for now. Your people need to locate Mark LoNigro, and we need to narrow down the list of vessels that could be carrying the bomb."

Morgan and Cofield used the Houston refueling stop to grab an hour of sleep. Each found a leather lounger that converted to a recliner. Seventy minutes later, Morgan awoke as the Hawker leveled off at forty thousand feet. Cofield was checking her email.

Balding copilot Rich Paleo entered the cabin with a flight status update. He didn't need to duck to clear the cabin's ceiling. "We should be touching down in two hours. Currently we have landing priority status and will be cleared to taxi to the end of the runway, where a helicopter will be waiting."

"Thank you, Captain. It's going to get hectic in a few hours."

Morgan brought roast beef sandwiches and two water bottles back to their seats. "We need to keep our blood sugar up and stay hydrated."

Cofield wrinkled her nose as she read the latest message from Agent Soler. "Looks like the Panama Canal Authority isn't anxious to suspend its transit of ships without more details. They've basically ignored the threat. Soler says each ship pays a toll of about ninety dollars per container. Every ship not going through the canal is costing Panama between five hundred thousand and a million dollars."

"Typical shortsightedness. How much would they lose if the whole canal were out of commission?" Just then, Morgan's phone pulsed with a new message from Rilee.

"We need good news."

"We have it. It seems that while your people were processing Conti's body and condo, Rilee took it upon herself to plug in his router. While the FBI was waiting for a warrant to remove and run diagnostics of his computer, she was still obtaining files using a malware she had installed."

"My God, Brick, she's either a cybertechnology scholar or a sociopath!"

"Maybe both, but it gets better. He opened a file that describes using two batches of C-4. The plan is to use one explosion to stop the ship and another explosion to detonate the dirty bomb."

"Tell her to figure out the target ship."

"I did. She's still perusing Mott's files. She did identify three ships to watch. Write these down. On the Atlantic side is the *Scorpion Flyer*, Barbados registration, traveling from Baltimore to Taiwan. She's one-thousand-seventy feet by a hundred forty-four and in the queue for today at five o'clock. She listed two that are on the Pacific side. The *Cobalt Crystal,* a Hong Kong-flagged vessel that sailed out of San Diego; no date assigned. Here's an interesting entry: the *Harmony Pogy,* eleven-hundred-ten feet, Panama registration, sailed out of San Francisco two days ago and will enter the third lock this morning."

For the next hour, Morgan analyzed all the little dots that represented ships identified by the AIS marine tracking system. He entered the three names provided by Rilee and located their positions on the marine traffic display.

"Thirty minutes out of Tocumen," announced Paleo.

"Shit!" bellowed Morgan suddenly, looking at a new text from Rilee and punching the air with his fist. "Rilee now says it's a cruise ship. The *Rose Diamond*. She says the bad guys made a change from using a cargo ship to a cruise ship to better control access to the new third lock."

"I'll inform the bureau. Maybe they can stop the ship."

"Let Agent Soler know. He might be able to contact the Panama Canal Authority."

Morgan downloaded a deck plan for the *Rose Diamond* and sent a message to Diamond's Director of Fleet Security Vasco Deluca, asking him to scan his manifest for any singles that booked in the last thirty days."

"How in the world would they get a radioactive bomb on a cruise ship?" Cofield asked.

"I doubt they smuggled kryptonite in watermelons," said Morgan as their plane settled through wispy clouds into its final approach to Tocumen International Airport. "The *Rose* is a sister ship of the *Terra Diamond*. It's big, Nicole, thirty-four hundred passengers and over a hundred twenty thousand tons. Let's ask Agent Copeland to get a driver's license photo of LoNigro from the Washington Department of Licensing and do a forensic photo analysis with the passenger embarkation photos."

"I'm on it."

Panama City, the capital and largest city in Panama, was founded in 1519 by Spanish explorers and became a launching point for the exploration and conquest of the Inca Empire in Peru and a transit point for gold and silver headed back to Spain, much of which was lost to shipwrecks along the Florida coast and countless other locales. The city, located at the Pacific entrance to the Panama Canal, has a population of nearly 900,000 and is the political and administrative center of the country and a hub for international banking. Its Tocumen International Airport is the largest and busiest airport in Central America. Today, the canal was receiving two unexpected guests who were trying to save the city and its people from almost unbelievable horror.

Air traffic controllers had been instructed to give the Hawker immediate landing clearance, and Captain Bowgren set it down as directed and taxied toward the north end of the terminal's 10,000-foot main runway, where a man awaited them next to his parked sedan.

Cofield finished sending her traffic to the FBI, and Morgan made a final check of his go bag as the Hawker rolled to a stop. A minute later, Copilot Paleo turned the silver handle that unlocked the cabin door from the top and popped it open. His two passengers exited the plane to the steaming-hot tarmac.

"Agent Cofield, Mr. Morgan, welcome. I'm Agent Marcos Soler." He shook hands with them both. "We need to get off this active runway and get to your next ride." He nodded toward a bright red Bell 429 Global Ranger helicopter awaiting them on an adjacent runway. As they walked toward the chopper, their charter departed, moving off the runway to a taxi strip and heading for its assigned parking area.

Soler reached into the helicopter's cabin and then handed Morgan a small canvas bag. "It's a Sig .40. Don't lose it or I'll be reassigned to the Congo." Soler was on his second embassy tour, his first having been a three-year stint at the US embassy in San Jose, Costa Rica. His twenty-six-year FBI career was triggered in 1992 during the LA riots. His first job after graduating from the UCLA School of Law was clerking for a federal judge in Los Angeles. While driving home from the courthouse in April 1992, his car was surrounded by a dozen marauding blacks angry over a jury's acquittal of four white police officers who had beaten black motorist Rodney King a year earlier after a traffic stop. Soler barely escaped with his life after his car was rocked violently and a Molotov cocktail was thrown inside, causing the vehicle to explode. The next day, he resigned from the District Court, left Los Angeles, and applied to the FBI.

"Jump in and I'll brief you." Soler handed each of them aviation headsets plugged into a console as their pilot, Agent Clarence "Chico" Rodriguez, lifted the chopper and banked toward the canal.

"Chico, has this bird got a four-twenty-seven and a five-speed in it?" asked Morgan.

"Two tame. I've got a big-block four-fifty-five supercharged Buick in here. She'll do zero to sixty in three-point-two seconds and one forty flat in the quarter mile."

"We may need all she's got, bud."

"Ready when you are."

Soler began rattling off information. "We're five minutes out. Thirty minutes ago, the *Rose Diamond* entered the second of the Cocoli lock's three chambers, where she is right now."

"So there's no way to back up the ship to freeze her in that first chamber where we could have better access to board her?" asked Cofield.

"Afraid not. When the Canal Authority received word that the *Rose* was the potential threat, they just froze. Some people wanted to move her along and dump her into Gatun Lake—a minimum of two more hours. Another group wanted to move her back into chamber one and drag her back toward the Pacific Ocean, as you indicated."

"So they wasted time and did nothing," said Cofield sarcastically.

"It's frustrating as hell. While the Authority officers were arguing, Cocoli's second chamber was continuing to fill with water. All three of Cocoli's chambers lift ships a total of eighty-five feet, the height of Gatun Lake. Next, a big container ship, the *Harmony Pogy*, entered chamber one, effectively blocking the *Rose* from backing up. When chamber two was near its twenty-eight-foot level and chamber one was at the halfway mark, all hell broke loose. Somebody at the Maritime Authority informed security officers about a radiation threat. They activated a security alarm, and when the operators and tug crews heard about a nuclear alarm, they dropped their lines, tied up the tugs, and left the locks."

Morgan couldn't believe his ears. "So both ships are now stuck in the Cocoli chambers. Is that about it, Marcos?"

"No, three ships are stuck! There's a big LPG tanker in chamber three. Its tugboat crews also dropped their lines."

Cofield looked puzzled. "What real difference does it make to us which part of the lock the *Rose* is in? We just need to find the ship, wherever it is, and get aboard. What's the good news, Marcos?"

"The canal is loaded with radiation monitors. So far no alarms."

"Let me get this straight," said Morgan heatedly. "No radiation alarms were triggered in the canal itself, but some imbecile in the Maritime Authority set off their own alarm and the Panamanian crewmen all ran away."

"So much for bravery," said Cofield.

"These guys wouldn't have been useful on D-Day," Soler chimed in.

"This is bullshit!"

"No argument there, Brick."

"Look out the window," Soler said. "That's the *Rose Diamond* high in Cocoli's second chamber."

The helicopter leveled to about forty feet above a grass field connecting three maintenance sheds. As Rodriguez prepared to set it down, Morgan observed a small puff of smoke amidships on the starboard side of the *Rose*. He keyed his mike to deliver the obvious.

"Detonation!"

Tick . . .

Chapter Thirty-Five

Tock . . .

LoNigro, dressed in a dirty brown Carhartt jumpsuit, looked no different than any other member of the *Rose*'s belowdecks crew, except for the small canvas bag he carried with him on deck four below the waterline. He moved quickly and unchallenged past three bulkheads toward the bow of the ship while crewmen, spooked by klaxons and other alarms that blared throughout the ship, scrambled to get topside. The near panic, resulting from the Panama Maritime Authority's badly timed warning of a potential nuclear attack in the canal, caused grown crewmen to stumble over one another in their haste to abandon their posts. The *Rose*'s captain was forced to use his starboard thrusters to hold the ship against the portside of the lock after tugboat crews, assigned to hold the ship in place, cut their lines and fled.

The timing couldn't have been better for LoNigro, who slipped unnoticed into the empty crew's bar with his bag containing tools and explosives. His luck was doubled when he spotted a pool table near the far side of the bar. In less than three minutes, he removed enough insulation and wall material to expose the ship's hull. He then broke one of the wine bottles in which he had smuggled the C-4 aboard and pressed a block of the putty-like substance against the steel. Next, he inserted an M-6 military blasting cap into the C-4 and attached wires from a cell phone to the cap.

LoNigro then used his massive bulk to tip over the pool table and push it up against the C-4 to help direct the blast toward the hull. He left the bar and walked down a long, deserted passageway before using a second cell phone to make the call detonating the charge. A broad smile creased his features when he felt the green linoleum-covered deck shake under his feet.

Ignoring the continuing loud alarms and chaos in the passageways, LoNigro returned to his cabin on deck eight and placed his two green oxygen cylinders in an appropriated laundry cart. He added another set of electric detonators and as a backup an Abrams nonelectric blasting cap and fourteen inches of time fuse. He covered the hazardous load with a blanket.

In the crew's bar, the blast had ripped a three-by-four-foot hole in the hull. Its force had blown the pool table across the room and out against a forward bulkhead where the watertight doors were situated. When the doors tried to close automatically, the pool table, with its heavy wooden frame and inch-thick slate tabletop, prevented them from doing so fully, and outside water poured unabated into the ship.

LoNigro's next destination was the number seven refrigeration room on deck four. Reefer seven would be perfect for detonation of the dirty bomb, as the temperature was maintained at thirty-seven degrees Fahrenheit to keep its fruit and vegetable contents fresh. He hoped the room's coolant would become contaminated with radioactive dust and spread throughout the ship. He pushed the cart out of his cabin door and headed to a service elevator that would take him to deck four. By now, the ship's air horn was signaling seven short blasts followed by one long blast. Abandon ship!

By the time LoNigro reached the refrigeration room, water was pouring into deck four at a rate he hadn't expected. He bulled his way into the cold-storage room and set to work.

Morgan watched Rodriguez slowly lower the collective lever, apply a little pressure to the right antitorque pedal, and let the full weight of the Bell 429 settle on the grass. He removed his headphones and asked Agent Soler if the copter was on call for other duties.

"It's ours for the day. Leave what you want inside."

DETONATION

Morgan climbed from the chopper and kneeled on the grass with his bag. He holstered the service weapon he received from Soler and grabbed a SureFire flashlight, a Cold Steel Recon knife and the bag containing the Wolfhound detector. He threw the rest of his go bag's contents into the cabin and turned to Cofield and Soler.

They had landed about two hundred feet from the edge of Cocoli's middle chamber. "Looks like the *Rose* had already started evacuation before the bomb went off," said Cofield, gesturing toward four orange evacuation tubes running from the promenade deck seven directly to the shore. "They also have two gangways on deck four running up to the chamber's side and two gangways slanting down from deck five. How fast can they get everyone off the ship?"

"My guess is two hundred, maybe two fifty a minute," Morgan replied. "With the captain using the thrusters, the ship should hold tight to this side of the lock."

While the thrusters kept the *Rose Diamond* in place, there were no bollards or anything else for the ship to tie up to, and the flooding from the blast in the crew's bar finally took its toll as the bow of the *Rose* slowly drooped to the bottom of the sixty-foot-deep channel. Disembarking passengers and those waiting their turns at exit points screamed in terror as water swirled over the ship's first hundred feet of decking, causing a forward gangway to bend sideways, throwing three passengers off to the ground fifty feet below. None moved after landing.

Belowdecks, eleven crewmen injured by the blast on deck four and left to fend for themselves drowned as the in-rushing water covered them where they fell.

Soler's radio monitored the frequency of the Panamanian National Police. "The Canal Authority received a message in both English and Spanish that a nuclear bomb was aboard the *Rose Diamond*," he said. "Plus the FBI's request to stop all traffic was enough to tell the pilot aboard the *Rose* to abandon ship."

Soler removed his radio and nodded toward the ship's stern. "There comes the crew bailing out as fast as possible down to the chamber's walkway, passengers be damned."

Morgan took a moment to analyze the situation. "How much freedom are the Panamanians giving us, Marcos?"

"If we wait for permission, the three of us will be drawing social security before our request is answered. Everyone is paralyzed. The Canal Authority is still arguing whether to move the *Harmony Pogy* and drag the Rose back through chamber one and into the Pacific, or continue forward and get her into Lake Gatun. It's academic because the tugboat operators can't be located."

"Nicole and I didn't fly down here just to sit on the bank and watch the *Rose* sink. We're going aboard, and anyone who tries to stop us will be going for a swim."

Cofield motioned that she had received an update. "The bureau just heard from Diamond Cruise Line. I have five cabins that have singles and were booked during the last thirty days."

"Go for it," urged Soler as he pulled out a pen and a three-by-five card.

"Ortega, deck ten, cabin three-oh-two. Reed, deck eleven, cabin five-one-seven. Karsuyama, deck ten, cabin three-six-oh. Stevenson, deck nine, cabin four-six-three. McGuire, deck eight, cabin two-one-two."

"We have five leads. Let's go," said Morgan.

Soler handed the card to Morgan. "You two give it a try. I need to stay here and meet a group of ATF agents who just flew in from Chile. I've also requested a couple of Geiger counters."

"Wish us luck! Let's try that gangway coming up from deck four." It was obvious that Panama's immigrations and customs protocols had completely broken down. "I see two men and a woman who appear to be assigned guard duty at the gangway. Get out your FBI credentials out and act tough."

"I am tough, Brick!" replied Cofield, throwing him a dagger glare.

"Follow me. I have a secret weapon," Morgan said as he pulled the Wolfhound from its case.

"What the hell is . . ."

The three members of the National Police made a move to block their attempt to board until Morgan pressed a button on the Wolfhound, causing it to emit a series of loud beeps, and started shouting, "Radioactive—peligro—bomba!"

The policia couldn't move away from them fast enough, and after weaving through the crowd of disembarking passengers, Morgan and Cofield found themselves on deck four.

Only when the group of passengers was behind them did they realize a third person had followed them aboard the *Rose*.

When Morgan and Cofield turned to face the stranger, the man, who appeared frightened, lifted both hands, trying to signal that he meant no harm. "You're Morgan, right?"

Cofield stepped to one side and rested her hand on her weapon.

"And who the hell are you?" Morgan asked hotly.

"I know you're looking for Mark LoNigro. I can help you."

"Keep talking!"

"My name is Mitch Steinberg, and I want to stop this madness."

"So do we, and we don't have much time!"

"LoNigro is using the name Bart Stevenson and is pretending to be disabled so he can carry nuclear material in oxygen tanks."

Cofield moved back next to Morgan and asked what else Steinberg knew.

"He's using C-4 to stop the ship, and after the ship is empty, he will use a cell phone to explode the rest of the C-4 that's wrapped around the dirty bomb. I know how crazy this sounds. I tried to change his mind, but he wouldn't listen."

"Why don't we arrest you right now?" asked Cofield.

"Because I know what Mark looks like."

Morgan looked at the five cabins he had written down and spotted the name Stevenson assigned to cabin H-463. He grabbed Steinberg by the arm and led him to the interior of the ship and in the direction of stairs that would take them to deck five.

"Most of the elevators start on deck five," he explained as Cofield dialed the FBI about their encounter with Steinberg. Morgan continued to interrogate the stranger while the lift took them to deck nine.

"Who's running the operation?"

"A man named Barry Mott found the money and contracted with our group."

Morgan thought he would try the shock treatment. "You know that Mott and Conti are dead?" He had never seen a man turn pale so quickly. For a second, he thought he might have a heart attack. When the door opened on deck nine, all two hundred thirty pounds of Morgan lifted Steinberg and pressed him against a wall. "Okay, asshole, who's the leader of the pack?"

Sweat was pouring off Steinberg as he tried to answer. "Rizzo, Gaston Rizzo. He should be here in Panama to meet up with Mark LoNigro."

Morgan let him slide back down the wall, and all three headed for cabin H-463.

Cofield took charge when they reached the cabin. "Use your toy and see if there's a cell phone inside, Brick. Then we crash the door." She aimed her service pistol at the lock, closed her eyes, and pulled the trigger. Before she opened her eyes, Morgan had kicked open the cabin's door.

"Clear left, Nicole! I'll clear right."

Cofield entered and cleared the closet and the bathroom. There was no "right," so Morgan charged into the main cabin and then cleared the balcony.

"Not here, and no oxygen tanks either." Cofield looked under the bed. "What next, Brick?"

"I think he'll explode the bomb below the waterline so the blast is not disbursed into the air. Let's get to decks three and four below the waterline."

"I just got a message from my supervisor ordering us off the ship, Brick. A special bomb-disposal unit is flying in from Colombia—ETA twenty minutes."

Morgan shook his head. "You get off. My client hired me to stop the bomb."

Cofield ignored him. "What do we do with Steinberg? Handcuff him to a handicap rail?"

"We need him to ID LoNigro. Let's go to deck three first."

A service elevator took them below the waterline to deck three. Cofield hesitated when they reached the long corridor that was filled with hand trucks, forklifts, and hundreds of pallets. Water inside had stabilized, but they still were nearly knee deep.

"My God, it's huge."

"It's called I-95, named after the East Coast Interstate."

"This is my first time on a cruise ship."

"Really? After we find and defuse the bomb, we'll have a drink in the bar. Let's get to work." Morgan pulled out the Wolfhound and scanned various food service stations. They inspected the bakery, dessert station, meat storage, and even the printing press room. "I've got a hit!" He directed the detector toward the loudest beeps emanating from the Wolfhound and entered a wine-storage room. On a desk was an abandoned Moto Z Droid. "Well, we know this thing works."

He held the detector with both hands, directing it in half-moon segments and picking up two more false alarms before settling on a strong signal coming from a fruit-preparation station on his left. That signal was overshadowed by a much stronger one that grew in intensity as he aimed the Wolfhound toward the ceiling. "Come on," he said. "It's on deck four!"

They ran up a steel staircase that was covered with yellow-and-black-striped caution tape.

"Let's start aft. I would try to contaminate the engineering space if I was LoNigro."

They passed a half-dozen freezers with various signage for poultry, fish, and beef. Each freezer displayed large digital thermometers displaying temperatures below twenty degrees Celsius.

"Bingo!" whispered Morgan as he stood outside a fruit and vegetable

refrigeration unit. "Steinberg, give us a little space. We can't wait for the cavalry. Are you game, Nicole?"

She nodded as she pulled out her Glock. "Same as before. I clear left, you go right."

Morgan held up three fingers, then two, and finally one. He pulled down the stainless steel handle and turned it to open the large walk-in reefer. Upon entering, they encountered a cold curtain of plastic strips used to keep the cold from escaping the large room that was filled with stainless steel pallets stacked throughout with fresh fruit. He then saw a large man dressed in blue overalls in a far corner of the room working on two green cylinders perched on a double crate of apples. Morgan and Cofield held their fire and were edging closer when Steinberg suddenly ran past them and stopped ten feet from LoNigro.

"Mark, stop! There's still time to stop this insanity! Conti and Mott are dead. Mark, it's over. Think of Karen!"

"Too late," said the big man who barely glanced at Steinberg. He saw Morgan and Cofield, guns drawn, but acted almost like he was in a trance as he calmly returned to his work fusing the C-4 around the bomb. Cofield's announcement of "FBI! It's all over, Mr. LoNigro. Stop what you're doing, raise your hands, and come over here" was greeted with stony silence.

"Mark, you have to give up!" yelled Steinberg, who then charged the three-hundred-pounder like a twenty-year-old linebacker. He was no match for the big man, but he did cause LoNigro to drop his phone on the linoleum floor.

LoNigro pushed Steinberg away, but in doing so he tripped and both men crashed into the crate of apples, crushing it. Not only did the hundreds of apples spill, but the two oxygen cylinders also slammed to the hard floor and broke apart, shattering the electrified radiation-protective glass inside each cylinder. That event changed the equation in a heartbeat.

Morgan motioned to Cofield. "Get out of here now, Nicole!" he yelled, backing toward the door.

Almost as fast as the struggle between Steinberg and LoNigro started, it stopped. Morgan felt a strange warmth on his face, neck, and arms. He then observed that both men were in extreme distress. An eerie, glassy film now covered their eyes, and LoNigro had blood running from his nose.

Morgan grabbed Cofield, threw her over his shoulder, opened the door, and dumped her on the passageway deck. He then remembered LoNigro's cell phone and darted back into the reefer.

He found the phone about six feet from the men, used a water hose to loop it and pull it to him, and took a quick photo of Steinberg and LoNigro, both of whom had collapsed. The heat in the room was unbearable, and it was clear to Morgan that the two men were dead and that some of their facial skin had melted. He also observed sparks coming from what appeared to be lithium-ion batteries. A few seconds later, he was out of the reefer, wondering how much radiation he had absorbed.

"Let's get out of here. This place is hot. You might want to keep a few feet away from me until I can get decontaminated."

"You're just saying that so I won't arrest you. You dumped me on the floor like a bag of potatoes."

"They're both dead—very dead."

"Looks like we stopped the bomb. What will happen—"

A thunderous explosion from the walk-in refrigerator they had just left slammed them both to the deck.

Morgan struggled to his knees, ears ringing. "We failed!" he yelled, pounding his fists on the deck. "Damn it! Damn it!! We blew it, Nicole!"

She grabbed his left arm and pulled like a woman possessed. "Let's get away from here while we still can."

Morgan wore a hospital gown after being hosed down in a makeshift decontamination tent set up by the ATF unit. After a similar shower several minutes earlier, Nicole had changed into a jumpsuit borrowed from one of the ATF agents.

"We were lucky, Brick. The Geiger counter indicates we won't glow after dark."

"We still have to take iodine for ten days. Regardless, the bomb went off and I was hired to stop it."

"Don't be so hard on yourself. The word is we're heroes."

"Not hardly."

"While you were still relaxing in decontamination, I was working. The ATF team put on their fancy yellow suits and entered the reefer. They said LoNigro had set a timed fuse and that sparks from the lithium batteries caught the paper that wrapped the apples on fire. That fire ignited the fuse and one of the C-4 blocks exploded. It didn't even breach the steel cylinders. Their Geiger counters have hot readings in the reefer, the freezer next door, and part of the deck on I-95. Bottom line, the dirty bomb didn't work."

"We still need to catch Rizzo."

"More good news. I gave LoNigro's cell phone to Soler. Between the wonderful FBI technology team and our partners at the NSA, they found four numbers on his burner. One of the numbers pinged at a tower next to the Gamboa Rainforest Resort. The resort is located near the canal on the Chagres River."

"I want the guy, Nicole."

"Well, now comes the bad news. Panama's National Police are now fully engaged and want to take control. The United States National Security Council, the National Counterterrorism Center, and probably the Girl Scouts also want to take over."

Morgan waved over Agent Soler. "About Mr. Rizzo. I want him, Marcos. I don't give a rat's ass who takes credit for it. I'm not trying to turn a disagreement into an international incident, but I've earned him."

"The National Police don't have evidence to hold him, but they have him under surveillance at the resort. My contact with the policia says he doesn't know he's being watched."

"Can you get us another car, Marcos?"

"Not from here. The ATF borrowed a car from the embassy, but that's *their* car."

Morgan looked across the field where the Bell 439 they had used to reach dockside was parked. Chico Rodriguez was asleep in his pilot's seat, feet protruding from a window.

"I believe we just found a solution."

"Wait a second, Brick. That's an embassy chopper—for official use only!" Soler exclaimed. "We're not cops."

"No, but we're concerned citizens acting in the best interests of the Panamanian people."

"Maybe, but we have no police authority here."

"He's right," added Cofield, crossing her arms.

Morgan knew that the longer they waited, the greater would be the international hubbub. He turned and walked quickly toward the Bell 429 with Cofield and Soler in tow.

"I don't like this one bit, Brick," murmured Nicole, trying to keep up.

"Why not?"

"Well, for one thing, you're not wearing any pants."

"My pants are in my go bag, and it's in the chopper."

"And for another thing, this is an *embassy* helicopter," said Soler loudly enough that he awoke Rodriguez, who looked over at them.

"Morgan here wants to commandeer the chopper to go get the guy behind all this mayhem!" Soler shouted.

"Remember when you told me you had a big-block Buick in here capable of warp speed, Chico?" asked Morgan. "Well, we need that speed right now. We have to find the Gamboa Resort where the bad guy is staying before he hauls ass out of town. Can you do it?"

"Oh, hell yes!" crowed Rodriguez enthusiastically. "Hop in!"

"Brick, Chico—don't do this!" yelled Soler as the helicopter rotors began spinning.

Morgan first retrieved new pants from his go bag. "Cover your eyes, Nicole. I don't want to frighten you."

He got into the helicopter behind her, followed by Soler, who groaned, "Now, I *know* they'll send me to the Congo on my next assignment." All three buckled in and put on their earphones and mikes.

"Don't worry, Marcos," said Cofield. "I'll be at the next desk."

"We're twelve minutes out," Rodriguez declared as the chopper lifted into the air.

Morgan turned to Nicole. "We don't care who has custody of Rizzo, but we do need to find out who remains in his organization plus the money trail. Marcos, what's the name of the chairman of the board of the Panama Canal Authority?"

"His name is Francisco Cabello. My God, Brick, what are you up to?"

"See if you can stall the policia for more time. I need to make a phone call."

Morgan and Soler each dialed numbers on their cell phones. Morgan's was busy.

But Soler got a hit. A thirty-second conversation in Spanish ended abruptly. "It's been arranged that we have twenty minutes with Rizzo. After that, he's the property of the National Police."

"I thought they had no evidence," said Cofield, giving Soler a quizzical look.

"Once we get him, the police will have all the evidence they need," said Morgan. He tried a number again, and this one went through. He was patched through from the US Embassy to Pogy Oceanic Shipping, which had a business office four miles from Gamboa. Five minutes later, Morgan asked Rodriguez if he could set down on a helipad at the Pogy office.

"Know right where it's at, bro."

Three minutes after that, Morgan, Cofield, and Soler took stairs down to the office lobby where they were met by office manager Guillermo Vasquez, who had been alerted to the critical nature of the visit. Vasquez took them outside, where they were greeted by a driver in a BMW sedan. All three shook hands again with Vasquez and waved to Rodriguez, who gave a thumbs-up before shutting down his engine on the pad.

Soler took the front seat; Morgan and Cofield got in back. The driver wore a white shirt with three gold bars on the shoulder epaulettes. "Brick, who the hell did you call?" asked Soler with a big grin.

"It seems that money talks. Pogy Oceanic Shipping pays over three hundred million a year in canal tolls and fees. Three years ago, I was able to help them with a charge of illegal hydrocarbon dumping. The chairman likes me and offered the company's services. He called Señor Vasquez, and this nice BMW showed up."

"We're going to have one shot at this, gentlemen," Cofield observed. "Don't screw it up."

"We need the names of everyone involved in the organization," Morgan said again.

Cofield peaked over the top of her red reading glasses. "We may be there already, Brick. Rizzo may be the end of it."

Soler said they were about five minutes from the 164-room resort. He wondered aloud how much money might have been involved in the canal plot. "There must be tens of millions floating around. A lot of people would be happy if we recovered it."

"Ten-four on that, my friend."

"You'll find this interesting, Nicole," said Soler. He read from his Blackberry. "The ATF says the C-4 and nuclear juice could have been a successful dirty bomb. It might have taken years to clean up. The message ends with 'Bravo Zulu.'"

"What's Bravo Zulu?" she asked.

"One of the ATF team explosive experts is an ex-Navy SEAL. 'Bravo Zulu' is

navy jargon for 'well done.'"

When their car arrived at the Gamboa, Morgan and Cofield eyeballed their surroundings for a moment, as brilliantly colored scarlet macaws and toucans preened and fluttered around them.

"This place is a combination of a tropical garden and an exotic bird sanctuary," said Soler.

As they approached an orchid nursery, three armed members of the police met them, led by Captain Ernesto Silva. While Soler translated introductions, a group of monkeys was pestering a crocodile iguana in a palm tree barely fifteen feet away.

Silva's eyes narrowed to slits as Soler explained the reason they had come for Rizzo. "Perhaps this man should attempt to escape," he said in Spanish. "My men could help with that situation."

"No, no, please," said Soler. "He should be tried in a Panamanian court and imprisoned here for life—a fate worse than death."

Silva nodded and then a broad smile crossed his features. "*Me gusta mucho tu idea*," he said.

"Okay, Rizzo is on the second floor. They believe he has no idea we're here. He's been out on his balcony using a cell phone. We'll have twenty minutes. When we enter, two guards will follow us into his room and proceed to the balcony. There also will be three additional guards at the door."

"Let's do it!" prompted Morgan as he followed the police up the stairs.

"By the way, he's using the name Lawrence Willow," said Soler. "The embassy located a picture of Gaston Rizzo of Tacoma, Washington, and forwarded it to the National Police. He's our man."

Cofield tapped on Rizzo's door and feigned an accent. "Meester Willow, hosekeeping pleese."

When the door opened an inch, Morgan threw his weight against it, sending Rizzo crashing to the floor. Before he could move, Soler stuck his weapon in Rizzo's mouth. Two guards wearing ball caps pushed through and took up duty on the balcony.

Cofield put a handcuff on one wrist while Morgan and Soler rolled Rizzo to his stomach. Morgan leaned a knee into his back while Soler hooked up the other wrist. After checking him for weapons, they dragged him to the end of the bed and pulled him into a partial sitting position.

"Who the hell are you people?" Rizzo demanded.

"We are your worst nightmare come true," said Morgan.

"That doesn't answer my question."

"Okay, the lady on my right is Agent Nicole Cofield of the FBI, and the man is FBI agent Marcos Soler of the American Embassy in Panama City. I'm Brick Morgan, a maritime investigator from Tacoma."

"What do you want with me?" Rizzo shouted.

Morgan pulled two chairs over by Rizzo, and Soler retrieved a third from the balcony. No one reacted to Rizzo's protest.

"Gaston Rizzo, the next few minutes will be the most important of your life. Don't foul it up," warned Morgan, returning his pistol to its holster.

"Who are you, you can't—"

Morgan leaned into Rizzo. "Mott is dead, but he told us about the plan. Conti is also dead and so are Steinberg and LoNigro! Your answer to my question will be the most important of your life. Who else was involved in this scheme? Names, Mr. Rizzo. Who were your partners? Who was paying you? You can take the fall—and I do mean fall—alone, or you can retire to a country club prison for a while. It's your choice."

"I don't know what you're talking about. I'm an electrician on vacation. And I'm an American. You can't just waltz in here, make accusations, and threaten me. I've got rights."

"Maybe it hasn't occurred to you yet that you're not in America. You're in Panama, Mr. Rizzo. You have no rights here. If anything, we're trying to help you make the best of a very bad situation. Once more: Conti, Mott, LoNigro, and Steinberg are dead. Take a long look at this photo. This is what's left of Mark LoNigro and Mitch Steinberg inside the *Rose Diamond* cruise liner. The nuke device failed, but it toasted them."

"Steinberg . . .?" mumbled Rizzo, a faraway look on his face.

"You weren't expecting him here today? Neither were we. He helped us find you. Apparently his conscience got the best of him."

Rizzo refused to look at the photo on LoNigro's cell phone. "None of you has any authority here," he said, his voice getting louder.

Morgan ignored him and calmly repeated the questions. He was determined to stay in control and avoid getting the FBI agents in hot water over an excessive force issue. Rizzo continued his refusal to acknowledge the names of Mott, Conti, LoNigro, and Steinberg. Morgan could tell Rizzo was in shock and seemed about to pee his pants. He held the phone directly under Rizzo's face until he looked at the photo. He appeared ready to vomit at the sight of his friends' melted faces.

Morgan recalled his conversation with attorney Patrizio Bianchi and the threat of a foreign prison. "I don't think you understand your situation, Mr. Rizzo. You are part of a gang that just tried to destroy the canal. The livelihood of Panama. The National Police want you very badly. Steinberg provided the FBI with a statement implicating you as the leader of this crime. If you continue refusing to provide the names of your group, we will turn you over to the Panamanians. Within weeks, you will be sent to Penitenciaria Federal de Chitré, considered the deadliest prison in the world. It was built for nine hundred and now has four thousand prisoners.

"Three gangs run the prison, Mr. Rizzo. The guards never enter; they only guard the outside. The prison has no bathrooms or showers. It's so crowded that most of the prisoners have to stand and, as a result, their feet rot, and because of the shit on the dirt floor, gangrene is rampant. Mr. Soler, tell him about the Lung Gang."

"The Lung Gang is a group of cannibals, Mr. Rizzo. Every Wednesday, they select a couple of prisoners and mark them for that Friday's barbeque. Cutting off their ears marks them. On Friday, they are chopped up and put on the barbeque. Because the lungs are considered a delicacy, the gang is named the Lung Gang. The only way anyone leaves Chitré is by the loading dock out back. The prison doctor, who never enters the prison, retrieves and disposes of the dead prisoners who are dumped on the dock."

Morgan added, "If you don't speak Spanish, you will be a June bug for a big bubba. Remember, Chitré has no guards inside. They won't enter."

"Listen up, Rizzo." It was Cofield's turn to try getting through to him. "If you answer our questions, you will be turned over to the United States and spend your years at a cozy federal country club. Is it door number one or door number two?"

"Screw you, bitch! All of you are Americans. I'm an American, and I demand to see an attorney. I've got rights, you bastards!"

"I *am* an attorney, Mr. Rizzo, and I'm here to tell you once again that you have no rights in Panama," Morgan said. "You turned down our offer. After a few formalities, your next stop will be Chitré penitentiary.

Morgan and Soler reached under Rizzo's armpits and lifted him to his feet. They then signaled to the National Police on the balcony that he was now theirs. As the three Americans started to leave the room, Soler turned to the police guards.

"¿Dónde puedo encontrar una buena barbacoa, *amigos?*"

"What did you say?" asked Cofield as she opened the door.

"I asked them if they knew where there was a good barbeque."

Acknowledgments

I am immensely grateful for the support and patience of my wife, Nancy, during *Detonation*'s maturation. Nancy read multiple drafts of each chapter before they were forwarded to my editors.

My gratitude continues to the following special people in my life for their priceless contribution to *Detonation*:

One of my first clients in the financial service business, Dick Walters, provided an historical perspective of the Port of Tacoma and insight into the workings of the port's governance.

Mike Ervin and I met when he rescued our blind cocker spaniel, Layla, who had escaped our Puget Sound cabin. The following month, Mike shared his wisdom of today's cybersecurity threats and provided "Rilee" with the tools needed to bring down "The Business."

My friends for fifty years, my S.A.E. fraternity brothers, were present during an annual Portland lunch when the Panama Canal was selected as the novel's focal point. Thank you, Jim (Bud) Clary, Dan Martin, Craig Mendenhal, Jerry Reilly, and Craig Vogel, for your confidence and motivation.

My brother-in-law, Larry King, has been with me from my first novel, *The Drummer*. For *Detonation*, Larry and his son, Matt, made a fact-finding road trip to the Hanford Nuclear Reservation. "Dr. Dunbar" can thank the Kings for his success with the heist of the radioactive material.

A special shout-out to my three sons, Kris, Kyle, and Zach, for their help with rewrites and website development. Thanks, kids, for making your father appear smart.

Over forty-five years ago, Joe Boyle and I worked together selling life insurance. Recently our paths crossed again, and the talented Joe recently loaned me his extensive law enforcement experience and helped Brick Morgan deal with that tenacious criminal syndicate.

During the Cold War, Bill Noe and I were shipmates on the USS *Sea Owl*. During the writing of *Detonation*, Bill coordinated my training in the field of radioactive isotopes.

George Mills has been a great supporter of my writing since my return to the Pacific Northwest and provided his strong interest in the period to the Panama Canal's history.

My longtime friend, Dick Sypher, generously volunteered uncountable hours to bring his genius to character development and plot evolution. Fans of Brick Morgan are in Dick's debt.

I so appreciate Diana Schramer of Write Way Copyediting LLC for applying her super knowledge and copyediting skills to *Detonation*. Diana corrected countless author-created faux pas and made the manuscript as smooth as glass. If a reader finds a blooper, it would be my flub, not Diana's.

Finally, although no animals were injured during the development of this manuscript, in the spirit of full disclosure I must confess that my son Zach's springer spaniel, Scorsese, sat on my lap with my MacBook Pro during many writing sessions.

CPSIA information can be obtained
at www.ICGtesting.com
Printed in the USA
FFOW04n0835201017
41353FF